CW01642780

IF I HAD MY TIME AGAIN

LINDA GREEN

Boldwood

First published in Great Britain in 2026 by Boldwood Books Ltd.

Cover Design by Alice Moore Design

Cover Images: Depositphotos and Shutterstock

A CIP catalogue record for this book is available from the British Library.

Paperback ISBN 978-1-83633-983-0

Large Print ISBN 978-1-83633-982-3

Hardback ISBN 978-1-83633-981-6

Trade Paperback ISBN 978-1-80656-352-4

Ebook ISBN 978-1-83633-984-7

Kindle ISBN 978-1-83633-985-4

Audio CD ISBN 978-1-83633-976-2

MP3 CD ISBN 978-1-83633-977-9

Digital audio download ISBN 978-1-83633-979-3

This book is printed on certified sustainable paper. Boldwood Books is dedicated to putting sustainability at the heart of our business. For more information please visit https://www.boldwoodbooks.com/about-us/sustainability/

Boldwood Books Ltd, 23 Bowerdean Street, London, SW6 3TN

www.boldwoodbooks.com

For everyone who has lost a loved one.

AUTHOR'S NOTE

This novel is set in an imaginary afterlife and therefore deals with death, grief and loss. In particular, there are sections relating to suicide and baby loss, which I wanted to give readers advance warning of. While I appreciate these topics can be difficult and some may wish to avoid them, I hope I've tackled them in a sensitive way, and they are balanced throughout the novel with warmth, love and humour, where appropriate. I also hope that by encouraging people to read, think and talk about these important issues, it may make things easier for those who have gone through grief and loss to speak about their experiences and us to be able to offer support.

I will be making donations to The Samaritans and Sands, the baby loss charity, from the royalties of this novel and if any readers would like to make donations, that would be greatly appreciated.

The Samaritans can be contacted on 116 123 in the UK or via www.samaritans.org.

PROLOGUE

Sometimes the pain is simply too much to bear. Physically and emotionally. Perhaps other people would struggle through it, but I am not brave like them. Not in the slightest. I have nothing left to fight with. I am consumed by the intense, twisting pain in my flesh. The shards of hurt from a lost love, an unlived life, pressing ever deeper into my heart. And the absolute emptiness of my existence.

The wind tugs at my hair, calling me, gently coaxing me forwards. Whispering to me that it can take the pain away. I am old enough and wise enough to know it is a con artist. That nothing can be as easy as it makes it sound. There are terms and conditions, such as the fact that for a few fleeting seconds the pain will be far worse than this. Excruciating, I imagine. But nobody reads the small print because they want to believe what they are being promised: that they will be thinner, richer or happier. Life will be better, more exciting or easier. And I am no different to anyone else. So, I take the wind at its word and sign on the dotted line by shuffling my feet forward.

I can feel the bridge swaying ever so slightly. Or maybe it is me, it's hard to tell. I teeter on the edge and for an agonising moment I'm not sure I'll be able to do it. To fulfil my side of the contract. I think of her, standing on Clifton Suspension Bridge one hundred and forty years ago. Her heart wounded. Feeling this was her only way out. Unaware that her huge, billowing petticoats would talk her body out of it on the way down. Acting as a parachute to allow her to land softly in the mud beneath. I look down. I am wearing black leggings. Below me is only tarmac. There are no escape clauses in my contract. No cooldown period. I have signed my life away. People won't talk about me next century because I won't be the miracle woman who survived. I was not special in life, and I will be unremarkable in death too. I open my mouth to let out one last anguished howl. And then I lean over. Letting the wind take me. Aware there is nothing to break my fall.

1

JULES

I woke up as a door banged shut. A few seconds later came the sound of what appeared to be someone peeing in close proximity to my head. I sat up quickly, remembering the time Rob had returned home drunk and forgotten to open the door to the ensuite before relieving himself. Fortunately, he wasn't in the room. The sound was coming from the other side of the wall. And this wasn't my bedroom. So, if I wasn't in my own house, where the hell was I?

It was the taste of fear on my lips that came back to me first. Followed by the sensation of hurtling through the air and wishing to God I'd packed a parachute. Shit. I'd only gone and done it. For the briefest of moments, I felt a shot of elation. When your list of lifetime achievements was as short as mine, this had to count for something. It was surely up there with winning second place in the potato and spoon race at sports day when I was ten. And then the consequences of my actions hit home. The main one being that I was dead.

I sat up and looked around. Being someone who set the bar low, it wasn't as if I'd expected gold fixtures and fittings and a bird of paradise on the bedside cabinet in Heaven, but surely something a little more luxurious was in order than what appeared to be a bog-standard Travel Inn room – which smelt of a leftover takeaway and had all the character of an empty cardboard box.

Another door slammed shut. Someone started hoovering outside. Which was when it occurred to me that my actions had presumably booked a one-way ticket to Hell. In which case, this wasn't bad at all. There'd been no one to do the hoovering for me at home. If this place came with a cleaner, it may as well be Heaven as far as I was concerned, and the whole 'do not sin or you'll end up in Hell' thing must have been invented to prevent overcrowding.

I wasn't sure how long it had taken me to get here, but I wondered if Rob had missed me yet or would do when he got home from work and discovered that his tea hadn't been made and no one had put the washing out. I certainly didn't flatter myself by thinking his heart would be broken, but I did suspect he'd be pissed off I hadn't emptied the dishwasher before I'd left. To be honest, it was the cats I was most concerned about, having no expectation that Rob would think to feed them, or even knew where their food was kept.

I swung my legs around and sat on the edge of the bed. It was only then I realised I was pain-free. Which was surprising when you considered what state my body must have been in on the dual carriageway when they found me. And even more surprising when you took into account that I'd been in physical pain for years before that. Still, here I was, neatly put back together again and healed. There was no need to think about the mess I'd left behind. For once, someone else would have to clear up after me.

A quick glance down confirmed that I appeared to be

wearing the same clothes as when I'd left the house that morning. I was either the 'after' scene in an advert for a highly impressive brand of washing powder, or something beyond my understanding had taken place. I stood up tentatively. I'd feared my legs would buckle, but they appeared solid enough to support my not insubstantial weight. Everything seemed to be in full working order, which was not something I'd been able to say for a long time.

I walked over to the window, curious to know what the view was from Hell. Turned out it was of the A629 into Halifax. It was hard to know whether to laugh or cry. All the times I'd driven past this place and had no idea that Hell was located on the top floor of a mill redevelopment of the world's largest carpet manufacturer on the outskirts of my hometown.

It was only as I headed back across the room that I noticed the TV on the wall. I supposed if they had TVs in prisons, there was no reason to think they wouldn't have them in Hell. They probably wouldn't include any streaming services but when you were old enough to remember being excited at the launch of Channel 4, having anything more than three channels was still something of a luxury.

There was a message in large letters on the TV screen.

'Welcome. Please go to Room 010 in the basement, where your induction programme will begin. You are requested to arrive at 9.45 a.m. for a 10 a.m. start. Thank you.'

At least I wasn't being summoned to Room 101, because I'd always felt it would be an impossible task to whittle down all the things I hated to a mere handful of offenders. The clock in the corner of the screen said it was nine thirty, which meant I still had time to freshen up. It occurred to me that I may have already been bathed as part of the extensive repair process which had seemingly taken place before I'd got here. A quick sniff of my armpits suggested that I had. Perhaps it had been like that scene in *The Wizard of Oz* where they got Dorothy and her friends scrubbed up before their meeting with the Wizard. That would explain why I bore no trace of what had happened earlier today. But I decided I should still make the effort to smarten myself up a bit for a meeting.

I opened the wardrobe next to the bed. Inside, hanging neatly on the rail, were a selection of clothes. Not just any clothes, my clothes from home, although admittedly they appeared to be freshly washed and ironed, which is why it took me a moment to recognise them. I felt like one of those cardboard figures I'd had as a child, who came complete with a cut-out-and-keep wardrobe that I could attach to myself with little tabs. I pulled out a red top, thinking a splash of colour would be better than the sombre black T-shirt I'd chosen for my death. I was glad to see my bag was in the bottom of the wardrobe too, as it contained my make-up, a hairbrush and a small can of body spray – which was pretty much all I needed.

Inside the bathroom, I was greeted in the mirror by the sight of a pasty-looking middle-aged woman with dyed reddish-brown hair and dark shadows under her eyes. Clearly, my hope that they might have managed a facelift as part of the clean-up operation had been misguided. I took my lipstick and eyeliner from my bag, aware that a slick of my trusty red lippy and a line of kohl was the best I was going to be able to do. For a second, I thought I caught sight of Nina's reflection in the far end of the mirror. I used to stand next to her in the ladies' and marvel at her cheekbones and huge eyes as we reapplied our make-up during our many nights out in Bristol. Part of the appeal of being a goth for me had been that you were accepted for simply wearing eyeliner and dyeing your hair black; there was no beauty or size-related entrance exam, but you still got to hang out with the beautiful people.

The toilet seat had been left down; another advantage Hell had compared to home. It was only as I squatted that I realised I wasn't desperate to go, nor did I have any shooting nerve pains. If Hell could do away with perimenopause symptoms and birth injuries, then it really had been getting an unfairly bad press.

When I was ready, I headed for the door, not being at all sure what would greet me on the other side. The corridor was disappointingly similar to every other budget hotel I'd ever stayed in. It was only as I pulled the door shut behind me that I noticed my room number was 666. Somebody here, it seemed, had a sense of humour. I followed the sign to the lift. As I got there, another door opposite opened and a skinny teenage girl with long chestnut brown hair stepped out, visibly flinching when she saw me. I was about to say she looked like she'd seen a ghost when it occurred to me that she had.

'Sorry,' she said. 'I wasn't expecting to see anyone.'

'Me neither,' I replied. We stared at each other for a moment, presumably both wondering the same thing. I called the lift and the doors opened instantly, as if it had been waiting for us. I stepped inside. The girl followed me, somewhat gingerly.

'Which floor?' I asked.

'Basement,' she said, in a voice barely more than a whisper.

I nodded and pressed the button. She looked down at her feet. Poor kid, she couldn't have been more than eighteen. Pretty, with rosebud lips which would no doubt be good at the obligatory teenage girl selfie pout, but also eyes which were full of unbearable sadness. I wondered how she'd got here. I hoped to God it wasn't the same way I had, but then you never had a clue what someone else had been through. I felt the need to say something vaguely comforting. Anything.

'I don't understand it either,' I said. 'I'm only following instructions.'

'On your TV?' she asked.

I nodded. 'Don't know why I'm doing what I'm told, to be honest. Can't say I usually do. But I guess curiosity got the better of me.'

'Have you still got your phone?' she asked.

It was the first time I'd even thought about it. I fished around in my bag but there was no sign. I shook my head.

'Me neither.'

It was clear from the expression on her face that this was probably the biggest concern to her right now. I suspected Thomas and Noah would have been the same. Phone deprivation would certainly be their idea of hell. She wound the ends of her hair around the index finger of her left hand. It was only then I noticed that she was wearing what looked like an engagement ring. I frowned. She glanced up and caught me looking.

'Ten days,' she said. 'We were engaged for ten days.'

For someone who a few minutes ago had appeared to be a regular teenage girl fretting about her missing phone, she suddenly had the air of a woman several times her age, who had been through two world wars and lost her entire family. I was about to say something, perhaps even reach for her hand, when there was a ping and the doors opened.

We stepped out onto another corridor. There was a man standing outside the door opposite us. Probably in his thirties or forties; bald, clean shaven and wearing glasses with a dark rim on the top edge only. He nodded and gave us a thin smile.

'Hi, I'm Carl,' he said, offering his hand.

I shook it. He had a very firm handshake.

'Jules,' I said.

'And this is?' He looked at the girl and back to me.

'Oh, we're not together,' I said. 'We just met in the lift coming down.'

'Sorry,' he said. 'I thought you were her mum.'

I turned to face the girl, who appeared appalled by the suggestion.

'I'm Emily,' she said quietly.

'Pleased to meet you both,' said Carl, like it was a wedding reception, not a chance encounter in Hell.

'Did you get the same message?' I asked, nodding towards the door of Room 010 opposite.

'It appears so,' said Carl. 'No idea what's going on, mind.'

'Has anyone else come down in the lift?' I asked.

'Nope. Only you two.'

'It's like we're the three reprobates standing outside the headteacher's office,' I said. Emily stared at me blankly.

'You've never had to stand outside a headteacher's office, have you?' I asked.

She shook her head. I turned to Carl with a questioning look.

''Fraid not,' he replied. 'I was annoyingly well-behaved and responsible at all times.'

I frowned. How could this be Hell if I'd ended up with two people who had never even been in trouble at school? Perhaps it was like *The Good Place,* and they'd got me mixed up with another Julie Smith who'd lived a blameless life.

The door opened and a woman with an unruly mass of wild grey hair and sporting an ancient black leather jacket greeted us cheerily.

'Welcome, all,' she said. 'I'm Suzi, as in Quatro. Surname Parker, as in nosey. Come on in and I'll go through the whole shebang with you.'

She turned and retreated into the room, her jacket squeaking as she went. I looked at Carl. He shrugged and gestured for me to go first.

'Who's Suzi Quatro?' whispered Emily as she followed me into the room.

'The original female rock chick,' I said. 'Bit before your time, mind.'

Suzi's room had black walls, shiny black floor tiles and three black and chrome chairs positioned on one side of a desk with a huge red leather swivel chair behind it.

'Take a seat, ladies and gent,' she said, practically leaping into her own chair and turning a full 360 degrees in the process.

'Now, before we get down to business, we've got to get some boring admin out of the way.'

She turned to the laptop in front of her and tapped a few keys.

'Most of your details have already been uploaded, only a few gaps to fill in. Julie,' she said, turning to me. 'Can I just check we have the correct name for your next of kin?'

'It's Jules, actually,' I said. 'And my husband's name is Robert Smith.'

Suzi threw back her head and laughed.

'Excellent, thought it might be an error with our computer programme. Glad to hear it's genuine. And this from the woman whose email address starts with gothgirl75. Did you marry him for a bet?'

I hesitated before replying, not keen to admit it but appreciating that if I was already in Hell, there was little point in trying to save face.

'I went on our first date for a bet,' I replied. 'The marriage thing just kind of happened.'

I noticed Emily frowning at us, as did Suzi.

'I can see I'm going to need to translate for the Gen Z girl here,' Suzi said, before turning to Emily. 'Robert Smith, lead singer of The Cure. Her favourite band.'

'How do you know that?' I asked. 'And how do you know my email address?'

'Have you never stopped to think about all the personal information you put online? You can hardly complain when it's used to create your file,' she replied.

'Why do you have a file on me?'

'You've all got one. But I can tell you that some are more embarrassing than others. Goody-two-shoes here,' she said, nodding towards Emily, 'has a blemish-free record.'

'So why is she here?' I asked. 'I thought this was...' My voice trailed off when I saw the look on Emily's face. If she hadn't clocked it by now, I really didn't want to be the one to break it to her.

'All in good time,' said Suzi, holding up her hand. 'Now, Emily, I've got two different names for your next of kin here.'

'It's Harry Sanders,' she said, sounding clearer than I'd heard her so far. 'My fiancé.'

'Ah,' said Suzi, checking her screen, 'I'm afraid next of kin have to be eighteen or over.'

Carl and I exchanged a glance. How the hell had she been engaged at seventeen?

'My dad then,' said Emily. 'Simon Mottram.'

'Great, that's the other name I had. And last but by no means least, Carl. I have your most recent occupation down here as "motorcycle rider" and I wanted to check if you meant a stunt one, like Eddie Kidd?' asked Suzi, turning to Emily and adding, 'Think hot seventies guy in biking gear jumping over buses.'

'More like Deliveroo, sadly,' replied Carl.

'OK. Not nearly as impressive,' said Suzi. 'Right, now we've got that out of the way, I can get down to business.'

She took off her oversized, black-rimmed glasses and looked at us.

'I expect you're all wondering why you're here.'

We nodded in unison, seemingly all wanting her to say it out loud rather than be forced to voice it ourselves. Although I sensed Suzi was not someone who was going to be diplomatic about breaking the news.

'Well, if you haven't clocked it by now, you're all deceased, passed on, no more. You have expired, gone off to meet your maker. You are, in effect, ex-people.'

I managed a smile at the Monty Python reference. Carl bowed his head. Emily continued staring at her in bemusement.

2

EMILY

Suzi looked at me and said, 'Sorry, sweetie. I know that may have sounded brutal, but I've done this talk enough times to know that subtle doesn't tend to work, people need it spelt out to them. Take all the time you need to get your head around it; you're probably in shock.'

She was doing what they always did, treating me like a kid. As if I didn't know I was dead. I'd known I was dying for months. I'd hardly thought about anything else, even if Dad had tried his best to avoid the subject. To talk about what we could do together next year as if I was still going to be alive. In my experience, it was the adults who liked to play make-believe and dance around the truth instead of confronting it.

It had been the same in hospital; first being stuck on a children's ward because I wasn't old enough to be on an adult one, and even when I turned sixteen, they still treated me like I was a kid. I wasn't old enough to be recognised as a grown-up, but I was old enough to die.

And now I was here, and it was the first time in what felt like forever that I hadn't been ill or in pain and all I wanted to do was listen to music, look at photos of Harry and grieve for my lost life. But I couldn't do that because I didn't have my phone.

'When do we get our phones back?' I asked.

Suzi, who was still banging on about us being dead, stopped mid-sentence.

'I'm sorry?' she said.

'I'd like my phone back, please. I get that we can't make calls or send messages, but it's got my photos and music on.'

All three of them stared at me. I sighed and rolled my eyes.

'Look, I'm not a kid and I'm not stupid. I died; I get that. It was a long time coming. Unlike you guys, I'm over it. I just want my phone back, please.'

Suzi raised her eyebrows. 'Well, I must say you've taken the news better than most. But I'm afraid you're out of luck because there are no phones allowed here.'

I frowned.

'You can't do that. What sort of Heaven is this if there are no phones? Or is Heaven designed by old people who still consider mobiles a nuisance?'

Jules immediately looked down at the ground. I turned to Carl, but he was busy cleaning his glasses.

'Houston, we have a problem,' said Suzi.

'Will you please just talk normally?' I asked her.

Jules reached over to me and patted my hand, which she had no right to do because she wasn't my mum.

'I'm afraid we're not in Heaven, Emily,' she said quietly. I stared at her. It took a moment for the words to sink in.

'You mean...?'

Jules nodded.

'This is our "welcome to Hell" talk,' she said.

Suzi spurted out the coffee she'd just taken a mouthful of as she started laughing.

'Hey,' said Jules, scowling at her. 'What is wrong with you? That's not an easy thing to hear, especially at her age.'

I rolled my eyes.

'Please don't patronise me,' I said to Jules. 'I don't need protecting from anything. Especially the truth.' I turned back to Suzi.

'But I would like you to explain how I ended up in Hell because if you look at my school reports, you'll see it's all "hard-working and conscientious" and "she was a pleasure to have in the classroom". The *Halifax Courier* described me as a "plucky fundraising hero", and I never even argued with my parents or shouted "this is so fucking unfair" after they told me I was going to die.'

The room was quiet again for a moment. It was Suzi who spoke first.

'Firstly, take no notice of her,' she said, gesturing towards Jules. 'This isn't Hell.'

'Isn't it?' asked Jules, frowning.

'No.'

'But it can't be Heaven because phones aren't allowed,' I pointed out.

'Your reasoning skills are suspect, but your conclusion is spot on,' said Suzi.

We all sat there staring blankly at her.

Suzi sighed.

'OK, you, quiet guy at the end, can you work it out?'

She looked at Carl, who appeared to be weighing up his answer carefully like a quiz show contestant.

'Is it a kind of holding place?' he ventured. 'Like a processing centre?'

'Correct!' Suzi shouted, punching the air. 'You win Bully's star prize of a caravan holiday in Skegness.'

I screwed my face up. She really was the weirdest woman.

'I don't understand,' said Jules. 'Why didn't we go straight to whichever one we're destined for? I thought I'd booked a direct flight.'

Suzi rolled her eyes.

'Have you any idea how much admin is involved every time someone pops their clogs? And it's twenty times more paperwork since we left the EU. Perhaps you lot should have thought about that before you voted for Brexit.'

'Don't blame me,' I protested. 'I was too young to vote. It was all the old ones who messed everything up, as usual.'

'I voted Remain, thank you,' said Jules, indignantly. We all looked at Carl.

'Er, I ended up working a double shift, so I was too late to vote.'

'There you go,' said Suzi. 'This is what happens when a country puts its desire to scoff a bucket of chicken wings before long-term future and prosperity.'

'Oh no, it wasn't when I was delivering takeaways, it was a previous job,' said Carl.

'Don't let the facts get in the way of a good story,' said Suzi. 'That's what a career in journalism teaches you. And that anything can happen to anyone at any time, which is why you're all stuck here, and I've been landed with a shitload of admin to do.'

'So, is it like having to sleep on the airport floor for a night when your plane's been delayed?' asked Jules.

'Not exactly. You'll be here for about a month.'

'A *month*?' Jules replied. 'What are we supposed to do for that long?'

'Well, it's certainly not a holiday camp. You'll be working while you're here.'

'It doesn't involve cleaning, does it?' asked Jules. 'Because I've done enough of that for four lifetimes.'

'No, we have permanent staff as cleaners,' replied Suzi. 'People who took up seats on trains with their bags or put their feet up on them. And those who played their music or YouTube videos loudly enough for the whole carriage to hear. They thought they'd got away with it, but they're doing payback time here.'

'So, is that like community service for the dead?' asked Jules.

'I prefer to call it VAA – Vengeance Against Arseholes – but whatever floats your boat,' said Suzi, waving her hand.

'So, what about us?' asked Carl. 'What do we have to do?'

Suzi pointed to the wall behind her as a screen dropped down from the ceiling with a photo of a coffin with an 'End Credits' logo on it.

'Don't worry,' she said. 'This is the only photo. I don't do PowerPoint presentations because I understand that you've already lost the will to live once. This will be painless in comparison.'

She reached for a laser pointer and shined it at the screen.

'You have arrived at the headquarters of the film production company End Credits, of which I'm the Executive Producer. The good news is that you lovely lot get to be film directors.'

'What, like Martin Scorsese or Steven Spielberg?' asked Carl, looking the most excited he'd been since we arrived.

'Not exactly. I'm afraid we're talking low-budget movies here. You'll be working on the films of your lives.'

'I'm sorry?' Carl replied.

'Right, buckle up,' said Suzi, 'because this is where the ride gets wild. The significant moments of your lives have been filmed. It shouldn't be too much of a shock, especially as you all spend so much time filming stuff on your phones.'

'Woah... Who? What? Why? When? Where? How?' stuttered Carl.

'That's a lot of questions,' Suzi replied. 'And the very ones we were taught to ask at journalism college, so let me try to answer them for you. We monitor everyone's lives with remote cameras and hacked footage that feed into a huge production gallery. Obviously, it's a lot easier nowadays, what with CCTV everywhere, security cameras, webcams, Ring doorbells and mobile phones, all of which we can access. Again, save your complaints, you're the ones who use all that stuff.'

'You won't have much of my youth then,' said Jules.

'Nope. I'm told that before I arrived here ten years ago, they had very limited resources. Originally, they did manage to convert some old cinefilms people had made – if you've seen ads for companies offering to digitise cinefilms and video tapes, that's us, excellent way to get our hands on footage without the public realising – but that was about it.

'Fortunately, from the nineties, CCTV was rolled out across the UK and people started sticking up Sky dishes on their roofs, meaning the satellite technology could be used to transmit footage from anywhere.'

'I was at uni in Bristol in 1995,' said Jules. 'Best days of my life.'

'Well, there'll be no keeping secrets from your student days,' said Suzi with a laugh before she continued.

'And then came the internet, video cameras in many households, mobile phones, home security cameras, facial recognition software, drones and everything else. It seems you lot can't get enough of yourselves on camera.'

'But the logistics involved in that must be immense,' said Carl.

'How did I know you'd be the logistics dude?' said Suzi. 'We developed algorithms which allow us to get alerts whenever significant moments are expected: someone buys an engagement ring, gets a job interview, arranges a first date, texts someone to end a relationship – your generation really are savages. I would never have believed civilisation would come to that.

'Anyway, we focus on those people instead of the 99 per cent of folks having boring humdrum days. Our production gallery monitors have seen a lot of lives and deaths; they know the signs to look for. And you lot are boringly predictable most of the time. And when it appears something major is brewing – whether that's good or bad – we dispatch one of our crack professional camera crews.'

'But that makes no sense,' said Jules. 'Surely we'd see them?'

Suzi rolled her eyes.

'Ghost camera crews, obviously. Whenever they die, they get offered the opportunity to stay on here in a job for the afterlife and it turns out playing around with cameras and booms is their idea of Heaven.'

'So, we couldn't see them, but they could see us?' I asked, 'Like in *The Sixth Sense?*'

Suzi punched the air and pointed at me.

'Hey, so you're not completely clueless about cultural references from before you were born.'

'Of course not. Mum did eighties and nineties film nights with me.'

'Excellent,' said Suzi, 'that's one less thing for me to explain.'

'But why did you let invisible men film me without me

knowing? What about our privacy?' I demanded. 'There are laws against that sort of thing.'

'Don't worry, we operate a strict no bedrooms or bathrooms policy,' said Suzi. 'Although if you were in the habit of walking around your house in your underwear' – she broke off for a second to look at Carl – 'we may well have that on film.'

I thought of all the times Harry had sat with me in my bedroom. A part of me wished they had filmed that because watching it would make me feel like I was with him again. His hand stroking my head as he whispered into my ear. Telling me how much he loved me. How he would never stop loving me.

Suzi had stopped talking and was looking at me. So were the others.

'Do you need to take a moment?' Jules asked. I realised a tear was rolling down my cheek and I quickly brushed it away, telling myself that there would be plenty of other footage of us together. Harry asking me out, us taking Slinky Dog for walks in the park, him singing to me at our engagement. I was going to see him again. That was the important thing.

'No. I want to see it now. Everything that's been filmed.'

Suzi held up her hand.

'Not so fast, missy, there's work to do first. The films aren't quite finished yet and that's where you come in. You'll each be directing your final filming unit before you get to watch what's already in the can.'

'But if it's the highlights of our lives and we're dead, what's there left to film?' asked Carl.

'I didn't say highlights, I said significant moments, and your departure is undoubtedly one of them. Plus, we need a big emotional ending,' said Suzi. 'You know, grieving family and friends, lots of weeping. Otherwise, it can all fall a bit flat.'

I let out an audible gasp. I was going to see Harry again in real life. He wouldn't be able to see me but maybe he'd be able to sense I was there. It would be like *Ghost* but without the pottery, which was good as I hated getting my hands dirty.

'What if they're not doing major grieving?' asked Jules. 'What if they're simply trying to find the manual for the dishwasher and wondering where I kept the cat food? I mean that's not going to make much of an ending, is it?'

'Nothing I can do about that,' said Suzi with a shrug. 'You'd better hope someone does a good eulogy.'

'Fat chance,' said Jules. 'Rob hasn't said a nice word to me in years, so I can't imagine he'd say any in death.'

I stared at her, unable to work out why the hell she was still married to him if he was such a bastard.

'Well, the good news is you haven't got to share a bed with him because we'll put you up in your own film trailer with three separate rooms while you're on location,' said Suzi. 'Obviously your folks won't be able to see you, the film crew or the trailer. And as soon as you're in the ground, it's a wrap.'

'I'm having a cremation,' said Carl.

'Well, the frying pan then,' said Suzi.

Jules frowned at Carl.

'How do you know you're having a cremation?'

'It was in my will,' he replied.

'Your will? Did you know you were going to die?'

'No. It was an accident.'

'And how old are you, late thirties?'

'Thirty-one, actually,' Carl said.

I resisted the temptation to say 'awkward'.

'So how come you made a will?' Jules continued. 'I haven't got one and I'm fifty, married with two stepsons and a mortgage.'

Carl looked flustered.

'I guess I'm a practical sort of person,' he said. 'Always prepared for anything.'

Suzi scrolled down her laptop screen.

'There. Suspected as much,' she said. 'Former boy scout. Dib, dib, dib, dob, dob, dob and all that.'

I was starting to think Suzi literally spoke a different language to me.

Carl shook his head. It was probably the closest he got to being angry.

'Isn't this whole thing a bit much?' he asked. 'Expecting us to attend our own funerals and cremations.'

'Hardly, you're going to be there anyway,' said Suzi.

'You know what I mean,' he replied firmly.

I knew what he meant too. Although I was desperate to see Harry, I was not so keen on having to watch him grieving for me. Mum would be in such a state. And I had no idea if Dad would be able to get through it.

We all stared at Suzi, making it clear we were expecting a better answer. Her expression changed and she put down the pen she'd been twiddling between her fingers.

'Look, death is like one of those rock-hard toffees that everyone avoids by choosing the soft centres. But the truth is, it's the one thing you're guaranteed to get from the selection box in the end and the sooner you realise that, the better.'

The three of us sat there in silence for a moment. I realised I'd had a lot longer to come to terms with it than the other two had.

'So, what happens then?' I asked. 'After the funerals.'

'That's the good bit,' said Suzi. 'You come back here and start editing the films of your lives, only there's a twist. You get to do a director's cut.'

'What's a director's cut?' I asked.

'Jeez, these youngsters,' said Suzi, shaking her head. 'Go and google *Blade Runner*, sweetie.'

'I can't,' I reply. 'You've stolen my phone.'

'Seriously,' said Carl. 'Ridley Scott's version of *Blade Runner* is epic. You should watch it.'

I pulled a face, still having no idea what any of them were talking about.

'Basically, we get to pick an ending of our own choice,' said Jules, 'instead of the one we actually got.'

'Well, sort of,' said Suzi. 'Although there are a few rules to follow. It's about regrets.'

'Unfortunately, I've got so many regrets, I wouldn't know where to start,' said Jules.

'Not as catchy as the Frank Sinatra line,' replied Suzi.

'But no one will ever get to see our director's cut,' said Carl. 'Which seems a bit of a waste.'

'The three of you will,' said Suzi. 'We'll give you a big private screening and a copy of the film to keep that you can watch for all eternity. We'll even throw in a tub of popcorn. No expense spared here. Now, any questions before we get this show on the road?'

'But what's the point of it?' asked Carl. 'It sounds like you're forcing us to go through some tough things to make a film that no one else will see apart from us. Are you sure this isn't all some ruse to keep you in a job?'

Suzi raised an eyebrow at Carl, but he showed no sign of taking back what he'd said.

'Believe me, I've got better things I could do with my time,' she replied. 'The point of it is, you need to rest in peace.'

'Don't go all religious on me,' said Carl, 'because I'm really not interested.'

Suzi sighed.

'You can't move on to wherever it is you're going until you find some kind of peace with your life and the decisions you made.'

'And what if that's impossible?' asked Carl.

'Well, Suzi Parker's director's cut is not the same as Ridley Scott's. My version of it allows you to actually make a change which could have a huge impact on your final film – not just the ending. Although there are three rules which I should draw your attention to.'

'Like what?' asked Carl.

She pressed a clicker, and three rules appeared on the screen behind her.

'I lied. There is another slide. It's like the Covid press conferences all over again,' said Suzi, before she started reading.

'Rule one: You can't save your own life or anyone else's. No exceptions and that includes changing the way you died. Two: You can't kill anyone. Three: You can make one cut that changes the life of someone you've left behind. And when you do, everything that happened afterwards will change too, like in that *Sliding Doors* movie, have you seen that one?' she asked, turning to me.

'Yes,' I replied. 'Gwyneth Paltrow had two different haircuts, so you knew which version it was. I thought she looked really good with short hair.'

'You can always rely on Gen Z to focus on the most trivial aspect of anything,' said Suzi, shaking her head. 'Now, any further questions?' There was so much weird crap to get my head around, it was hard to know where to start. I went with the first one which came to mind.

'Why are the three of us here together when we've, like, never met each other before?'

'Timing and geography,' Suzi replied. 'You all died on the same day in Halifax. And this is your local processing centre.'

'You mean there are places like this in towns and cities all over the UK?' asked Carl.

'Yep,' said Suzi. 'Best-kept secret there is. You'll never get a room on the top floor of a Travel Inn unless you've bitten the dust.'

'But where are all the old people?' asked Jules.

'Sorry, I should have explained that. We only take those under retirement age here. There are a lot more older folks, so they have to be processed offshore.'

'Offshore?' asked Carl. 'That sounds a bit extreme. Is it like Rishi Sunak putting asylum seekers on that Bibby Stockholm barge? Only I thought that was just some madcap idea the Tories adopted when they got desperate.'

'No, cruise ships, darling,' said Suzi. 'Plenty of room and some of the pensioners are already there anyway. They simply have to move down to the lowest deck. Doesn't matter if you're below the waterline in that situation.'

We all nodded, as if that was totally acceptable, and I tried not to think about my great-nan, who wouldn't go on boats because she got seasick.

'Anyway,' continued Suzi. 'Our usual intake is pushing sixty or above. It's a refreshing change to get some young blood, to be honest.'

She looked at me as she said it, and I saw a hint of colour rise in her cheeks. Jules and Carl were both glaring at her, but it didn't bother me. I'd got used to other people's awkwardness about me dying so young. I thought instead about the people who'd be arriving tomorrow. They probably didn't know it yet. Or, if they were young like me, maybe they did. They just weren't expecting to end up in this place.

'So, no one else under sixty-six died in Halifax yesterday?' asked Carl.

'Nope. We'll probably get a bumper intake tomorrow to make up for it. Any other questions?'

Carl looked down and blew out.

'What about the children?' I asked.

The room went quiet. They were clearly a bit squeamish about this stuff. It even took Suzi a moment to answer.

'The babies and toddlers are looked after in special crèches. Those under thirteen go to Disney-style holiday resorts complete with chaperones. And the teenagers under sixteen get an afterlife pass to the UK's theme parks. You did well to miss out on that.'

'What about pets?' I asked. 'Where do they go when they die? Only my Slinky Dog is nine and I want to know if I'm going to see him again.'

'Wow, you certainly do ask the big questions,' said Suzi. 'The good news is that pets are well cared for, although separately from us. We have dog play parks with ball-throwing machines – which is where Slinky Dog will go – cat cardboard box hotels and guinea pig carrot cottages with fleece-lined interiors, so basically, they do better than us, exactly as in real life.'

'Good,' I said, sad that I wouldn't see Slinky Dog in the afterlife but happy that he'd love the play park.

'And why are you still here?' I asked Suzi. 'Why haven't you moved on to your final destination?'

For a second, I actually thought I'd succeeded in flooring her. It took her a while to come up with an answer.

'Tough question,' she replied, pointing at me. 'You would have had journalistic potential. I guess I thought being an executive film producer and having a swanky office with a massive swivel chair was a way better deal than what I was going to get anywhere else.'

I nodded. It was the first time I'd detected a catch in her voice, and I decided not to push it.

Carl piped up again.

'The message on the TV said this was the start of our induction programme, so what else do we have to do before we head off on location?'

'Nothing gets past you, does it, Sherlock?' said Suzi. 'And I can exclusively reveal that your next challenge is to do a practice director's cut of your favourite children's film. Same three rules apply.'

I sat there looking at her, trying to work out if she was joking or not.

'Seriously?' I asked.

'Absolutely. Children's films are the perfect training ground, and you'll only be dealing with scenes of mild peril instead of the serious shit in your own lives.'

I thought for a moment. She had a point. Although I wouldn't have called the peril in my favourite children's film mild.

'Easy. I'll do *Finding Nemo*,' I said. 'I used to be scared to go swimming in case I went over the drop-off.'

The others smiled and nodded but didn't make any suggestions of their own.

'And is that it?' asked Carl. 'Only I have a bad feeling you're holding something back.'

Suzi hesitated before she replied.

'First thing tomorrow, you lucky people get to watch the final scenes of each other's lives,' she said, her eyes firmly on her laptop screen. There was a pause before any of us spoke.

'You mean... our deaths?' Carl asked. 'We have to watch each other dying?'

'Like I said,' replied Suzi. 'It's all part of the grieving process. You can't move on until you come to terms with what's happened. You'll need to help each other through it. Like a sort of team-building exercise.'

I looked at Jules and Carl, unable to see how we'd ever be part of the same team. The colour had drained from their faces. They didn't want to do this; I could see that. But I didn't mind. I would happily watch myself die a thousand times because it meant I could see Harry again.

3

CARL

I stared at Suzi, unsure I'd be able to watch. Not because of me; I had no qualms about seeing myself die. But watching Lewis, that was a different matter. I hadn't known if he'd survived the accident. Not until Suzi had said the three of us were the only people of working age from Halifax to have died yesterday. But Lewis could be one of the new arrivals tomorrow. He might have clung to life overnight but not be able to hang on into a second day. At least when we went on location, I'd be able to go to the hospital and find out what had happened to him. But before that I was going to have to watch what I'd done to him in front of Jules and Emily. They would ask questions: who he was, why he'd been a passenger on my bike, why I'd lost control going into that bend. I'd lie, of course, make some excuse about the road conditions. But I knew the real reason and not even death had obliterated it from my mind. I may have been regenerated, *Doctor-Who*-style, but it seemed no one had been able to wipe my brain of the horrors that lurked within.

'Right, off you all trot, then,' said Suzi. 'Faz, our tech whizz-kid editor, is outside. He'll take you to the editing suite to get started on your children's film director's cuts and I'll pop along soon to see how you're getting on.'

I stood up with the others, and we trooped out of Suzi's office to be greeted in the corridor by a young guy in a retro Choose Life T-shirt – which felt highly inappropriate in the circumstances – ripped jeans and red Converse. He smiled broadly at us with perfect teeth which looked like they had been chemically enhanced.

'Hey guys, welcome to End Credits, I hope you're feeling refreshed after your journeys here.'

He said it with no hint of irony and a rising inflection which suggested it was a question he expected an answer to. I glanced at Jules, who rolled her eyes. He carried on, seemingly unperturbed by our silence.

'Perfect! So, I'm Faz and I'll be leading you through the rest of the induction programme. If you'd like to come with me, I can get you set up.'

He gave another dazzling smile, turned on his heel, keeping a firm hold of his reusable coffee cup as he did so, and set off down the corridor at breakneck speed.

'Jesus, I thought I was done working with people who are straight out of uni and unable to contain their enthusiasm,' Jules whispered to me as we followed him.

'He's just trying to be positive,' said Emily, who was walking a step behind us. 'And he must be at least twenty-five.'

'Sorry,' Jules said over her shoulder. 'It must be tough being stuck with a couple of grumpy old farts like us.'

She said it kindly, so I decided not to remind her that thirty-one wasn't exactly 'old fart' territory and I was actually closer to Emily's age than hers. That was the trouble when you went bald before your time. People always aged you at least ten years in their heads.

'OK, guys,' said Faz, stopping at the end of the corridor. 'This is us.'

He opened the door and led us into a production studio full of monitors, mixing desks and other tech equipment.

'Grab a seat, and I'll give you a quick run-through of the basics.'

I sat down in the chair at the far end of the desk and watched intently as Faz showed us how to play, fast forward and rewind the film, mark the start and end points of cuts and move sections of footage.

'You need to remember the rules Suzi gave you. You can't save any characters who died or kill ones who didn't. It's simply about making one cut which then impacts the rest of the film,' he explained.

'And what happens after we've made our cut?' I ask.

'You add any editorial notes, send it through to me, I'll input it into our system and our computer programme will generate the new version of the film. You'll get to watch it before you do your own director's cuts on your films.'

I nodded. Still not sure I was ready for the children's film task, let alone messing with the film of my own life.

'Right,' said Faz. 'Let's get you all started. What children's films have you chosen to practise on?'

He looked at Emily first.

'*Finding Nemo*,' she said.

'Amazing!' replied Faz. 'How much do we all love Ellen DeGeneres?'

Emily didn't look at all sure whether she should attempt to answer this question, but Faz was already moving on to Jules.

'*Bambi*,' she said.

'Perfect, all the nans like that one. I'm not familiar with it myself but I've seen some *hilarious* Thumper memes.'

Jules looked as if she might thump Faz, but he moved quickly along the line to me.

'*The Lion King*,' I mumbled.

'Fab-u-lous! Love Elton John, and the costumes in the musical are to die for. Have you seen it?'

'Er, yes. A couple of times. Bradford and Broadway.'

'Hey, we have a musical theatre luvvie in our midst!' Faz exclaimed, with a knowing smile. I was used to this by now. The quick assumptions. It didn't help being single either. Or taking care with my appearance. It felt like being an older version of the 'wee English lad' in *Derry Girls*, who everyone just assumes is gay.

Jules looked at me as Faz walked away. I shrugged, not bothering to deny anything because I didn't want the conversation that would inevitably follow.

'OK,' he said, a few minutes later. 'I've loaded those films into the system now, so I'll leave you to get on with it, but please feel free to reach out to me if you need any help.' He disappeared into a booth at the far end of the studio.

We stared blankly at our screens for what felt like a very long time.

'We need to work through this methodically,' said Emily after a while. 'Plan out exactly what we're doing in a storyboard before we start cutting anything.'

'There speaks a young woman who used Post-it notes and highlighters for her GCSE revision,' said Jules with a smile.

The colour rose in Emily's cheeks.

'I've watched documentaries about Disney Pixar,' she said. 'They have slides and cereal bars in their HQ, it's dead cool.'

'It doesn't look like they run to that here,' said Jules. 'I'm bloody starving and I haven't seen as much as a vending machine.'

'Anyway,' said Emily, who clearly wasn't bothered about Jules's sugar cravings. 'Have you both watched *Finding Nemo*?'

Jules and I nodded.

'Here's why I'm stuck. What I really want to do is save Nemo's mum Coral from dying but the rules say I can't do that. So, the next best thing I can come up with is to cut the line where Dory tells Marlin she has short-term memory loss.'

'But that would ruin the whole film,' pointed out Jules.

'I know. And it would also mean my second-favourite film, *Finding Dory*, wouldn't even exist but sometimes you have to make tough decisions.'

I looked at her and nodded. She clearly knew her own mind.

'I've got a similar problem,' I said. 'The obvious thing is to save Simba's dad, Mufasa – but I'm not allowed to do that. Maybe I should change it by having Scar die trying to save Mufasa instead of throwing him off the cliff.'

'Oooh, that would be good,' said Jules. 'The brothers plunging to their deaths together.'

I realised as soon as she said it that, in the circumstances, I really didn't want to go down that route.

'Actually, no,' I said. 'I'll have Mufasa fall off the cliff accidentally first and Scar can just lurk in the background until he dies later on. I can't kill off the baddie so early. Probably upset the critics.'

'Believe me, it would be nothing compared to mine,' said Jules. 'I'd like to turn *Bambi* into a bloodbath.'

I stared at her, wondering what on earth this woman I'd been holed up with was capable of.

'You can't do that,' I said. 'It was bad enough Bambi's mum getting killed.'

'Oh my God! Bambi's mum gets killed?' screeched Emily. 'No wonder my dad wouldn't let me watch it.'

'It bloody traumatised me as a kid,' said Jules. 'But thinking about it now, the whole film is a pile of sexist crap and should be erased from the archives.'

'What do you mean?' I asked, sensing I might regret inviting her to expand her theory.

'Well, Bambi's mother had no big scenes or lines, did she? She was only there so we could feel sorry for her little boy fawn when she got shot.'

'She was shot?' said Emily. 'That's even more horrific.'

'I know. And, unlike Mufasa, she didn't even have a name,' continued Jules. 'She was simply reduced to being "Bambi's mum". I mean his dad was called "The Great Prince of the Forest", but she was "Bambi's mum". I know what that's like. I've spent years being "Thomas's stepmum" and "Noah's stepmum" and I can tell you, it's a crock of shit. You lose your entire identity. Everyone forgets there's a real person under there. A person who had a life before they took on parenting duties and spent all their time cooking meals for them, washing dirty PE kits and picking their socks up off the floor. Plus, everyone calls you the evil stepmother behind your back and Disney are to blame for that too.'

I looked at her, one eyebrow raised. She wasn't exactly coming over as a devoted earth-mother type. She hadn't finished yet though.

'No, Bambi's mum deserves to have her own name in lights, and we all need to shout it loud and proud for all the mums out there who have forgotten they even have a name.'

Jules stopped to draw breath and realised Emily and I were staring at her. I wasn't sure whether to be impressed or scared.

'Have I gone off on one?' she said. 'I don't really care if I have, because it needed to be said. Anyway, back to *Bambi*. Faline, his love interest, that's all she's there for, to simper at him and look pretty. Bloody Thumper has a love interest too. Her name is "Miss Bunny". I mean that's still not a real name, is it? And she's only in one scene where she spots him, falls in love instantly and tricks him into noticing her, because us females are so sneaky like that. She got to say one word, one fucking word, which was "hello", and other than that she got to stroke his ear. I mean, come on.'

Jules drew breath again. Emily was managing the closest thing I'd seen to a smile.

'But if you hate it that much, why did you choose it as your favourite children's film?' I asked.

'Because it was my favourite when I was seven, I watched it so many times, despite the trauma. But when I watched it with the boys years later, I realised what a pile of sexist crap it was, which is why I'd now like to make the feminist version.'

'Go on then,' I said, worried I might regret this. 'What are you planning to do with it?'

'I'll call Bambi's mother Titania, Queen of the Forest – because that's a name you won't bloody forget in a hurry. Obviously, I'd like her to dodge the bullet,' continued Jules, 'but the rules say I can't do that. So instead, she'll charge the hunter, and as he shoots her at close range, his second bullet ricochets back off the bronze name tag she wears and maims him for life. So at least she gets her own back on the bastard. Then, when Faline meets Bambi, she'll tell him to get lost, and Miss Bunny, who I'll rename Persephone, the goddess of persuasion and seduction, will give Thumper myxomatosis, which would leave him seriously ill, even if he doesn't die before the end. Faline and Persephone would then head off together *Thelma & Louise* style, as the ghost of Titania rises up and roars – or whatever noise female deer make – her approval across the land.'

Someone started applauding. I looked around and saw Suzi standing in the doorway with a grin on her face.

'Now that,' she said, 'is a director's cut that would go down in history.'

Jules stood up and bowed.

'I tell you, I bloody wasted my life,' she said. 'I should have started a new Disney universe franchise of animated female character revenge movies.'

'Would have been huge,' Suzi agreed. 'Made you a small fortune.'

'Jeez, if I could have my time again,' Jules said.

And that was when it hit me. We couldn't. This was it. Game over. And what had I done? Where had I made a difference? I hadn't invented anything or changed anyone's life for the better. I hadn't even been able to save anyone. Not the people that mattered. Including my own brother.

'And what about you, quiet guy?' Suzi said, turning to me. I opened my mouth, knowing that no one would have found it easy to follow Jules, but that my effort was going to be particularly lame in comparison.

'I'm going to have Simba's father, Mufasa, and his brother, Scar, bury their differences before Mufasa dies,' I said. 'Turn it into a tragic accident. And then Simba's mum—'

'Her name's Sarabi,' said Jules pointedly.

'Sorry, Sarabi – she can be caretaker leader of the pride until Simba's old enough to take over and Scar would simply fall off Pride Rock due to failing eyesight.'

'Boring as hell,' said Suzi, turning her nose up.

'Simba should have an older sister who becomes leader,' said Jules. 'That whole male succession thing is so last century. Even the Royal Family has scrapped it now. Simba's sister can ensure the hyenas are there to eat Scar when he falls, and Simba can just prat about with Timon and Pumbaa for some funny bits.'

'I'd listen to her,' said Suzi, looking at me while nodding towards Jules. 'You're seriously outnumbered by females here, and I wouldn't count on Faz for support.'

'OK,' I said. 'I guess I'm sorted then.'

Suzi turned to face Emily.

'Right, your turn. Let's see what Gen Z are made of.'

'I'm going to cut Dory having short-term memory loss,' Emily said. 'I know it ruins my favourite film and means my second favourite wouldn't even get made, but it's the right thing to do. It would save Marlin from his misery because Dory would be able to take him straight to the boat.'

'But what would happen in the rest of the film?' I asked. 'Because Nemo wouldn't be lost long enough for anyone to have to find him.'

'I dunno,' she said with a shrug. 'Maybe they could just save the coral reef or something. I could turn them into eco-warriors and have Greta Thunberg voice Dory instead.'

Suzi threw her hands up in despair.

'You see, this is what we have to put up with from teenagers nowadays. Bloody bunch of do-gooders and bleeding hearts. Too concerned with saving the planet and being nice to each other to come up with a gripping storyline.'

Emily rolled her eyes at Suzi. Jules appeared to be plotting her feminist revenge movie franchise. I stared at my screen, still wishing I could save both Mufasa and Scar.

* * *

Suzi said we could have a late-afternoon siesta when we'd finished editing so we went back to our rooms. I didn't want to be on my own, to be honest. As crazy as the day had been, it had at least given me a welcome respite from replaying the accident in my head. Ruminating over the mistakes I'd made, not just on that afternoon but over my entire life.

I still hadn't plucked up the courage to tell the others what my real job had been, or why I'd lied about it. And all I could think of was that tomorrow they were going to watch my final moments on earth in full technicolour. I had a choice; I could come clean about everything, or I could continue this pretence of acting as Mufasa when I had far more in common with Scar. Because although I may not have caused my brother's death yet, it was surely only a matter of time, and even in the best-case scenario, I must have inflicted life-changing injuries. It would have been impossible for him to have gone off the edge of that road and not done a hell of a lot of damage to himself by the time he came to rest on the steep valley side below.

I slumped down onto the bed, holding my head in my hands. It was time to fess up. To reveal what sort of person I was. This whole nice-guy persona was a charade which had gone on for too long.

* * *

We'd been told that our evening meal would be served at 7 p.m. in the exclusive sixth-floor restaurant. For once, I wasn't the first to arrive, despite being early. Most of the other diners were, as Suzi had said, considerably older than me and sixty-somethings always loved a good queue. When the doors opened, I waited to be seated as those in front of me were shown to their tables, seemingly grouped by their arrival dates, which a man on the front desk was asking for. I answered 'today' and received a particularly warm smile in return.

'Welcome to Food to Die For,' he said. 'We do hope you'll enjoy dining with us. My colleague Elsie will show you to your table.'

Elsie stepped forward from where she'd been polishing cutlery. To my surprise, she must have been in her seventies and looked like an unsuccessful auditionee from *Downton Abbey*, in a neatly pressed black uniform, white apron and cap.

'Wow, you look incredibly well turned out,' I said to her. 'I used to wear a uniform so it's nice to see someone else taking a pride in theirs.'

'Thank you,' she said. 'I can't be doing with slovenly waiting staff. I'm silver-service trained, you know, which is why I polish that cutlery until I can see my face in it.' She leant towards me and lowered her voice, which was full-on Yorkshire. 'Some of our younger staff here don't have such exacting standards. I think that's why they let me have this job, even though I'm a teensy bit over retirement age. That and the fact my birth certificate had been lost years ago and couldn't be traced in records, so I were able to tell a little white lie about my age.'

'Good for you,' I said, 'and your secret's safe with me.'

I winked at Elsie and she led me over to a table in the far corner which was set for three and had the date on a stand in the centre. Elsie appeared to take a moment to get her breath back before she could speak.

'Sorry. I'll be back to take your order when your friends have arrived,' she said before heading back towards the cutlery pile. I couldn't help feeling 'friends' was a bit strong when the three of us had only met this morning and hadn't had any choice in our grouping.

Five minutes later, Elsie was heading back towards me with Jules, who was trying very hard to stifle a laugh.

'They didn't tell us the elderly waitress from the Victoria Wood sketch was working here,' she said as she sat down and Elsie headed off. 'It's not a problem, because no one here's going to be in a hurry. Although you do realise, we're going to have to ask for two soups when we order.'

Emily was the last to join us. She spotted us before Elsie had the chance to show her to our table. As she made her way over, I was aware of other diners looking in her direction.

'They're all staring at me,' said Emily as she sat down. 'I wish they'd stop it, I'm so sick of all the sympathy looks.'

'Surely there's worse things than sympathy?' I asked.

'Not when you've had nothing else for eighteen months. "Poor little dying girl" and all that crap. Only now it's poor little dead girl.'

I looked down at my hands, unsure what to say for a moment.

'It was leukaemia,' Emily said. 'I know that's what you're both wondering, and I just want to get it out the way before we eat.'

'I'm sorry,' I said.

'Yeah. You and everyone else.'

'Life's not fair,' said Jules. 'It absolutely sucks, to be honest.'

'Is that supposed to make me feel better?' asked Emily.

'No, love. It was my cack-handed way of trying to say something appropriate without saying sorry.'

Emily fell silent. I glanced at Jules, wondering if she was going to volunteer how she'd died, which would put all the pressure on me. Fortunately, the wine waiter arrived at our table with the bottle she'd ordered before she had the chance. He uncorked it and went to pour some in Jules's glass, but she waved him away.

'It's fine, thanks. And I'll do the honours.'

He nodded and left.

'I can't stand all that tasting it first bollocks,' she said when he was safely out of earshot. 'I don't know about you, but I just want to get rat-arsed.'

She poured some for herself then held the bottle over my glass.

'No thanks,' I said, quickly placing my hand over the top.

'Jeez, it's not going to kill you, you know.'

'Just not in the mood,' I said.

Jules shrugged and turned to Emily, who shook her head.

'No one's going to mind that you're not eighteen,' Jules said.

'I know. I still don't want any, thanks,' Emily replied.

'Well, looks like I'm going to get plastered on my own,' Jules said. 'And I'm very much hoping that the one perk of being dead is that I won't have a hangover tomorrow.'

I said nothing. I was hardly in a position to. Instead, I picked up the menu and a smile spread across my face.

'What is it?' Jules asked.

'Death by Chocolate is one of the desserts,' I replied.

I started laughing. A deep, throaty laugh that soon had other diners looking over.

'I thought you were the quiet, respectful one?' said Emily.

'I'm sorry,' I replied. 'People in my line of work tend to have quite a dark sense of humour.'

Both Emily and Jules frowned at me. It was a second before I realised what I'd said. And that as far as they were concerned, I'd been a Deliveroo rider. I scrambled to cover myself.

'Er, because of the idiots on the roads, I mean. And the

abuse. You wouldn't believe how angry some people get when they're kept waiting for their food.'

I wasn't sure if I'd got away with it, but Jules shrugged and looked back down at the menu. A minute later it was her turn to start laughing.

'What?' I asked.

'I'm having the pan-fried venison. The butcher of *Bambi* strikes again.'

I smiled at her. Although I also felt a stab of guilt, because I knew that I wasn't going to be able to bring myself to tell them the truth about what I'd done. Not tonight, at least.

4

JULES

I lay in bed the next morning unable to stop thinking about Emily. A teenage girl would never imagine she would die of leukaemia. The worst thing you'd envisage happening to you at that age would be getting pregnant or a bad dose of the clap. You were supposed to have your whole life ahead of you at seventeen. That was certainly how I'd seen it. I could still remember the excitement of being offered a place at Bristol. The thrill of thinking about leaving my hometown and heading off to a city with actual clubs worth going to and gigs worth seeing. Of living in halls and making new friends and meeting cool people. It really had felt as if anything was possible. The thought of my life ending before I'd experienced any of that was horrific. I'd never have danced at goth clubs until two in the morning, sat up all night talking with Nina and watched the sunrise from Clifton Suspension Bridge. All the time imagining what amazing, crazy, wonderful lives we would lead. Emily had been denied all of that. I was at least relieved that she had tasted first love. I understood now why they'd got engaged: the stark realisation that they'd never get the chance to marry in their twenties or thirties, like other people did. Her mum must have been in bits when she'd told her, knowing there would never be a wedding.

Would Thomas and Noah ever get married? I hadn't really thought that far ahead, too busy clearing up after them to consider that one day it may be someone else's job. But now I realised that if there was a future wedding, I wouldn't be there. Would they think about me? Notice the gap where their stepmum should have been at the top table? Or would they simply be angry that I had abandoned them like their real mum? I hoped not. I didn't want them to think badly of the woman who had raised them. But perhaps it was a bit late for that.

I sighed and stretched out in bed. I still couldn't get over being pain-free when I woke. For so many years the shooting pains deep inside my pelvis had been the last thing I was conscious of before I fell asleep and the first thing I remembered when I woke in the morning. I didn't think I would ever get tired of waking pain-free and not having to pack spare knickers and pain killers every time I went out.

I couldn't deny it was also lovely having a whole double bed to myself for the first time in years. I immediately felt bad for thinking it, even if it was true. I wondered if this was what it would be like now; my stepmum guilt simply replaced by suicide guilt. I decided to go for breakfast and try not to feel guilty about eating a croissant because if you couldn't stuff your face without worrying about putting on weight, what really was the point of being dead?

I realised as soon as I saw Emily sitting at our table that I hadn't thought the guilt-free breakfast idea through properly. She smiled weakly at me.

'Morning,' I said. 'This hasn't got any easier, has it?'

She shrugged and pushed her cereal around the bowl. Her

hair, still damp from the shower, was hanging over one side of her face but couldn't hide her pained expression. I wanted to give her a hug, or at least squeeze her hand, but I had the feeling this would not be appreciated.

After a few more agonising moments of silence, Emily put her spoon down and stood up.

'See you later,' she mumbled, without making eye contact.

'OK,' I replied, deciding not to say that she should really eat something, in case she pointed out that it was a bit late to be concerned about her health.

As she left, I scanned the room to see if I could spot any new arrivals, but they appeared to be the same groups as last night. I guessed the newbies were getting ready to meet Suzi in the basement, as we had been yesterday. For a second, I thought it would be nice for Emily if someone her own age arrived for company, then quickly chased that from my mind as I realised what I was wishing for.

There was no sign of Carl, so I ate breakfast on my own. I was relieved, to be honest. Today was going to be hard enough without having to make small talk before we watched each other take our last breaths. I wasn't proud of what I'd done. Far from it. But it was also fair to say I hadn't known I was going to be required to justify my actions in front of a panel that included a seventeen-year-old girl who had died from leukaemia. Maybe if they put that warning on bridges, it might be more effective in stopping people jumping.

When I stepped out of the lift in the basement a short time later, Carl was already waiting outside the editing suite.

'You're keen,' I said.

'Not really. Just like to be early for things.'

I nodded and decided not to mention that arriving early to watch your own death seemed a little strange. Carl stared resolutely down at his shoes, which were impeccably clean, and brushed imaginary specks from the sleeve of his jacket. I got the distinct impression he was as anxious about this as I was, though I couldn't imagine why. The lift doors opened again, and Emily stepped out. The three of us stood there in silence for a moment.

'Who wants to go first?' I asked.

'I don't know. Maybe Suzi or Faz will decide,' Carl replied. 'But I'm happy to let you ladies go first if you want to get it over with.'

I looked at Emily.

'Shall we put age before beauty?'

'Whatever,' she replied.

'Right, that's sorted. Only, there's something I want to tell you both before you see mine.'

'You weren't murdered, were you?' asked Emily, her face ashen.

'No, nothing like that. And I didn't die of cancer or any other awful disease or medical condition. Nor was it an accident.'

They both looked at me. I imagined them going through all the possibilities in their heads until there was only one option left. Carl got there first. I could tell by his expression. I couldn't quite work out what he thought of me, but it was safe to say it wasn't positive.

'Pills?' he asked quietly. I shook my head. Before he could say anything, the editing suite door opened and Faz stuck his head out and beamed at us.

'Perfect, you're all here!' he said. 'Come in, front-row seats are still available.'

He said it as if we were queuing to see the latest blockbuster release, not to watch each other die. We filed into the room and took the same seats we'd been in yesterday.

'Do you have any 3D glasses?' I asked.

'You're so funny and so noughties!' said Faz, waving me away with his hand. I didn't like to admit I seriously wanted them to blur my vision for the screening ahead. 'And you're first up,' he continued, fiddling with some buttons on his control desk. 'Press play whenever you're ready. I'll be in the sound booth if you need me.'

An image came up on our screens of an overweight, middle-aged woman with windswept hair, teetering on the edge of a bridge and looking deathly pale. There was a gasp to my right, and I could feel the intensity of Emily's eyes boring into me.

'You didn't?' she said.

There was absolutely no point trying to deny it.

'I'm afraid I did.'

'That is so bloody inconsiderate.'

I had been expecting Emily's wrath. Carl's, I was quite unprepared for. I turned to face him.

'Clearly, I wasn't thinking straight at the time.'

'Plenty of people manage to take their own lives without putting others at risk.'

'What do you mean?'

'The motorists below, you could have killed one of them.'

'Well, I didn't because they're not here, are they? If they were, I'd totally understand if they had a go at me, but I'm not sure what my chosen means of departure has got to do with you.'

Carl's eyes flashed darker still.

'Did you not think about the emergency services? Some poor sod had to scrape you off the road, you know. And then went home to their wife and kids pretending it had been an average day at work because they didn't want to upset them by talking about it.'

'I was in a bad way. I didn't think about anything beyond

stepping off. I wanted to get it over with before anyone tried to talk me down.'

It was only as I said it that it dawned on me. There had been people there who could have intervened. The bloody camera crew had been filming me the whole time. I waved my arms at Faz in his booth. He was doing a good job of pretending not to notice me, so I walked over and banged on the door. He opened it, still smiling.

'Hi, how are you getting on?'

He was evidently hopeless at reading the room.

'The film crew,' I said. 'Why didn't they do anything? Why didn't they stop me?'

'I'm afraid I can only deal with technical queries,' said Faz. 'Anything else is outside my remit.'

'Well, I'd like to speak to Suzi then.'

'Perfect, I'll message her to come through. Take a seat, she won't be a minute.'

I was half expecting him to put annoying telephone-hold music on while we waited. Emily was still staring at me. I couldn't work out if it was a good or bad thing that she hadn't said anything yet.

The door opened and Suzi appeared, still wearing the leather jacket despite it being a warm day. I suspected she never took it off.

'Morning, apprentice directors, are we not happy bunnies this morning?'

'Your camera crew filmed me jumping off a bridge.'

'Yes... the clue is in the job title.'

I really wasn't in the mood for her humour.

'They fucking stood there and watched me jump. Why the hell didn't they try to save me?'

'OK, two things,' said Suzi. 'Firstly, they were there to do their job—'

'Oh great, you make it sound like some sick reality TV show where the contestants are allowed to kill themselves for entertainment purposes.'

'I think what Suzi means,' said Carl, interrupting, 'is that it's probably in their contracts. An ethical code of practice which states they are not to interfere with life on earth. Like the David Attenborough documentaries on the BBC. They simply film what happens in front of them; you don't see a sound guy shooting a tranquiliser into the lion so the gazelle can get away.'

'There was a David Attenborough programme where they intervened,' said Emily. 'They dug a ramp in the snow for some penguins who were trapped so they could get back to their chicks. I remember it made my dad cry.'

Suzi looked at us in turn and shook her head.

'Will you all stop it with your David Attenborough conspiracy theories and use your heads? What power would any of you have now to stop a human doing anything? They can't see you or hear you. If you touched them, they wouldn't even feel it, so you certainly couldn't grab on to them and stop them jumping.'

'OK, so they couldn't physically stop me, but they could have done the equivalent of the penguin thing. Laid down a rope ladder or something.'

'Come on,' said Suzi. 'You climbed the steps to get up there, you could quite easily have used them to get down again. Gone home to your partner and your chicks. But you didn't, did you? You've got to take responsibility for what you did and stop trying to blame other people.'

I stared at her, for once rendered speechless, because I knew she was right. And so did everyone else in the room.

Suzi threw what appeared to be a sympathetic look in my direction before leaving. I could have done with a moment to try to compose myself, but I wasn't going to get it.

'How could you do that to your family?' asked Emily.

I looked down at my hands.

'It felt like the only way out at the time.'

'It wasn't though, was it? If you didn't love your husband, you could have divorced him, that's what other people do.'

'It wasn't that simple; you have no idea what I'd been through.'

'Try me. We can compare notes if you like,' said Emily.

I knew I was beaten before I'd even started. I hadn't had cancer, a disease, a chronic illness, something people would immediately say, 'Oh no, you poor thing,' or cluck sympathetically about. No, I had a pain that couldn't speak its name. People understand that childbirth is painful, but not that you can still be in emotional and physical pain from it thirteen years on. No one thinks that is even possible because we don't talk about it. In the same way we don't talk about stillbirth. Women who are pregnant and don't bring home a baby at the end of it are about as taboo as you can get. No one wanted to hear about my fourth-degree tear, the thirty-eight stitches I'd had, the damage to my bowel as well as the birth canal. When people asked how I was – and not many did – they were referring to my emotional healing. Not the physical pain which still seared through me. As for saying things had got so much worse during the perimenopause, she would think I'd had a few hot flushes, maybe forgotten what I'd gone upstairs for. A few cheap laughs in sit-coms. That's what the menopause was to most people. They had no fucking idea that the scar tissue from a birth injury could wreak havoc with your bodily functions, that the depression could run so deep it was a daily struggle to keep your head above the dark waters of it, or the crushing anxiety. Because they weren't things you were supposed to talk about either. Nor could I speak about the pain of a lost love when I couldn't even name the person or tell stories of the tender moments we'd shared. Because Emily had already cornered the tragic lost love market. And nothing I had would compare.

'I've no excuses,' I said. 'It was an appalling thing to do, to my stepsons particularly. All I can say is that I'm sorry. And I know that doesn't cut it. Not in the slightest.'

'The paramedic or traffic cop who was first on the scene, this will have done them in, you know,' said Carl. 'They'll be having nightmares. They'll probably need professional counselling. It's the same with train drivers when someone steps off the platform. Screws people up for life, it does.'

'Look, I'm sorry. I couldn't take it any more. I know nothing I say will make up for what I've done, so let's get this over with.'

I reached out and pressed play. I didn't want to see it any more than they did, but I knew none of us had a choice.

I lean into the wind and hover there for a moment before allowing myself to topple forward. In my head, I had imagined floating down like Sarah Ann Henley, who jumped from the Clifton Suspension Bridge and survived, her huge skirt and petticoats puffing out like a parachute, slowing her descent to allow her to land softly in the mud. In reality, of course, I am wearing black leggings and a top. I plummet. It is sheer, unadulterated terror I see on my face as I hurtle towards the road below. I shut my eyes, or maybe the speed I am travelling forces them shut; it's hard to tell. I know I'm about to hit the ground at any second. I scream but there's no one to save me, no cord to pull on my parachute. It's too late for regrets. I hear my body meet the ground with a sickening thud. And then nothing.

The footage cut off straight away. I imagined Faz had done that on purpose to prevent me seeing the messy aftermath. I looked to my right. Both Emily and Carl had averted their gaze from the screen. I wasn't sure if it was out of respect to me or simply an unwillingness to watch something so unbearably awful.

The room was silent for a few moments. A silence which weighed heavily on me.

'I'm sorry,' I whispered. 'I wish you hadn't been made to watch that.'

Neither of them said anything for a while. When Emily finally turned to me, she had tears in her eyes.

'I tried so hard to cling on,' she said. 'I did everything they told me, took whatever drugs and medicines they gave me, smiled through the pain, all because I wanted so desperately to live a day, an hour, a second longer. And yet you threw your life away in an instant, with no regard for the people who loved you. You disgust me. You really do.'

5

EMILY

I turned back to the screen. I had nothing more to say. I didn't want to be in the same room as Jules or even look at her. I had the perfect response though. I didn't wait for Faz to come out and tell me it was my turn. I pressed a button and a frozen frame of me appeared on the screen, lying in my bed at the hospice. Mum and Dad sitting on one side, Harry on the other. You could practically smell the love in the air. All the tubes and monitors had gone because it was the end. A nurse was hovering attentively. It was Nurse Redfern, Louise to me. She'd been my favourite. If I could have chosen the nurse to be with me at the end, it would have been her. She used to tease me about Harry, say she'd have made a move on him herself if she'd been thirty years younger. I didn't mind though because she explained everything without being patronising. Treated me like a grown-up. It was her who'd told me the day before to say anything I wanted to say because time was running out.

Jules and Carl didn't want to watch this. They were already shifting uncomfortably in their seats. But I didn't care if it made Jules feel bad. I wanted her to regret what she'd done and the pain and hurt she'd caused. And if this was the only way to make her do that, then so be it. I pressed play.

I have everyone around me. Everyone I need. Harry is holding my hand. He's been holding it pretty much non-stop for the last forty-eight hours. When he does finally let go, I suspect he'll leave me with the imprint of his hand on mine. I hope so, at least.

Dad is holding my other hand; Mum's arm is across my leg. It's as if they're pinning me down with their love. It's a nice feeling though. Like one of those weighted blankets. Heavy but gentle and comforting at the same time.

My breaths are getting shallower, I can sense that, so I'm sure they can too. Dad's talking to me about things we used to do when I was little. It's his way of coping, I know that. I tune in and out intermittently.

'You spent most of that holiday fishing in the rock pool at Robin Hood's Bay. We could probably have left you there, gone to the pub for lunch and come back and you wouldn't have even realised we'd gone.

'You were looking for Nemo, of course. Said you wanted to find him and get him back to Marlin. And then when we went on a boat trip, you were fretting we'd go over the drop-off.'

I gently squeeze his fingers. And that is when he starts to cry. Big tears that roll down his face and plop onto the bed. It's good though, it means he knows it's happening. Mum takes his other hand; she'll be there for him. I'm so glad they'll have each other.

I feel the life draining out of me, like water going down the plughole after a bath. There is nothing I can do to stop it. I muster the remains of my strength to squeeze Harry's hand.

'Always,' I whisper, barely loud enough to hear.

'Always,' he replies softly. And then he lays his head on my chest, maybe so I don't see his tears. He lies there for a long time. Until finally, I try to take another breath, but there is nothing there. I've said my goodbyes, but I still don't want to go; I want to fight to hang

on to my life, but I have nothing left to fight with. Louise says something to Dad. He nods. My eyelids close. I have the image of Harry, Mum and Dad imprinted on the inside of them. I hope it will stay with me always.

Everybody is crying. It weirdly sounds like music. My death symphony. I imagine Harry writing the lyrics to it later. I hear him singing them softly into my ear.

It's the last note I hear.

The video stopped and the screen turned black. Jules stared blankly ahead. Carl was pinching the bridge of his nose as if to stop himself crying.

'I'm sorry,' Jules said eventually. 'Sorry for saying sorry, sorry that happened to you, sorry you had to lose everyone you loved, sorry they all lost you. And sorry I've been such a stupid fucking cow.'

She got up and ran from the room.

'I'm sorry too,' said Carl.

'For being a stupid fucking cow?'

'Maybe not that,' he said with a hint of a smile. 'But for everything else. I can't imagine how tough that was for you all.'

His voice broke, like he really meant it.

'Thanks,' I said with a shrug.

'People don't talk about it, do they?' continued Carl. 'Young people dying, I mean. But it happens and that silence makes it even more difficult for everyone who goes through it.'

'My dad was in denial,' I said. 'Right to the end. He was always so positive about everything. Even when I was little, he used to tell me there was no such word as can't, that everything was possible if I put my mind to it, worked hard and believed in my dreams. His little girl had the world at her feet. That's what he used to say to me.'

Carl shook his head and blew out.

'It must have been so hard for him.'

I nodded.

'He's the one I'm worried most about seeing again. The one I think won't be coping. He'll probably be pretending it never happened now, throwing himself into his work or the fundraising again. We raised a lot of money for Leukaemia Research doing walks and stuff. It was all his idea. Made him feel like he was doing something. And maybe that money will help to stop other people going through it. I hope so. But what he really wanted to do was save me and he couldn't do that. Couldn't save his own daughter, and I think that's what he found hardest of all.'

Carl was silent. But he nodded, like he understood what I was talking about.

'Nothing prepares you for death. We're not even very good at dealing with it in old age but with teenagers…' His voice trailed off.

'Who are you not looking forward to seeing in your dying film?' I asked.

Carl looked up at me.

'Is it that obvious?'

I nodded.

'My little brother,' he said.

'Why?'

'He was on the back of my bike when I skidded off the road.'

He hung his head as he said it.

'What happened to him?'

'I don't know. I'm dreading him turning up here today or tomorrow. He must be in a bad way. He could die too.'

'Sorry, that's rough. How did it happen?'

'You'll see in a moment.'

'I think we've got to wait for Jules to come back. Though I'm not sure if she's going to.'

'Maybe I should ask Faz what we're supposed to do,' said Carl.

I looked across at Faz who was sitting in his sound booth with AirPods in and appeared to be chair dancing while mouthing along to the song.

'I don't know. He seems a bit of a prick.'

Carl smiled. Before we could decide what to do, the door opened and Suzi walked in, followed by a red-eyed Jules.

'OK,' Suzi said, shutting the door behind them. 'Team meeting. Jules here thinks she's not worthy of being in the same place as you two, thinks she should have gone straight to Hell.'

I looked at Jules, who was staring down at her feet, avoiding eye contact.

'I've told her that's not how it works here,' Suzi continued. 'And I'm telling all of you to remember that what you're watching here are your final scenes. People are very quick to make judgements these days. Bloody social media did that to you. Everyone's got an opinion and everyone's quick to voice it. But none of you know what came before these scenes, so I suggest you hold your judgements until you do, OK?'

Suzi looked at me as she said it. For the first time since I arrived here, for the last two years in fact, I felt like I was being told off. It came as something of a relief.

'Like I said, you've got to work as a team. This isn't *Big Brother* or I'm a Knobhead Get Me Out of Here, or whatever the latest reality TV crap everyone's watching nowadays is. You're not competing against each other and there are no prizes for living or dying well. Is everyone clear?'

We all nodded. Carl raised a hand.

'Yes, quiet guy who thinks he's still at school,' she said, pointing to him.

'Have the new people arrived yet?' he asked.

'They have indeed.'

'Are there any young ones? Under thirty, I mean.'

'No, all in their fifties and sixties today. Lots of talk about having paid their National Insurance for years and being cheated out of their pensions.'

Carl nodded. I saw him swallow hard. His brother was still alive. I gave him a little smile.

'Right then,' said Suzi. 'Let's get this show back on the road. Quiet guy. I believe it's your turn. I'll leave you to it.'

6

CARL

I am riding fast. Not too fast, because I know this road well enough to handle it, but faster than would be safe for many people. I've taken these bends in the dark and in far worse conditions, so navigating them in daylight in the summer is not a problem for me. I feel the weight of Lewis against my back. He's not scared. He's been riding pillion since he was thirteen. He knows to lean with me on the bends. And I haven't drunk enough for it to be a problem. Sure, the police might not see it like that, but I know what I can handle and I'm an experienced rider. I've taken every advanced course there is and I've never come off my bike. So, if I say I'm not going too fast, I haven't drunk too much and I know what I'm doing, there's no need to ask any further questions. Besides, the police wouldn't give me any grief if they did stop me. Not once they found out I was one of them. Or had been, at least.

It's the only time I'm free, when I'm on my bike. I don't mean free as in free of responsibilities. I still have those. But free of the images in my head. The memories. The pain. I'm not sure why they don't bother me when I'm riding. You'd think they would, given the circumstances. But somehow, they leave me alone. Let me ride in peace. It's at night they come to me. And any moment I'm sitting still. That's why I need to keep moving.

It's only as I navigate the first corner that I see the road ahead is still wet. It's sheltered here, under the trees. Tends to be one of the last spots to dry out. I feel Lewis start to lean ever so slightly in anticipation of the bend ahead. I squeeze the brake. Not too much, just enough to be able to take it as normal. The sun is glinting onto my visor from between gaps in the trees, casting shafts of light across the glistening surface. The truck comes out of the darkness from nowhere. It's also over the centre line in the road. I am a fraction slow in my reaction, so I brake harder to try to compensate. My back wheel starts to go. Lewis feels it too because he takes one hand off the passenger bar and grabs my jacket. I try to correct it, but the surface is too wet, and the tyres aren't gripping well enough. We're going into a slide. It's all I can do to steer clear of the truck, but as it passes, I realise that we'll not be able to stay on the road. The momentum will carry us over the edge. The barrier won't be enough to stop us either. Not the speed we're going. Lewis has both arms around my waist. He knows it too. But clinging onto me won't save him. We're done for. We hurtle into the barrier and are thrown up into the air. Me, Lewis, the bike. We all leave the road at the same time. I see a jumble of trees, sky, Lewis, bike, and the valley bottom below as I somersault through the air. And all I can think is, 'Please let Lewis be OK. Please, God who I don't believe in, forget about me, just save my brother.'

The video stopped with me lying motionless on a rock on the hillside. Blood oozing out from under my helmet. It must have been instant. I can see at least part of the bike further down the hillside. I can't see Lewis.

'Where's my brother?' I shouted. Jules looked at me and reached out a hand.

'I'm so sorry,' she said.

I stood up and rushed to hammer on Faz's sound booth.

'Come on,' I said when he came out. 'Run the film. I want to see what happened to my brother.'

'Hey bro, thanks for reaching out,' he started.

'I'm not reaching out. I'm telling you to run my fucking film.'

The smile disappeared from Faz's face instantly, replaced by a look of sheer terror.

'I'll message Suzi,' he said, seemingly incapable of dealing with anything himself.

I shook my head and returned to my seat.

'It wasn't your fault,' Emily said.

'You can't say that.'

'That truck forced you to swerve.'

She didn't have a clue, of course, and I could hardly tell her I'd been slow to react because I'd been drinking. Not after the way she'd reacted to what Jules had done.

'It's not that simple,' I said. 'He shouldn't even have been on the back of my bike. I was going out on my own, but he begged me for a lift into town. Said he was going to be late for his appointment at the job centre. I didn't want them to sanction him, and I've ended up killing him in the process.'

'OK, quiet-boy-turned-drama-queen,' said Suzi, coming into the room. 'I understand you have asked for more.'

She said it in the style of Mr Bumble from *Oliver!* Her complete failure to take any of this seriously was becoming incredibly annoying.

'I want to see what happened to my brother. You have no right to keep that from me,' I told her.

Suzi sighed. 'He's not dead. That's as much as I can tell you.'

'How do you know?' I asked. 'He could have died this morning. He could arrive tomorrow.'

'We get alerted as soon as someone dies,' she said. 'We've

already got two booked in for tomorrow. Your brother isn't one of them.'

I stared at her, relieved Lewis wasn't dead but immediately feeling bad for those who were. And aware that Lewis wasn't out of the woods yet.

'But he could still die at any time. I want you to run the film on so I can see what happened to him. I want to know how bad it was.'

'I'm afraid we can't do that. The rest of the film is part of your brother's story. We don't have access to it because he's still alive,' Suzi explained. 'That's how it works.'

'And what about the film crew?' asked Jules. 'Or are you going to tell us they couldn't do anything because of the rules too?'

'Or because of the David Attenborough thing?' said Emily.

Suzi looked at each of us in turn.

'It's good to see the team starting to support each other but as I've already told you, there is no David Attenborough thing. The film crew did an amazing job, I thought, going fast enough to keep up with you and capturing all that on a jib arm from a car. Nice bit of work.'

I stared at her, wondering if this casual cruelty was intentional.

'What is wrong with you?' I asked.

'Like I said before, they're simply doing their job.'

'How did they even know to follow him?' asked Jules. 'Presumably they didn't go on every bike ride with him?'

Shit. It was the drinking. That's what would have alerted them. An intoxicated man putting on bike leathers would have set off the alarms, and the crew would have been dispatched immediately. Unlike the emergency services, they at least got advance notice of what was to come.

'Everything's monitored from on high,' said Suzi. 'There are algorithms. Various things that had happened in the run-up to that moment must have given them reason for concern.'

She glanced at me as she said it. She knew. And she was covering for me. The other two were looking at me. Waiting for some kind of explanation. I supposed I should be grateful the film hadn't started with me drinking. I could tell them. I should tell them. But somehow, I still couldn't find the words. So, I did what every coward does. I tried to shift the blame. In my case, onto Suzi.

'Will you stop trying to make out I'm the one at fault here? You may not have had anyone in your life that you cared about, but you could at least try to understand how hard this is for me, when I'm worried sick about my brother.'

Her face dropped and she blinked hard and turned away. I immediately regretted my words. It took a few moments for her to recover herself.

'OK. Now you've got that off your chest, I was going to tell you that you can see your brother soon because you'll be heading straight out on location with the film crew after lunch.'

'What, just me?' I asked.

'No, all of you. You'll be working together filming each other's families in turn. Think of it like a team-building exercise but a way deeper one than playing paintball or doing some stupid assault course.'

'What's good about intruding on other people's grief?' asked Emily.

'It will help you bond. You'll be supporting each other through it as you work with the film crew.'

'Are they the same people that filmed our deaths?' I asked.

'No, we always make sure they're a different team. We have got some ethics, you know. But pack an overnight bag because you'll be staying in your rooms in the film trailer while you're on location. I expect you to do a professional job and I have no time for prima donnas, so don't get any grand ideas about demanding luxury items in riders. Like I said, yours are low-budget films. Now bugger off and I can but hope that the new arrivals are less trouble than you lot.'

'I think I've offended her,' I said as soon as Suzi had left the room.

'I shouldn't worry,' said Jules, 'she's got a Teflon coating, that one.'

I looked at Emily. It had been a tough morning for all of us, but especially for her.

'Are you OK?' I asked.

'I thought people were going to stop asking me that, once I was dead. I told you; I don't need protecting. I just want to get out of here as quickly as possible so I can see Harry again.'

7

JULES

I might have known I'd be first – supposedly on account of having died first. The only one who wasn't desperate to see their loved ones, and I got to have the pleasure of my family's company while the other two waited impatiently for their turn. I wasn't sure whether I should warn them that Rob and the boys might not have even noticed I was missing yet, only that the cats seemed hungry, but I figured it was best for them to discover how sad my life had been for themselves.

We'd been told to meet outside the hotel where the production unit car would pick us up. I'd packed my suitcase as instructed and was relieved we'd be staying in our own rooms in the trailer instead of coming back to the Travel Inn every night, as that did at least save me from the awkwardness of our enforced meals together in the restaurant. I was under no illusions as to my status in the group. I was the one the others tolerated simply because they had no choice. I'd been expecting Emily's wrath, and having watched her unbearably sad death, I couldn't say I blamed her. My seventeen-year-old self would probably hate the cynical, despairing fifty-year-old version I'd become, too. You're so full of hope at that age. Hope and utterly unrealistic expectations. Where everyone loves everyone else and doesn't regret anything and your best days lie ahead of you. I don't think you necessarily get wiser as you get older, simply more realistic because of all the crap that's happened to you.

What I hadn't bargained for was Carl having a pop at me too. I mean, if my own mental health had deteriorated to the point where I'd thought hurling myself off a bridge seemed like a good idea, I was hardly going to be considering the mental health of the poor sod who found me, was I? Anyway, it was clear that my mode of death had determined that I was public enemy number one, and even my obvious sympathy for their suffering was not going to redeem me. And now they were going to have to watch my family barely bothering to grieve for me, instead of going straight to their own loved ones.

I sighed and wheeled my case out of my room to the lift.

When I stepped out into the foyer, I immediately felt conspicuous and had to remind myself that I was invisible to the living. It struck me that as no one had paid much attention to me as a fifty-year-old perimenopausal woman when I was alive, it wouldn't be hard to get used to being ignored completely now I was dead. I suspected you could have some fun with it, but I didn't feel in the mood for pranks. I simply wanted to get this over with and take my rightful place in Hell, where I could be left to fester with my own kind.

I could see Carl and Emily standing outside, deep in conversation. A conversation which stopped abruptly when I appeared next to them.

'Look, for what it's worth, I think I'm the scum of the earth too, so you don't have to pretend with me,' I said. 'And I apologise in advance that my lot aren't going to pull on your heartstrings, apart from maybe the cats, if they haven't been fed.'

'What are their names?' asked Emily, presumably deciding they were more worthy of sympathy than me.

'Victor and Hugo,' I replied.

'Ah, is someone in your family a big *Les Mis* fan?' Carl asked.

'Come again?'

'Victor Hugo, the French novelist who wrote *Les Misérables*.'

I stared at Carl. Clearly, he thought my family possessed cultural sophistication way beyond them.

'Sorry to disappoint you,' I said, 'but we got them from a rescue centre on the day Leeds United boss Victor Orta signed Hugo Diaz and that's why the boys picked their names.'

'Oh,' said Carl, his illusions well and truly shattered.

'Anyway,' I went on. 'How come you're so well up on French literature?'

'I'm not. It's just that *Les Mis* is my favourite musical.'

'First *The Lion King*, now *Les Mis*. I thought you were a biker, although not a hairy one, admittedly.'

'Guess I like breaking down stereotypes,' he said with a shrug.

A battered Ford Mondeo pulled up in front of us – a sure indicator that our life stories weren't worthy of a big-budget movie. The driver had an 'End Credits' sign in the windscreen. We looked at each other. Carl gestured to me to go first. I opened the front passenger door and got in.

'Hi there, I'm Jules.'

'Hiya,' the driver said in a broad Yorkshire accent. 'I'm Majid and you're a bit younger than my usual passengers.'

'Wait till you see who gets in next,' I replied.

The rear passenger door opened, and Emily climbed in.

'Oooff,' said Majid, wincing. 'I see what you mean.'

'Hello, actual person with eyes and ears here,' said Emily.

'Sorry, love,' said Majid. 'When you mainly ferry older

people about it comes as a bit of a shock to get a young lass like you, that's all.'

Emily said nothing and stared out of the window.

'She doesn't like people feeling sorry for her,' I hissed at Majid.

'Again, I can still hear you,' said Emily with a sigh.

Carl got in and introduced himself.

'Well,' said Majid. 'At least a younger group are less likely than my usual customers to ask me where I really come from and complain about immigration.'

I laughed, deciding not to tell him that my husband would probably have done just that.

'Do you know where you're going?' I asked as Majid pulled away.

'Yeah. I may not have a sat nav in here, but I've been driving these streets for years. And I have an A–Z of Halifax in me glove compartment as a backup for any new roads I don't know.'

I smiled. He reminded me of my mum before she'd had to give up being behind the wheel. She'd held out against any modern technology in the car too, even if it had meant her having to stop to ask for directions all the time.

A pang of regret surged through me, and I had to remind myself that as Mum hadn't known who I was for the last few months since she'd gone into the home, she wouldn't miss me or my visits.

'So, who's going to be at home?' asked Majid, glancing across at me as he pulled out onto the main road.

I hadn't thought about it until that point. Rob must have had a visit from the police by now and called Thomas and Noah. Would they have come home from their unis? Noah probably, because he was only in Manchester and commuted, but whether Thomas would have come back from Warwick, I wasn't sure.

Would Rob be on compassionate leave from work? Maybe they'd be clustered together in mourning around the kitchen island, telling stories of happier times over a brew. Somehow, I doubted it. I struggled to think of any happier times to think of, for a start.

'Not sure. Maybe my husband and stepsons. They're probably busy clearing all my stuff out so they can have more space for their music gear.'

'What do they play?'

'Guitar,' I replied. 'Thomas, the eldest, is very talented. Could make a career out of it if he wanted to. I encouraged him to apply for music degrees, but his dad told him to do something that leads to a proper job. So, he's on a production technician course instead.'

'My little brother Lewis is the same,' said Carl. 'He's a brilliant drummer but never had the motivation or confidence to take it any further.'

'He should start a band,' said Majid.

'I think he's missed his chance now,' replied Carl, his voice catching.

I glanced back at Carl, who was staring out the window, blinking hard. Poor bastard. I hoped his brother did pull through. Hoped he wasn't as badly injured as he feared. It hadn't looked good for him on the film, though. Not good at all.

I gazed out of the window as we turned into my road. The others seemed to have picked up on my silence as we pulled up outside my house. It was so weird seeing it again. It felt like it had been both forever and only two minutes ago since I'd left. I'd never had an emotional attachment to the place; it was an average three-bedroom semi in an average street in an average town. It had pretty much summed up my entire existence. But seeing it again, I noticed things I hadn't been aware of before:

the bright blue of the lobelia in the planters either side of the front door, the newly washed windows, the fact that our front drive was in a better state than next door's, whatever Rob said.

It was Majid who broke the silence.

'There you go, your crew are waiting for you.'

He nodded towards the alley at the side of my house where a man in his sixties and a young, tall woman dressed in black were lurking with their camera and sound gear respectively. The whole thing felt surreal.

'Right,' I replied, not sounding at all sure of what I was supposed to do now.

'I'll be back for you in a day or so,' said Majid.

'Why that long?' asked Carl.

'Your families will probably still be in shock. And our crew will need to get some denial and anger on film for a bit of variety.'

The idea that my family would obligingly go through different stages of grief seemed unlikely. I wasn't sure either Thomas or Noah would look up from their phone screens for long enough to allow us to capture one emotion, let alone a range. And I wouldn't put it past Rob to be back at work tomorrow.

'But we need to see our families too,' said Carl. 'Can't you take us on your way back? You can drop me at the hospital, that's where I need to be.'

''Fraid not,' said Majid. 'If it's not on my call sheet, I don't go there. I'll be back when Suzi tells me. You'd better get cracking; our Gerry doesn't like being kept waiting.'

We clambered out of the car and Majid gave a quick wave before pulling away. In a few moments I would be expected to go inside and see my husband and stepsons and I really wasn't sure if I was ready for that.

'Er, do you want to lead the way?' asked Carl.

I nodded. Just get it over with, I told myself. Put on a brave face and smile so no one will be any the wiser about the pain inside. I strode over to the camera crew.

'Hiya, I'm Jules and this is my gaffe, or ex-gaffe, I should say.'

The man, whose face was craggy and weather-beaten, removed the cigarette from his mouth, tossed it on the paving stone and stubbed it out with his foot before offering his hand.

'Gerry Madden, cameraman extraordinaire and proud Yorkshireman, at your service,' he said.

I smiled and shook it, deciding not to say anything about him leaving fag-ends on our path, as I supposed it was none of my business now.

'And I'm Alice, your shit-hot sound operator,' said the woman, who was probably in her late twenties, although for some reason I always found it harder to tell with tall, skinny people.

'Now, if you don't mind,' continued Gerry, 'we'd better get our arses in gear as we've lots to get through. Where do you want to start?'

I stared at him blankly.

'I don't know. We're all new to this and I'm not sure what we're supposed to be doing.'

Gerry nodded. Presumably he'd heard it all before.

'Right,' he said to me. 'As director, you decide what shots you want and shout "cut" when we've got them.'

'And what shots do we want?' I asked.

'Grief, basically. Unbearable sadness and people bawling their eyes out and saying how much you meant to them.'

'And what if they don't do that?'

'A good old-fashioned family bust-up is always welcome. Anger, things being thrown, fistfights, that sort of thing.'

'The more dangerous the weapons and the more blood, the better,' added Alice.

'Right,' I said, feeling increasingly unsure about this whole thing.

'And what do we do?' asked Carl. 'I'm a bit of a film buff, into cinematography and arthouse movies, so happy to take on any role.'

Gerry turned to him with a look of thinly veiled contempt.

'Keep yoursen out of our way, mainly. You can be 1st AD, that's assistant director. You're responsible for the logistics and smooth operation of the shoot. You also get to call "action".'

'Great,' said Carl, who appeared genuinely thrilled by the prospect. Gerry turned to Emily.

'And you can be 1st AC, assistant camera operator.'

'Is that because I'm a girl?' she asked indignantly.

'Nope. Because I think you'll be better with a clapperboard than that fella,' Gerry said, nodding towards Carl.

Emily managed a little smile. Gerry and Alice picked up their gear and headed for the front door.

'Shit,' I said, checking my pockets, 'I haven't got my key.'

Gerry turned to look at me and sighed.

'And there were I, hoping you'd be brighter than our last lot.'

'Is it like Harry Potter?' asked Emily. 'Do we just run at the door?'

Gerry shook his head.

'No, not unless you want a bloody nose. I have skeleton keys that can get us into anywhere. How else do you think we do our job?'

I watched as he fiddled with the bunch of keys in his hand then brazenly opened the front door. I couldn't help thinking that our neighbourhood WhatsApp group would have a field day with this, if they had any inkling.

I followed him inside, but it still felt wrong to appear in my own cramped hallway without having alerted the occupants.

We waited for a moment as Alice untangled the boom from the cheap pendant lightshade in the hall, which Rob had bought from Wilko because he couldn't be bothered to go elsewhere and find a better one.

'Er, kitchen's at the end on the right,' I said, realising they were waiting for my instructions. 'That's probably where they'll be.'

Gerry set off down the hall, the others followed, and I brought up the rear, feeling slightly sick about the prospect of what was in store.

It was the silence that hit me first. Silence was OK when there was only one person in the room. Even with two people, it could be a momentary lull in conversation, but with three people present, silence was always crushing.

Rob was pouring the tea, which was about the only domestic job he'd ever excelled at. Thomas and Noah sat slumped over the kitchen island, phones in hands, eyes glued to their screens. Rob put their mugs down in front of them and they didn't even look up or acknowledge him. He stared at the wall opposite, although he was unwittingly looking straight at me. His face had a pallor I didn't recognise. His eyes an unfamiliar darkness. If I didn't know better, I'd have thought he was genuinely grieving.

I turned to see Gerry had set up his tripod and was ready to roll and Alice was poised with her boom. Emily brandished the clapperboard, Carl called 'action' and Hugo obligingly strolled into the kitchen and gave what was possibly the loudest miaow ever recorded.

'Jeez, haven't you fed him?' asked Thomas, looking up at Rob.

'I gave him a tin that had been left out. Not my fault if he turned his nose up at it.'

'He doesn't have tins, he has pouches,' said Noah, without looking up from his phone.

'You what?' asked Rob.

'Victor has tins. Hugo has pouches.'

'What are they when they're at home?'

'Those little plastic packets you tear the tops off of,' explained Noah.

'Well, where did she keep them?'

'I dunno,' replied Noah with a shrug. 'I just remember seeing her feeding him them.'

Rob stood up and went over to the food cupboards and started rifling through them, as if I might have randomly mixed them in with the rice and pasta.

'Where are they?' Emily whispered in my ear. I pointed to the bottom cupboard in the corner.

'Next to the cat litter with Victor's tins. He must have found the tin I'd left out to give to Sue next door for her cat because Victor had gone off them.'

'Shall we open the cupboard door when they're not looking, to try to help him?'

'I'm not sure we can, and it would probably violate the David Attenborough thing, even if it isn't a rule. We'll have to let them fend for themselves.'

Hugo chose that moment to rub around my legs, as if he could see me, or at least sense that I was there. I wondered if I dared bend to stroke him, but when I glanced across at Alice, she was shaking her head. The food cupboard door slammed shut.

'Bloody great,' said Rob. 'She doesn't leave a suicide note or instructions about where to find cat food.' Thomas and Noah both looked up at him. They said nothing but they didn't have to.

'Sorry,' said Rob, sitting back down on the stool. 'I shouldn't have said that, but I still don't understand why she did this.'

'I guess none of us were paying much attention,' said Thomas.

'I was,' said Noah. 'I knew Hugo has pouches.'

The kitchen fell silent again. I looked at Thomas, wondering why he didn't tell Noah that he hadn't been talking about the cat food. He'd always been the most sensitive and perceptive one of the three. Admittedly that wasn't saying much because the bar was set low, but I suspected he at least had an inkling of how unhappy I'd been.

'Why don't you go and buy some?' asked Noah, looking back up at Rob.

'I don't know what to buy, do I?' he replied. 'What brands or flavours they have, or owt like that.'

'Then get one of each and we'll try them in turn till we find out what they like,' said Noah.

'That'll cost a bloody fortune,' replied Rob.

'Fine,' said Thomas. 'Let them starve then. I'm sure that's what Jules would have wanted.'

I'd never wanted them to call me 'Mum'. And the fact that their own mum was still alive but had simply abandoned them for her new fella had meant there'd never been a vacancy under that name. Simply an unpaid one, for someone to look after, feed and clothe them like a real mother would but receive none of the benefits usually associated with that. On Mother's Day, if I was lucky, and only when my mum was still well enough to give Rob or the boys a nudge, I received a card saying thank you for being 'like a mother' to them. You never saw that on gravestones, did you? 'Here lies Julie Smith, beloved wife, "like a mother" and daughter.' Mum used to say that I was still their mother. Certainly, a better one than their actual mother. But it meant nothing. No one had ever called me Mum. And that had never stopped hurting.

Rob walked out and a moment later the front door slammed shut. It was all I could do to whisper 'cut'.

'Let's take ten,' said Carl, who clearly knew all the lingo for his role, as I left the kitchen.

* * *

Carl found me a few minutes later sitting on the end of Thomas's bed.

'You OK?' he asked.

'It doesn't really matter, does it? I'm dead. What's done is done.'

He nodded slowly and looked around.

'Whose room is this?'

'Thomas, the eldest's. Him with wavy hair.'

'The one who said none of them had been paying attention.'

Carl, at least, clearly had been.

'Yeah. He wasn't wrong there.'

'Lewis is the same. Totally oblivious to what's going on in anyone else's life. When Mum announced she was moving to Spain with her new bloke, he couldn't understand it. I had to point out what a crap life she'd had, putting up with my dad's verbal abuse for years before he left her and dealing with all the grief we caused her. She'd finally found a little bit of happiness, and she wanted to make the most of it. Couldn't say I blamed her.'

I nodded, wondering why I hadn't done that; buggered off to somewhere warm instead of chucking myself off a bridge.

Maybe I didn't think I deserved any happiness. Or simply didn't have anyone to share it with.

'How old was your brother when she left?'

'Nineteen.'

I nodded. 'These two were much younger when their mum left. Noah was barely out of nappies. I can understand her wanting to be shot of Rob, but I will never get how you can walk out on your own children. Your own flesh and blood.'

'Did she not try to take them with her?' asked Carl.

'No. Wanted a child-free life, apparently. She should have thought of that before having them.'

'At least they had their dad.'

'I guess so. Although he was struggling with it when I met him. Didn't have a bloody clue, to be honest.'

'So, you stepped in and made them a family again.'

I'd never really thought of it like that; me being the permanent replacement piece in the jigsaw puzzle of their lives.

'Something like that,' I said.

'It's not easy taking over that role, I do know that much. Lewis was working and the mortgage on our house was paid off when our mum left, so there was no financial responsibility. All I had to do was look after him for her...'

His voice trailed off.

'It wasn't your fault,' I said gently.

Carl shrugged and gazed out of the window.

'Didn't look after my kid brother, did I? That's as good as being asleep at the wheel.'

'But not as bad as jumping off a bridge,' I replied.

He was quiet for a minute.

'How long have you been with him – your fella?'

'Sixteen years,' I said. 'Married for fourteen. You get less for murder, that's what he used to say.'

'So why did you stay with him?'

I hesitated. I didn't want to talk about it, but I had a feeling Carl was going to ask a lot of questions if I didn't.

'I got pregnant within a few months of marrying him. It was planned. Much longed-for, on my part at least.'

Carl frowned.

'So—'

'My daughter, Grace, was stillborn,' I said.

'Oh God. I'm so sorry.'

'It's OK. It's not something people talk about, is it? People only want to ask if it's a boy or girl. Maybe what weight it was. No one asks if it was born alive.'

We were both silent for a long time. A silence I appreciated. All I'd had at the time were people landing themselves on the world's-worst-thing-to-say step. 'Never mind, you can try again.' 'At least you have your stepsons.' 'Everything happens for a reason.' None of them understanding that all I wanted to do was grieve for my daughter.

'How long ago was this?' Carl asked eventually.

It was a moment or two before I could reply.

'She would have been thirteen this July,' I said. 'All her birthdays were hard, but I really couldn't bear the thought of that one.'

Carl seemed to be deep in thought for a few moments.

'You never know, do you?' he said, eventually. 'The heartache people are carrying.'

I looked at him. He appeared genuinely upset for me. I hadn't expected that from him. Not after the way he'd reacted when he'd watched my final scene.

'I didn't handle it very well. Never got any help. And to save you wondering, although another baby would never have replaced Grace, we did try again after a while. But there were medical complications from the birth, and, for whatever reason, it didn't happen. I was getting on a bit by then. So, I simply resigned myself to looking after someone else's kids. Because, as people said, I was lucky to have my stepsons.'

'But you didn't see it that way?'

I sighed. Not wanting to appear ungrateful.

'Don't get me wrong. I do love them. I stepped up to the plate. Did everything that was asked of me. Tried not to be the evil stepmum from hell. But inside I was just going through the motions.'

'The pain of loss never goes away, does it?'

I looked across at him. Perhaps it was true that the quiet ones were simply taking it all in.

'No. It doesn't.'

'And you stayed because you had to.'

I shrugged. 'I could hardly be the second mum to abandon them, could I?'

There was a pause. I could almost hear Carl's head fast-forwarding and getting to the bit which didn't make sense.

'But?'

'I know. I suppose I figured they were old enough to be fine without me now. And I simply couldn't hack it any longer. I was in a lot of pain, physically and emotionally. And something just tipped me over the edge.'

We were interrupted by Thomas coming into the room, closely followed by Noah. For a second I thought they could see me and that I had some serious explaining to do. But then my brain caught up with my instinct, and I did as Carl had and moved to the landing, where Gerry and Alice were ready to start filming. Carl called 'action'.

Thomas flopped down onto the bed.

'I fucking hate Dad,' he said.

'It's not his fault,' said Noah.

'It's all our faults,' replied Thomas. 'But he was her husband. He should have seen it coming. Done something about it.'

'Like what?'

'I dunno. Got her some professional help. Rang the Samaritans. Just made a bit of an effort for once in his life.'

'No,' said Noah, shaking his head. 'She didn't love us. She didn't care about any of us. She wouldn't have done that if she had, would she?'

'That's not true. She just wasn't thinking straight,' replied Thomas. 'If I hadn't been away at uni, I might have noticed that something was up.'

'So, it's my fault now, is it?'

'I told you, it's all our faults!' shouted Thomas. 'We all took her for granted. None of us ever did anything for her, did we?'

Noah had no response.

'She asked one thing of us that I can remember, and we didn't even manage that. We all let her down.'

Thomas broke down in tears. Noah tried to put his arm round him, but he pushed him off.

I called 'cut', turned and ran back downstairs and out of the front door just as Rob was coming back up the path with a carrier bag, presumably full of cat food pouches.

I hurried down the side alley, aware he couldn't see me but still not wanting to be in his presence. What I wasn't expecting was to be greeted with a huge mobile trailer taking up most of the back garden.

'Jesus Christ,' I said out loud.

'No, not his work,' said Gerry from the back step, where he was having a fag. 'Majid reversed it up your driveway, and me and a couple of other lads moved some of your stuff out of way.'

I looked around and noticed a couple of planters had been

shifted and the rotary washing line had been repositioned. I turned to stare at Gerry.

'Don't worry. They can't see it, remember. And I can't imagine any of them will notice your washing line's been moved.'

'You're right on that front,' I said.

'There are three separate rooms inside. Nearest door's yours. Young lass is in middle, and Carl's is at far end.'

'All mod cons, is it?' I asked, nodding towards the trailer. 'Only I'm not taking a crap in my own back yard.'

'Oh, aye. Got everything you need in there and a few things you won't be expecting.'

'What do you mean?' I asked.

'They're personalised, see. Designed to reflect your individual personalities. And you'll find lots of mementoes from your old life, including things you won't have seen for a while.'

'How do they do that?'

'Ours is not to question,' replied Gerry, taking a long drag on his fag. 'That's first thing you need to learn here. Anyway, we're wrapped for day, so why don't you go ahead and have a look for yoursen.'

He handed me a key.

'OK,' I said. 'I will.'

I climbed the three metal steps leading up to the door. There was a doormat outside which had '*FFS. What do you want now?*' printed on it. I managed a half-smile and let myself in.

The interior was a sea of red and black. A bit of an assault on the senses, to be honest, but as many people had said that about me over the years, I couldn't really complain. There was a large red sofa, which I presumed opened out into my bed, and a black blind over the small rectangular window which looked out on my old house, seemingly offering a small mark of respect. The fridge was a big red Smeg one, the sort I'd coveted my entire life but had never been able to justify shelling out for because I never put myself at the top of the list for handouts.

In the corner of the little kitchen unit was a sorry-looking pot plant, which I swore I remembered from my student digs, and posters of gigs I'd been to with Nina were plastered all over the walls; two of The Cure, Echo and the Bunnymen, The Damned and The Smiths for good measure. And taking pride of place on the little coffee table was my old record-player from uni. The one with the broken stylus. Only when I checked, it was in its pre-broken days. Next to it was a box of LPs. I knelt down and started flicking through them. The covers so familiar, the album tracks already playing in my head. Somehow, they were still in the alphabetical order I'd kept them in then. 'Worryingly anal.' That's what Nina had said about it and which I'd told her sounded like a good name for an indie band. Not the first night when she'd knocked on my door to introduce herself, but months later, when we got drunk one night and she confessed she'd had a quick gander while I'd gone to the loo and had nearly made a hasty exit.

Talking of the loo, presumably the bathroom was behind the only other door in the room. I squeezed inside. It was like one of those tiny cubicles in public toilets which forced you to perform weird contortions simply to do your business and leave with all your body parts intact. But my gaze was drawn instantly to what was sitting on top of the cistern. Just like I knew it would be.

It's the last day of autumn term in our third year before we break up for Christmas and I'm packing. I don't want to go home. This is home now. Halifax is a distant memory. My family are relics from my past. I'm a different person to the one who left home more than two years ago. I don't want to go home because I don't want to go back to the person I was then. Bristol is who I am now.

Nina is going home too. She's not as dead set against it as me; she gets on OK with her parents and confesses to missing Cardiff a little – or the sound of Welsh voices, at least. But I don't detect much enthusiasm from her either. I think if we had the choice, we would both rather stay here. We share a flat now, just the two of us. Life couldn't be more perfect here, as far as I'm concerned. And yet the expectation is that we should both be with our families.

I don't know how old you have to be before there is not that expectation. Perhaps once you are married or have children of your own, that is when it would be considered acceptable. I want to tell them Nina is my family now. But they would just laugh at that.

Nina knocks on the door.

'You decent, Jules?'

'As I'll ever be,' I call.

She enters my room. She has a neatly gift-wrapped box in her hand.

'I've got you something,' she says, holding it out to me.

I knew she would. I've got something for her too. I went to a second-hand bookshop and found old editions of three of her favourite books. I take the box from her.

'Do you want me to save it for Christmas Day or open it now?' I ask.

'It's up to you. It's your present.'

I want to open it now. I want this to be our little pre-Christmas ritual. I rip the paper and open the box inside. There's red tissue paper on top. I remove it and pull out what's inside. It's one of those knitted toilet-roll cover dolls, like my nan has. Except its knitted off-the-shoulder dress is red and black, the exact same design as the ballgown I'm saving up to hire for the graduation ball. Her hair is dark. Nina has tied a black lace shawl around her. I look up at her. It's a second before I'm able to speak.

'You made this, didn't you?'

'Is it that obvious?'

'You made it for me.'

'I couldn't think of anyone else who'd appreciate it,' she says with a smile.

'I love it,' I say. 'No one's ever made anything for me before.'

'Well, I couldn't afford the real thing for you, so I thought I'd make you a mini replica.'

'I'll treasure her forever. She'll take pride of place on my toilet, wherever I live.'

'I should hope so,' says Nina. 'It took me ages to knit that pattern.'

I laugh and hug her, wondering if I'll ever be able to open a present again, knowing it will never be as good as this.

I pick the toilet-roll holder up now, unable to stop myself smiling at the memory. Or to forget the sound of Nina's laughter, when I said I would name her after Sarah Ann Henley, the woman who had thrown herself from the Clifton Suspension Bridge after being jilted but been saved by her huge dress and petticoats acting like a parachute.

'Mind you don't drop her down the bog then,' Nina had said, 'because I didn't knit any petticoats for her, so she probably wouldn't survive.'

8

EMILY

I lay in my bed the next morning, snuggled under my *Friends* duvet, and gazed around me. My trailer room was so much me, it was as if someone had downloaded the contents of my head. It was decorated in various shades of lilac and was full of *Friends* memorabilia and photos of New York. It hurt, of course. Because I knew I would never go to those places now; never ice-skate in Central Park holding hands with Harry or drive across the Brooklyn Bridge in an open-topped car with shades on and the wind blowing through my hair. They were silly dreams, girlhood dreams. Things I wanted to do before life got real. Or rather, death got real.

It was the signs dotted around the trailer that hurt most of all, though. The ones Dad had put up all over the house when I was first diagnosed, telling me:

'Every day is a new beginning. Smile. Start again.'

'Wake up. Today is your day. Be awesome. Inspire someone. Smile. You rock.'

They had been exposed now for what they were: empty, hollow, meaningless words. Because I had run out of todays and tomorrows. And no amount of smiling or putting a brave face on or being fucking awesome was going to change that.

The truth was that life is cruel. A seventeen-year-old could get leukaemia through no fault of her own and there was absolutely nothing she could do about it. But they don't make signs saying that because no one would buy them. So, people go on pretending it doesn't happen.

I sat up. My sloth slippers were on the floor next to my bed. I smiled and as I did so, I was aware how alien it felt. Smiling. And how I wished I could go back to a time when I did nothing but laugh.

Ava insists I put my sloth slippers on as soon as I open them.

'Hi, sloth face,' she says, moving one of her own capybara slippers next to mine. 'How you doin'?'

I snort with laughter at the Joey Tribbiani reference, and this makes her laugh too.

'Could I be *any happier to be here with you?' I reply in my best sloth voice. It's the morning of my thirteenth birthday and Ava has slept over. I'm not sure if I got any sleep at all as my mouth still aches from laughing all night.*

'I know!' says the capybara slipper in her best Monica voice.

'We were on a break!' replies sloth slipper.

'Please don't tell me you're a palaeontologist,' says capybara slipper, 'because they are so boring.'

Ava doesn't like Ross. He is her least favourite one from Friends.

'Sorry, I was only joking,' says my sloth slipper. 'I'm a singer songwriter and I'm going to sing something for you.'

I break into a mangled rendition of Phoebe's 'Smelly Cat' song. Slinky Dog pushes my bedroom door open with his nose and starts howling when he hears me singing. Ava is laughing so much she is bent double and I know this is my best birthday ever because finally

I'm a teenager and I'm here with my best friend and we have SO much to look forward to that I can't wait to get on with it.

'Come on,' I say, 'Mum said she was going to make us American pancakes for breakfast.'

There were no pancakes this morning, of course. No Mum, no Ava, no Slinky Dog and I suddenly missed them all more than I thought possible. I stood up and went to the fridge. There were strawberry milkshakes inside and those corner yogurts where you tipped the puree portion into the rest and mixed it up. Dad hadn't let me have them after I was diagnosed. Said that sugar inhibited my immune system, and I needed to fight it with everything I had. Fat lot of good that had done.

I took one out and sat on the end of the bed, taking pleasure in seeing the yogurt turn pink as I mixed it. I had forgotten how good they tasted. How good life tasted. Before everything had turned bitter and sour.

As I looked up, I saw Harry's face smiling down at me from the corkboard on the wall. Not just one Harry, but seventeen selfies of us together, all with his face nestled against mine, which he'd given to me for my seventeenth birthday. I wondered if he was looking at the similar photo-board I'd made for his seventeenth. If he was, I hoped it was providing him with a shred of comfort. Helping him to cope. Whatever 'coping' meant. I'd talked to him about it; what would happen after I'd gone. Said I wanted him to be able to get on with his own life without me. Even though I knew I wouldn't have been able to do that if our positions had been reversed.

I stood up and gazed out of the window. Wondering what the flat or house I may have one day lived in with Harry would have looked like. It wouldn't have mattered to me how big or small it was. All I'd ever wanted was a place I could be together with him. A place we could call our own.

Gerry had said yesterday that we might be done here by lunchtime, in which case we could move on to the next location. Mine. Which was why I was counting down the minutes until we left. I suspected Jules felt the same. It had been awkward, yesterday. Seeing her upset like that. Feeling as if we were intruding on her family's private grief. Even if Thomas was the only one who had been able to talk about it. I still hated what Jules had done, throwing her life away like that. But to be fair, her husband was a complete knob. God knows what she'd ever seen in him. When I finally got to see Harry, Jules would realise that he loved me, really loved me, and he would never speak about me like her husband did about her. Which was all a bit embarrassing, what with her being ancient and me only seventeen. I almost felt sorry for her. Almost, but not quite.

When I emerged from the trailer, Jules was already sitting on the steps.

'Morning,' she said. 'Just soaking up a bit of sun.'

'Are Gerry and Alice here yet?' I asked.

'I think I heard Majid dropping them off out the front.'

Before I could respond, the back door opened and her husband came out into the garden, holding a mug of tea.

'Shit,' Jules said. 'It's a bit early for him to be up. And we're not ready to start shooting.'

'I hope we don't miss anything important,' I replied.

'You're sounding keen.'

'I want to get this over with and go and see Harry, that's all.'

She fell silent. I felt like a bit of a cow for saying it, but it was true.

Rob was staring right at us.

'Are you sure he can't see us?' I asked. 'Maybe he's got a sense that you're watching him. Your cat knew you were there, didn't he?'

'Yeah, but my cats have always been a lot more perceptive than my husband,' replied Jules.

I looked at her for a long time before I spoke.

'When did you stop loving him?' I asked. 'I mean you must have loved him once, otherwise you wouldn't have married him, would you?'

She hesitated before replying.

'One of the things you'll learn as you get older is that life isn't as simple as you thought it would be.'

'But I'll never get older to find that out, will I?'

She turned to look at me. Her eyes were full of sadness.

'Shit,' she said. 'No, of course not. I'm sorry.'

Gerry and Alice clattered noisily down the side alley with their gear and arrived in the back garden as Carl emerged from the end trailer room.

'Morning. Shall we crack on?' Gerry asked, nodding towards Rob before turning to Jules. 'I hope you don't mind me saying this, but I want to get wrapped here because I can't put up with your waste-of-space husband much longer.'

'Now you know why I had to get out,' she replied.

'Bloody hell,' said Gerry. 'You mean you…?' His voice trailed off, and he mimed hanging himself.

'Not like that,' said Jules.

'So, did you…?' Gerry put a two-fingered pistol to his head and raised his eyebrows questioningly.

'Jesus, have a bit of respect,' said Carl.

Jules appeared as surprised by his intervention as I was.

'Sorry,' said Gerry. 'I usually find it's a good icebreaker, you know, asking how people copped it.'

'Jumped off a bridge, if you must know,' said Jules with a sigh.

Gerry visibly winced.

'Not nice for emergency services.'

'Yes, we've done that one already, thanks,' Jules replied. 'And to save you asking, Emily here had leukaemia, and Carl was in a motorbike accident.'

'Sorry, love,' he said to me, before looking across at Carl.

'Didn't have you down as a biker,' he said. 'Bloody dangerous things, motorbikes. There's a dead-bikers club here, we get that many.'

'What about you, then?' asked Jules. 'Do we get to know how you died?'

'Got hit by a dolly-cart while filming,' he replied. 'One blow and I toppled back and hit me head on concrete. Felt like quite an apt way to go, to be honest. Like that time Boy George narrowly survived being killed by a glitterball. I couldn't help thinking he'd never have got a better ending than that.'

'And you were happy to go early if it meant you got a suitable death?' asked Jules.

Gerry shrugged.

'Always someone younger ready to take your place in my line of work. I were gutted, mind, because I'd been booked in to do first series of *Last Tango in Halifax* next and I would have liked that. I worked with Sarah Lancashire on *Corrie*, you know?'

'Wow!' said Carl, unable to hide the fact he was impressed.

'Oh aye, I've done *Emmerdale* and *Brookside* too. That's all you got to do up north in those days. Course, they're bloody falling over themselves to film round here now. Even Samuel L Jackson were up here shooting a Marvel film at Piece Hall. You can't move in Halifax or Hebden Bridge without bumping into a film crew.'

'I worked on the first series of *Happy Valley*,' chipped in Alice.

'You didn't come a cropper on the film set too, did you?'

asked Jules. 'Get run over by Catherine Cawood's police car or something?'

'Oh no. I severed an artery when I tried to swat a wasp away at a barbecue and forgot I had a steak knife in my hand.'

Jules started laughing. 'Sorry.'

'No, it's OK,' said Alice. 'That's how most people react. On the plus side, I'd just had the best burger I'd ever eaten, so at least I went happy. And it was such a freak accident that it made the local TV news.'

I hadn't thought about that. My death being on the news. It probably would have been because of all the fundraising stuff Dad had organised. I'd been on the local news with that, so they'd have been bound to cover my death as well. Which meant everyone would know. All the kids from school. Which would be making it even harder for Harry.

We were interrupted by the sound of Rob's mug smashing on the patio. Gerry grabbed his camera and started filming without waiting for Carl. Rob squatted down on the step, holding his head in his hands, and rocked quietly to and fro. Jules said nothing. Hugo came out of the back door licking his lips and completely ignoring Rob.

'That's good,' Jules whispered to me. 'At least it looks like he's been fed.'

As soon as Majid turned up at lunchtime, I jumped in the passenger seat next to him.

'So, I've got an address for Harry Sanders to go to. Is he your dad?'

'My fiancé,' I said. I thought I saw him glance in his mirror to look at the other two in the back, as if he didn't know whether to believe me or not.

'Right you are,' he said. 'We'll be there in two ticks, love.'

I nodded. Not even taking him up on the 'love' thing. He

was way over forty; he wouldn't understand. I let Jules and Carl do all the talking. I wasn't in a chatty mood. I was in a getting-there-and-seeing-Harry-and-not-caring-about-anything-else kind of mood. I flipped down the visor and took my brush out of my bag, pulling it through my hair, before applying some lipstick. I could see Jules in the mirror giving me a look from the back seat. I knew what she was thinking; that someone should say something to me, remind me that he wouldn't be able to see me. But I didn't care about that. He was my Harry and if I wanted to look my best for him then I would. I wasn't going to stop making an effort simply because I was dead.

As we pulled up outside Harry's house, I looked up and saw his bedroom curtains were closed. He would never have left them like that normally. He loved the sun pouring into his room at this time of day. Even said he felt bad sometimes because his little sister had got the bedroom at the back which never used to get any sun.

Gerry and Alice were already waiting outside. Majid said all cameramen drove like maniacs. It was why so many of them died young. He turned to look at me.

'Suzi may say our loved ones can't see us and have no idea we're there, but I think they can feel our presence,' he said. 'I think you'll be a comfort to him.'

I managed a little smile before I got out. Carl came over and put his hand lightly on my shoulder.

'Let us know when you're ready,' he said. 'And remember, you can stop the filming at any time.'

I nodded. It was like they were all auditioning to be my father figure or something.

'I'm fine,' I replied. 'I just need to see him.'

Carl nodded. I knew he was desperate to get this over with so he could go to see his brother. Though he was probably dreading it, too.

'Where to, love?' asked Gerry. What was it with old men and 'love'?

'That bedroom,' I said, pointing up. 'I don't know if there'll be anyone else in. Maybe his mum.'

Gerry opened the front door. The rest of us followed him. The scent of Harry hit me first. His jacket was hanging up at the bottom of the stairs, and I swear I must have been one of those sniffer dogs in a previous life because I could have picked it out from a hundred others in an instant. I touched it lightly then hurried straight upstairs and into his room.

Harry was lying on his bed. His mop of wavy hair, usually squeaky clean, was unwashed. He had unfamiliar stubble on his chin and his eyes looked so heavy they were in danger of pulling down his face. I gave an involuntary gasp. Carl said 'action' in a respectfully quiet voice and Jules, who had swapped with me to be assistant camera operator while I directed, did the clap-perboard.

There was no action, of course. Because his grief wasn't a moving thing. It weighed him down motionless to the bed. He was hugging my T-shirt, the one I'd given to him when I'd gone into hospital so he could keep me close. He held it like if he pressed it hard enough against his heart, he could somehow get mine started again. I wanted to go to him, let him know I was there. I stepped forward, waiting for one of the others to pull me back, but they didn't. So, I knelt at the side of the bed and reached out one tentative hand towards him. I didn't touch him, I figured that would probably be against the rules, but I left it so close to him that I could feel the warmth coming from his body. He turned his head and looked straight at me. Majid was right. He could feel my presence. I was certain of it. I blinked at him.

Willed him to reach out and squeeze my hand, even though I knew he couldn't. And then the tears came. His tears. Which rapidly turned into more of a howl. I heard footsteps hurrying up the stairs. A few moments later his mum, Cath, flew into the room and threw herself over him from the other side of the bed, scooping him up in her arms and rocking him like he was a baby.

'It's OK,' she said.

'It's not,' Harry sobbed. 'I want Emily. And Emily will never be here again. I've lost her. I didn't cling on hard enough. I let her down.'

'You mustn't say that,' said Cath. 'You couldn't have done any more for her than you did. She would have felt the strength of your love right to the end.'

'I did!' I shouted. 'You couldn't have loved me any harder. I was so lucky to have you.'

Harry fiddled with his engagement ring. He'd wanted to have one too, probably because he knew we'd never exchange wedding rings. I held my hand up.

'I'm still wearing mine,' I told him. 'I won't ever take it off. We'll always be joined together.'

'I can't cope without her,' he said. 'I miss her more every second. I don't know how I'm going to survive.'

'You will, though.' I thought it was Cath's voice for a moment until I realised she was unable to speak for crying and it was actually mine. 'You've got to carry on and live your life. That's what we agreed. Even though I miss you too. So, so much.'

I felt someone come and scoop me up off the floor as I started crying. Put their arms around me and hold on tight. I stupidly hoped it was Harry, although I knew it couldn't be because I was still looking at Cath holding him.

'It's OK,' a voice said. I lifted my head. It was Jules.

'It's not though, is it?' I replied. 'Because, unlike you, I never wanted to leave this world. I never wanted to leave his side. I planned to spend the rest of my life with him. But you wouldn't understand that because you've never loved anyone, and you threw your life away.'

For a second, I thought she was going to slap me across the face. I probably deserved it. She didn't though. Instead, she whispered something so quietly that I wasn't sure any of the others could hear.

'I'm sorry,' she said. 'And no, I never had what you had and believe me, that hurts like hell.'

* * *

I didn't want to leave Harry. He was the only reason I'd wanted to do this 'on location' thing. And I totally didn't get why they couldn't have parked the trailer in Harry's back garden. It was bigger than ours for a start. But Majid had already taken it to my parents' house, because they were officially my next of kin. I hated that. It made me wish I'd married Harry instead of just got engaged. We'd talked about it at one point. Harry hadn't thought my dad would agree to it, and he was probably right. It wasn't that Dad had any beef with Harry, but he did have a problem accepting that his little girl had grown up. I would have fought him over it, but I decided that I didn't want to be responsible for making Harry a widower at seventeen. That would have been wrong. Anyway, according to Suzi, it wouldn't have mattered anyway because even if I'd married Harry, he still wouldn't have been old enough to be my next of kin. I hated that; we'd been through more stuff than most people go through in a lifetime, but they still wouldn't take us seriously as grown-ups. And now I had to spend the night outside my mum and dad's house like I was some little kid camping out in their back yard.

When Majid arrived for us, we got in the car without saying a word.

'Off to your folks' place, is it?' he asked. I nodded. Carl made polite conversation with Majid but Jules, who was sitting opposite me in the back, stared out of the window in silence. I suspected she was still mad at me for having a go at her.

We pulled up outside my house. Gerry was smoking by the side gate, and Alice was picking at a scab on her arm, which was weird because you would have thought she'd have had enough of making herself bleed.

'Trailer's in back yard if you all want to freshen up first,' said Gerry.

'Are you saying we stink?' asked Jules.

'No, but I do want to finish my fag before we get started.'

I led the others down the drive to the back of the house, still thinking about Harry and how awful he'd looked. How I hated myself for what I'd done to him. Which was why I wasn't prepared for the scene that greeted me. Mum and Dad sitting at the table on the patio, half of Mum's face in the sun, as if she was trying to become a 'before and after' advert for fake tan. She'd always tanned easily, unlike me. I had Dad's skin. Everyone said that. Which is why he never let me leave the house in the summer without a tube of factor fifty. He saved me from sunburn, but the leukaemia got me instead. Pity he couldn't get a tube of something to protect me from that.

My parents sat there looking like someone had punched a hole in their stomachs and they may either throw up or pass out at any moment.

'Bloody hell,' said Gerry, coming round the corner, 'you could have shouted for us.'

'You haven't missed anything,' I said. 'Just some more shots of people looking sad.'

Gerry wasn't listening to me, though. Or waiting for Carl. He was already filming.

Mum pushed a bit of salad and some cold chicken around her plate. Dad pretended not to notice. Eventually, he broke the silence.

'I've put together a piece for the *Courier*. More of a tribute, really. And I've included the details of the funeral so people can come and pay their respects.'

Mum dropped her fork on the plate and looked at him.

'Are you actually going to grieve for her at any point?'

'I'm sorry?' Dad wasn't used to the tone of her voice. Nor was I.

'Our daughter, Emily. She died three days ago, and you've been so busy organising her funeral, it's like you're not allowing yourself to stop in case you have to acknowledge what's happened.'

'I want to make sure she gets the best possible send-off, that's all.'

Mum stared at him and shook her head.

'Send-off? You make it sound like it's a leaving do. She *died*, Simon. Our beautiful seventeen-year-old daughter died and at some point, you've got to face up to that. And maybe when you do, you might be able to offer me a bit of support.'

Mum stood up, her chair scraping across the stone, and fled into the house. Dad sat there, staring at the empty chair where I used to sit, as Slinky Dog trotted down the steps and sat down next to him, looking up and whining. It was like he was grieving too. I hated that I'd hurt all the people I loved most in the world and the best dog ever.

I wiped my eyes, knowing we couldn't have scripted it better if we'd tried. And wishing like hell I could go over and give them both a cuddle.

9

CARL

I lay in my trailer in Emily's back garden that night, trying, unsuccessfully, to stop myself thinking about them. The parents. All of them. Those who'd lost the most precious thing in their lives. No one should have to go through that. It wasn't the natural order of things. You expect to have to bury your parents. It should never be the other way around. Nothing prepares you for that. There's no manual. Which is why they're left to struggle and stumble through it, flailing around for something to hold on to. Something to make them believe life can ever be worth living again. It was better if they had another child. Not because it in any way eased the pain of losing one, but because it gave them a reason to carry on. Without one, they developed that haunted expression. The one I had seen so many times over the years. While doing my job and when I shut my eyes to try to get to sleep at night.

Would Emily's parents manage to stay together? She'd been their only child. Clearly, she meant the world to them. But without her, the cracks were already beginning to show. Everyone grieved differently, including parents of the same child. It was whether they found the strength to accept that – and help each other – that would determine if they got through it.

Emily didn't understand that, of course. She was too hurt and angry with the world to think about what might happen to her parents, poor kid.

I sighed, got up and padded across the trailer in my bare feet to open the fridge. The bottles of lager stared back at me. I wasn't sure if everyone had got the same. I wouldn't put it past Suzi to have found out all our favourite tipples; she seemed to have a stack of information about us on file. Maybe she knew more than she'd let on. She could have put it in here for me as a test. Knowing that I was weak. That I might not have the willpower to resist. I had no idea if they had AA meetings in the afterlife, but I was sure I didn't want to go to one if they did. I took the bottles out of the fridge one by one and emptied them down the sink. It wasn't the first time I'd done that, of course, and it still felt ridiculously wasteful but there was no other option. I'd learnt that the hard way. When I was done, I drank a glass of water and sat there on the end of my bed, staring into the darkness.

They were queueing up in my head now, ready to keep me awake. The sights, the sounds, the smells that could take me back to that night in an instant. Only if I let them, mind, and I wasn't going to, not tonight. I needed my head clear for the morning because we were moving on. There was only so much grief you could wring out of each set of loved ones and Gerry had said we were done here for now.

We wouldn't be going to my house, though, because there would be no one there. We'd be off to Calderdale Royal Hospital. Though how the hell Majid would find a space for the trailer in that hospital car park, I did not know.

* * *

I must have gone back to bed and fallen asleep at some point because the next thing I knew, I was woken by a tap on my door and Jules's voice calling out, 'Only me.'

I fumbled for my glasses on the bedside table, pulled on my dressing gown and opened the door.

'Sorry,' said Jules. 'I've run out of milk, and something told me you would have rationed yours wisely.'

'Sure,' I said. 'I'll get you some.'

Jules stepped inside without being invited.

'Like it,' she said, nodding towards the heavy-duty '*Life is short. Try not to be a dick*' doormat.

'Yeah. Can't think why they chose that for me.'

I turned to go to the fridge, at which point she caught sight of all the empty lager bottles on the draining board.

'Bloody hell, you didn't ration the booze, did you? Good night, was it?'

'I didn't drink them,' I said quickly.

'Oh, you had some ghost buddies around to help you out, did you? Quite a few of them, by the looks of it.'

I wasn't sure what to say. I'd had conversations like this before when I'd tried to stop, and they always tended to go the same way, as for some reason being teetotal seemed to be on a par with admitting mass murder to some people. Still, I didn't have any other options.

'I don't drink,' I said. 'The contents went down the plughole.'

Jules nodded slowly. I sensed she was trying not to say anything too judgemental.

'Bit of a waste.'

'Better than me being wasted.'

'I guess so. Though I knocked back half a bottle of red last night and I've got a perfectly clear head, so I've got a feeling you don't get hangovers here.'

I nodded, took one of the two milk bottles from the fridge and handed it to her, hoping to change the subject.

'Thanks,' she said. 'Promise I won't chuck it down the sink.'

I smiled weakly.

'You worried about seeing your brother?' she asked.

'He's not going to be in a good way, is he?'

'It's bloody brilliant what doctors can do nowadays.'

'They couldn't save Emily, could they?'

'I know but leukaemia's different. This is about putting your brother back together again after an accident. That's the sort of stuff they do all the time, and they can work miracles.'

'Not always,' I said.

'Look on the bright side, why don't you?'

'That's a bit rich, coming from you.'

Jules fell silent. I cursed myself for overstepping the mark.

'Sorry,' I said.

'It's OK. I deserved it.'

'I'll be better once I've seen him,' I said. 'At least, I hope I will.'

Jules nodded and looked around the trailer properly for the first time.

'It's a bit drab in here,' she said.

'Is it? I thought they were all plain and functional.'

'Well, mine's in your face red and black. Looks like an eighties party venue.'

I surveyed my magnolia walls, the serviceable vinyl floor. The only things that stood out were the red flag propped up in the corner and a poster of a Harley-Davidson on the wall. I'd already hidden my old police ID badge which had been on the table.

'What's that about?' asked Jules, pointing to the flag.

'It's a *Les Mis* prop, they wave it in the barricade scene. It was my mum's favourite show too and she got it for me one Christmas because she knew I'd appreciate it a lot more than socks.'

'Glad I asked. And I suppose you've got a shitload of musical theatre stuff to listen to,' she said, nodding towards the stack of CDs next to the hi-fi.

'Yeah. All my favourites. I'd offer to lend you some, but I don't imagine it's your cup of tea.'

'You're right there. And if you hear The Cure coming from my gaffe, bang the wall and I'll turn it down. It'll be like being in my first flat again.'

I managed a smile. Jules headed for the door.

'Thanks for the milk,' she said. 'And if they do restock your booze, let me know before chucking it away next time and I'll take it off your hands.'

As soon as she left, I started worrying about what she must be thinking. What questions she would ask me later. How I was going to deflect them. Because if she started to peel back the layers, I felt sure she would get to the truth. And the truth was ugly, and I was brittle. Too brittle for life and apparently now too brittle for the afterlife.

* * *

Majid arrived at the front of the house at nine thirty sharp, as promised. Emily was the last to emerge from her trailer room and come out to the front.

She took a final look over her shoulder at the house before getting into the back of the car.

'Straight to the hospital, please,' I said to Majid as I sat in the passenger seat next to him.

'Who are you going to see?' he asked.

'It's my younger brother, Lewis. He was on the back of my bike.'

Majid pulled a face.

'I'm sorry to hear that. Dangerous things, bikes.'

'So everyone keeps telling me,' I replied. 'Only it's a bit late for that.'

It was only a ten-minute drive from Emily's house. I clenched my fists, torn between being desperate to see Lewis and not wanting to think about the state he'd be in. Majid pulled up outside the main entrance.

'There you go. Hope it's not as bad as you think,' he said, patting me on the arm before I clambered from the car.

I spotted Gerry stubbing out his cigarette at the hospital entrance. Alice was gawping at a man with blood streaming down his face who was being helped towards A & E by paramedics.

'Your brother's in bed two in intensive care, which is on level three,' said Gerry.

'How do you know?'

'I know my way around this place,' he said, tapping his nose. 'I used to work for *Look North*.'

'What state's he in?' I asked.

'I'm not allowed to tell you that. But you'll see soon enough.'

I waited till there were no living people around, called the lift and we all squeezed in, Alice's boom in serious danger of doing one of us an injury. The doors opened outside the ICU. I looked at Gerry, who got out a card and proceeded to swipe us all through. It seemed wrong to go in without pressing the buzzer and waiting for someone to come, but we had no choice.

The deep-clean smell hit me first. And the noise of machines whirring and monitors beeping. The silence from patients was what told you they were teetering on the edge of death. The wards where people complained to nurses and called out in pain, that was a different level of illness. Here, people were beyond speech. They had to rely on monitors to do their complaining for them. They were all only a single continuous beep away from crossing over to the other side. Our side. And the most important thing to me right now was that Lewis didn't join us.

He was in a bed in the far corner. Not that I recognised him; I saw only a figure with a respirator on his face, bandages around his head, a neck brace, a cast on one arm, tubes and lines seemingly connected to every part of him and a raised sheet covering the lower half of his body. It was Mum who I recognised, sitting at the side of the bed, looking broken and battered herself, but without anything to cover it up or hold her together. She must have come straight over from Spain. I supposed that was the benefit of me having an In Case of Emergency number on my phone. Because looking at Lewis, he wouldn't have been in a fit state to call anyone.

He was lying there motionless. The only thing that indicated he was still alive was the intermittent beeping of the monitors he was hooked up to. Jesus, what had I done to him? To my own little brother.

I glanced back at the others and nodded at Jules, who had taken over my job, so she knew to say 'action'. Gerry started the camera rolling. But there was no action. All that happened was that Lewis continued to lie motionless, and Mum carried on staring at him, wringing her hands and looking utterly bereft.

She was one of those parents now. The ones who had lost a child. I had done that to her, and I had also left her second child as good as dead, which was maybe worse. At least you could grieve someone who was dead. A lifetime of sitting at the bedside of the living dead didn't even afford you that release.

A nurse came over, checked Lewis, or what she could see of him, and all the monitors, before turning to speak to Mum.

'No change this morning, I'm afraid. If you'd like to come with me, Mr Henderson has got the results of the scans and would like to speak to you.'

Mum nodded and stood up. Her legs appeared shaky, as if she knew what was to come. It wasn't going to be good news. One look at Lewis could tell you that. I hated that she was on her own to hear it. Presumably Colin, her new fella, hadn't been able to leave the bar he ran in Spain at such short notice. He was due to retire next year. That's what Mum had told me the last time we'd spoken. They were planning to go on a big cruise. Plans that now lay in tatters. Because Mum wouldn't leave Lewis, I knew that. That was supposing he survived, of course.

I watched as she followed the nurse into a small room off the ICU corridor where a tall, balding man shook her hand and asked her to sit down. The nurse came out. There was barely room for me and Gerry and Alice's boom to squeeze into the room.

Mr Henderson started speaking. He did, at least, spare Mum any long preamble.

'I'm afraid the results are as we feared. Your son has suffered a severe spinal cord injury to his T1 vertebra, which has caused irreversible damage to his spinal cord. He's paralysed from the neck down and, as such, is classed as a tetraplegic, which is what used to be known as a quadriplegic.'

The word hit me hard. It was so brutal, so final. No glimmer of hope included. No way I could kid myself he might be able to play drums again one day. No way I would ever forgive myself for what I had taken from him.

Mum nodded. I could see her biting down hard on her lip. Mr Henderson continued, perhaps sensing she was unable to ask the questions she wanted to.

'The broken collarbone and arm will heal, and we'll gradually be able to reduce the level of sedation, but he faces a long, hard road ahead.'

Mum nodded again, seemingly still unable to speak.

'I'm sorry I can't offer you anything more hopeful but it's important to be realistic about what lies ahead. Obviously, our priority now is to stabilise him and get him breathing independently again but once that's happened, we will be looking at securing him a place at a rehabilitation centre, so he can continue his recovery with the specialist physio and support he needs. Do you have any questions?'

I looked at Mum, her face contorted in pain.

'He won't be able to play the drums again, will he? He's an excellent drummer. At least, he was.'

Her voice trailed off, and she looked down at her lap.

'I'm afraid not,' said Mr Henderson. 'I've got a few leaflets here which explain things further and should answer all your questions but please do feel free to come back to me if you think of anything else.'

Mum took the leaflets from him with a shaking hand and stood up.

'Thank you,' she whispered, before leaving the room.

I stood there staring at Mr Henderson, wanting to force the words back down his throat. Tell him he was wrong. A fraud who had no idea what he was talking about. But I knew none of this was true and that it wouldn't help. Nothing could help Lewis now. That was the truth, however unpalatable it was.

I stepped outside. The camera was still turning. I sensed the others were looking at me. I mumbled the word 'cut'.

I couldn't get my head around what I had done to my brother. I was supposed to be the responsible, reliable one. That was what Mum had always said. I remembered how proud she'd been when I'd qualified as a police officer. And prouder still when I'd made the motorcycle unit and completed the advanced training. She wouldn't be so proud of me now, if she knew the truth.

I started to shake. Jules tried to put her hand on my arm, but I pushed her away.

'This is all my fault,' I said. 'So please do not waste your sympathy on me or say that at least Lewis is alive and maybe he could still have a fulfilling life, because remember Christopher Reeve. Lewis is not fucking Superman and there is nothing remotely positive about being a quadriplegic at twenty-one. Nothing at all. My brother did not deserve this. Sure, he was a lazy sod and could be a bit of a dick at times, but he didn't deserve this.'

Jules opened her mouth to say something, but I held up my hand to stop her.

'Don't waste your breath on me. I'm no better than you. If anything, I'm worse because it wasn't my life I took. It was someone else's.'

I turned and strode off along the corridor. As I'd hoped, no one came after me.

10

JULES

Majid took us back to the Travel Inn afterwards. The journey was silent. Carl stared forlornly out of the window in the front passenger seat. I suspected he was trying to hide his glistening eyes from Majid, but I could see them reflected in the glass.

'That'll be twelve pounds fifty then,' said Majid with a wink as he pulled into the car park. His attempt at humour fell flat and Carl got out without a word. I patted Majid on the shoulder before leaving.

'Tough day for him,' I said.

'It gets easier,' he replied.

'What, like watching our own funerals?'

'After that,' he said. 'It brings some closure.'

I nodded. Though I couldn't imagine what closure it would bring for Carl. It wasn't his own death he was mourning; it was what had happened to his brother. And that was a living hell.

To be honest, I couldn't imagine my funeral bringing any closure either. When you borrowed a book you didn't enjoy from the library, it didn't bring closure when you returned it. Only a frustration that you didn't take out a better one in the first place.

At least with a library you got a chance to find something better next time. But this was me done. *Finito*. I'd had one life, and I'd screwed it up big time. All that lay ahead for me was regrets. And there really were too many to mention.

* * *

Carl was already seated at our table in Food to Die For when I arrived that evening. He'd clearly had a shower, put a fresh shirt on and made an effort, but if anything, he looked worse than earlier. I sat down to his left and leant over to him.

'I'm so sorry about your brother,' I said.

'It should have been me.'

'What do you mean?' I asked.

'Well, I got off lightly, didn't I? A split second and it was all over for me. He's got a bloody life sentence to serve.'

'But at least he survived,' I said.

'And you'd be happy with that life, would you?' asked Carl. 'The one he's going to have, unable to move from the neck down?'

I said nothing for a moment. Mainly because I knew full well that I'd not consider it a blessing if I'd survived but ended up in that state. And then it came to me. The thing Carl could do. The thing that would change everything.

'He could be your director's cut,' I blurted out.

'What? Sorry?' said Carl.

'Lewis. You can still save him. Suzi said you can't save your own life or anyone else's. So as long as he doesn't die, you could do something to save him.'

I watched as Carl's expression changed from one of utter dejection, going into neutral as his brain processed what I'd just said and then transforming into a look of wonder.

'Jesus, of course. Why didn't I think of that?'

'Because you've been so busy beating yourself up about it being your fault. And I'm a bloody genius, of course.'

Carl smiled at me, his eyes conveying the first glimmer of hope I'd seen since I'd met him.

'You're right. This is fixable. I can press the rewind button. Leave home before Lewis has the chance to ask me for a ride.'

I looked up to see Emily staring at us, or, more specifically, Carl.

'What's up with you?' she asked.

'I can save my brother. Jules has pointed out that if he doesn't die, I can save him with my director's cut. You know, turn back time and edit out him getting on my bike.'

'Right,' Emily said, sitting down at the table without another word. I knew what she was thinking. It was good news for him and his brother, at least. But it didn't help her. She'd left Harry mourning for her and there was nothing she could do to change that.

Elsie arrived at our table, gasping for breath as if she'd just scaled Everest. She held up her hand as if to ask for a moment.

'Sorry,' she said eventually. 'Bloody long Covid.'

I frowned at her, not understanding why she hadn't been healed on arrival like the rest of us.

'I had it twice,' she said. 'They did away with second bout of infection that killed me but somehow forgot about my long Covid.'

'That's no good. Have you complained?' I asked her. 'They still might be able to sort it out here.'

'Not worth it,' she replied. 'I mean, I'm dead as a dodo, aren't I? And nobody could do owt about it when I were alive, so I can hardly expect them to be any better now I'm dead. I blame Boris Johnson.'

'What for?' I asked.

'Absolutely bloody everything,' she said. 'Now, are you ready to order?'

She said it with the same inflection as the Julie Walters character. I gestured to the others to go first while I tried to stifle my laughter.

Carl ordered fish and chips.

'To celebrate,' he said, before glancing at Emily and looking awkwardly down at his plate. Emily ordered a pasta dish as usual, and I went for the salmon. Elsie licked her fingertip in order to turn over the page in her notebook. I stifled another laugh.

'Haven't they offered you a digital order device, Elsie?' asked Carl.

'They have but I told them they could stick it where sun don't shine. I managed fine without one for nearly sixty years and it would take me another sixty to learn how to use it. So I'll stick with my notepad and pencil, thank you very much.'

She turned and walked off before any of us had a chance to reply.

'Well, that told you,' I said to Carl with a smile. 'She's comedy gold, that one. Which is a bit of luck, after the last few days we've had.'

Emily looked at me with a raised eyebrow. Clearly, she didn't consider my suffering as being in the same league.

'Tough for you two, I mean. I know my lot failed miserably in the ramping-up-the-sympathy department.'

'You can't blame them for being angry at you,' snapped Emily.

'I've got no problem with the anger,' I said. 'It made a welcome change to the indifference, to be honest.'

'Yeah, well, it was your decision to end it all. Some of us didn't have a choice.'

Carl turned to look at Emily.

'Maybe don't assume you know everything about someone else's life, OK?'

'What's that supposed to mean?'

'Exactly what I said. None of us know each other's full stories.'

'You're the one who had a go at her for traumatising the emergency services.'

'Yeah, well. Maybe I was a bit quick to judge, too.'

Emily looked at Carl and me in turn.

'What is this? The oldies ganging up on me or something?'

I tried to give Carl a look to indicate that I didn't want him to say anything more, but I suspected he was too disgruntled by being called an oldie to notice, so I decided to try to change the subject.

'What do you think your funerals will be like?' I asked.

They both turned to stare at me.

'What sort of question is that?' asked Emily.

'The sort you ask when you are in an afterlife processing centre waiting to attend your own funerals,' I replied.

'Fairplay,' said Emily.

'I'm being cremated,' said Carl.

I rolled my eyes.

'Yes, you already told us that. Did you leave instructions for the entire proceedings or were you not that organised?'

Carl sighed.

'I'd completed an online funeral wishes document which I'd saved on my computer and emailed to Lewis.'

'Oh,' I said. 'So, no one's going to see it in time?'

'It's OK. I filed a hard copy with the solicitors who hold my will too.'

'Wow,' I replied. 'What kind of person does funeral planning to that degree in their thirties?'

'One who understands that anything can happen to anyone at any time,' said Carl.

He said it seriously, with his gaze on the table.

'Isn't that what Suzi said?' I asked.

Carl sighed and looked up.

'Yeah, and she's right. I used to be in the police,' he said. 'In the motorcycle section.'

'What, delivering takeaways for them?' asked Emily.

I shook my head. Sometimes I had genuine fears for the future of the planet, with Gen Z in charge.

'You lied to us?' I asked.

'No. I've just been economical with the truth.'

'And there was I thinking we'd bonded in a truth and reconciliation session.'

'Please don't take it the wrong way,' said Carl. 'I just couldn't cope with all the questions at the time.'

'So why are you telling us now?' I asked.

'Because you're going to find out at the funeral anyway. There'll be some kind of turnout from the police. There always is.'

'So, you never worked for Deliveroo?' asked Emily, who appeared to be disappointed at Carl's revelation. Food delivery courier presumably ranked higher up than the police in her desirable jobs list.

'Only briefly,' said Carl. 'In the last couple of years since I left the police.'

'Why did you leave?' I asked.

Carl hesitated. I sensed this was why he hadn't told us in the first place.

'I'd done my time,' he said. 'It gets to you after a while. Relentless death and carnage, you know?'

I nodded. I couldn't help feeling there was more to it than that, but he clearly didn't want to go there.

'So, what's your order of service?' I asked instead.

Carl took a deep breath.

'My body will be brought in to "Bring Him Home" from *Les Mis.*'

'That's wild,' said Emily. 'You actually know what music will be playing.'

'Yep, everything planned down to the last detail.'

'I hadn't even thought about the music,' said Emily. 'And I'm the one who actually knew I was going to die.'

'What would you like it to be?' I asked.

She hesitated before replying.

'Something Harry has written for me. Maybe not actually him singing live, he probably won't be up to that, but a recording of it or a piece of music he composed.'

I was rendered speechless for a moment. It was so bloody beautiful.

'That's a lovely idea,' said Carl.

Emily shrugged and looked down at the table. Carl turned to me.

'What about you?'

I thought for a moment. Although there was only really one choice.

'"Lovesong" by The Cure,' I said.

'Never heard of it,' said Emily.

'I have,' replied Carl. 'It doesn't get played nearly as much as "The Lovecats" but it should do. It's gorgeous.'

He said it as if he was surprised I had such good taste. That he'd expected my choice to be something obviously tongue in cheek like 'New York, New York', that everyone would smile at and say, 'She was always a laugh, that Jules.' I felt somewhat affronted.

'Who's it for?' asked Emily.

I hadn't been expecting the question. I looked at Carl, as if he'd somehow be able to help me out of the hole I'd dug myself. He had nothing though.

'Me,' I said eventually. 'It reminds me of my student days in Bristol.'

It was a lot more than that, of course. But I didn't want to tell Emily who it was really for. Fortunately, my answer appeared to satisfy her.

'And I'd be carried out to "Baby, I Love You" by The Ramones, just to get everyone singing in the aisles,' I continued. 'It would be like a Richard Curtis film.'

That wasn't why I wanted it either. It was because I'd sung it to Grace every day in the shower, from the moment I'd found out I was pregnant. I would have had it at *her* funeral, if I'd had my head together. As it was, I'd been in emotional and physical bits. I couldn't even remember if we'd had music. If we did, I certainly hadn't chosen it.

I turned to look at Carl, wanting to steer the conversation back to the topic of his funeral, rather than my own.

'Come on, then,' I said. 'Let's have the full itinerary, as you're the only one who's got the whole thing planned out.'

'Well,' he replied. 'After "Bring Him Home", there's a welcome by the celebrant. It'll be a non-religious ceremony.'

'Don't you believe in God?' asked Emily.

Carl shook his head. 'No. I mean, you wouldn't be here if there was one, would you?'

She nodded, presumably in recognition that this was a fair point.

'There's supposed to be a eulogy from Lewis,' he went on. 'But obviously that's out of the question now, not that he'd probably have had much to say anyway. So, unless they rope in anyone else to do it, it'll be straight into "Highway to Hell" by AC/DC for the exit music.'

'Oof, that's quite a change of tempo,' I said. Emily went to pick up her phone to search for it and got annoyed about not having one all over again.

'Yeah, thought I'd better put something in there to keep the bikers happy.'

'Are there going to be bikers at your funeral?' I asked.

'Cremation,' he said again. 'And yes, I expect so. I've been going out for a Sunday ride with them for years.'

'Like the Hairy Bikers on TV?' asked Emily. 'My dad loves them. He's got one of their cookbooks.'

'Sort of. Only none of them can cook. They're great, though. Got a heart of gold, most of them.'

'So, you were the non-hairy biker then?' I asked with a smile.

'Well,' said Carl, smoothing his bald head. 'I do like to buck a trend.'

'Will there be lots of them there?' asked Emily. 'Like when that Hairy Biker died?'

'I mean, not that many, obviously. But they usually give fellow bikers a good send-off.'

I hadn't stopped to think about it – how many people would be at my funeral. Or rather how few. My brother and his wife, Tracey, my old friend from high school, a handful from work, a neighbour or two. I'd be lucky to get to double figures. Maybe Rob would bring the cats to try to make up the numbers.

Not that I was really bothered about how many people

would show up. There was only one person I wanted to be there, and she wouldn't be because she wouldn't even know I was gone. We'd not been in touch since uni. Obviously, me not leaving her my home address hadn't helped. She had phoned my parents' house once. The Christmas after we'd left uni. Mum had told her that I didn't live there any more and asked if she'd wanted to leave a message, but she'd just said to wish me a happy Christmas. And that was the last I'd heard of her. My bad, as Emily would have said.

Carl turned to Emily.

'I bet you'll have a fair few too, what with all that fundraising you did.'

Emily groaned. Clearly, she hadn't thought that far ahead either.

'Oh God. Dad will organise the whole thing. He'll probably invite the local TV news. There'll be cameras and journalists and nosey people who didn't even know me but read about it in the *Halifax Courier* and come along anyway, so they can stick it on their socials.'

'Hey, I wouldn't knock going viral,' I said. 'At least your death won't go unnoticed.'

'But I don't want a huge fuss. I never wanted any of this. I just wanted to live and be a normal seventeen-year-old girl. Death is for losers. No offence,' she adds quickly, looking at me and Carl.

'None taken,' I said. 'Just a shame we can't swap dos. I'll be having a very quiet affair. I'm not even sure Rob and the boys will make it. Depends if they have any better offers.'

Carl and Emily looked awkward and said nothing. They didn't seem to appreciate my self-deprecating sense of humour.

'So, back to your itinerary,' I said, looking at Carl. 'Anything else you've not mentioned?'

'Er, a reading from *Les Misérables* by Victor Hugo.'

'What is it?' I asked.

'You'll hear it soon enough,' he replied.

'I bet it's a bit highbrow. Do you not think I'll get it?'

'I've got to save something for the day, haven't I? Otherwise, it'll be like watching a film where you already know everything that happens.'

I shrugged. Clearly it was as much as I was going to get for now.

'I'd have a reading from *Winnie the Pooh*,' Emily said.

'Which one?' asked Carl.

'The one about living to be a hundred minus one day so Pooh would never have to live without Piglet.'

I nodded, unable to say anything in response.

'What would you have?' Emily asked me.

'Also something from *Winnie the Pooh*. The one where Eeyore thanks them for noticing him.'

* * *

When I went back to my room after the meal, I immediately missed my trailer. All the personal touches, the mementoes, Sarah, my crinoline lady toilet-roll holder. Nina wouldn't be there at my funeral, and I couldn't get past that. My life had ended up as empty and soulless as a Travel Inn room. No love. No light. No laughter. It was the laughter I missed more than anything. The laughter that haunted me. Taunted me, in truth, because it reminded me that I hadn't laughed like that since. Not once since I'd left her.

11

EMILY

Waiting for your own funeral was a weird thing. It felt like I'd spent most of the last couple of years waiting for my death and now I'd done that, the waiting still wasn't over. It wasn't even as if I could do anything to help or prepare for it. Suzi had made it clear that we would not be allowed out to visit our families again before being laid to rest.

Dad was good at organising, I knew that. So, it was possible that my funeral would be first. But he would also want it to be perfect and to invite everyone I'd ever met and some I hadn't *and* check their availability before committing to a date. I imagined him analysing the data on a spreadsheet he'd made specially for the occasion, working out which date would have the maximum attendance.

Because he'd want a big turnout. It would mean he could treat it like one of his fundraising events and organise the hell out of it, instead of stopping for a moment to think about what it was he was doing. Dad didn't do standing still. Or silences. Not since I'd first been diagnosed. He'd done research and ran around like a maniac and googled stuff and made me smoothies

– as if organic berries could somehow soak up those bad cells that were killing me. He never once admitted defeat. Even when I'd got engaged to Harry because I knew I was going to die, he was still talking about the fucking wedding.

Mum had known. She never once mentioned a wedding, and I heard her crying once when she thought I was asleep. I think Mum had known from the start. Though she had never let on. She'd gone along with all Dad's weird crap and his fundraising but there was something in her eyes that told me she didn't believe I was going to survive, any more than I did.

Not that I didn't hope I would. I even prayed once, when I was so desperate to stay with Harry that I decided to overlook the fact that I didn't believe in God. But a) there's clearly not a god of any kind and b) sometimes the odds are stacked so much against you that you don't have a chance, not even with everything medical science can do to help. That's why I hated all that crap about 'bravely fighting leukaemia or cancer'. It makes it sound like it's a fair fight and it's not. Mainly because the battlefield is your own body, so you can't exactly bomb the hell out of it. And it suggests that if you die, you were too weak or you weren't fighting hard enough and it's all your fault.

If anyone at my funeral said the word 'brave', I'd be so mad at them. I wasn't brave. I got ill and there was nothing I could do about it. Harry was the one who was brave. He could have dumped me when I first found out or gradually stopped coming round before ending it. He had a choice, and he chose to stay. In sickness and in health. That's what he'd have said if we had got married. If. If. If.

I turned over on my bed, curled into a ball and screwed up my eyes. I couldn't bear to remember how he'd been when I'd seen him last. Broken and empty. Grief had destroyed him, and I was worried he would never recover from it. I needed to see him. And it wouldn't wait until the funeral.

I sat up, a surge of energy pulsing through my body as the idea came to me. I was going to visit Harry. Now. I had no idea yet how I was going to achieve this but surely it couldn't be that hard? I mean, I had an invisibility cloak to start with, and that had got Harry Potter into places he wasn't supposed to go – and out of a few scrapes when he got there.

The clock on the TV said it was ten past eight. I would go now to give myself time to get there and back. I put on my jacket and picked up my bag. I didn't have my phone or any money, but I wasn't going to let that stop me. I could get a bus most of the way. Sneak on at the same time as someone else. I tried to work it all out in my head as I shut the door quietly behind me. I turned around just as Jules opened her door.

'Going out, are we?'

She said it like she was my mum. She seemed to get off on trying to be a mum to people who weren't her kids. I had two choices: I could either deny it, make some kind of excuse and go back into my room, in which case I'd probably not dare come out again, or I could tell her the truth and see what happened. She may have been many things, but I didn't have her down as a grass.

'I'm going to see Harry,' I said.

She nodded and seemed to think carefully about her response.

'I see. You do know that's against the rules?'

'Yep.'

'Only you don't strike me as the sort of girl who's used to breaking rules.'

'What's that got to do with anything?' I asked.

'Well, it suggests you may benefit from having an accomplice with you. Someone who has broken pretty much every rule in the book, in her time.'

'You're not suggesting you come with me?'

'Nope. I'm telling you I am. It's either that or have me shout at you in the corridor and get all the dead people to come out.'

I started laughing. I couldn't help it. She seemed to like the fact that she'd made me laugh. Her face softened slightly. Her shoulders too.

'We off then?' she asked.

'I don't seem to have any choice.'

'Okey dokey. Stay there a minute while I nip to the loo. You can't go anywhere at my age without going for a wee first.'

I was about to tell her that was too much information, but I figured it would only slow things down, so I kept quiet. When she came back, she'd put her red lipstick on as well.

'No one's going to see you,' I said.

'We're going to see Harry, aren't we? I like to make an effort when it's something important.'

I nodded. That was probably the nicest thing anyone had said to me since we got here.

'So, what's the plan?' she asked as we went down in the lift.

'To get the bus. You know, sneak on, like.'

'I bet you've never evaded a bus fare either, have you?' she asked.

I shook my head.

'I knew a guy called Dave at university whose brother worked for London Underground, and he gave him his spare work donkey jacket so that whenever Dave went on the Tube, he'd wear it, go up to the dude in the ticket box and say, 'All right, mate,' and they'd wave him through without him having to pay. Must have saved him a fortune. I bet he was gutted when they brought in the ticket barriers, mind.'

She smiled and looked at me.

'You don't get it, do you?'

'There is so much in what you just said that I don't understand. Like what a donkey jacket is and haven't there always been ticket barriers on the Underground?'

'Jesus, how to make me feel even more ancient than I am. I'm not going to bother trying to explain but I'll try to keep my anecdotes to the last ten years from now on, although I'm not sure I've got any good ones, as my life's been boring as fuck for a good while now.'

I stared at her. I thought I'd decided I hated her for what she'd done. But then she went and did or said something that made me not quite so sure and that confused me. Life was much simpler when everything was black and white.

The lift doors opened, and we stepped out into the corridor. There was no one else around as we walked into the foyer. The woman on reception didn't even look up. I was starting to like this being invisible thing. I could have done with it sometimes when I'd been in hospital, to stop all the fuss and sympathetic looks.

I followed Jules outside and up onto the main road.

'There. That was easy enough,' she said. 'Now for the bus.'

I reached into my pocket to check the time of the next bus and groaned as I remembered that my phone wasn't there.

'Back in my day,' said Jules, 'you just rocked up at the bus stop and there was no way of telling what time the next bus would come. It was wild, I tell you.'

'So how did you get anywhere on time?' I asked.

'You didn't. You were usually really early or very late. Nina reckoned she spent at least half her time at uni waiting for me.'

'Was she your best friend?'

Jules walked on for a bit before she answered.

'Yeah. Yeah, she was.'

'At least you'll get to see her at your funeral.'

She shook her head.

'No, we lost touch years ago, I'm afraid.'

'How come?'

Jules shrugged.

'That's just how it was before everyone had Facebook and whatnot.'

'Haven't you looked her up since, though?'

'No,' said Jules. 'A lot of water under the bridge since then. Anyway, is this the bus stop?'

I looked up.

'Yeah. We need the 510.'

'Only ten minutes to wait, then,' said Jules, looking at the digital display. 'That was lucky. Or it will be if someone else shows up in the meantime so we can actually get on the bloody thing.'

We stood in silence for at least the first two minutes until Jules asked the question she'd probably been gearing up to.

'Why not wait till the funeral to see him?'

I looked at her.

'You were there. You saw what he was like. I need to know he's OK. That he's hanging on in there.'

'You don't think he'd—'

'No. Of course not. He's not an id—'

My voice cut off abruptly as I realised.

'Sorry,' I said.

Jules raised her hands.

'No offence taken. I was a complete idiot, to be fair. And I wasn't suggesting he is. But it is a hell of a lot for someone to go through at that age.'

It was a moment before I decided to tell her.

'We talked about it,' I said.

'Really?' She seemed genuinely taken aback.

'I was worried about him. For that exact reason. I told him I didn't want him to do anything silly. That it wasn't *Romeo and Juliet*. I mean, how stupid were they? There was nothing romantic about it. I asked Harry to promise me that he wouldn't try to take his own life. I told him that was the last thing I wanted. That it was bad enough me having to die but him choosing to would be such a waste. Sorry,' I repeated, as I looked up at her.

Jules put her hands up again and shook her head.

'Don't be. You really have your head screwed on. I'd say you're ten times more mature than my stepsons and you're several years younger than them.'

I shrugged.

'It makes you grow up quickly. The whole dying thing.'

She nodded.

'But you still need to see him? Even though you know he wouldn't do anything daft.'

'Yep. I mean, I know he's still going to be in a bad way. And when I saw him last time, I had some weird feeling that he could sense it.'

'I think maybe he did.'

I stared at her. I hadn't expected that response.

'Really? You're not just saying that?'

'No. You clearly have something so strong that it's probably unbreakable. Not in a *Titanic* "Our Love Will Go On" way. But in a way that you can feel. Almost touch.'

'Good,' I said. 'I'm hoping he'll know when I'm with him again. That he'll be able to take some kind of comfort from it.'

'He was very lucky to have you,' she said.

'No,' I replied. 'He wasn't. I wouldn't wish this much pain on anyone. And especially not the person I love most in the world.'

Jules said nothing. Another person joined us at the bus stop. A man in his twenties.

'Yes!' I whispered. Jules took my arm and grinned at me. I didn't push her away this time. I didn't even want to. When the bus came, we jumped on as soon as the doors opened, so there was no chance we'd get left behind. Jules led me to the seat nearest the exit doors, which was free.

'So, we can get off quickly when we get the chance,' she whispered.

'Why are you whispering?' I asked.

'Because it makes it seem more exciting, and I like that.'

I smiled at her then. A proper smile. I really couldn't work her out.

Someone rang the bell to get off two stops before the nearest to Harry's road, so I decided we should take the chance while we could. Jules called out her thanks to the driver before the doors opened.

'Don't,' I said.

'Why? No one's going to hear us.'

She was right, of course. But the whole thing still felt so wrong. I started walking in the direction of Harry's house, Jules a few steps behind.

'Wait for an overweight, out-of-shape, menopausal woman, will you?' she called after me.

'Sorry,' I said, slowing down a little. 'I can't wait to see him again, that's all.'

It was only as we got closer that I started to worry if this had been a stupid thing to do. What if he'd been doing well? Starting to get himself together, and him sensing me turning up would unsettle him and make him worse again? Maybe I was being selfish. Just because I needed to be with him, it didn't mean that was what was best for him. It was too late now though. I was turning into his road. I could see his house. The light on in his bedroom. It was only then that I realised. I stopped and turned round to Jules.

'We won't be able to get in, will we? Not without Gerry's keys.'

The realisation hit Jules too. She looked annoyed at herself. Like she was supposed to be the responsible adult here.

'Sorry. Shit for brains, I've got,' she said.

'It's not your fault. It was my idea.'

'Yeah, and I was supposed to be your accomplice. Some kickass sidekick I'd make.'

We stood for a moment. Unsure what to do.

'Maybe it will be enough just being outside his house,' I said. 'I mean, it might make me feel like some weird stalker girl, but I could try it. See if it helps.'

'Sure. Whatever you think,' said Jules.

I carried on walking until I was directly outside his house. I looked around for Jules. She was eyeing up the tree opposite.

'How about it?' she said.

'I've never climbed a tree,' I replied.

'Don't be daft, you must have.'

'No, really. My dad was always worried about me falling.'

'Well, you've got nothing to lose now,' she said. 'I mean, you're hardly going to kill yourself, are you?'

I started laughing. Proper laughing, like I hadn't done in a long time. Jules laughed too and for a moment, I almost forgot where we were and why we were there. But then I looked up, and Harry was standing at the window, staring straight at me. I stopped laughing immediately, feeling weirdly guilty that I'd been having a good time – even if it was for only a split second – when he still looked so unbearably sad.

And then his mum Cath opened the door, car keys in hand. It was Jules who started running first. Although the word 'run' was probably not the right one to describe what she was doing. Whatever the word would be for a middle-aged, overweight woman in unsuitable footwear legging it as if her life depended on it, that would be it.

Within a second, I was right behind her. A moment later, I'd overtaken her and somehow, as Cath rummaged in the boot of her car, we both piled into the hallway.

'Jesus, that was lucky,' Jules said, bent double as she got her breath back.

I wasn't listening, though. I was already halfway up the stairs. When I got to Harry's room, he was still standing at the window, looking out for me. I knew that was what he was doing, even if he didn't know it himself. He was wearing jeans and a T-shirt. They both looked crumpled, or maybe *he* simply looked crumpled. It was hard to tell.

'It's OK, I'm here,' I said.

He stayed at the window for a moment, sighed deeply and then turned and walked back to his bed. I wanted to join him. More than anything in the world I wanted to climb on next to him, hold him and tell him that he was going to be OK. But I didn't know if that was allowed. Or even if it would somehow unsettle him.

So, I sat down next to the bed, my head resting on the mattress, and gazed up at him like a loyal Labrador. It was hard to tell if he felt my presence or if I was imagining it. But his face and shoulders softened, his breathing became calmer, the tension in his body released slightly. And that's why I sat there for so long. Because, rightly or wrongly, I felt it was helping him.

It was helping me too, of course, but that wasn't the reason I was doing it. It was for Harry. Everything had always been for Harry.

Eventually, he got up and went into the bathroom, presumably to get ready for bed. I wanted to stay the night. More than anything, I wanted to stay with him, but I wasn't sure I could do that. I crept outside the room to find Jules sitting on the top step of the stairs.

'What are you doing?' I asked.

'Just waiting here in case you needed me. I didn't want to intrude.'

I nodded my thanks.

'How's he doing?'

'He's a bit calmer. Less restless maybe.'

'He knows,' said Jules.

'I think maybe he does,' I replied. 'I want to stay the night. Do you think that's allowed?'

'Who gives a toss?' said Jules. 'You're doing it anyway.'

'You don't have to stay. I'll be fine.'

'Don't be daft. I'll kip on the sofa downstairs. I'm not deserting you. I'm your kickass sidekick, remember?'

I smiled at her and decided to tell her the thing that had been eating away at me for too long.

'I never had sex with Harry. I was waiting for my eighteenth birthday, like a good girl. It's one of my biggest regrets.'

Jules shook her head and reached out to hold my hand.

'That's not a regret. A regret is missing out on the love of your life. Of not risking doing what you want to do because there's a chance it could go wrong.'

I looked at her. She was being serious. I could see it in her eyes.

'But it makes me feel like we weren't a proper couple sometimes,' I said.

'Bollocks,' said Jules. 'Sex is overrated. People have sex but don't love each other. They cheat on each other for it. Too often it's about power, not love. What you and Harry had was way more important than sex. Loads of people never had what you had. What you still have.'

I looked down at the floor and rubbed my toes back and forth on the carpet.

'Do you mean that?' I asked eventually.

'Yes. Now get back in there and spend the night with the love of your life. Although don't get up to any funny business because that would be all kinds of wrong now. I'll see you in the morning.'

* * *

When I woke up, I was still in the same position as when we went to sleep. Curled into Harry on my side, his body enveloping me as if he was protecting me. As if he would never let me go. I had to go, though. I knew that. I'd already left him. This was simply a visit. A check to ensure he was doing OK. Trying to comfort him the only way I knew how. It was impossible to know if it had helped.

I could hear his mum busying herself in the kitchen downstairs, probably preparing breakfast for him before she went to work. I liked his mum. Always had done. I heard her footsteps coming up the stairs and a soft tap on the door before she poked her head around it.

'Morning, love. How did you sleep?'

'A bit better,' said Harry.

'That's good. One day at a time, remember? I've left breakfast for you downstairs when you're ready.'

She walked over and kissed the top of his head. He reached out and clutched her hand.

'I'm dreading her funeral,' he said.

'I know. Me too. But we're going to get through this, OK? We'll all be there to support you. Mia's insisting she's coming too.'

He nodded but didn't seem too sure. The thought of his younger sister having to go through that was clearly difficult for him too.

'I'll see you later. Call me if you need me,' his mum said.

I knew I had to go now too. It would be the perfect opportunity to leave the house, and, on some level, I knew that I couldn't stay here forever. I really couldn't. But Harry started crying again the moment she left the room. Tears that plopped down onto my bare shoulder and served as a reminder that Harry was not OK and maybe never would be. Perhaps this would be the defining moment of his life, and he would simply go into long-term mourning mode. Sometimes people never recover from a loss like this. Especially at such a young age. Maybe I had screwed up his entire fucking life.

I got up and fled from the room in one quick movement, not daring to look back, and bolted downstairs. Jules was waiting for me in the hallway, her hair and clothes all dishevelled.

'You OK?' she asked.

'Why do people keep asking me and Harry that? Of course we're not fucking OK!'

Harry's mum hurried out of the kitchen, jacket on and work bag in hand.

'I take it we've leaving?' asked Jules.

'Leaving and not coming back,' I said, pushing past her to the door.

12

CARL

I ate breakfast on my own. I had no idea where the other two were, but I had no intention of going to knock on their doors to find out. To be honest, I was grateful for the solitude. I didn't want to be questioned about Lewis again or what may have happened to prompt End Credits to send their camera crew to film me. Jules and Emily would find out soon enough. Presumably at the point where we watched the significant moments of our lives. I wasn't looking forward to that because I was well aware what mine were and none of them were positive.

I finished my poached eggs on toast and stood up to leave. The significant moments were crowding my head. Jostling for position so they could taunt me afresh. I walked back down the corridor towards my room but when I got there, I decided to keep going, right to the end of the corridor where the numbers on the doors stopped and instead there were a pair of double doors with the words 'Room of Reflection' above.

My first thought was that it was a bit late to pray. We were all dead and merely waiting to be processed so, unless there was some dodgy bribery going on and you could offer a financial incentive to a man of the cloth to bump you upstairs, I really didn't see the point.

Having said that, the thought of going back to my room to be alone with my thoughts didn't appeal either. I decided to have a quick look with a back-up plan of making my excuses and a quick exit if a chaplain came anywhere near me.

I pushed the door open. Inside, the lighting was dimmed, the music sounded as if it had been the first option on a search for 'peaceful contemplation', and there was a faint smell of some kind of essential oil. I was relieved to see there were no rows of pews facing a giant altar. Instead, there were a few easy chairs and a couple of beanbags. A water feature gurgled away to itself. There were no overtly religious artefacts, just a sign saying it was a place to find 'pastoral care, solace and reflection'.

I wasn't fussed about the pastoral care, but solace and reflection felt like good things to have right now, so I chose a comfortable-looking chair and sat myself down. It was only as I did so that a screen at the far end of the room pulled back to reveal a strange-looking cross between a confessional booth and two toilet cubicles. The right-hand one had a red curtain across the front and the word 'Engaged' above it in neon lights. The left-hand one had a green curtain which was pulled back and the word 'Vacant' was lit up above it.

In any normal situation I'd have been running for the door, but nothing about this place was normal. So, despite the fact that I had no desire to confess my sins to a man of the cloth, my curiosity got the better of me. I stood up and headed towards the vacant booth. If anyone started preaching at me, I would make my excuses and leave but I may as well see if there was anything useful in the way of absolution available.

I sat down on the little stool in the booth and pulled the curtain across. A green light flashed and I was half expecting a countdown to begin before a passport-style photo was taken. Instead, a sign appeared on the little screen saying 'Ready for reflection'. There was no question mark at the end, so I assumed it was an instruction. There was a speaker panel on the side neighbouring the other booth, which suggested someone was listening, if only I could find the right words to say.

'Hello?' I ventured. 'I just want to check there's someone real there and it's not like a chatbot situation.'

There was a pause before a female voice answered.

'And do you often find yourself talking to chatbots?'

'Only online,' I said. 'I did once have a conversation with someone on the phone from the bank before I realised they were automated.'

There was what sounded like a stifled snort from next door.

'Well, I can assure you I'm real, Carl, so fire away.'

There was something vaguely familiar about her voice but I couldn't quite place it.

'How do you know my name?' I asked.

'I'm all-seeing and all-knowing, I thought you understood that?'

'Wait, are you religious? Because I don't believe in all that stuff.'

'That's OK. You don't have to call me Rev, just rev up your bike and we can get going.'

The laughter from the other side of the partition was not disguised this time. It was accompanied by a thud and a shriek. I stuck my head out from behind the curtain to see a familiar figure lying laughing on the floor.

'Suzi!' I yelled. 'What the hell do you think you're playing at?'

'Steady on,' she said, wiping her eyes. 'I was only having a bit of fun. How was I to know you'd fall for it and make me collapse off my stool laughing?'

'That's out of order. You were trying to get me talking by impersonating a chaplain.'

'Where does it say that?' she asked, gesturing around the room. 'You were offered a place for quiet reflection and a cool booth to do your confession in. It's not my fault you decided you were talking to the female Pope.'

She had a point. I felt small and slightly ridiculous.

'What were you going to say when I confessed?'

'Let's carry on and you'll find out,' she said, picking herself up off the floor.

'I can't continue now I know it's you, can I?'

'Why not? You said you didn't want someone religious and you've struck lucky.'

'Can't we at least do this face to face?'

'Nope. It doesn't work as well and there's no way you'll get me sitting on a beanbag because I'm not twelve.'

She disappeared back inside the booth and closed the curtain. I had two choices. One of them was to walk out and go back to the grim silence of my room and the images in my head. The other was to tackle them head on.

I thought of the girls. Of the haunted look in their parents' eyes at the funerals. One which would also never leave them. Or me.

I returned to sit on the stool. We sat in silence for a while.

'How much do you know?' I asked finally.

'I've seen all of your films in their entirety.'

She knew the worst of me, but she was still here and still willing to hear my side of things. I was grateful for that at least.

'I still feel angry at God for letting the girls die,' I said.

'At God or yourself?' Suzi asked. 'Only you said you don't believe in God.'

For someone who was a pain in the arse most of the time, she was unnervingly good at this.

'I joined the police motorcycle unit because I loved bikes. Wanted to be out there riding for a living. Helping people. I hadn't stopped to think about all the things I would witness. What I might be responding to. I was only twenty-five.'

I stopped, aware that my voice was faltering. All the emotions that I kept locked up inside, secured with several layers of gaffer tape and a padlocked chain, were starting to work themselves free. Perform some kind of escapology act in front of a washed-up film executive with a penchant for practical jokes.

I jumped up off my stool, powered by such intensity that I was surprised I didn't shoot straight out through the ceiling.

'I hate him!' I shouted. 'I hate him for what he let happen. They were eleven and twelve years old, for fuck's sake. They were on their way back from a netball tournament in Leeds. And theirs was a Church of England school, too. If he'd been protecting anyone, he should have been protecting them. But he wasn't. And all of them died. Nine girls and two teachers. I got there first, before the fire and ambulance crews. A sack of netballs had escaped across the motorway, and they were bouncing around all over the carriageway and I am still so fucking angry with him for saving the stupid netballs and not the girls!'

'Hey, I thought you were supposed to be the quiet one?' said Suzi.

'Yeah, well I'm not quiet inside, am I? I'm not anything people think I am, as the others are about to find out.'

'Maybe it's time for you to reveal your true self,' she said. 'You might find others don't find you quite as objectionable as you seem to think you are.'

I sighed and shook my head, even though I knew she couldn't see me.

'Can't you see how hard this is for me? I don't want to play your stupid games any more. I buried all this stuff because it was the best place for it and now, you're insisting I have to live through it all again so you can get some kind of kick out of it.'

'Believe me, that's not why I'm here,' she said.

'Yes, it is. You could have gone peacefully on to the afterlife like everyone else. You chose to stay here and act out your big exec-producer fantasy by getting your minions to film us as we died. What level of sick is that?'

Suzi remained silent for a long time, which wasn't like her at all.

'Sorry,' I said. 'I went in a bit hard there.'

'No apology needed,' she said, her voice sounding shaky. 'Although, in my defence, I should say that I don't get a kick out of seeing anyone suffer. But I do like helping people to come to terms with things that have happened.'

'Watch it, you're starting to come over all touchy-feely. Doesn't really fit the image.'

'Look, Carl, I'm not going to lie to you. Part of the reason you're here is because you need to deal with it before you go on anywhere else.'

'You said this was a processing centre, where we stay while all the admin is sorted.'

'Yeah, it is. But it's also a bit more than that. You know all that RIP stuff? Well, peace is actually a pretty hard thing to find.'

'How do you know that? Because you've never even moved on.'

'Maybe that's because I'm still working on this finding peace lark,' she said.

'Is that why you're really still here?' I asked.

'You're a better person than me, Carl. And no one's asking you to forgive anyone for stuff that's happened or even to make sense of it all. Sometimes life makes no sense whatsoever. But if you could try to make some kind of peace with it – and with yourself – that will help.'

I heard her pull back the curtain and stuck my head out as she headed towards the door before turning.

'And send me the bloody instruction manual on how to do that if you do work it out, eh?'

* * *

All three of us were subdued in the restaurant that evening. I noticed Jules and Emily exchanging several glances during the meal. At one point Jules mouthed, 'Are you OK?' to her and didn't get a mouthful or a scowl in return. Just a brief nod. I couldn't work out what had brought about this change in their relationship but decided it was best not to ask. I didn't tell them about my weird afternoon with Suzi either, because it had felt like a private exchange between the two of us. Plus, I was aware that the whole thing would have sounded ridiculous.

We were just about finished when I spotted Suzi striding towards us. I thought for a moment she was going to mention our get-together earlier. But that was not the case.

'Make the most of the good food, guys,' she said. 'You're going to be back on the Deliveroos tomorrow.'

We all stared at her blankly.

'Trailer food. You're heading out on location. It's funeral time.'

She did jazz hands as she said it, which felt wildly inappropriate.

'Would you be so good as to tell us whose?' I asked.

'Jules has the honour. First thing Friday morning, so Majid will be picking you up at 4 p.m. tomorrow.'

I looked at Jules. Her face was pale at the best of times, but I was sure it had found a new level of pallor that was in danger of becoming transparent.

'Shit,' was all she said.

13

JULES

'How are you feeling?' Majid asked as he drove us to my old house the next day.

'Like I'm about to go and watch my own funeral and, quite frankly, I'd rather poke my eye out with a fork.'

'Fair enough,' he replied.

'And before anyone else says anything, I know I brought it on myself, but I didn't know I'd be expected to film the whole bloody aftermath, did I?'

No one had a reply for that. I was aware that Emily and Carl were not exactly looking forward to this either. I mean, why would you want to go to the funeral of some random woman who you'd never met when she was alive? And it wasn't as if it would be one of those 'join us to celebrate the life of' affairs. I was struggling to think of anything positive to celebrate and it had been my life. My method of departure wouldn't help matters either. At least if it had been cancer, people could have passed on their sympathies to my loved ones, muttered something about my life being cruelly cut short. I imagined those attending – and I still wasn't sure they'd make it into double figures – would attempt to leg it out at the end without having to exchange one awkward word about my own sharp exit.

'Maybe it won't be as bad as you think,' said Majid as he pulled up outside my house.

'Did you say that before Liz Truss became Prime Minister? Only it's likely to turn out the same way.'

'Be thinking of you, anyway.'

'Thanks. You can do a drive past if you want. Give me a little toot of support. Like I'm on a picket line or something.'

Majid gave me a thumbs-up. We all clambered out of the car. Gerry and Alice were slumped against the alley wall. Judging by the pile of cigarette butts on the floor, they'd probably been there a while.

'Didn't think you'd be here till the morning,' I said.

'Delighted to see you too, pet,' Gerry replied. 'We're here in case there's any last-minute fireworks.'

'I can tell you now that Rob will not have forked out for a display as a send-off, if that's what you mean.'

'No, sometimes, the stress of it all blows up,' said Alice. 'Especially when the family don't get on. We've had fistfights and smashed glasses before. Once someone was cut in a big family bust-up and they bled all over the funeral flowers. It made great footage, you know, the blood dripping on the white lilies.'

I exchanged glances with Emily, who pulled a horrified face, and Carl, who simply shrugged. I was never going to work this woman out.

'Right, well I apologise in advance if my lot don't give you the big blood-and-guts finale you're looking for. If it's any help, my favourite colour is red, but they probably don't know that, so you might not even get a splash of colour.'

'You ready to go in, then?' asked Gerry, nodding towards the house. 'Or do you want to go to your room first? Trailer's parked up if you want it.'

'Maybe the trailer,' I said, feeling the need to gather myself privately before I entered the house. 'If we can take ten, then I'll be with you.'

Gerry nodded and we all trooped down the side alley to find the trailer waiting for us in the back garden. I went straight into my room without so much as a sideways glance at the others. It was oddly comforting and familiar inside. A slice of my life served up to me for my death. And the cherry on the top which I was looking for was in the bathroom. Sarah was still there. My crinoline lady toilet-roll holder. Resplendent in her scarlet knitted dress with black lace trim. I picked her up. Pulled her to me. I was aware how fucking sad and ridiculous it was, but I was past caring. She was my only link with Nina.

'Wish you were here,' I whispered. 'Wish I'd done everything differently. Wish I hadn't been such a coward.'

I stood there in the tiny loo, clutching her to me, and shed a tear for a lost love, a life unlived and the empty space where Nina should have been at my funeral. What got me most was that no one would know she wasn't there. No one in the life I'd ended even knew she existed. It would be like she'd been airbrushed out of my life. And the worst thing about it all was that it was me who had done it.

By the time I pulled myself together enough to go back outside again, everyone else was waiting and Gerry was on his umpteenth cigarette.

'You know that will kill you, right?' I said to him.

He laughed and followed me in through the open kitchen door, where Rob was on the phone. Carl whispered, 'Action.'

'Yeah, that sounds great,' he said. 'And no need to bring your own cleaning stuff as we've still got plenty here. If you could start next Friday, that would be fantastic, as I'll be going back to work the Monday after.'

It took me a moment to compute what he was saying. Mainly because I didn't want to think that he could possibly be that insensitive, but then I remembered this was Rob we were talking about.

'Fucking hell,' I said, 'he's getting a cleaner to replace me.'

Alice put her finger to her lips, even though I knew my voice wouldn't come out on the film. When I turned to look at Carl and Emily, they were both conveniently looking at the kitchen floor.

'I know it needs a good mop,' I said, 'but he could at least have waited until I was in the bloody ground before he hired my replacement.'

'I'm sure he's not replacing you,' whispered Carl. 'Probably just trying to be practical.'

I laughed.

'The man's never been practical in his life. Lazy, yes. That's why he's prepared to fork out good money for someone to do what I've been doing for years. He never paid me, did he? Offered me fifteen pounds an hour for my work around the home. I'd have been a damn sight better off if he had.'

Rob ended the call. I looked at him to see if I could detect any semblance of guilt that he was replacing my services in such a blatant way. Nothing. If anything, he looked pleased with himself. I supposed I should be relieved we hadn't had sex for a long time, otherwise a prostitute would have been next on the list.

Thomas entered the kitchen.

'What you looking so pleased about?' he asked Rob.

'I've sorted a cleaner. She's starting a week tomorrow.'

Thomas rolled his eyes.

'Good for you. Hope you feel super proud.'

'What's that supposed to mean?' asked Rob.

'You know exactly what my beef is. You're gonna be nicer to the cleaner than you ever were to Jules.'

'Take that back immediately!' Rob shouted.

'Why? Because the truth hurts? If you were so nice to Jules. If you'd appreciated her. If any of us did. Then she wouldn't have done what she did, would she?'

Thomas turned and stomped back upstairs. Rob stood there, looking like he had no understanding of what just happened. And somewhere, a cleaner was setting a reminder in her phone to come to our house a week tomorrow.

'I think that's a wrap for today,' I said, when we all went back outside. 'I doubt you'll get anything better than that unless the cats launch a full-scale attack on Rob.'

'I was still kind of hoping that would happen,' said Alice. 'Him screaming as the cats' claws cut through his bare skin and the blood trickles down his arms would have made such great footage.'

We all looked at her with an assortment of frowns and head shaking.

'Well, there's no sign of the cats,' I said. 'He's probably given them up for adoption. So, I suggest we call it a night.'

Alice appeared disappointed but didn't put up an argument. Gerry lit up another cigarette and the three of us headed into our rooms. I'd barely taken my shoes off and slumped down on the sofa when there was a tap at the door. When I answered it, Carl was standing there.

'I just wanted to check you're OK,' he said.

'Why wouldn't I be?'

'When you're a former police officer, you're used to looking behind the mask.'

I nodded.

'It's a fair cop. To be honest, I'm disappointed you weren't still with Deliveroo. I could have ordered a Chinese.'

Carl smiled. I held the door open for him to come in.

'Fancy a brew?' I asked.

'Wouldn't say no,' he replied.

He went through my record collection while I made the tea.

'Your teenage years were basically filled with the music of doom and gloom and abject misery.'

'Yep. The Smiths have a lot to answer for. You'd have thought they'd have tipped me over the edge then.'

'So why didn't they?'

'I was young, optimistic and had good people around me,' I said, putting our mugs down on the coffee table.

'Family?'

'No. They had no idea who I really was. It was friends who got me through. Well, one friend.'

'Do you think they'll be there tomorrow?'

'Nope,' I said. 'I lost touch with her years ago. You know what it's like.'

Carl nodded. But I couldn't help wondering if he did know.

'Did you have anyone special?' I asked.

'When?'

'Before you died.'

'Nah.'

'Why not?' I asked.

Carl shrugged. 'Being in the police wasn't conducive to having a relationship. All the unsociable hours and that.'

I nodded slowly. Aware that he might still be struggling with the same thing I'd been struggling with my whole life.

'You can tell me, you know. I went on the Section 28 protest marches back in the day. And *Pride* is one of my favourite films.'

Carl groaned. 'Why does everyone assume I'm gay?'

'You're not?'

'No. Just painfully shy with the opposite sex, if you must know. And a bit rubbish at the whole dating business.'

'Oh. Sorry. I'm afraid I can't be much help there.'

'Why not?'

'Did you not see and hear what just went on in that kitchen? I'm hardly in a position to dispense relationship advice, am I?'

There was a pause.

'It's so sad,' said Carl, eventually.

'What, that my husband is replacing me with a cleaner?'

'That you never felt able to put your needs first.'

'Welcome to life as a woman.'

'Is it really that bad?' he asked.

'It's the expectation that you're there to serve. There to conform. There to do whatever society expects you to do.'

'And you're not allowed to be happy?'

'Not unless it fits in with everyone else's needs and only on their terms.'

'Fucking hell.'

'My thoughts exactly,' I said, 'which is part of the reason I'm here.'

I waved my arm around the trailer room. It was only as I did so that I noticed I'd left the crinoline lady toilet-roll holder on the coffee table. I saw Carl's gaze fall on her as mine did. He looked at me with a questioning raised eyebrow.

'Present from my friend Nina at uni,' I said.

'Must have been a special one,' he replied, 'for it to end up here, I mean.'

'Best present I ever had.'

'I take it that's the Nina who's not coming to your funeral? Did she knit it for you?'

'Yep, guilty on both counts.'

'Is that what's eating you up most about this? That she's not going to be there?'

I had to take a moment to compose myself before answering.

'Yeah. Nina would have known what music to play,' I said.

* * *

I woke to the sound of it pissing down with rain on the trailer roof. I was channelling Eeyore even before the day had started. I got up and took a quick shower before having to address the thorny issue of what to wear to my own funeral. While I liked to think Rob would have sent out a suggestion that everyone wore something red to my funeral, as it was my favourite colour, I knew the reality would be different. No dress code would have been issued and those attending would no doubt do the safe thing and stick to black. Not even gothic black with lace and zips and a bit of oomph. It would be the dullest funeral black imaginable.

There was only one thing for it. I opened the wardrobe door. I knew my red and black gothic ballgown wouldn't be there. That really would have been too much to ask. But there, hanging on the far side of the rail, was my favourite red lacy top with black leather corset and my black fishtail skirt. They weren't *actually* my clothes, of course. Because if they had been, they wouldn't fit. I was definitely no longer 1990 size. But whatever afterlife replica clothes service I had seemingly subscribed to on my arrival had conveniently delivered them in my current size.

I got dressed quickly. Keen to see how they looked. And as I stared in the mirror, I saw that the answer was they looked OK. For the first time in God knows how many years, I didn't pull a face and turn away. Didn't feel revulsion or dejection or a burning desire to go for liposuction in my lunch hour. I felt – good. Yeah, that's what it was. A sensation so unfamiliar to me that I had to check the mirror again to ensure it hadn't been playing tricks on me. The only frustration was when it dawned on me that no one attending would be able to see me. The real me. The one who had been fighting to break free all these years.

When I stepped outside, the others were all lined up in regulation black. Carl looking particularly well turned out and Emily heartbreakingly beautiful in a black minidress and Dr. Martens. As they heard my footsteps they looked up and visibly gawped.

'Bloody hell,' said Gerry. 'You're not going quietly, are you?'

'If you can't make an effort for your own funeral, when can you?'

Emily smiled at me.

'Looking good,' she said. 'But what's with the shoes?'

She nodded to the pointy black stiletto boots which were already pinching my toes.

'In the last millennium we hadn't stopped to question why we were crippling our feet in the name of fashion. We have you lot to thank for that and it makes us smile every time we see you in your comfortable flat boots.'

'I think mine need breaking in a bit, actually,' said Emily.

'Then we'll both go barefoot later, if necessary,' I replied.

'Right, well we'd better hotfoot it round the front,' said Gerry. 'Majid's following your funeral cortege and they're not far off.'

I hadn't stopped to think about how we would get to the church until that moment. The idea that I'd be following my own body – my actual messed-up, scraped-off-the-road body – in a coffin in a hearse was such a weird one.

We emerged from the alleyway just in time to see the hearse pull up outside, followed by a funeral car and Majid in his battered red Mondeo. He, at least, had got the memo about coming in something red.

'Action,' Carl hissed to Gerry.

He turned his camera immediately to the front door as we heard it open. Rob was standing there in his black suit – the one he'd worn to my dad's funeral. He looked sombre but he could hardly look anything else in the circumstances. As he stepped down onto the path, he immediately put on a pair of sunglasses. It was a knobbish thing to do, not least because it was still raining but also because he wasn't a film star or anyone famous who could get away with wearing shades because they didn't want to be recognised. I wondered if it was so people couldn't see that he *wasn't* crying. That was the sort of thing he'd do. Play the part of the grieving husband while all the time being pleased with himself for sorting the cleaner.

Thomas and Noah came out after him. Both wearing ill-fitting black suits that they looked awkward and self-conscious in. Neither was wearing sunglasses. Thomas stared straight ahead at the hearse. Noah looked down at his feet. And then, just when I'd given up on seeing either of the cats again, Hugo ran out from under Rob's van, went straight to the hearse, raised his tail and pissed against the rear passenger wheel.

I started laughing. Uncontrollable laughter that was hardly fitting in the circumstances.

'That's my boy,' I said, before turning to Gerry. 'Did you get that?' I called.

He gave me a quick thumbs-up and carried on filming. Carl and Emily were both stifling laughs.

'It's OK. It's the perfect send-off for a mad cat lady,' I said. 'I feel suitably honoured.'

I watched Rob and the boys get in the car. Gerry took one last lingering shot through the window and as Thomas started to cry, I called 'cut'. Gerry and Alice headed off and we clambered sombrely into Majid's cab.

'Wow, you look like you're dressed for a night out rather than a funeral,' said Majid.

'Thought I may as well see myself out in style, even if no one else does,' I replied.

'What do you think you're actually wearing?' asked Emily. 'You know, in there.'

She nodded towards the hearse, and I shuddered as I realised Rob would have been asked to choose something for me to wear. He wouldn't have had a clue.

'Oh God, I don't know. He's probably taken in an old onesie for them to put me in.'

I undid the seatbelt and went to open the door.

'What are you doing?' asked Majid.

'I need to check I'm not being buried in something embarrassing.'

He put his hand on my arm.

'We can't do anything, remember. We're out of the game now. We're simply spectators.'

His words hit me hard. He was right, though. That's all I was. A spectator at my own funeral. I plugged my seatbelt back in again and Majid set off, the secret third car in the funeral cortege. The others were quiet, as if in a mark of respect, which was weird when you considered that I was sitting next to them.

The journey to the church was entirely unremarkable. The rain continued to fall. People in town continued going about their business, most not even giving my hearse a second glance. We arrived outside the church, which was also unremarkable and not the beautiful one a few streets down, although part of me was relieved about that and guessed why Rob hadn't chosen it. There were no crowds outside, no special welcome. A man simply moved a couple of traffic cones so we could park. It appeared my funeral was going to be as insignificant and unremarkable as my life.

We got out and hurried up to Gerry and Alice, who were already set up. Carl said 'action' and Gerry started filming as the coffin containing my body was rolled out of the hearse. It was only then that I saw it properly for the first time.

'It's made out of fucking cardboard!' I shouted.

'It's OK, they do that now,' said Carl. 'It's the eco-friendly option.'

'Bollocks. Rob's never done anything eco-friendly in his life. He used to complain about putting the recycling out and having too many bins. It's the "being a tight-arsed prick" option. That's what it is.'

'It doesn't really matter though, does it?' asked Emily. 'I mean it's going to go straight into the ground anyway.'

'Exactly,' said Carl. 'That's why I specified a cardboard one in my will. No point in spending money on something that will be going up in the flames at the end of it.'

'Jeez,' I said, looking at them both in turn. 'A little moral support would be appreciated. If I say my husband's being a tight-arsed prick, I expect you to back me.'

'Sure,' said Carl. 'What an absolute wanker and utter bastard he is.'

'OK, that's enough. He is still my husband.'

'He should have treated you with more respect,' added Emily. 'You deserved better than that.'

And that's what made me start crying. That little bit of human kindness which was missing from my actual funeral but was there in a seventeen-year-old girl I'd only known for a week or so.

Emily and Carl reached out and took a hand each as my

coffin was lifted onto the shoulders of half a dozen men I had never met in my life. Rob and the boys walked behind them. And though I may have lived with them for years, they didn't know me either. Not really. The handful of other mourners – I counted twelve – filed in after them. My brother, Dean, and his wife, who must have made a special journey from Newcastle and had probably complained about it all the way; Tracey, my best friend from high school; a better turnout from work than I'd expected, although that was probably because they would have been given paid time off; a couple of neighbours and a few people I didn't even recognise who must have been work colleagues of Rob's who'd come to support him.

No one had brought Mum. I hadn't expected them to, and I was glad, to be honest. The last time I'd been to visit her in the home, she'd not even shown a flicker of recognition. She'd called me Carole and repeatedly asked if I'd come to do her hair. It wouldn't have been fair to bring her to the funeral of a daughter she couldn't even recognise. At least this way I could stay alive in her head, albeit as a much younger version of myself. She wouldn't miss my visits; wouldn't know I was gone. And it was best to leave it that way. At least for her.

We followed them into the church, Gerry wanted to get a filming position looking out at the mourners, so I ended up standing behind my own coffin staring at... well, it wasn't a sea of faces, more of a small pond. But the only face I really saw was the one that wasn't there. Smiling out at me from an empty space on one of the front pews. Rolling her eyes when they played 'All Things Bright and Beautiful' instead of 'Lovesong' by The Cure. Grimacing through the Lord's Prayer and mouthing 'what the fuck?' when the vicar, who I had never met in my life, spoke of the kind-hearted wife and stepmum who always put others first.

I shrugged and smiled at her. Wanting to reach out my hand and take hers. To escape as far away from this place and these people as possible. To be back in Clifton, running along the bridge laughing and screaming. Having a picnic, where the only rule was that everything had to be chocolate, up on the downs and talking and talking until the sun went down. Visiting Bristol Zoo and telling her I was going to be a big cat keeper one day and her pointing at a group of schoolkids with their teacher and saying she would bring her pupils here to visit me. Innocently thinking our lives were going to go on forever and no one would ever tear us apart.

I felt a hand in mine and turned to see it was Emily's. Carl was on my other side. He offered me a tissue as they started playing 'Angels' by Robbie Williams.

'Really?' I said. 'It's the first thing that comes up if you google songs to play at a funeral. And I fucking hated Take That.'

* * *

It was a short drive to the cemetery where I was to be buried. It was the only thing Rob had got right. I understood why he'd avoided my funeral being in the same church as Grace's, although it was probably to protect himself as much as anything. But at least he'd thought to lay me to rest at the same place as Grace. As I stepped inside the gate, everything about that day flooded back, and I knew straight away I couldn't face it. Too many memories. Too much pain.

'Are you OK?' asked Carl, seeing my anguished expression. I shook my head.

'Not really,' I whispered. 'This is where Grace is buried.'

'Oh God, I'm sorry. I didn't think,' said Carl. 'Is there anything I can do to help?'

'Yeah, can you take over as director please?'

He nodded and walked over to point Gerry in the direction of the best filming spot, much to his obvious disdain.

'Sleep tight, Grace,' I whispered. 'Mummy's here to watch over you now.'

At that point, Majid beeped his horn as promised as he drove past. I turned to see him wave out of the window, having no idea he'd picked the most inopportune moment to do it.

I headed back to the car and collapsed into the front passenger seat.

'Tell me something funny,' I said. 'The worst and weirdest passengers you've had in your cab. When you were alive and since you've been dead. I want to hear them all.'

Majid patted my shoulder and nodded.

'You'll never guess who I had in the back of my cab once,' he began.

14

EMILY

We had to wait the whole weekend for my funeral. Dad had organised it for 11 a.m. on Monday morning. Not too early for those travelling a long way. Not so late that people were hungry before the sandwiches at the wake. Sandwiches which would no doubt be suitable for all dietary requirements. Nothing would be left to chance. No detail overlooked. All of it designed so that he would be able to say he gave me a good send-off, even if he couldn't save me.

He would probably call it a 'celebration of life', in the hope it would look good in gold lettering on the invitations. And if he avoided calling it a funeral, he wouldn't have to accept the fact that I was dead. Which meant he would never get to help me organise my wedding or my eighteenth birthday party or a baby shower or any of the other landmark moments that I'd been denied.

I didn't want to go. Obviously, I wanted to see Harry again, but I didn't really want to see him in these circumstances when he'd be upset and probably beating himself up about why he couldn't save me. What is it about men that they feel the constant need to save us women? Like we have no ability to save ourselves.

I tried. It didn't work. Nothing to do with Harry or Dad. It was my body that failed and my body that was being buried. I knew that it was a burial because Mum had managed to ask me if that was what I wanted. It was very near the end, and she probably thought she'd phrase it that way because it would be easier to say 'yes', than insist I wanted to be cremated. I didn't want to be cremated, as it happened. But even if I had, I wouldn't have been able to tell her that because I knew she and Dad couldn't bear it. If they put me in the ground, it would just be like tucking me up in bed for the night, like they used to do when I was little. Letting my body go up in flames would have been another thing entirely. Another failure to protect me on their part. I can't say I blamed them. I hated the thought of being set fire to as well. It struck me as the most violent thing you could do to a body. Burn it so that there was only a pile of bones left, ready for someone to grind down and pretend it was still me.

I would have hated to be reduced to that. I wanted to lie where people could visit me. Harry, in particular. And Dad could come and talk to me like I was still there, which I knew was what he wanted. As if I was a kid again and he was coming home from work and telling me about his day.

But until then, I had to wait. Jules and Carl had both asked if I wanted company, but I didn't. Tomorrow evening, we'd be going back to the trailer at Mum and Dad's house. For now, I would simply lie on my bed and try to remember the good bits. My life may not have lasted very long but there were plenty of good bits.

I suspected from Jules's funeral that her life hadn't had many good bits at all. So, I was determined to appreciate mine.

That's what Dad had always said. That we had to appreciate each moment we had together. He used to say that before I even got leukaemia. Maybe he'd had a hunch it was heading my way.

I knew that after our funerals we'd get to see our significant moments on screen, but that wasn't how I wanted to remember them. I wanted to close my eyes and see them in my head. Picture the people and the places. Taste the moments. Feel my way through them and breathe them in. Appreciating everything about them. Just like Dad said.

* * *

The others were quiet in Majid's car. I suspected because of my age. Everything is always because of my age. It's like they could deal with Jules's funeral because she's fifty years old and she'd taken her own life anyway, so it wasn't like she hadn't wanted to die. But they didn't want to think about a seventeen-year-old girl being buried because that was tragic and they didn't know how to handle it.

'I'm OK about this, you know,' I said with a sigh. 'You haven't got to pretend it's not happening and we're all going on a nice picnic or something.'

My comments were greeted with silence at first. They really couldn't handle it. Carl was sitting next to me in the back. I noticed his knuckles were white where he was clenching his fists. Like he was super stressed or something. Which made no sense at all because it wasn't even his funeral.

'The thing is,' said Majid from the front, 'we're not used to dealing with a person your age dying. I don't think I've ever had someone so young in the back of my cab before.'

'Well, sorry to be the bearer of bad news but young people

die too, you know,' I replied. 'And it would really help us if older people stopped being so weird about it.'

'So, how do you want us to be?' asked Jules.

'I dunno. Just not weird.'

'Where do you think the funeral will be?'

I sighed. I had a pretty good idea. Because none of us were religious, a church funeral would have been wrong, so it didn't leave many options really.

'My mum showed me this woodland burial place once. Only online, I didn't go there. I mean that would be a super weird day out, wouldn't it? Like a transition day for high school that turned pretty dark. Anyway, it was between Halifax and Huddersfield. So, she and Dad and Harry could all visit easily. And they plant a tree for you, where you're buried. A little one, like, so it grows big over time and it's in a nice, quiet spot and there are benches where you can sit and that.'

The others all went quiet again. I heard Jules sniffing from the front.

'Jeez, I can't say anything, can I?'

'It sounds lovely,' said Jules.

'It does,' agreed Carl.

I shrugged, trying to imagine Mum and Dad sitting on the bench while Dad wittered on about stuff. Maybe Harry would sing for me. I didn't want to admit it, but I thought it sounded nice too. Well, as good as you could hope for in the circumstances.

Majid pulled up outside my parents' house.

'Trailer's already parked up at back for you,' he said. 'Enjoy that lovely burial spot you've got waiting for you.'

'I am coming back afterwards,' I pointed out.

'I know, it's on my call sheet. We'll be heading off to Carl's place, though. It's his turn on Wednesday, first thing. They've decided to give you a day off for rest and relaxation on Tuesday rather than you having to go back and forth to your hotel again.'

'That's the first I've heard of it,' said Carl.

'That's best bit about being unit driver,' said Majid. 'I get to know what's going on before you guys do.'

We all got out. I spotted Gerry's car but there was no sign of him or Alice. When we arrived around the back they were sitting on the trailer steps, camera and boom at the ready.

'Here we go. Ready for round two,' said Gerry.

'Thank you for being normal about this. These two are being all squeamish,' I said, nodding towards Jules and Carl.

'But there wasn't any blood involved in your death, was there?' asked Alice, who appeared disappointed by this fact.

'No, I mean squeamish about my age.'

'Right. Gone too soon and all that,' said Gerry, nodding knowingly.

'We all went too soon,' said Carl. 'Just some more so than others.'

'Anyway. Have you seen my parents yet?' I asked Gerry.

'Only some movement inside. A lot of movement, actually. They seem pretty busy in there.'

It didn't surprise me. Dad would have lists, or probably a spreadsheet, and Mum would be pulling her hair out trying to calm him down and sort everything with the minimum of fuss.

'We'd better go in then,' I said. 'If you want boring footage of a middle-aged man organising the hell out of a funeral, that is.'

Gerry opened the back door. I couldn't help thinking how freaked Dad would be if he realised strange men could just walk into the house, despite the high-tech lock he had spent ages choosing.

We followed him and Alice into the kitchen. Fortunately, there was little going on there as presumably they had catering booked for the wake or celebration of life or whatever it was Dad had organised. But the dining room was another matter. The table was covered with photos of me from every age from birth till death. Mum was sitting there, clearly struggling to hold herself together.

Carl whispered 'action', as if he didn't want to disturb her.

She had a pair of scissors in her hand, which appeared to be shaking slightly. She picked up a large photo and started cutting around me. Detaching me from my location. When she was finished, she punched a hole through one end of the photo and threaded some brown string on, so it looked like a large gift tag.

And then Dad appeared with a fresh pile of photographs which he'd obviously printed out upstairs and put them on the table.

'I think that's probably enough now, love,' she said gently.

'I've got half a dozen more I've just found on the computer. Ones we took when we went to Cornwall when she was eleven. Do you remember, we went to the Minack Theatre, and it was blowing a gale, but she loved it so much she wrapped herself up in the picnic blanket and had a huge grin on her face the whole time?'

Mum nodded. She did remember. I knew that. So did I. I'd snuggled into her side as we'd struggled to hear the words of the actors above the waves crashing against the cliff below. It had felt wild and raw and alive. Everything all at once. And I'd loved that. Yes, Dad had booked the tickets and packed the hamper, and I seemed to remember there were some lush strawberries and homemade custard tarts he'd picked up from a little stall outside someone's house on the way and it was all predictably perfect. But what I'd really loved was the unpredictability of the weather and how suddenly everything had felt possible. Although it hadn't been, of course.

'Maybe just those last few then,' she said. 'Then it's time to leave it. You've got to let her go now.'

'I know,' Dad said, his voice breaking.

'Besides, Harry and her friends are all bringing photos to tie on too. We've got to be sure there's room for them.'

I realised what they were doing then. They were going to decorate my coffin with photos. Trying to blot out my death with my life. You couldn't fault Dad for trying. Right up to the very end.

* * *

I sat in my trailer room later, surrounded by the memorabilia of my life. The *Friends* doormat and matching mugs and coasters. Phoebe was always my favourite. She was Harry's favourite too, probably because she played guitar. I liked her best because she wasn't afraid to do her own thing. She'd look at the others being obsessed with their hair or generally a bit anal and just make up a song about a smelly cat. I'd once asked Harry to play it at my funeral. I don't think he knew whether to take me seriously or not. I guessed I'd soon find out.

There was a knock on my door. I opened it to find Jules standing there, holding a glass of something alcoholic.

'Thought you might want company. Completely understand if not but I'll be a bit sad drinking a pint of snakebite on my own at my age.'

I stood aside to let her in.

'What's even in that?' I asked, pointing at the glass.

'Half lager, half cider. It was all the rage at the clubs I went to when I was at uni.'

'I'm surprised you remember any of it,' I said.

'I try to only remember the good bits,' she replied.

'I can't believe we'll be watching them soon. All the significant moments. I still think it's dead creepy.'

'Yeah, but at least you haven't done anything bad you need to worry about,' said Jules.

'True. But my film will probably have a 12 certificate, which is a bit lame.'

'Nothing to be ashamed of about that. *Finding Nemo* was a U and that's your favourite film.'

I smiled at her and got myself a Diet Coke from the fridge. Jules sat herself down on the sofa.

'Right, what we watching, then? I reckon you've got the box set of every series of *Friends* in there,' she said, pointing at the cabinet under the TV. 'That should take your mind off things for a while.'

'How did you know?' I asked, opening the cabinet door to reveal the stacked DVD boxes.

'Female intuition,' said Jules. 'That and the fact that your entire trailer is full of *Friends* stuff.'

I took the first season box set out.

'From the beginning then,' I said.

'Absolutely,' she replied.

* * *

I woke up to see sunlight streaming through the trailer window. It was a beautiful day for a funeral. That was what Dad would be saying while running around the house ticking off things on his list. I realised that although I was supposedly directing the filming of my funeral, Dad would very much be the executive producer – although with a lot more empathy than Suzi had. And he would make my job incredibly easy because all I had to do was tell Gerry that it would be perfectly choreographed and he simply needed to keep filming.

There was a croissant in a plastic wrapper on the breakfast bar, but I couldn't face food. There was too much going on inside me. All I could think about was Harry. He wouldn't eat either. I knew that. I imagined his mum coaxing him into a suit which they'd probably had to buy specially because I was pretty sure he hadn't owned one. He'd been dreading this day for so long. There was no pretending after this. No chance of it all being some horrible mistake and I would rock up at his front door as if nothing had happened.

I hoped Mum and Dad would have asked him to come to our house to be in the lead car with them. I couldn't imagine leaving here without him. And I hoped in some way it would provide a shred of comfort to him. That I'd be following him as he followed my body. A weird sort of Emily sandwich.

After I'd showered, I went to the wardrobe and took out my outfit. It was an obvious choice, really; the lilac dress I'd worn for my engagement. The one Harry loved so much. If I couldn't wear lilac for my wedding, at least I could wear it for my funeral.

It was a while before I plucked up the courage to go outside. Not because I couldn't face it but because I knew how the others would react. Sure enough, as soon as Jules caught sight of me, she had to turn away. What I wasn't expecting was that Carl looked even more upset and walked straight off.

'It's like I'm in some gruesome horror movie and no one can bear to look at me,' I said to Alice.

'Yeah, and they'd be vampires, and they'd bite you and get blood all down that gorgeous dress.'

'Take no notice of her,' said Gerry, stubbing out his cigarette. 'She needs her head looking at.'

'You look lovely,' said Jules, recovering her composure. 'Lilac really suits you.'

'It's a *Friends* colour,' I explained. 'Because of the inside of the door in Monica's apartment.'

'Of course it is. Should have realised. We watched enough of it last night. Is that going to be the colour theme today, then?'

'I don't know. Depends on my dad, I guess. It doesn't matter if not.'

'It did to me,' said Jules. 'And not one bloody bugger wore red.'

I gave her what I hoped was a sympathetic look and headed round to the front of the house. Carl was standing there, his head bowed.

'Are you OK?' I asked.

'Yeah. I'm going to find this tough, that's all.'

'But it's my funeral.'

'In my head, it's lots of different funerals.'

I shrugged, though I had no idea what he was talking about.

Right on cue, the front door opened. I told Gerry to start filming as Mum and Dad stood there, eyes already teary. Mum in a lilac dress and Dad in a grey suit with a lilac shirt and tie.

'See, told you,' Jules said, coming up and squeezing my hand. 'This is going to be perfect.'

As if to prove the point, I heard the sound of hooves and looked up to see a carriage coming down our road, pulled by two white horses with lilac plumes.

'Oh my God,' I said. 'If Disney did funerals, this would be a Disney Princess one.'

The horse-drawn hearse stopped outside our house. Neighbours started coming out. Some of them were holding lilac or white flowers. I waited for Mum and Dad to get in but they didn't. They went back inside again before emerging with Harry by their side.

I gasped. I hadn't even realised he was in there. He must have come earlier that morning before I was up. I was so pleased they'd done what I wanted because he was my family too.

'And there's your Prince Charming,' said Jules.

'Actually, I always thought Prince Eric was hotter,' I replied.

She grinned.

'Good call. And you have something of Ariel about you. Obviously, I've come as Ursula the sea witch,' she said, giving a twirl in her black and purple dress. 'In case you hadn't noticed.'

I tried not to laugh. It seemed wrong when the three people I loved most in the world looked so desperately unhappy, but I figured that if I was going to get through this day, I would have to find the humour in it.

'Do you think you're dressed as Ariel in there?' Jules added, pointing to the hearse. 'Maybe a little lilac bikini top and a full-size mermaid tail.'

I snorted a laugh.

'Are you two OK?' asked Carl.

'Yeah,' said Jules. 'We're just trying to keep our spirits up.'

Carl nodded and mouthed 'thank you' to Jules. And I couldn't help thinking how much Dad would appreciate them supporting me like this. He and Mum walked with Harry to the pavement. Harry couldn't even bring himself to look at the hearse. Just got in the funeral car parked behind it, my parents on either side of him. I told Gerry to cut there.

I hadn't even noticed Majid until now. He was parked behind them, his head bowed in respect.

'Wow, your folks have knocked it out of the park with this,' Majid said as we got in, gesturing towards the horses.

'Are we going to the woodland burial site near Huddersfield?' I asked.

'That's what it says on my call sheet.'

'Told you,' said Jules. 'Everything you wanted.'

We pulled away slowly behind them. As we made our way down the road, the neighbours who had gathered outside their houses threw flowers on top of the hearse.

'Bloody hell,' said Jules. 'It's like Princess Di's funeral. They've probably booked Elton John to sing at the service.'

'What are you talking about?' I asked.

'Oh God, you weren't even born when Princess Di died, were you? Google it.'

'I would if I had a phone.'

She sighed.

'Ordinary people came out on the streets like this and threw flowers as the coffin went past. And Elton rewrote "Candle in the Wind" for her, which made everyone cry.'

'Tell me about it,' said Majid, shaking his head. 'She were our People's Princess and look how they treated her. My aunties still mutter under their breaths and turn their TV off if Charles or Camilla come on.'

'One of my colleagues was in the motorcade,' said Carl. 'A white rose landed on his bike at one point. His wife pressed it when he got home. He said they were going to sell it on eBay if they ever hit hard times.'

We turned the corner and there were more people. More flowers being thrown.

'I don't understand. I don't even know them,' I said.

'It'll be all that fundraising for leukaemia,' said Majid. 'It were on Calendar news last night.'

'Was it? Why would they bother about me?'

The car went silent for a bit. It was Jules who finally spoke.

'Because you're seventeen, beautiful inside and out and you did all that stuff to help others. Everyone's sad that you went way, way too soon and they were all rooting for you to pull through because they want to believe in fairy tales.'

I got it. They wanted to see Ariel marry her Prince Eric. They felt cheated. So did I. But not even my director's cut could give them the ending they wanted. Because I couldn't save myself.

* * *

It wasn't until we got out of Halifax that the onlookers disappeared. Dad would be crying in the car in front. I knew that. But with some good tears mixed in with the sad. Because he would know he had done well, got the whole town to come out for me to say goodbye. Made me feel like royalty – or someone famous, at least.

He wasn't finished yet, though. Because when we turned into the natural burial ground, the narrow lane was lined with mourners, most of them wearing something lilac, and the flower throwing started all over again.

I caught glimpses of people I knew. Kids from school, teachers too. Nurses from hospital and staff from the hospice. It was like my life was already flashing before my eyes. And then the horses come to a halt and Mum, Dad and Harry got out of the car behind. I thought for a second Dad was supporting Harry, but it was actually the other way around. Mum was on Dad's other side, and it was hard to know who was supporting who there. More like they were clinging on to each other as if they had been shipwrecked, which I supposed, in a way, they had. The leukaemia iceberg had always been there, looming in the distance, but they thought they could navigate safely around it. They simply didn't know how big it was underneath.

As we got out, Gerry and Alice were already set up outside the gothic chapel where the service would take place. Carl gave them the nod to start filming and we hurried inside. I was hit by a sea of lilac. Flowers were draped through the rafters and in displays dotted around the chapel and at the end of every pew. As the mourners came in, I got up close enough to see they were all wearing little lilac ribbons saying 'Emily – Always in our hearts' before 'Angel' by Sarah McLachlan started playing as my coffin was carried into the chapel.

The one good thing was that you couldn't hear Harry or Dad's crying above anyone else's. They all blended in to one giant wall of sobbing. Harry sat down next to my parents on the front row. His mum and little sister, Mia, and my best friend, Ava, were sitting behind and they all reached out to put a hand on his shoulder.

Jules reached out and clutched my arm.

Next to me, Carl had his head bowed, unable to bring himself to watch as his shoulders shook silently.

'You OK?' I asked.

'I'm the one who should be asking you that.'

'Yeah, but we're the touchy-feely generation who actually ask stuff.'

He managed to turn up the edges of his mouth but said nothing.

The celebrant was a woman. She was wearing lilac too. I wondered if she'd had to buy her dress specially or if she had one in every shade to enable her to be prepared for every colour scheme. She said her name was Rachel and made a joke about being on a break from Ross. Clearly, Dad had briefed her well. She went on to say it was a celebration of my life and that I'd packed more into it than many people did in a lifetime. It was like she was talking about someone else, not me at all. And I was doing OK until the point where she invited my family and friends to come up and tie photos of their memories of me to the willow coffin. And they started playing 'I'll be There for You' by the Rembrandts.

I watched as first Mum and Dad came up and tied their photos on. Soon they were joined by Harry, his mum, Cath, and Ava and then everyone else queued to tie their pictures on, until the point where my coffin had disappeared underneath all the photos. Only Dad was still there, still tying the last one, before Mum took his hand and led him back to their seats.

There was more talk. Stuff about leukaemia, the wonderful care I'd received and the fundraising, before Rachel invited Dad up to say a few words. He composed himself for a moment, managed to thank everyone for coming and embracing the spirit of the day. And then he opened his mouth to say something, but no words came out. He tried again. Nothing. He looked up helplessly, his eyes swimming in tears. At which point, Mum stood up and walked over to the lectern, took the piece of paper he had his speech on from his shaking hand and carried on.

'Our daughter was special. Everyone says that about their own child. But she wasn't just special to us, she was special to everyone she met, whose lives she touched. We know that by all the support and love we've been shown since we lost her and the marvellous turnout today.

'And now Harry, Emily's fiancé, is going to sing and play a piece he wrote especially for her.'

She smiled at Harry as he walked past on his way to the piano, where he sat, took a deep breath and began to sing. The sound of his voice was like a comfort blanket being thrown over my shoulders. It enveloped me and warmed me and made me want to disappear inside it forever. I was so, so glad Alice was there to record it for me. They could keep my phone. If they would just let me listen to this on a loop forever, it would be enough.

At the end of the service, it was announced that Harry would sing a final song for me. He picked up his guitar, which had been placed on a chair next to the lectern, sat down and started singing and playing Phoebe's 'Smelly Cat' song from *Friends*.

I smiled. He'd done it for me. Just like he said he would. It was a shame it was my funeral because other than that, it really would have been the perfect day.

* * *

We went out of the front of the chapel and waited by the hole that had been dug for me.

Gerry and Alice, who nearly slipped and fell into my plot, boom and all, as she hurried towards us to set up, arrived, both slightly out of breath.

'Who's the girl with your fella?' Alice asked.

I glanced over to where Harry and Ava were walking towards us with their arms around each other.

'Ava. She's my best friend.'

'Right. Only your Harry just told her that he's not going to apply for uni because he can't bear to leave you behind.'

I stared at her.

'How did you hear that?' I asked.

'I've got a fucking great boom, remember,' she said.

'But he has to go to uni,' I said. 'He can't stop living just because I have. We talked about that beforehand. He had it all planned out. He was going to apply for a place on a music degree at LIPA in Liverpool. It's the performing arts school Paul McCartney set up.'

'Well, he's not any longer,' said Alice. 'He's going to be serenading you at your graveside every night from the sounds of it.'

We were interrupted by the arrival of my coffin. I knew I was supposed to be directing the film, but I couldn't give a toss at that moment. I simply wanted to grab hold of Harry and shake him and tell him he couldn't do this. Not because of me.

But it was too late for me to say anything. My coffin was being lowered into the ground. Mum and Dad each threw a lilac rose on top of it. Harry stepped forward and crouched down to drop in a red rose. Rachel was inviting people to throw earth on top. Instructing them to cover me over with a blanket of warmth and security. And as I watched myself disappear into the ground, all I could think of was that Harry's hopes and dreams were disappearing with me.

15

CARL

There was a time in my old life when a day off would have been something to look forward to. Not in the last few years, of course. But back when Mum still lived with us, before everything turned to shit. In those days, I'd have probably had a long lie-in to catch up on my sleep after a run of gruelling shifts. If I was lucky, Mum would do me a cooked breakfast, or I'd fix my own. And then I'd have gone out for a ride on my bike. Out of Halifax, up over the tops on some winding road stretching across the moors. It didn't matter what the weather was like; I preferred it when it was wild and desolate because it gave me such a sense of freedom. Of it just being me and the bike and the road.

All that was very much in the past now. For a start, I was dead. And anyway, there was no chance of a long lie-in because I'd barely got any sleep. The second I closed my eyes I saw Emily's parents' faces. They then morphed into the faces of the parents of every one of those girls who hadn't survived the minibus crash. When people talked about being haunted by the dead, what they didn't realise was that it was far worse to be haunted by the living. The pain etched into the eyes of a parent who has lost a child was something you could never erase. Even with alcohol. I knew that from bitter experience. And those flashbacks still haunted me. When they'd opened the back doors of Emily's hearse, I'd seen the netballs come bouncing out over the road. Haunted by day and by night. I'd hoped the one benefit of dying might be that it would have erased those memories. Clearly, that was not the case. So instead of a nice lie-in, I was sitting in a trailer, barely able to keep my eyes open, while eating a dried-up croissant.

There would be no cooked breakfast. No bike ride. Instead, I would leave before either of the others had woken and catch a bus to the hospital to see Lewis. Because the only positive thing I could think of doing with my day off was to check that Lewis was out of danger so I knew I could save him in my director's cut.

I almost got away with it too. I shut the trailer door quietly behind me, crept down the steps and round to the front of my house. I tightened the tabs on my backpack and was about to set off without a backward glance when I heard a voice.

'Hey, if you've dragged me out of bed at silly o'clock in the morning, the least you can do is wait for me.'

I looked around. Jules was perched on the front wall of my house. I stared at her in confusion.

'I didn't ask you to get up early.'

'No but it was a no-brainer that you'd try to leave before we woke up, so I set my alarm accordingly. I may not have been a boy scout, but I can still be prepared for an expedition, you know.'

I looked at her and sighed.

'Do I have a choice in whether you come?'

'Absolutely not. Give a man a choice and he'll always make the wrong one. That's my motto.'

'That definitely wasn't a boy scout one,' I replied, managing a small smile.

'So, what's the plan today?' she asked.

'Check in on Lewis. I'm hoping he's out of danger and breathing unaided, in which case I can go ahead and save his life. Then I can be cremated tomorrow knowing that I've at least done one good thing.'

'I'm sure you've chalked up more than one in your life. There must have been lots of people you helped along the way.'

'Yeah, but think of all the people I didn't save. The ones I let down.'

Jules looked at me.

'Are you worried about going to Hell?'

'I'm not religious, am I?'

'So where do you think you're going when we're done here?'

It dawned on me that I hadn't really thought about it. I'd been so busy beating myself up over Lewis, trying to save him and being haunted by the past, that I'd given scant regard to the future.

'I don't know. Maybe some big biker's holiday where I just get to ride over the moors for eternity.'

'That sounds like a good call,' said Jules.

'What about you?' I asked.

She thought for a minute before replying.

'I'd like to go back to Bristol,' she said. 'Though I don't suppose I'd get to do the good bits or live in Clifton again. I'd probably be sent to be a troll under Clifton Suspension Bridge. That would be my lot.'

'I'm sure they've got something better than that in mind for you,' I said.

Jules shrugged.

'So how do you plan to get to the hospital?'

'Walk, I guess,' I replied.

'Bit of luck I've got a lift sorted then. Majid should be here in five minutes.'

I frowned at her.

'We've been given a day off,' she said. 'It's like when the boiler broke at high school and they sent you home early. You didn't actually go home, you went into town to have some fun.'

I realised, not for the first time, that I missed out on a lot during my teenage years.

'Go on,' I said.

'Majid's taking us on an End Credits outing.'

'How have you wangled that?'

'He offered. Said he'd like to do something for us after a tough week.'

'Wow. He's such a lovely guy. Well, I'm in. Is Emily not coming with us?'

'We're coming back for her afterwards,' Jules said. 'I figured she'd have had enough of hospitals and she could do with a lie-in after yesterday.'

Majid's Mondeo appeared around the corner and came to a smooth stop in front of us.

'Morning,' he said as we got in. 'Where to first?'

'Calderdale Royal Hospital, please,' I said.

'I thought this was supposed to be a fun day out?' he asked.

'It is. This is Carl's special request. We're doing the serious bit first before we come back for Emily.'

'Right you are, then,' Majid replied, heading off.

When Jules and I arrived, we had to wait for some other visitors to be buzzed into the critical care unit before we could go in. Lewis was still lying in his bed not moving, Mum was still sitting by his side looking, if anything, more tired and gaunt than on my last visit. But there was one change. Lewis did not have an oxygen mask over his face.

'He's breathing unaided,' I said. 'Which must mean he's out of danger. I can do this. I'm going to be able to save him.'

And that was all that mattered because now I had the power to hit rewind and make it all go away. Not my death, obviously, but this utter torture. In my director's cut, Lewis would be fine. Grieving me, obviously, but with his life and limbs otherwise intact. And his future ahead of him for the taking, instead of lying in tatters on the hospital floor.

Jules smiled and squeezed my hand.

'What about your mum?' she asked.

'I think she can deal with the death of one son if she has the other one to live for. I can make it bearable for her. And that's the best I can do.'

We stayed for a while. Absorbed the silence and the stillness. Watched as Mum stroked Lewis's hand. Mourned the loss of everything. And what I wanted more than anything was to let her know that I was on it. I was going to fix this. For once in my life, I was going to save someone.

* * *

When we got back to the trailer, Jules went to knock on Emily's door. She was at least up and dressed but looked understandably confused when she saw us standing there.

'Come on,' said Jules. 'We're on an End Credits day out and you get to decide where we go next.'

She frowned at us.

'Does Suzi know about this?' she asked.

'Absolutely not,' said Jules.

Emily nodded, went to pick up her backpack and followed us out to the car.

'Morning. Gang's back together,' said Majid.

'What have I missed?' asked Emily, who was in the back with me.

'We went to the hospital first thing,' I said. 'Lewis is breathing unaided. Looks like I'll be able to save him.'

'Great,' she said, although I knew it was hard for her because she couldn't perform any miracles for Harry.

'So, Carl's had his turn. Where would you like to go?' asked Jules from the front. 'Somewhere in Halifax that you used to love.'

She thought for a moment. I suspected she was ruling out all the places she used to go with Harry because they'd be too painful to return to.

'Eureka!' she said finally.

'Have you discovered the displacement of water theory?' asked Jules, who clearly knew very well that she was referring to the children's museum.

'Very funny,' replied Emily. 'Mum and Dad used to take me there when I was little. I loved it, especially the pretend shopping area bit. I knocked someone over once with my mini trolley.'

'Eureka! it is then, Majid,' instructed Jules.

'That's good. I used to take my children there too. It were fairly new then, mind. They've probably changed it a lot since my day.'

It occurred to me that we knew nothing about Majid's life, or death, for that matter.

'When did you, um, er...'

'1999,' said Majid, stepping in to save my embarrassment. 'Although it may actually have been 2000.'

'How can you not know when you died?' asked Jules.

'It were Millennium Eve,' said Majid. 'I had a heart attack during firework display at midnight. My folks were that busy watching, they didn't notice straight away.'

I looked at Jules, who appeared to not know whether to laugh or cry.

'It's OK,' said Majid. 'I can see t' funny side of it now. I were worried about Millennium Bug and that everything would stop working at midnight and turned out only thing that did was my heart.'

I allowed myself a smile.

'That must have been tough for your family,' I said.

'It were very difficult. My wife Rabia worked long hours and my brothers and cousins supported her. I felt bad because men of my generation feel they should provide for their family. And it spoilt firework displays for my family, they loved fireworks, especially Rabia, we had them at our wedding.'

'Did you stay here because you couldn't bear to leave her?' asked Emily.

I caught Jules's eye in the front mirror. We both knew why Emily had asked that.

'Yes. This job gave me chance to keep an eye on all of them. See my three sons grow up. I have six grandchildren now, you know.'

'Congratulations,' said Jules. 'If that's the right thing to say.'

'Oh, it is,' said Majid. 'I'm very proud of them all. And Rabia, she's seventy-two now, she tells them that every day.'

We turned into the Eureka! car park and I patted Majid on the shoulder.

'Do you want to come in with us?' I asked him.

'Thank you but if you don't mind, I'm going to visit my family until you're ready. What time would you like me back?'

I looked at Jules.

'Let's say four thirty. I'm sure we can amuse ourselves until then. You go and see your wife and kids.'

'Thank you. And you enjoy your packed lunches,' he said, handing Jules a bag. 'I always used to make them for our family. It was nice to be able to do it again.'

Jules took the bag and gave Majid a hug. We watched as he drove off.

'He must really love her,' said Emily.

'Yep. And he's a top bloke,' said Jules. 'Anyway, let's go and relive your childhood memories.'

Eureka! was fairly quiet. We slipped in past the queue of paying guests.

'It's like having one of those fast passes for a theme park,' said Emily.

'Where to first?' asked Jules.

'The shopping area,' said Emily over her shoulder as she hurried off.

I'd never been there before, so it was all new to me. I followed Jules through the different zones until we spotted Emily laughing as she watched small children pick up an assortment of fake food items from the racks.

'Mum and Dad used to watch me do that for ages,' she said. 'Mum always said I was in training for a supermarket trolley dash when I was older.'

It was so nice seeing Emily enjoying herself that I had to blank out the thought that she never got to go to the supermarket as an adult. After she'd had her fix in the shopping area, Emily headed off around the corner.

'Oh my God, the bank,' she called out. 'I'd forgotten about the bank. I used to say it was Gringotts from Harry Potter and Dad would joke about watching out for the goblins.'

I looked at Jules and we smiled at each other.

'It's like she's rediscovering the childhood she'd forgotten she had,' said Jules.

And that was exactly it. The life she'd had before leukaemia. A reminder of all the good days she'd had before the bad ones had taken over.

She ran over to us breathless with excitement.

'I've just remembered the train carriage outside,' she said. 'We're going to eat our packed lunches in the train carriage.'

* * *

By the time Majid came to collect us later, I felt certain Emily had run the equivalent of a marathon in one day.

'Did you have a good time?' Majid asked as we got in the car.

'It was great,' said Emily. 'I remembered so much of it and there was new stuff too and your packed lunch was amazing.'

'I'll second that,' said Jules. 'I'd ask for the recipe for the samosas, but I imagine they're a fiercely guarded family secret.'

Majid smiled.

'Rabia's mother passed it down to her. I tried to copy it best I could.'

'You did an excellent job,' I said. 'How was Rabia?'

'She's struggling with her mobility but she lives with my oldest son and daughter-in-law and gets a lot of support.'

'That's good to hear,' said Jules. 'My mum's in a home. She's got dementia. We couldn't give her the care she needed.'

'I'm sorry to hear that,' said Majid. 'But it makes me even more glad about our next stop.'

'What do you mean?' asked Jules. 'I thought we were going back to the trailer now.'

'Not just yet,' said Majid.

He pulled away and headed off through the town centre traffic. I had no more idea what was going on than Jules did. I glanced at Emily, but she shrugged. A little later he pulled up outside The Piece Hall.

'If you open my boot when you get out, there's a padded bag with curries and rice for everyone. I've put a reserved sign on one of their picnic tables, so you can eat there. Emily, if you could take out my smaller black bag from t' boot. When you've finished your meal, there's a note in there explaining what to do. Faz has helped me with it, so hopefully everything works. I'll be back to collect you at nine.'

We thanked Majid and did as we were told, I took the food bag and Emily peered inside the smaller one and smiled.

'I have no idea what's going on,' said Jules.

'Relax,' I replied. 'The food, at least, smells amazing.'

So we sat on our reserved picnic table in The Piece Hall, surrounded by other people eating, drinking and enjoying the evening sunshine. And for a brief moment, it felt like we were alive, and were out here having a good time without a care in the world.

The food tasted as good as it smelt and when we'd finished and had sat a while to let it all go down, Emily delved into the other bag and read out the note she pulled out.

'Tonight, for one night only, The Cure are going to be playing at The Piece Hall. Not in person, unfortunately, we couldn't make that happen, but through the headphones attached to your Walkmans. Dance like no one is watching, because they're not. Faz.'

Emily held up the note, which contained a lot of emojis, all of them unnecessary in my opinion, then proceeded to give out the headphones and Walkmans.

'How do these things even work?' she asked.

Jules groaned.

'You press the play button,' she said, pointing to it. 'Our lives were simple back then.'

We put on our headphones and Jules gave us a countdown to pressing play, allegedly so our dancing would be synchronised. Clearly she'd never seen me dance. The first notes of 'Friday I'm In Love' came on. Emily grinned at me and pointed. Jules was off, her eyes shut, a smile on her face as she danced. She was back there in Bristol. I knew that. Back at the only time in her life she'd ever seemed to be happy. And I for one never wanted it to end.

* * *

I woke early on the day of my funeral. It still felt weird to think of people gathering to say goodbye to me. Lewis wouldn't be there, of course. The only person I knew who definitely would be was Mum. She would come to my funeral to mourn me then go back to the hospital to mourn Lewis. Who'd be a parent? Mum used to say that sometimes, half in jest. Or at least, that's what I'd thought at the time. But she was right about the constant worry. How it got worse once we were old enough to go out on our own. Live our own lives. Young men are addicted to risk taking. They believe they are invincible. It's a lethal combination. I knew that from my work. Mum must have thought that she was over the worst. That at least she only had Lewis left to worry about. And then I, who was old enough to know better, caused her this much grief.

My suit was hanging in the trailer wardrobe. Utterly spotless. My white shirt was neatly pressed and my black shoes polished to within an inch of their lives. My old sergeant, Roger, liked his officers to be smart. Smart to look at and with their brains. He used to say that while tapping the side of his head. I wondered if he'd be at the service today. Word would have got around. It was like that when you were in the force. Hotel California, they used to call it. Because you could check out but never leave.

I took one last look in the mirror. I'd have the sharpest suit at the crematorium. Not that any of the mourners would see. I trusted that Mum would have taken my best suit to the funeral directors for them to dress me in. She knew the care I took over my personal appearance.

'Give his head a final polish.' That's what she would have told them.

When I stepped outside and the others turned to see me, Gerry stood to attention and saluted me and Jules gave me a wolf whistle.

'You scrub up OK,' she said. 'Shame you never put it to any use.'

'I thought you were going to be wearing all your biker gear,' said Emily.

'No. I don't do stereotypes. Or fit into convenient boxes.'

'Right. Better get this show on t' road,' said Gerry. 'Reckon you're getting horses or owt fancy?'

'I suspect there may be an entourage,' I replied.

I heard the bike throttles before I saw the hearse. Jules gave the go-ahead for Gerry and Alice to start recording just at the point where they came around the corner. I thought there might be a dozen or so riding behind the funeral car but there were at least four times that. A mixture of bikers and my former colleagues from the police motorcycle unit.

'Bloody hell,' said Jules. 'And there you were, making out you hadn't meant anything to anyone.'

I looked at her and back to the bikers as they came to a halt outside. They trailed back along our entire street. My front door opened and Mum came out, clutching her fella Colin's hand. Her sister, Carole, bringing up the rear. I watched Mum's expression change as she clocked the bikers. Saw Carole reach into her handbag and pass her a tissue, before they walked steadily to the funeral car and climbed inside. I told Gerry and Alice to run down to the end of the street where they'd parked so they could get footage of the procession leaving, then beat them to the crematorium. We got into Majid's car, which was parked across the road.

'I've not seen owt like this before,' he said. 'I'll have to follow on behind them all. I never had you down as a biker.'

'Looks can be deceiving,' I said.

'So it seems.'

We crept along at the back of the entourage. People in the street stopped to stare. I had caused quite a scene, which was not like me at all. It felt good, though. Felt like I mattered. That for all my fuck-ups, some people still cared about me.

The crematorium was a drab concrete building. I supposed it was designed that way. Purely to be functional.

'This is a bit grim. I'm glad I had the woodland burial,' said Emily, as we got out of the car.

'I'm glad you had it too,' I replied. 'This is for those of us who just want to go quickly and quietly without too much fuss.'

'Try telling that to your hairy biker friends,' Jules said. I looked over to see a mass of long hair and beards wrapped in leather moving as one towards the small chapel. I was grateful to them for coming. For lending some interest to the bland backdrop of my exit.

I watched as my coffin was removed from the hearse. Cardboard, as I'd requested. On top were two floral tributes. One saying 'son', the other, 'brother'. Everyone knew that Lewis hadn't got that himself. It was Mum's way of placing him here. Of ensuring he was not forgotten.

As the pallbearers hoisted my coffin onto their shoulders and entered the chapel, the first notes of 'Bring Him Home' from *Les Mis* rang out. A ripple of confused looks passed between the bikers. They were probably wondering if they'd come to the wrong funeral. But then a few eyes were blinking back tears. A few calloused hands belonging to tattooed arms brushed them away.

'It's just as you planned it,' whispered Jules. And I couldn't help wishing that the same could have been said of my life.

A man at the front introduced himself as the celebrant. Said his name was John. I had no idea where they had got him from. He'd been well briefed though. Gave a potted outline of my life. Or 'significant moments' as Suzi would have called them. Although he glossed over the difficult bits by using the phrase 'testing times'.

John said he was going to do a reading from *Les Misérables,* the book not the musical – that got a ripple of laughter. The reading ended with the words, 'The greatest happiness of life is the conviction that we are loved; loved for ourselves, or rather, loved in spite of ourselves.'

'Not bad,' whispered Jules, 'but I'd still have gone for *Winnie the Pooh*.'

And then they got to the point where Lewis would have spoken. Not that he'd have been capable of saying much. He'd never been a great one for public speaking. I knew Mum wouldn't be able to get up there. She was barely holding it together while clinging onto Colin and Auntie Carole. But John was inviting someone else to come forward and speak. Someone I recognised, although he was noticeably older than the last time I saw him.

He stepped up to the podium and introduced himself.

'My name's Sergeant Roger Lockwood of West Yorkshire Police's motorcycle unit. I wish I wasn't here today. I've only got a few weeks left before I retire and I wanted to be marking that in any way other than attending the funeral of a former colleague. But of all the officers I've worked with, Carl is the one that stands out in my memory. Which is why I didn't want to let this occasion pass without talking about the officer and the man I knew.'

I frowned. He'd got the wrong person, surely? Had he mixed me up with another Carl? But he continued.

'Carl joined the unit as one of those mustard-keen young officers. Loved his bikes. Loved serving in the police. It was his dream job. He was trustworthy and reliable. Not hot-headed like some lads his age. The sort of officer who you knew was always going to get it right. Was never going to cause you any problems.

'He'd witnessed his fair share of accidents, or at least the aftermath of them, just as we all have. But on the particular October day in question, he saw things that no one should ever see. He was the first response officer on the scene of the minibus crash on the M62 which killed nine girls and two teachers. He never described to me exactly what he saw but I could see it written in his eyes.

'All I knew was that he was never the same officer or man again. He did everything he could and went far beyond the call of duty. He insisted on attending every one of those girls' funerals. Said it was the least he could do in the circumstances.'

Jules reached out and took my hand, giving it a squeeze. I was vaguely aware of the sound of sniffing in the congregation.

'By the time he had to give evidence at the inquest, he was unrecognisable as the bright-eyed officer with a zest for life and a passion for his job. He read from his notebook as if each word was carved out of him in blood. He stared blank-eyed at solicitors as he was asked questions. He did everything required of him, but it took an enormous toll on him.

'He began drinking. I was aware of that, as were most of his colleagues. Many of us had been there ourselves and tried to blot things out with alcohol. It never worked. But Carl went on trying.

'It was his coping mechanism. I'd insisted he took time off. Sent him to see the police psychologist for the PTSD which he undoubtedly had. But the counselling had little impact. He refused to take more time off work. Said it only made things worse, having time at home to dwell on it. But unfortunately, the drinking put paid to his career. I urged him to retire on health grounds. Said I'd sort out the paperwork for him. He wouldn't have it, though. I don't think he wanted to accept that it had beaten him. And he certainly didn't want any sympathy or have anyone say he was a victim too.

'He'd simply shake his head and talk about the girls' parents. How they were the ones who had truly suffered. It was his decision to leave the force but only because he knew he'd get kicked out sooner or later and he couldn't bear that. On a purely selfish level, I was relieved I didn't have to do that to a young man I had huge respect for.

'Carl was the best of officers. The best of humans. This is a tragic ending to the life of someone who deserved so much more but never complained about what had happened to him.'

He stopped for a moment to compose himself. Looked over at my coffin.

'I'm sorry for the years this tortured you, Carl. Thank you for your service. You were one of our finest. May you now rest in peace.'

As he stepped unsteadily down from the podium, people

clapped spontaneously. All except Jules and Emily, who took an arm each and supported me as my body shook.

I don't think so many people had ever been so relieved to hear 'Highway to Hell'. The tears were replaced with smiles. There were a few fist bumps from the bikers. And as Mum walked past me on her way to touch my coffin, I whispered to her.

'Don't worry. I'm going to sort this. I'm going to make sure Lewis is here with you in the final version.'

16

JULES

I took a coffee to Carl's trailer room the following morning. I figured he'd need it. I mean, what he actually needed was something far stronger, but I understood that he couldn't have that. Poor bastard.

He opened the door looking better than I'd expected. Like something had lifted from his eyes.

'Thanks,' he said, taking the mug from me. I followed him inside. Sat down on his boring grey sofa.

'Well, that was a turn up for the books,' I said. 'Who knew that you were bloody Saint Carl of Boothtown.'

Carl looked at me.

'Hardly. He revealed me as a pisshead who screwed everything up through drink.'

'That's not what I heard. I heard about a remarkable man who witnessed something no one should have to see and struggled to deal with it. You might be an obstinate fucker who should have accepted help but that's not a crime.'

Carl didn't respond for a moment or two.

'Do you really think he meant what he said? What if he was

just saying nice things because it was my funeral and no one likes speaking ill of the dead?'

'He didn't have to say anything, did he? And he didn't strike me as the sort that would make stuff up. Was he an honest copper?'

'Yeah.'

'There's your answer then.'

We sat for a moment. Carl stared into his coffee. I remembered coming to his trailer room the first time. The bottles of lager he'd emptied down the sink. So much of it made sense after yesterday.

'Did you get your drinking under control?' I asked.

'Well, it doesn't matter now, does it? It's not as if I can do any more damage.'

'What do you mean by that?'

'You'll find out soon enough. Just don't go around saying I'm a saint before you know all the facts.'

* * *

I went back to my room for one last look around before I left. It felt like leaving Nina all over again. Leaving my past. The happy part of it, at least. The bit I didn't want to forget. I took one final pee in the bathroom, washed my hands and turned to look at Nina's knitted toilet-roll holder.

'I'm fucking having that,' I said out loud.

I grabbed hold of it and hurried outside, brandishing her above my head. Carl and Emily were already out there waiting.

'You need to take a souvenir back with you,' I said.

'You mean nick something?' asked Carl.

'What's your problem? You're not a copper any more, you know. You don't have to be such a goody-goody.'

I turned to Emily.

'I spent all my life as a goody-goody,' she said.

'Well, here's a chance for both of you to do something about that. Get back inside and take the thing that's important to you. The memento you want for wherever it is we'll be heading off to when we're done here.'

They exchanged a quick glance, before both heading back inside their rooms. Carl emerged first, carrying his red *Les Mis* flag.

'Really?' I asked. 'You couldn't have picked something more portable?'

'This is what I wanted to take with me,' he said. I shrugged and turned back to see Emily coming out of her trailer holding the giant pinboard with the seventeen selfies of her and Harry.

'I'm glad I wasn't washed up on a desert island with you two, I'd have had no space to myself.'

Majid was out the front waiting for us. He sighed as Carl tried to position his flag where it wouldn't obscure his vision.

'When most people take things from hotels, it's a little set of toiletries that doesn't take up much room,' he said.

'Yeah, well. I've never taken anything from a hotel in my entire life, so I'm making up for it in death.'

Majid smiled at him.

'Right. Back to the hotel it is then. Suzi's got a treat in store for you.'

'What do you mean?' I asked.

'Has she not told you? It's wrap party time.'

'You what?'

'A party, to celebrate the fact that you've wrapped filming.'

'But I was only cremated yesterday,' pointed out Carl. 'I'm hardly in the party mood.'

'Think of it like a joint wake you never got to go to,' said Majid.

'Will there be booze?' I asked.

'I imagine so.'

'And soft drinks?' I added quickly, remembering Carl.

'Of course. All your usual party stuff.'

'A Colin the Caterpillar cake?' asked Emily.

'I thought you didn't want to be treated like a kid,' I said.

'Colin the Caterpillar cakes are for all ages,' said Emily firmly.

'Are you coming, Majid?' asked Carl.

'I am indeed.'

'Great,' I said. 'We'll save you a bit of cake then.'

Suzi was waiting for us when we arrived back at the hotel. She whooped as we walked through the foyer, like she was some crazy woman on an HRT overdose, and shepherded us into the lift.

'We're going down to the basement,' she told us, very matter-of-factly.

'What for?'

'Debrief in my office.'

* * *

'Take a pew,' said Suzi, showing us in. 'Although I promise you there'll be no hymns here. "All Things Bright and Beautiful" really was hideously inappropriate in the circumstances, wasn't it?'

She looked at me, but I decided not to respond. 'So, how are we all feeling now we're dead and buried?' she asked.

'Cremated,' Carl reminded her.

'That as well.'

'A bit flat,' I said. 'Especially as my send-off was so crap.'

'I know. It was like a knock-off funeral package he got from some bloke in a pub,' said Suzi.

'Thanks,' I said. 'You always know how to make a woman feel good.'

'You have friends for that,' she replied, 'I'm here to dispense the truth. Anyway, you'll be pleased to hear Gerry and Alice have downloaded all their footage and Faz has worked his magic on it, which is how I got a sneak preview of the best bits. Nice eulogy your ex-boss gave,' she said, turning to Carl. 'Wasn't expecting that.'

Carl shrugged.

'And nor was I expecting our youngest director here to have half the town turn out to throw flowers at her coffin.'

She turned and smiled appreciatively at Emily.

'It made great footage. I think Faz is putting it to music. Nothing I've ever heard of but he's too young to know "You Don't Bring Me Flowers". When I mentioned Neil Diamond, he thought it was a made-up TikTok name for a drag queen. Anyway, we'll let you loose on the footage soon enough. Tonight, it's the wrap party.'

'And what are we supposed to be celebrating exactly?' asked Carl.

'That the films of your lives have wrapped. You're free. It doesn't matter what you do now, it won't appear on celluloid.'

'What's that?' asked Emily.

'I keep forgetting about Gen Z here,' said Suzi. 'It means you haven't got to worry about anything you do from now appearing in the film of your life. Or on Instagram or TikTok and all those other weird things you do to increase social pressure and make yourselves feel like shit.'

It was a fair point. And there was some kind of release from knowing I was safely in the ground and I couldn't fuck things up any further. All that I had to do now was work out how to put right one of the mistakes I'd made. The biggest one by far.

'And what happens at this wrap party?' asked Emily. 'There aren't organised games, are there?'

'Nope, wouldn't dream of it,' said Suzi. 'There's food, booze, music and dancing. And the bloopers, of course.'

'You what?' I asked.

'You know, bloopers, outtakes. The funny or embarrassing bits that we caught on camera.'

Emily, Carl and I exchanged a look.

'You never mentioned this before,' I said.

'Didn't I? Don't worry about it. I mean, everyone loves the bloopers, don't they?'

I groaned. 'What if your life was one big blooper?'

'Faz has mentioned that you do feature quite heavily,' said Suzi.

'Great,' I said. 'The final nail in the coffin.'

* * *

It was a long time since I'd got ready for a party. Definitely years. Perhaps decades. I certainly couldn't remember one. I had no idea what you wore to a wrap party but when I opened my wardrobe in the hotel room, my red wrap dress was in there and it was too obvious a choice to ignore. I applied my make-up in the bathroom mirror. I didn't even try to cover up my wrinkles – there seemed little point at this stage. Just went with eyeliner and lippy, like back in the old days. Watched over by the knitted toilet-roll holder doll, who now had pride of place on top of the loo. She made me feel like Nina was still with me for this final stage of my journey. I may have had no idea where I was going but she was at least a familiar presence. Watching over me. Reminding me of happier times.

I took one last look in the mirror.

'Party time,' I said to the woman who looked back at me.

* * *

The wrap party was held in a function room opposite Food to Die For. It was the sort of soulless place with scratched laminate flooring, grubby magnolia walls and functional chairs that shouted 'unloved'.

To be fair, Faz had made an effort by bringing in some disco lights with his mixing desk and Elsie from the restaurant was laying out a little buffet spread that I suspected was a lot nicer than the food at my wake would have been.

'Hello, Elsie,' I said, 'Can I give you a hand?'

'No, you're OK, love,' she replied. 'You'll have spent your life volunteering for jobs you don't get paid for, you deserve a rest at your own wrap party. At least I'm getting paid for it.'

I smiled at her. The octogenarian telling me to take it easy.

'I've been meaning to ask,' I said. 'How do they pay you here? Is it just bed and board downstairs or do you get a wage as well?'

Elsie leant in closer to me.

'You can choose from various options,' she said. 'I went for those rude films.'

'I'm sorry?' I replied.

'You know, ones with an 18 certificate. I like sex and nudity as I'm not keen on violent ones. There's usually a good few male bottoms on display and some rather lovely chest hair. They send them to my hotel TV. That's best you can hope for at my age.'

I burst out laughing, relieved she hadn't been talking about anything hardcore.

'Good for you, Elsie,' I said. 'I'm glad they're keeping their employees happy.'

I left her to arrange the sausage rolls as I spotted Carl and Emily loitering in the far corner.

'What were you laughing at with Elsie?' asked Carl.

'Believe me, you don't want to know. All I'm telling you is that there's more to our elderly waitress than meets the eye.'

'This is really weird,' said Emily, scanning the room.

'It is,' I replied. 'Although, as we've nothing else in our social calendars, we may as well make the most of it and eat as much as possible.'

When I'd finished loading up my plate at the buffet, I turned to see Majid hovering by the door.

'Hey,' I said, going up to greet him with a hug. 'I want to thank you again for yesterday. It was the most fun I've had in ages.'

'Glad to be of service,' he replied.

'I'm going to ask you the same question I just asked Elsie. How do you get paid? Apart from your bed and board, that is.'

Majid also leant towards me and lowered his voice, and I thought for an awful moment he too received dodgy films to his hotel TV.

'My family are very lucky with The People's Postcode Lottery,' he said.

'Come again?'

'That is where my wages are paid into. My family win much more than other people do, they simply don't realise. Not big amounts, maybe £100 or so. And it's shared out between all my family members. Children, grandchildren, nieces and nephews and their children. And it's shared with their neighbours too, which helps not to arouse suspicion. They just assume everyone wins as often as they do.'

I started laughing, imagining those in charge scratching their heads over the clusters of lucky postcodes in Halifax.

'Is that Suzi's doing?' I asked.

'I think she has special powers,' Majid replied. 'Although she always pretends she knows nothing about it.'

'So, you have been providing for your family all these years,' I said.

'Yes,' said Majid. 'I suppose I have. Anyway, you three enjoy your party. I'll miss having you in my cab.'

'I'm sure your other passengers are a lot less trouble.'

'True,' he said. 'But they're a lot less fun too.'

The door opened again, and Gerry and Alice walked in. Although I nearly didn't recognise Alice without her boom.

'It's our crack crew,' I said. 'I'm surprised you're here. Thought you'd be glad to see the back of us.'

'You've kept us on our toes, but we'll be sorry to see you go. Plus, I'll go anywhere for free grub,' said Gerry.

'And I came to see if there were any gory bits in the outtakes,' added Alice.

'Are there usually?'

'No, but I live in hope.'

'I want to know how you both get paid,' I asked. 'Majid and Elsie have already spilt the beans and let me tell you, the one getting dodgy films streamed to their room is not the one you'd expect.'

Gerry snorted a laugh.

'Camera gear,' he said. 'I'm saving for a Blackmagic Cinema Camera.'

'Boring as fuck,' I replied. 'Alice, do better.'

'Sure. I buy fake blood on the afterweb and drop it off various public buildings so it looks like there's been a massacre.'

'See, knew I could rely on you,' I said. 'And at the same time I'm hugely relieved you're not still alive and dangerous.'

Suzi took to the floor with a mic in her hand. I was waiting for her to make a crack about it being a better turnout than for my funeral, but for once, she didn't go there.

'These three have really been put though the mill over the past week. But did they crumble? Did they lay down and die?'

I was worried she was about to break into a Gloria Gaynor impression, but she at least spared us that.

'Sorry, another one of my inappropriate jokes,' she continued.

'Anyway, they may have given me quite the interrogation on their first day and been a pain in the arse on more than one occasion since, but they've come together, supported each other and having seen the first rushes, I can congratulate them on having got some excellent footage from their departures.

'Tomorrow, they'll begin the task of editing their significant moments and creating their director's cuts, but before that process begins, it's only right that we show some of the bloopers from the lives which they starred in. And no, we haven't bleeped out the swearing because it's much more fun that way.'

Faz dimmed the lights. A grainy reel came up on the screen of a much younger Carl telling someone that he was going to go over and ask out one of the other police cadets. At which point he turned around and promptly fell over a wastepaper bin, landing at her feet with an empty bag of Wotsits on his head.

Carl groaned as Emily howled with laughter. But it was her turn next. A clip from school where she was sitting on a desk at the front of the class, with the male teacher on the other side, and you could just make out her foot rubbing up and down, not the table leg as she'd presumably thought, but the teacher's.

'Oh my God, that was Mr Pearce. I could never look him in the eye again,' she said, hiding her face behind her fingers.

And then I came up on the screen. Me and Nina, actually. It was CCTV footage. We'd been drunk and on our way home from a club at two in the morning when we'd sat down on a park bench. I'd scratched 'Jules & Nina Woz Ere' in the wood. At which point Nina had said she'd like to keep it as a memento. At which point I'd told her we were going to take it home to our flat. Which was why there was footage of us lifting up the bench, struggling to get it across roads and down steps and finally dropping it outside a butcher's when we heard a police siren, thought they were after us and decided to leg it.

People were still laughing when some Ring doorbell footage taken only a few years ago came on. I was taking out the recycling just as the boys left for school, as other kids passed our front gate. Only for me to drop the box and a year's worth of vaginal moisturiser tubes fell out at their feet, leaving them utterly mortified and me laughing so much I actually pissed myself.

Carl tried to suppress a snigger as Suzi roared with laughter.

'It's OK,' I said, 'go ahead. There'll be a lot worse than that to come.'

And there would be, tomorrow. I knew that. I just wasn't sure if I was ready for it.

17

EMILY

I wasn't excited about the next bit any more. I felt like the girl who had first arrived here and had been practically jumping up and down at the prospect of seeing all those clips of her with Harry was like a much younger, more naïve version of me. Maybe the others were right and she was still a kid, as much as I didn't want to think that.

All I knew was that three funerals later, that girl didn't exist any more. I'd grown; I'd changed. I'd seen and heard stuff people of my age shouldn't have to deal with and also stuff that had really made me think. Nothing was quite as black and white as I'd thought it was. And I was stuck with the knowledge that Harry was intending to ditch all his plans because I had basically screwed up his life. Not intentionally. But by going and dying on him. Grief didn't suit him. It really didn't. The Harry I used to know was always so chilled and positive. He sang, he played musical instruments, he saw the best in everyone, and he made the fucking sun come out. Now, he'd been reduced to a shell of what he once was. There was no light in his face or his voice. He was more dead than I was.

I hated that I'd caused pain to the people I loved most in the world. My mum and dad would get through it – although never over it, I already understood that much – because they had each other. But Harry was on his own with this hurt. And I feared that seeing the old Harry in these clips would make that even more painful.

* * *

When I stepped out of the lift in the basement, the others were already there, like it was the first day at school and they wanted to appear keen. I reckoned Carl would always have been the first in the queue for everything at school. I thought again about what his boss had said at his funeral. How what he went through had changed him and he was unrecognisable from the young man he'd once known. I couldn't let that happen to Harry. I knew that.

'Hey,' I said. 'This is going to be so weird.'

Jules nodded.

'We just need to get through it. Same as the funerals. Shut our eyes and hold each other's hands if necessary. Are we in?'

Carl and I nodded as a familiar voice called out from behind us.

'Hey guys,' said Faz. 'All looking good after the excitement last night. Jules, I didn't know you had those dance moves.'

'Nor did I till I'd downed a few drinks.'

'You are so funny! Let's go to the studio where Suzi's waiting for you.'

'Why does she want to see us? Are we in trouble?' asked Carl.

'No, it's just a debrief slash prebrief.'

We shrugged and followed him. Suzi was sitting on the desk

in the studio. Her leather jacket squeaked as she turned to face us.

'Hey, it's the three musketeers. Hope you enjoyed last night. We're cracking straight on with viewing your significant moments. We're going shortest life to longest lives, so Emily, we're starting with you.'

I nodded. At least this way I'd get it over with first.

'And remember, you're in this as a team,' said Suzi. 'But it's up to you all individually to edit your film and make the big call. No influencing the others. It's their life, they get to decide what their director's cut will be.'

We all nodded.

'Right. Faz will get you started. First job for each of you will be to watch your significant moments footage all the way through. And on your final day here, you'll make your directors' cuts.'

Suzi slithered down from the desk with more creaking of her jacket and left a strong smell of hairspray in the studio when she left.

'Ready to roll?' asked Faz. I nodded. 'Perfect,' he said.

They started with my baby videos which Dad had filmed and catalogued and saved in the cloud because, of course he had. I turned from the screen for a second as I heard Carl whisper, 'You OK?' to Jules. Which seemed a weird thing for him to ask when it wasn't her film.

And the footage kept coming. I suspected Dad would have catalogued everything in date order. Would have ensured he never missed a month of my life, so there were no gaps in my records. I wondered if he and Mum would have watched these since my death. If they would have provided a shred of comfort to them. I suspected not. It was probably too soon. But maybe in the months and years ahead they would watch and maybe it would bring back happy memories for them.

In the early clips, it was mostly Mum holding me. Her eyes tired but awash with love. And later Dad holding me as I took my first steps. Not wanting to let go even then.

There was a video of me as a toddler, sitting in that rock pool at Robin Hood's Bay. The holiday Dad had remembered. That he'd stuck a photo of on my coffin. I looked to be in my absolute element under the beach sun hat which Dad insisted I wore. Neither of us having any idea of what was going to happen years later.

Before I knew it, we were on my first day at school, me proudly standing in my uniform in front of the door as Dad encouraged me to say how old I was, what school I was starting and who my teacher was.

He took the same video every year. I watched myself grow up outside our front door. My first tooth missing in one of them. A whole load of them missing in another. Always I was smiling. Always I looked genuinely happy. Even when I got to high school there were no sullen faces or strops. Just a constant stream of smiles and laughter and good times.

'Wow,' said Carl. 'It's like you had the happiest childhood ever.'

And that's when it hit me that maybe I did. I just didn't realise at the time. And I'd kind of forgotten about it since.

'I know what I'm going to do with all this,' I said. 'I'm going to make it into a montage like at the beginning of *Up*. My mum always said that was the best bit of the film.'

'It was,' said Jules. 'I bawled my eyes out watching that. What came after was a bit of a let-down really.'

She realised as soon as she said it.

'Sorry, I've put my size sixes in it again, haven't I?'

'It's OK,' I said. 'And there's still some good stuff to go before we get to that.'

There were clips of me and Mum curled up on the sofa together for our eighties and nineties film nights, with a much younger Slinky Dog snuggling in between us, prompting some 'aaahhs' from the other two.

The screen changed abruptly, and we were no longer looking at home videos Dad had taken. It was properly shot footage that had somehow been taken at school. I guessed a film crew had been dispatched. I knew why they'd been alerted about a significant moment, too. I'd been interested in Harry for ages. Like years, not weeks or months. We'd talked at school and eventually online. All the time getting closer. Recently, we'd been flirting a bit too. And I'd sensed it was all coming to a head. I'd told Ava I thought he was going to ask me out and I knew as soon as I saw the screen that this was the day it happened.

I'm standing talking to Ava. It's summer and both of our skirts are shorter than they should be, probably because we have turned them up at the waist. My hair is tied in a high ponytail, but a few strands have come loose and are dangling around my face. A boy is hovering in the background. I know instantly who it is, simply from the way he stands and how he tries to smooth his hair.

Ava leans in and says, 'He's coming over.' I glance around and look straight back and even as I do so, Ava is walking away. She knows what's going to happen and she doesn't want to be a third wheel.

Harry smiles. I have seen that smile many times before, but it's still somehow the most dazzling thing on the planet.

'Hey,' he says.

'Hey.' It's all I can do to get the word out. My brain and mouth appear to be struggling to communicate with each other. My brain is

struggling to do pretty much anything other than stare at him, willing him to ask what I hope he's going to ask and put me out of my misery.

'I've got a couple of tickets for a gig next week—'

'Yes,' I say, before he has even finished asking me. He stares, as if not quite sure he has heard right and then he starts laughing.

'You don't know who and when yet,' he teases. I feel the colour rising in my cheeks. Worry I sound too keen. Too desperate. But I have said it now and there's no going back.

'Are you going to be there?' I ask.

'Well, yeah.'

'Then it doesn't matter, does it?'

It's my turn to smile at him. His turn to allow his hair to fall over his face to hide his blushes.

'No,' he replies. 'It doesn't.'

And we look at each other in a way that is so intense. So ridiculously serious. And he knows at that moment what I already know. That this is it. The start of us. And there will never be an end of us. Just the beginning.

'Wow, you guys,' said Jules. 'That was beyond cute. And that smile of his!'

'Did you see it flash?' I asked. 'That was like the flash of the camera at Carl and Ellie's wedding from *Up*. That's when my film really begins.'

And that's what came on next. Little clips of the hand holding, the cuddling, all leading up to the first kiss. And my face. I couldn't get over how much my face lit up when he kissed me. So many firsts. The first time he met my parents properly and my dad was being all serious and had a look that said 'what are your intentions towards my daughter?' and my mum just threw her arms around him because she loved him already for how happy he'd made me. And she knew he would never make me unhappy.

And all the time my dad was on high alert, trying to protect me from boys, or sunburn or speeding cars or anything else he could think of, he didn't know that the real enemy was lurking within me.

As the footage moved forward, I wondered if there were signs that we'd all missed. Was my skin paler than usual? Did I seem tired? Had I lost a bit of weight? I scanned the images trying to look for clues, but it was easy to think you could see things with the benefit of hindsight.

And then we got to the part where things were clearly not right. I was sent home from school because I'd had a bad nose-bleed that wouldn't stop. Unable to go into school because I was so tired and breathless when I moved. I seemed to be lying on the sofa watching TV an awful lot. Dad was looking worried and talking to Mum in the kitchen when I'd gone to bed early. There was a GP appointment. Some blood tests. A referral to hospital. A bone marrow test. All happening in a quick enough time that suggested they were worried. And then the three of us were walking into hospital. Going up in the lift and sitting in a waiting area until my name was called. It was the significant moment that changed everything.

I know as soon as I see the consultant's face. It has a sympathetic expression. One I imagine he keeps for situations like this. Mum knows too. I can tell by the way she grips my hand tighter. Dad is still doing everything he can to avoid the conversation to come. Talking about the weather and the traffic and anything that postpones for a moment the conversation we are about to have which will confirm his deepest, darkest fear.

We all sit down. I am between Mum and Dad, like they are still trying to protect me, when the truth is that I'm beyond protecting because it turns out the danger has been eating away at me from the inside and that's the one place they can't get to.

The consultant's name is Mr Abbas. He's good enough not to prolong the agony any further. As soon as Dad is over with the pleasantries, he turns to me and has the decency to look me in the eye as he tells me.

'I'm very sorry to say the bone marrow tests confirmed that you do indeed have Acute Myeloid Leukaemia. It's what we classify as stage M2, which means there is maturation in the cells. For this reason, we will need to begin the first induction block of chemotherapy as soon as possible.'

Each word slaps me around the face. My skin stings. My eyes sting but maybe that's because of the tears that are gathering in them. Mum squeezes my hand even harder. I'm pretty sure I'll have a bruise there tomorrow because I bruise so easily now. And when I look at Mum, I see that her eyes are glistening too. She is trying to keep a tiny smile on her face at the same time. Her attempt at putting on a brave face, I guess. She looks like a human rainbow.

Dad is not looking at either of us. Dad is asking Mr Abbas questions. Lots of questions. All of them with a positive slant. How long before I am better? What can they do to support my recovery? How much of an advantage will my age be in fighting this? Anything he can possibly think of which involves me getting better. Me being over this. And him never having to face up to the possibility of me dying.

I do not pay a huge amount of attention to the answers Mr Abbas gives. He's trying to be kind, I know that much. Trying to give us hope. Talking about the percentage of people who do survive for five years or more rather than those who don't. The odds. The probability. The statistics. I do not care about any of them. I only care about Harry. Because I'm going to have to tell him this later. I'm going to see his face when it crumples and falls. Watch as he tries to resurrect it into a brave face, like Mum and Dad have. And I don't want to do that to Harry. Don't want to break him. All he's ever given me is love and care and kindness. And yet somehow, I'm supposed to deliver this to him as if that's a fair swap.

And all the dreams I have for our future: taking a gap year and going travelling together, going to uni, seeing Harry make a success of his music, living together, getting married, having children... That's all gone now. I don't know if we'll ever be able to do those things because I don't even know if I'll still be alive in five years' time.

'Is there anything you want to ask, Emily?' I hear Mr Abbas say. And what I want to ask is why me? I've only ever been a good girl and done what I was told and worked hard at school and been kind to everyone, so why the fuck do I have leukaemia? But I don't say that because I don't want to upset my parents. Instead, I simply shake my head and look down at my hands.

There is talk of it being a lot to take in. Leaflets are passed to my dad with details of organisations who can offer support and advice. The hospital will be contacting us with the date my chemotherapy treatment will start and will provide all the information we need. And I am to rest and take things easy, which is all complete bollocks. Because I'm fifteen years old and I don't know how to deal with any of this, and I want to make it stop. Turn back the clock and make it all go away.

'Stop!' It was a moment before I realised I had shouted it out loud. In Faz's studio. Not in Mr Abass's room. Faz stopped the film. Jules reached over and put her arm around me.

'Can we take five?' asked Jules. Faz nodded and headed out of the studio, probably glad to get away.

'It's like Carl and Ellie's story in *Up*,' I said. 'It's the bit where it all starts to go horribly wrong.'

Jules nodded and rested her head against mine.

'I bet Ellie wished she didn't have to do that to her Carl,' I said. 'I bet she wished she could rewind their film and make it go away.'

Jules and Carl looked at each other. And I knew they knew what I was thinking.

When Faz returned, he had tubs of ice cream for everyone.

'Compliments of Suzi,' he said, handing them out. 'You've all got your favourite flavours. She said she used to eat a lot of ice cream during films that made her cry. And somehow, it always made her feel better.'

18

CARL

Jules went back with Emily to her room after her significant moments to make sure she was OK. And to continue watching the *Friends* box set. They stopped the film before Emily's death and her funeral, so at least she didn't have to go through watching that again. To be honest, I was relieved because I wasn't sure I could go through watching it again either.

I completely understood what she'd said. It was far harder to witness other people's pain than to deal with your own. Other people's pain and suffering rendered you helpless. Emily hadn't been able to do anything about it in life. It wasn't her fault she'd got leukaemia, but she still somehow felt responsible for the pain that had caused others.

I, on the other hand, *was* responsible. And the next day, Emily and Jules were going to find that out for themselves. I'd been the nice guy up until that point. I'd got pity at my funeral. But once the truth was out, I had no doubt that was going to change. I hadn't even had the guts to tell them myself. The lion in *The Wizard of Oz* had more courage than me.

* * *

I went for breakfast early the next morning, in an effort to avoid having to make small talk with Jules and Emily. Even though I'd seen Lewis breathing unaided at the hospital, I still did my usual thing of scanning the room for the new arrivals to check that he wasn't amongst them. Just a few days to go and I could put my plan into action. I had the power to do one good thing before I went on to wherever it was I was heading to. That was all I wanted to do.

'Hey, Mr Nice Guy,' said Suzi as I arrived outside the studio. 'Are you ready to do your Scorsese impression?'

I went to answer her, but no words came. Suzi looked at me. Her expression changed. I realised she knew what was about to come.

'It's going to be alright, you know.'

'Is it?'

'My husband had a drink problem, and he did a whole lot worse.'

'I doubt that's possible,' I said.

'Unfortunately, it is,' she replied, before turning and walking off as Jules and Emily got out of the lift.

'I thought you'd already be in there, raring to go,' said Jules.

'I couldn't cope with Faz's unrelenting positivity on my own,' I replied.

'I get that,' she said.

I looked at Emily. She had an air of calmness about her I hadn't seen before. She knew what she was going to do, and it had given her some peace. I needed to steel myself to get through this in the hope I could find peace on the other side too.

'Hey guys, you can't keep away from this place,' said Faz as we entered the studio. I resisted the temptation to point out that we had no choice and sat down at my screen. My film was already loaded. All I had to do was press play. I decided to approach the task with the detached air of Martin Scorsese. It wasn't my significant moments; it was the material I had to work with. I was the director. I would remain distant. I would not get emotionally involved. I hit play.

I was not a baby in the first shots. That was the price I paid for being in my thirties. Either that or there were no significant moments in my first ten years because that was when the film started. The baby on screen was Lewis, which made it seem as if my life didn't really start until he arrived. I was clearly already in responsible big brother mode; watching him everywhere he went, putting myself between him and any perceived danger.

The early footage was sporadic. Mum or Dad hovered in the background but there were no happy family vibes like in Emily's film. Mum looked tired, mostly. Dad appeared absent even when he was in the shot. Mainly it was just me shadowing Lewis. Telling him not to touch. To be careful. Completely oblivious to anything other than my big brother duties.

At some point in my teens, a BMX bike appeared. It was the first time I exhibited any excitement. Any interest in something of my own. At that point it was *the* significant thing in my life.

Dad disappeared from the reels, having become entirely insignificant in my life. And on my eighteenth birthday I woke to find a moped parked in our back yard. Suddenly, I was like a little kid on Christmas morning, beaming from ear to ear. I could hear Lewis in the background asking if he could have my BMX now and my answer was the same as it always was. If he was careful. If he rode it responsibly.

The moped was swapped for a light motorcycle a year later. At twenty-one, with me now working as a full-time police officer, I'd graduated to my first proper motorbike, bought from the showroom in Hipperholme that I'd spent way too many hours in. And that was when it appeared my life really began. All the footage was now of me on the open road. The backdrops when I was going over the tops were stunning. I started trying to work out all the biker anthems I would put on the soundtrack. I was actually beginning to enjoy myself.

Mum's proud face when I joined the police motorcycle unit came onto the screen. She'd never been one to voice her pride in either of us, but it was so often visible that perhaps she didn't need to.

'Is it all just bikes from now on?' Jules asked.

'Pretty much so,' I replied.

'There's a distinct lack of love interest, compared with Emily's.'

'Yeah, well you saw how lame my efforts were at the wrap party,' I replied.

And then I went quiet. Because it wasn't a time for wise-cracks. I knew what was coming. I felt everything within me tighten as I tried to brace myself for what was to come.

'You might not want to watch this,' I said. 'Jules, take Emily, I don't want her to see this.'

Emily shook her head.

'I'm not going anywhere.'

'All for one and one for all,' said Jules, gripping my arm tightly. And it was too late to argue further. I was back there.

It's late evening. The rush hour is over. The sun is low in the sky. It's the best time to be on the motorway. It's difficult to catch it at dawn without the traffic being heavy. But dusk is good, a rare time when you can get a sense of freedom.

The call is for an RTA involving a lorry and a minibus. I'm closest. Very close actually. I check my mirror and pull out into the fast lane. I can be there in a minute or two. Within a few moments the traffic in front of me has become stationary. Clearly the accident is blocking the road. I put on my lights and siren and swing onto the hard shoulder. My first job when I get there will be to manage the traffic. The paramedics will be on their way to deal with any casualties. I'll need to cordon off the scene to keep it safe and try to get at least one lane moving again.

That's what I'm assuming anyway, because I have no reason to think it's anything other than a run-of-the-mill RTA at this point. I draw closer. I can see two vehicles up ahead. The lorry, which is blocking the carriageway, and the minibus on its side. I radio in. Say I'll need fire and rescue too and some support from traffic management. That it will take some time to get the road open again.

And then I see the ball rolling towards me down the hard shoulder. It's large and orange and takes me by surprise. It's not the usual hazard we come across on the M62, though it's at least easily avoided. As I pull over at the scene and take my helmet off, I see that there are other balls rolling around the carriageway. Several people have got out of their cars and are surrounding the wreckage of the minibus, shouting and trying to get in. There could still be injured people inside. The paramedics haven't arrived yet. I will need to get to them first.

I am running now. A sense that this is bad, really fucking bad, is gripping me. The minibus has been completely mangled in the crash. I'm not sure I'll be able to get in or get anyone out until the fire crews get here. I call out that I'm a police officer, ask people to step aside and return to their cars. One woman is crying. A man still has his mobile in his hand; perhaps he's the one who called the emergency services. One of the back doors is slightly open. The bottom one, lying on the motorway. That is where the balls have rolled out from. I know I have to try to get inside, even if there's a risk the whole thing blows.

I stopped the film.

'Shut your eyes or look away,' I said to Emily and Jules. 'I mean it, I don't want you to see this. No one should have to see this. It'll be bad enough just hearing it. For me. Please.'

Emily shut her eyes. Jules looked down at the floor. I pressed play.

I get down on my belly and shine my torch inside. I immediately wish I hadn't. There are bodies and blood and hair. Lots of long hair. All in such a tangled mess that it's impossible to work out how many there are.

'Can anyone hear me?' I call out. I think I can detect a moan coming from the front but it's hard to be sure. I get straight back on the radio. Tell them it's a major incident with mass casualties involved. I listen as more ambulances and fire crews are scrambled.

Help is coming, I tell myself. You don't have to do this on your own. But for now, it's just me, and I have to try to save anyone who is alive in there. I start to crawl into the mangled wreckage, calling all the time. Desperately hoping for a response. I take the first arm I get to, a tiny bare arm with blood running down it, and feel for a pulse. There isn't one. I move on, unable to process what is happening. Tiny wrist after tiny wrist. Like lifeless dolls rather than human beings. They are dressed in P.E. kits, which somehow makes it even worse. And then my palm rests on something hard and metallic. I look down. It's a trophy. They won something today, these girls. And now they are dead. I hear sirens and crawl back out of the minibus. Two paramedics have arrived.

'It's not good,' I tell them, in the understatement of the year. 'The kids I could get to are all dead. I haven't tried the cab yet or gone to the lorry driver.'

The oldest man nods and gets down on his front to look, as I had. The first fire crew arrive, carrying cutting equipment, and get to work on the cab door. I go to the crash barrier and crouch to vomit onto the grass verge. I stand up, wipe my mouth with the back of my hand and look around. Another paramedic crew have brought the lorry driver out. He doesn't look too bad. I go back to my bike to get a couple of cones and that is what I do. Put out fucking traffic cones around the scene and pick netballs up from the carriageway and put them back in the sack which is lying in the road. I was the first responder who didn't know how to respond. I walk back to my bike, my head bowed as they bring out the first body.

'Faz, we need a break,' Jules called out. 'Some strong teas would be good too.' He nodded and left the studio without the usual spring in his step.

I realised for the first time that my body was shaking. That my knuckles were still white, my fingertips pressing hard into my palms.

'Fucking hell,' said Jules, putting her arm around me. 'I can't even imagine.'

I wasn't sure if she had looked up at any point. I hoped not. I turned to see Emily sitting beside me, her head bowed. She would have opened her eyes at some point. I was sure of it.

'I'm sorry you both had to sit through that,' I said.

'Will you quit apologising?' said Jules. 'Nothing is your fault. None of that was your fault. No one could have saved them.'

I nodded. On some deep level I knew that was true. They'd said so at the inquest. The only person who'd been alive when the paramedics arrived was the teacher in the driver's seat and it had taken fire crews with high-tech cutting equipment to get her out. Although she died before they got her to hospital. The teacher next to her was already dead, as were all the girls.

'I could never get past it,' I said. 'It was like part of me died on that motorway along with them. I don't mean that glibly. I simply can't remember laughing since then. Everything people talked about seemed so fucking trivial.

'I still see it and smell it and feel it, too. Not a day has gone past when I haven't thought about it. Not a night. And I didn't really drink until after that. The odd one after work, but that was it. I didn't have a problem with it. And I'm deeply ashamed of what you're going to see next. But I couldn't find another way of dealing with it.'

Faz returned with three strong teas. There was sugar in mine. I normally couldn't stand sugar in tea, but I decided not to say anything.

'Suzi sent chocolates this time,' he said, depositing three boxes of Heroes in front of us.

'Thanks,' I mumbled, knowing she was trying to tell me something that I still wasn't ready to hear.

'I used to bloody love Double Deckers,' said Jules, taking a dinky one from her box.

'I was more of a Crunchie guy myself,' I said, picking up a mini version.

'But that's the one nobody wants,' said Emily.

'As I said before, I like to buck trends,' I replied. 'What about you?' I asked.

'This,' she said, holding up a Wispa. 'Because it's got the most chocolate in. Simples.'

I glanced back at the box. 'Share good times' it said. But it seemed to work for sharing bad times too. I held my box out to Faz.

'Oooh, don't mind if I do,' he said, taking a couple of Twirls before heading back towards his sound booth. 'Just hit play when you guys are ready to carry on.'

'How old were they?' asked Emily.

'Eleven and twelve. They were all in Year Seven,' I replied. 'They'd been to Wakefield for a netball tournament. They'd won. They were on their way home to Halifax. Just didn't quite make it.'

Emily nodded sadly.

'They didn't even live long enough to have a Harry,' she said.

I shook my head slowly.

'No, they didn't.'

'What caused it?' asked Jules.

'The lorry driver had fallen asleep at the wheel when he ploughed into the back of them. There was nothing the teacher driving could have done.'

My voice broke as I finished. The therapist I'd seen afterwards said I had Post Traumatic Stress Disorder. I'd told her that was bollocks. That I wasn't going to claim to be a victim when so many people had suffered so much more than me.

I knew now that she'd been right. But it was too late. I'd created more victims and more grieving relatives. The whole thing was still going. I reached out and pressed play, determined to get this over with.

I'm standing in my uniform looking in the mirror. I want to check it's spotless. To ensure that when I pay my respects, I do not let myself down. And do not let them down any more than I already have done..

It's the last of the girls' funerals today. Olivia, her name is. She played wing attack in their netball team. I can reel off their names and positions like they were the England football team.

I asked for permission to attend the funerals, not wanting to add to the families' distress. Officially, I'm still signed off work sick. My therapist had backed me, saying it may be cathartic.

So, here I am, two weeks later, about to go to the last of the funerals. I haven't found it cathartic in the least. The emotion has been wrung out of me each time but only to be replaced with a fresh well of it, ready for the next one. I am mired in trauma and shock and grief. And my own inability to make a difference. That's why I'd joined the force; to help people and make a difference. Well, that and the chance to ride a bike for a living. But it turned out I was not as useful as I'd hoped I would be.

I drive to the church, the same one the majority of the funerals have been held at. It feels like a familiar ritual now. I keep a respectful distance, sit on a pew towards the back. Bow my head and pretend to pray when others do. After the service, I wait to approach the parents. To say how sorry I am for their loss. Olivia's mum grasps my hand tightly. I can't bring myself to tell her that this hand tried to take her daughter's pulse while she lay dead in the wreckage. That sometimes, in the middle of the night, I sit bolt upright in bed because I have dreamt that there was a pulse there after all and I simply walked away.

'Thank you,' she says. 'Thank you for everything you and your colleagues did.'

I nod, give a little smile and walk away. Still feeling her daughter's tiny wrist in my hand.

Emily leant over and put her hand on my shoulder.

'You OK?' she asked.

Her, a seventeen-year-old girl, asking if I, the former police officer, was OK. It was all kinds of wrong. But it was also all kinds of lovely. I nodded.

'Will you press play for me?' I asked. 'I think my hand's shaking too much to do it.'

She nodded. The film continued.

I go home that afternoon and sit, staring at the wall. Families and loved ones have been left to grieve in private. And the rest of us? We're supposed to get back to our own lives. I have two choices: take the extra time off sick they had offered me or go back to work as if I'm fine. Neither of the options appeal to me.

All I know is that I don't want to see it any more. Want to blot out every image, every sound from my head. So, I do what I know people do when they want to blot stuff out. I reach for alcohol. There is no lager in the house, but there's a bottle of vodka in the kitchen cupboard. Mum kept it there for emergencies, whatever that meant. I figure this constitutes an emergency. I take the bottle from cupboard, pour some in a glass and add some Diet Coke from the fridge, so it doesn't look bad if anyone comes in.

And I take the first drink. When the glass is drained, I feel a slight warmth inside, but the images are still clear in my head. I pour a second glass. And a third. When oblivion comes, there's no Diet Coke left in the fridge.

The film skipped forward. In each shot there was a constant, the bottle or glass in my hand. The glazed look in my eyes. I was chasing oblivion. Sometimes I found it. Sometimes I silenced the sounds, blurred the pictures. It gave me momentary relief and that was the best I could hope for.

I turned up for duty once still over the limit. I was sent to a doctor and signed off work on mental health grounds. That was a joke to me. I'd have been more worried about the officers who witnessed stuff like that and didn't turn to drink or drugs. Who went through it all robotically, storing it up inside. Because one day those guys were going to explode and when they did, God help the people who were on the end of it.

I went back to the therapist. She was the one who diagnosed me with PTSD. It meant nothing to me. A collection of letters which meant I was fucked up. I didn't see how talking about it could help. The very last thing I wanted to do was talk about it. So, I stopped going to sessions, drank more, chased oblivion. Until the point my boss called me into his office.

I like Sgt Lockwood. Always have done. Firm but fair, that's what they say about him and it's true. I knock on his door, very glad of the fair bit because I know he's going to be firm.

He calls for me to enter. Manages a hint of a smile and tells me to sit down. I don't want to but I'm not going to argue with him either.

'There are officers who cope with some of the things we get to see in this job like they're water off a duck's back. You're not one of them

and neither am I. The difference between letting it screw up your career and finding a way through is acknowledging the problem and accepting help.'

He pauses, clearly expecting me to say something.

'Talking about it makes things worse. That's why I stopped going.'

'I get that,' he replies, 'and maybe it's a bit too soon right now. But if you're going to try to self-medicate with alcohol, you're not going to stay in this job for long.'

Another pause. I can't think of anything to fill it.

'It gives me no pleasure to give you a written warning, Carl. But you cannot turn up for work in an inebriated state, and you should definitely not attempt to go out on your bike in one. If there's any further repeat of an incident like this, I will have no option but to bring disciplinary proceedings for gross misconduct which would result in you losing your job.'

He gets up and walks a few steps over to me.

'Please don't make me do that, Carl. You're far too good an officer for us to lose. Take the help. Take some time. Only come back when you're ready.'

'That's the guy who spoke at your service, isn't it?' asked Jules. 'Jeez, he gave good advice.'

'I should have listened to him,' I replied. 'Maybe I wouldn't be here if I had.'

'So, what did you do instead?'

I hit play.

There are shots of me drinking. Lots of them. I try to do it on my days between shifts but am not always able to abstain the rest of the time. When I fuck up again and go into work still half-cut, I remember Sgt Lockwood's words and take a handwritten resignation letter with me, so I don't force him to do it himself.

There is a leaving do. It's weird to watch it as I have no recollection of it from the first time around. I lie, of course. Tell people I'm going to work as a courier while saving for some big motorcycling road trips. Around the World in 80 Days. That sort of thing. People pat me on the back, say things like 'good for you' and 'do it while you're young, before you have responsibilities'. I have no intention of doing it, but I'm not going to tell them that. I want them to think this is a positive choice I've made, not that I was forced into it by my demons.

Only Sgt Lockwood knows that's not the case. He joins us for one drink, non-alcoholic. He looks me in the eye and shakes his head.

'It's not too late,' he says. 'There's still time to get yourself sorted. You'll be welcome back if you do.'

We both know that's not going to happen though. When you're on a downward spiral like I am, it's all snakes taking you further down. There are no ladders to help you back up.

'Thanks,' I say as someone presses another drink into my hand.

'Is that it?' asked Emily. 'Only I can't imagine you had many significant moments delivering people's chicken nuggets.'

'Oh, you'd be surprised,' I said, trying to make a joke. And then stopped, because I knew I needed to warn them about what they were going to see next.

'There's just one more scene,' I said. 'You probably won't like me afterwards and I wouldn't blame you for that.'

It's an item on the news which triggers me. Something about the parents of one of the girls who died in the minibus crash still campaigning for changes in the way lorry drivers' hours are monitored. I stop making myself a sandwich and listen. Their older daughter now has school-age children of her own and they're terrified that the same thing could happen to them. And that's when it hits me. It's a life sentence, losing a child like that. They will never recover from it.

I take the vodka bottle from the cupboard. I hide it behind cereal packets so that Lewis doesn't see it. I take my first shot neat. And the second. The third gets mixed with orange juice because it's all I have in the fridge. It's only as I shut the door that I remember I have an optician's appointment that afternoon. It's too late to cancel now and I don't do no-shows. Never have done. Besides, I know I need new glasses because I've been noticing my vision isn't as sharp when riding at night.

I start to get my things together. It's less than ten minutes into town and I'll be fine. Absolutely fine. Besides, if I get pulled over by the police, I'll probably know the officer and they're hardly going to breathalyse a former colleague.

I'm pulling on my boots and picking up my helmet when I hear Lewis shout from the landing.

'Are you going into town? Only I need to get to the job centre, and I'll end up sanctioned if I'm late again.'

'So, get the bloody bus,' I say.

'The buses are crap. Anyway, I've just checked and the next one isn't due for half an hour now, so I'll be well late.'

It's my hesitation which is fatal. Lewis seizes on it, comes down the stairs two steps at a time.

'Thanks, bro. Drop me off anywhere. You're a lifesaver.'

There is a second where I could argue with him. Put my foot down. But my brain is still throwing the word 'lifesaver' around in my head. Trying it out for size in case there is any way I can still make it fit.

Lewis pats me on the back. I open the front door. My bike is outside waiting for us.

The film ended there. We all knew what happened next. The studio was silent. If it had been school, a teacher would have said how disappointed they were in me. As it was, the silence spoke louder than words.

I stood up, still not daring to look at either of the others. I started heading for the door. And then they came at me. Both of them at once. Not with malice, arms flailing, hands pushing me away, but with love. Arms closing around me. Hands holding me tight.

'Why didn't you bloody tell us?' said Jules.

'I could hardly fess up after having a go at you for jumping off the bridge, could I?'

'Looks like we've all done stupid things,' said Jules.

'Apart from me,' pointed out Emily.

'Yes, apart from Mother bloody Teresa over there,' agreed Jules. 'It's time to forgive each other and ourselves.'

'That's what Suzi said in the Room of Reflection.'

'Wasn't that in Harry Potter?' asked Emily.

'That was the Room of Requirement. It's a long story,' I said.

'Well, you can tell it to us over tea,' said Jules. 'I think we could all do with some more Elsie in our lives. And more pasta, obviously.'

19

JULES

I woke up feeling sick knowing it was my turn. There was a lifetime of significant moments to get through, and it certainly wasn't going to be Disney. It struck me that the older you got, the more mistakes you had to hide. Emily hadn't kept anything from us because she had no secrets. Carl had held back so much pain and guilt that it had practically exploded out of him at the end. And now they were going to find out about my sad little life. My secrets, my lies. And the fact that my whole life had been one big one.

But there was also a weird frisson of excitement because I was going to see Nina again. For the first time in, what, almost thirty years, I would see her face, hear her voice, be transported back to a time when she was everything and we had our whole lives in front of us. And that bit, at least, I did want to see.

* * *

The others were already lined up outside the studio when I got down there.

'Bloody hell, this is like the time people queued around the block to see *Beetlejuice* when I was a teenager. I hate to tell you this, but I do not look as good as Winona Ryder and, as you've already seen, I'm not up there with Tim Burton in the director stakes.'

'It's OK. I'm expecting more of a gritty northern indie film full of humour and heartache,' said Carl.

'And I'm here for your uni days because I won't get to do that and I want to know what they're like,' added Emily.

I smiled at her.

'Come on in, then. I believe front-row seats are still available,' I said, opening the door to the studio.

'Hey guys,' said Faz, his smile and demeanour back to full-on, in-your-face brightness. 'Ready for Jules Unplugged?'

'Unhinged and unleashed, more like,' I said. 'Are you familiar with perimenopause symptoms?'

Faz did one of his over-the-top laughs with accompanying hand-flapping gestures.

'It's ready to roll when you are,' he said. 'I hope you've brought snacks because there's a lot there. *Oppenheimer* had nothing on this baby.'

Carl and Emily laughed and I groaned inwardly. I remembered what Suzi said about them not having much footage of me as a child. So, I wasn't surprised when my reel started with a series of still photographs of my childhood, which Faz had stuck some upbeat backing track to.

'Oh my God, you were so cute,' said Emily.

'And this makes me feel so old,' I said. 'It needs subtitles saying this person was born before the advent of modern technology.'

The birthday photos of me looking awkward standing or sitting behind a cake were coming to an end, and as soon as we passed the eighteenth birthday one – me in full goth make-up and dyed hair appearing utterly underwhelmed by the pink birthday cake in front of me – I knew what was coming next.

But even that knowledge couldn't prepare me for the shock of seeing Nina's face on screen. The laughter that emanated from her. The brightness that radiated within.

'Is that Nina?' asked Carl. 'The one who gave you the knitted toilet-roll holder?'

'It is,' I said, thinking how she would have laughed at that description of her.

'You never said how beautiful she was,' said Emily. And I realised I hadn't. Probably because I was too scared to remember. And too worried about giving my feelings away.

She is standing at the open door of our flat in halls, suitcase still in hand. It's brown and battered and she's carrying a guitar case in the other hand.

'Hi, I'm Nina,' she says.

'Sorry,' I reply. 'If you're auditioning for The Sound of Music, *you've got the wrong place.'*

There's a second when I worry I shouldn't have said it. That it was cheeky or downright rude. And then she starts laughing. A delightful, deep-throated giggle which is clearly genuine but also highly infectious. So now I'm laughing too, and we stand there like this until finally we both stop and draw breath.

'Sorry, probably shouldn't have said that. I'm Jules by the way, and I'm an expert at speaking first and thinking later.'

'Not at all, thanks for breaking the ice,' she replies. 'I was worried my flatmates might be swotty and serious and now I know one of them definitely isn't.'

'And if the others turn out to be, we can be the funny rebels together and really piss them off,' I say.

She laughs again and I step aside to let her in. She smells good as she passes me. Not of overpowering Dewberry body spray from The Body Shop, like me, but somehow naturally fresh.

Nina puts her case and guitar down.

'Are you on a music course?' I ask.

'God no. I just enjoy playing. I'm studying English Literature. How about you?'

'Biology.'

'Cool. What do you want to do after?'

'Probably a zoology Masters. I applied for the zoology degree course but didn't get on, so thought I'd do it the long way round and get to spend an extra year in Bristol.'

'Where are you from?' she asks.

'Halifax.'

'I've never been there,' she says.

'You haven't missed much. What about you?'

'Cardiff.'

'You haven't got a strong accent.'

'No. I'm adopted. Originally from Somerset and my adoptive parents are originally from Herefordshire. So, it's a bit of a mish-mash.'

I nod, aware that we already seem to know an awful lot about each other and she's only been here two minutes.

'Anyway. Pick a room. There are four and as it's first come, first served, I've already moved my stuff in, but you get to choose next,' I say.

'Have you nabbed the best one?' she says with a smile.

'No. The complete opposite. Mine doesn't have a window.'

'What? Why did you choose it then?'

'Because I love lie-ins and the daylight coming through the curtains always wakes me up, so this way I haven't got to worry.'

She grins.

'Can I see it?'

'Sure. Although if you're a fan of pretty boy bands, you might want to look away.'

I lead her through to my room and put the light on, illuminating Robert Smith, Morrisey and Echo and The Bunnymen in the process. Nina takes one look and screams.

'Jesus, they're not that scary,' I say.

'They're my favourite bands too,' she says, barely able to contain herself. 'I thought I was going to be the weirdo and my flatmates would all be into Take That.'

'No way! We can be goth girls together. We're gonna have the best time.'

Nina smiles at me.

'We absolutely are,' she says.

Emily reaches over and presses pause.

'She's so lovely, I can't believe you lost touch with her. She's like a BFF. Also, how come you're not a zookeeper?'

I shrugged.

'Because I'm brilliant at screwing things up.'

'What even was your job?' asked Emily.

I sighed heavily.

'I was an environmental health officer.'

'Why?' asked Emily.

'That's a good question. You'll soon find out.'

The film restarted with a huge vista of the Clifton Suspension Bridge bathed in sunlight, the mist lifting off the Clifton Gorge below. It took my breath away, even now. It was still my favourite place in the world. Not that I was at all well-travelled, but even if I had been, I couldn't imagine ever finding somewhere to match it. The cameras started zooming in. After a while, I could make out two figures running along the bridge. It was us.

We can barely run for laughing. It had been Nina's idea. We'd read that on the day the bridge was opened to the public, a twenty-three-year-old woman had raced a young man to be the first person to cross it – and she'd won. So, Nina had challenged me to do the same race with the prize of an ice cream for the victor. Which is why I'm now running at full pelt (which admittedly isn't that fast) in an attempt to recreate that moment.

'It said she'd gathered up her skirts first,' I gasped between breaths. 'But it didn't mention anything about running in DMs.'

Nina laughs. I live for that sound. And to see the way she throws back her head as she does it. Her long, dark hair is streaming out behind her as she runs. I stumble and she instinctively grabs my hand. We continue running and she doesn't let go. The sunlight is bathing everything in gold. The trees along the gorge are dazzling shades of orange and I think this might be the most perfect moment of my life. I try to drink it all in, in case it doesn't ever get any better than this. I want to be able to shut my eyes and see it, hear the joy in her laughter, taste the excitement on my lips.

And as we're approaching the far end of the bridge, I wish it were longer still so that this moment could go on forever. Even though I'm knackered and will need about an hour to recover from this, I'd keep on running if I could.

Nina lets go of my hand and sprints the last twenty yards, because of course, she's been holding back to stop me feeling bad. But also, she's still bloody competitive and would never stoop to letting me win.

We collapse on the railings on the other side. A tangled mess of hair and sweaty limbs. It is a few moments before I can even muster enough breath to speak.

'You were coasting that, weren't you?' I ask.

'Just pacing myself. I always like to keep something in reserve.'

'Well, thank you for doing me the honour of not publicly humiliating me by running it in half the time.'

'The honour was all mine,' she says. 'You were a noble opponent.'

'Noble or knobbly?' I ask, looking down at my knees. She laughs again and elbows me in the ribs.

'There's nothing wrong with your legs,' she says.

'No one's ever said that to me before.'

'How many people have you shown your legs to?' she asks.

'Probably not enough to get a representative sample,' I reply.

'There you go, then. Spoken as a true scientist. Your legs are fine specimens, and I'll challenge anyone who says otherwise to a race across this bridge.'

'How very gallant of you,' I say with a laugh. 'Now, I do believe I owe you an ice cream for your victory.'

'After the museum, please,' she says. 'I want to go to the museum first.'

The museum is in the visitor centre, a modern-looking oval stone building on the Leigh Woods side we ran to. It's bright, airy and welcoming, rather than the dark and musty ones I went to on school trips. Even the museums here are better, it seems. A life-size cardboard figure of Isambard Kingdom Brunel stands in the foyer. Nina walks up to the start of the huge timeline on the wall with accompanying photos and information.

'He was only twenty-four when he won the competition to design the bridge,' she calls out.

'No pressure to achieve greatness in six years' time then,' I say.

'He was dead by the time it was built though,' says Nina.

'There you go,' I say. 'That sounds more like my life trajectory. It doesn't matter if none of my plans get off the ground while I'm alive, I may achieve greatness after I die.'

The light dims on Nina's face.

'What?' I ask.

'I don't want to think about either of us dying. I want to live forever.'

'Ooohh, not sure about that,' I say. 'I'd get awfully smelly and wrinkly. You'd basically be living with a dried prune.'

'Who says I'll be living with you?' she asks, the smile returning to her face.

'Once flatmates, always flatmates,' I say. 'I mean, I'm unlikely to find anyone else who'll put up with me, aren't I? And who will sing "Lovesong" by The Cure with me at one in the morning.'

Nina smiles.

'Fair point,' she says. 'And I'll happily put up with your prune-like appearance.'

'Excellent. That's sorted then,' I say. And it does feel like a sort of betrothal. As if we've made a binding verbal contract. One that is beyond my wildest dreams.

I continue, ahead of Nina, along the timeline until I get to Friday 8 May 1885 and the heading 'Sarah Ann Henley'. She was a twenty-three-year-old barmaid, engaged to be married to a young porter on the Great Western Railway. Until after a big row, he wrote to her to break off the engagement and, in distress, she went up to the Clifton Suspension Bridge, climbed up to the parapet and hurled herself over the railings.

She somersaulted through the air, her huge petticoats acting as a parachute in the strong winds to slow her descent and she was blown to the side of the river, landing in the deep mud on the bank, miraculously without major injuries.

'Nina, you have to read this,' I say, tugging her arm. I watch her eyes open wide as she follows the story.

'That's incredible. Did you read what happened after? The doctor asked a horse-drawn cab to take her to hospital, but the driver refused because the mud would have messed up his cab. People had a go at him in the local newspaper and everything.'

'I mean, I've been refused when I've been eating a kebab, which is

fair enough because they are smelly and I do tend to drop stuff out of them.'

'Yeah, but the doctor told him she could die and he apparently said he didn't care.'

'Well, he was just a complete bastard then, wasn't he?'

'Absolutely,' she says.

'What happened to her?' I ask. We both edge forwards and read on together. She received numerous proposals of marriage afterwards and lived to be eighty-five.

'Nice work from her petticoats then,' I say. 'Perhaps I shall take to wearing petticoats to lectures just in case.'

'Can I make it clear that if you were covered in mud, I would absolutely still carry you to hospital?'

I look at her. She means it too. I have never experienced anything like this before. Such a rush of feelings. I don't know what to do with them. What can I do with them? We can't become an 'us', can we? This may be 1993, but Halifax isn't ready for this. My parents certainly aren't. They are of the 'it's not natural' generation who tut when there is any mention of homosexuality on TV. They would laugh if I told them, assuming it was a joke. Or set fire to my belongings in the back garden if they realised it wasn't.

'Come on,' I say. 'Let's finish up here and go and get your ice cream.'

I could feel Emily and Carl's eyes looking at me as if seeing me for the first time. They knew, I was sure of it. But I still couldn't bring myself to tell them. Still felt the need to distract.

'Can you imagine if an Uber driver did that today?' I said. 'Left a woman for dead because they didn't want her to mess up their car.'

'They'd be, like, majorly cancelled,' said Emily.

'The driver almost was at the time. He wrote a letter to the local newspaper making his defence. Saying he'd just spent all his money on getting his cab cleaned and that he legally couldn't accept a fare if it would leave his cab unfit for public hire. Reckoned his kiddies would have died if he'd lost his licence and his livelihood.'

'He had a fair point,' said Carl. 'And it wasn't his fault she threw herself off the bridge, was it?'

I frowned at him.

'Are we ending with the same argument we started with?' I asked.

'No. Of course not. Sorry. Carry on.'

There was no footage from any lectures at university. Which was probably because they were the most insignificant moments of my time there. Every clip we saw involved Nina. My significant other. Always we were laughing, dancing, listening to music, going to gigs, painstakingly applying make-up in bathroom mirrors, though the whole process felt pointless to me, because no amount of make-up could give me the radiant, natural beauty Nina possessed.

When it was time for the leavers' ball the first year we were there, we watched from afar as students headed off in frocks of various styles and colours. They were all pretty hideous to us. Nina promised that when it was our turn, she would take me shopping for something better. And that in the meantime, we would go window shopping to see what took our fancy.

'Where are we going?' I ask. Nina is dragging me down side streets I didn't know existed, into an area of Bristol I don't think we've ever been to before.

'This is the indie shopping area,' she says. 'We've been looking in all the wrong places. I did some searches on the computers in the library and found this place.'

She pulls me around the next corner, and I stop dead in my tracks. It's a quaint old shopfront and there, taking pride of place in the window display, is a huge black and red gothic ballgown. I gasp out loud.

'I know,' Nina says, jumping up and down by my side. 'I knew you'd love it. And the gowns are all for hire, so we might actually be able to afford them if we got jobs and saved up.'

'What about you?' I ask. 'Is there one you like?'

'Come inside, I'll show you,' she says.

She walks breezily into the shop; she has way more confidence than me.

'Hi, I've seen a purple and black velvet dress on your website,' she says to the assistant. 'And my friend would like to try on the dress in the window.'

'Yes, certainly,' she says, 'come through to the changing rooms.'

'We can't try them on,' I hiss.

'Why not?' Nina asks.

'I'll look crap in mine, for a start.'

'No, you won't,' she replies. 'I'm going to get you to see how good you can look.'

The shop assistant gets out a stunning crushed velvet dress from the rail which Nina holds up against her.

'I'd just stroke it all night,' she says with a laugh.

The assistant returns with my dress from the window. Nina is practically bursting with excitement.

'I'll leave you ladies to try them on,' says the assistant. We practically run into our individual changing rooms. I'm hot and sweaty and I fear I'll get stuck in the dress but somehow, I squeeze into it.

'Do you want lacing up at the back?' calls Nina.

'Yes please. Although it might be a little like squeezing a sausage into a fancy skin.'

She ignores my comment. I feel the touch of her fingers on my back and it's all I can do not to gasp out loud. When she's finished, she pulls back the curtain. We both stare at each other for a moment. She looks stunning, of course. The velvet dress fits her perfectly. But it's true that Nina looks stunning in absolutely everything.

'Look at you,' she says. 'I never knew you had such beautiful shoulders.'

I turn to look in the mirror, and I don't recognise the woman I see. My shoulders are nice, and the dress gives me an amazing cleavage without making me look huge. She steps back and grins at me in the mirror.

'Cinderella shall go to the ball,' she says.

'She'd better get a job and start saving up then,' I reply. When I'm back inside the curtained changing cubicle, the realisation hits. I am fucked. Completely fucked. Because I don't want Prince Charming, I want her. I'm never going to be able to forget what I'm feeling at this moment. And no one else will ever come close.

'Wow, you looked well fit in that dress,' said Emily, breaking the spell and bringing me back to reality.

'I like to think everyone has one moment in their life when they looked half-decent.'

'Did you hire the dress?' she asked. 'I want to see the ball.'

'Patience, child,' I said. 'We've got other stuff to see first.'

Carl looked at me. I knew what he was thinking. Why hadn't I told him? Especially when I'd been blathering on to him about how he could tell me anything and *Pride* being one of my favourite films. I felt bad I hadn't been able to confide in him, but the truth was that even here in the fucking afterlife, it had still felt too big to share. To be fair, it wasn't the revelation itself that I found most difficult now. It was the fact that I had hidden it all these years and lived a pathetic sham life which made it worse. I was so stuck in the bloody eighties that it was embarrassing. I knew what was coming next, but I was going to press play all the same.

I'm writing a letter. Not 'a' letter, actually. It's 'the' letter. The one

I've been planning in my head ever since I'd first set eyes on Nina. Because I'd known even then I'd never have the courage to voice my feelings in person. The fear of losing Nina as a friend was too great. I could cope with my unrequited love for her if I could still be her best friend. What I could not cope with was the thought of losing her entirely. And I had no doubt that's what would happen if she didn't reciprocate my feelings. It would be way too awkward to ever go back to being friends and flatmates. One of us would have to move out and we'd still see each other around the campus, and it would all be so unbearably embarrassing.

But now, on the day of the graduation ball, my feelings are shifting. Because, despite what everyone says about staying best friends when you leave uni, I know the reality is different. That life and geography and partners and children and work and new friends will all conspire against that. We will drift. It's inevitable. And I can't help fearing the drift will be almost as bad as a complete loss. The idea of reaching the point where we haven't seen each other or spoken for months. That our friendship becomes a once-a-year catch-up in Bristol and then every two years, then five, then, 'I'm really sorry but I just can't make it now with kids/partner/pets/career/whatever'.

So, I'm writing a letter. A proper old-fashioned love letter where I pour out my feelings, which I'm planning to put under her door before I leave early tomorrow. That way there will be no embarrassment if she doesn't feel the same way as I do. And our friendship will be severed here in an 'at least it's all over with in one go' manner, rather than face that horrible drift apart over time. I never want to be an inconvenience, so I've decided it's all or nothing. I win the only person I've ever loved and ever will love, or I leave empty handed. The stakes are that high, which is why the letter must be good. From the heart, honest and to the point. It's the most important letter I'll ever write in my life, I'm in no doubt of that.

When I've finished, I shall store it somewhere safe and get ready to go to the ball. Tonight will be ours, and I shall treasure every moment of it. And tomorrow, once she's read it, she'll decide whether she's to be the biggest part of my life or disappear from it entirely.

When I'm finally satisfied with the letter, I seal it into an envelope, write her name on the front with a big swirly 'N' and leave it on my desk for the morning.

I stand in my room, gazing at myself in the mirror. The dress is everything I dreamt it would be. I'm that woman I didn't recognise in the shop. The one Nina gazed admiringly at. It was worth all the hours of waitressing and washing dishes to be able to pay for hiring it. I take one last look around. Everything is packed, ready for a quick exit tomorrow. All my worldly goods, including my knitted toilet-roll holder, in one giant suitcase and a rucksack. Nina has already offered to take my dress back to the shop with hers, as her dad isn't collecting her until tomorrow evening.

When I open my bedroom door, she's already standing there in her beautiful purple gown. She looks stunning. As stunning as I've ever seen her. She grins at me.

'You look amazing.'

'Says you,' I reply. But I can't keep the smile off my face, the glow from warming my heart, as we clatter downstairs in our lace-up boots and head off towards the venue.

The hotel terrace overlooks the Clifton Suspension Bridge. I couldn't have picked a more perfect place if I'd tried. The evening is balmy; I'm already worrying about sweating too much in my dress. But nothing is going to spoil this night, I'm determined of this. Lots of the other students are milling about in their finery. Most of them in boring off-the-shelf tuxedos and black evening gowns. Some turn to look at us and smile as we pass. For most of my life, I've known those smiles have been mocking or pitying but no one is smiling at us like that this evening. They are smiling at Nina, who has always looked incredible, but most of them probably haven't noticed it because it's been hidden under baggy black jumpers and her long dark hair. But this evening her beauty is shining so brightly that no one can fail to notice. And even I, her shorter, dumpier friend, has scrubbed up beyond anyone's expectations. I hear a few people say 'wow' as we walk across the terrace.

'They're talking about you,' says Nina.

'Only because I normally look such a state.'

'Actually, it's because they haven't taken the time to notice you before. And now they feel a bit stupid about that.'

I look across at her.

'That's one of my favourite things about you,' I say. 'That you always manage to turn everything into a positive.'

'Perhaps I just tell the truth, which sometimes you don't recognise.'

She says it sweetly, gently. Like she says everything. But I know this is her way of trying to get me to believe in myself. To be able to survive in the big wide world without her.

We go inside. It all looks grand and sophisticated and I wonder, not for the first time, how a kid from a working-class family in Halifax ended up here. And what is going to happen to that kid once she is removed from this world and these people. I have no idea if I can make it on my own. If I can even survive away from here. These last three years have been everything. And Nina has been so much a part of that. The thought of having to prise myself from her tomorrow and leave all of this behind is starting to make me feel a bit sick.

'I need a drink,' I say.

* * *

An hour and several drinks later, I've nibbled at various things which I haven't been entirely sure what they are. And now we are standing at the edge of the dancefloor, watching as everyone dances to 'Ooh Aah...

Just a Little Bit' by Gina G and wondering how we could have spent three years in the company of people who would enjoy such a thing.

'Jesus,' I say. 'If this is the future talent pool, I worry for this country.'

Nina laughs.

'Maybe they'll grow out of it.'

'Maybe they'll get worse and all intelligent life in the UK will cease to exist,' I reply.

I'm about to suggest we get another drink or take a breather outside when a familiar intro starts. I turn to Nina.

'Did you request this?'

'Yep, because I knew they'd play a pile of crap most of the time and I wanted us to be able to dance in these gowns at least once.'

She grabs my hand and pulls me into the middle of the dancefloor as most of the other people are leaving and Robert Smith starts singing about moving like cagey tigers. The world closes in around us. We simply dance and sing, smiling and laughing and trying to create a private grungy mosh pit in the middle of this posh hotel. I want this moment to go on forever, I want the song to never end, our limbs to be swirling around each other like this for all eternity. When the song does end, when fucking Take That come on, we head straight for the ladies' loos to save ourselves.

We fall inside in a giggling tangle of bodies. The cubicles are empty. It's just us. My lips are still mouthing the words, my skin glowing, my body tingling with aliveness, and I realise suddenly that this is it. My life may have just peaked. This could be the last time we are alone together like this before the real world gets its claws into us and tears us in different directions. They have been the best three years of my life, and I don't want them to end. I have to do something now, anything to try to prolong this intensity, to prevent the air escaping entirely from us. I lean into Nina, take her face in my hands and kiss her. Softly, delicately, breathing the air back into our relationship.

Ensuring our hearts keep pumping, that we are not going to let this thing die. She pulls away from me.

'No!'

It's her voice. I see her lips move but I don't want to believe that she said it. There is fear in her eyes; a frown is creasing her brow.

'Jules, no!' she says again. And she is gone. Running out of the door. Fleeing the scene of the crime. The crime I committed because I could not bear to be torn from her. To risk her not replying to my letter and me never seeing her again. I thought I could seize the moment, do something brave and bold that may change our lives forever, but instead I've ruined it. Ruined everything. I break down in sobs and rush into the cubicle, locking the door behind me. If she comes back, I don't want her seeing me like this. I don't want anyone seeing me like this. I try to engage my brain to work out what to do. It only offers one suggestion. Run. Run and never come back.

I open the cubicle and flee the toilets. Tear through the hotel with my head bowed, hoping to avoid eye contact with anyone. When I get outside, I see the Clifton Suspension Bridge lit up against the gathering dusk. It is safe. It is home. It's where I'm heading. I feel sure Nina won't have gone there and I'm glad of that. She may have gone back to our flat. She may still be in the hotel. But I'll be OK at the bridge. No one will recognise me there. I can bawl my eyes out in privacy. The fresh air seems to jolt my brain into action, and I set off running. Once I'm out of sight of the hotel, I slow to a fast walk. Mainly because I'm not fit enough to run all the way but also because I don't want Nina to have to take this dress back reeking of sweat.

The bridge is calling me closer. Beckoning me to shelter in its safety. I watch it growing larger as I approach. Its size and reach comforting and familiar. It's only when I'm standing on it, clinging onto the railings as I'm feeling a little unsteady, that I think of Sarah Ann Henley standing here over one hundred years before me. Broken hearted after being rejected by her love. All her hopes and dreams for the future in tatters and feeling so utterly wretched that she was driven to do something desperate.

I climb up onto the railings, look down into the gorge below me in the gathering darkness. It would be so easy. All so very easy to put a stop to the pain.

'You OK, love?'

The man's voice comes from behind me. I turn to see a cab pulled up, the face of a bearded middle-aged man sticking out of the open window.

'Yes,' I reply, my voice shaky.

'Whoever he is, he's not worth it.'

I think for a moment about telling him that it's a 'she', actually. And that she is worth everything. But I don't want to make things any more complicated for myself than they already are.

'I'm happy to take you somewhere safe for free, if that helps,' he says.

I'm suddenly aware that I'm a slightly drunk young woman in a ballgown with tears streaming down my face. He's probably got a daughter around my age and hopes that someone would do the same for her if they ever spotted her climbing a bridge railing.

And I'm aware that a lot of cabbies may refuse my fare if I try to hail one later. They'd probably see the state of me and worry I was going to throw up in the back of their cab.

I step down from the railings and ask him to take me to Bristol Temple Meads station but to stop off at our flat on the way. I give him the address; he nods and looks relieved. I pile myself into the back of his cab, gathering my gown around me. He makes no attempt at conversation and I'm glad. I wonder for a second if Nina will be at the flat, but that's a chance I'll have to take. If she's there, I'll simply run in, get out of the dress, grab my stuff and leave again before she has the chance to say anything. I look out along the route in case we pass her but there's no sign. Maybe she's still at the hotel.

The cab pulls up outside our flat.

'Just give me a few minutes,' I say. 'I'll be straight back with my luggage.'

I tumble out, all gown and quivering legs, fumbling with my key for a moment before the door swings open. Nina isn't here. I can tell that straight away. I head into my room and start trying to peel myself out of the dress. It's not easy and I struggle with the bodice at the back, but after much grunting and swearing, I manage to pull it down and step out of it. I quickly put it on the hanger and lay it on my bed. If I'm lucky, Nina will still take it back to the shop in the morning. I open my case and pull on the first jeans and top I come to. I take one last look around and spot the envelope addressed to Nina on the desk. I can't leave it now. Not after what just happened. It included my home address and phone number, but she won't be wanting those now either. I pick it up and stuff it in my rucksack.

There. All trace of me is gone. Leaving just a ballgown behind. A memento of a night that promised so much but crashed and burned. My gown didn't save me. Nothing could.

I heave my rucksack on, pick up my case and leave the room without looking back.

20

EMILY

I stared at Jules, who was wiping away tears. I didn't get it.

'I don't understand,' I said.

'Which bit?' she asked.

'I get that you loved her. I just don't get what the big deal was? About telling her and her reaction and running away and never seeing her again and not telling us about any of it until now.'

Jules sighed and started to explain.

'It was different in our day. People couldn't just come out. There was no same-sex marriage, barely any openly gay couples. Colin kissed Barry on the side of his head in *EastEnders* and the whole world went batshit crazy. Most people of my parents' generation still considered homosexuality to be a hanging offence. And that was just gay guys. No one even mentioned that lesbians existed back then.'

'Really? It was that bad?'

'Absolutely. I'd never met a single lesbian. I mean, I must have, obviously, but no one that had been out about it. It simply wasn't an option.'

'Is that why you married Rob?' I asked.

'Yeah. I guess that's what we all did. A whole generation of gay people hid their sexuality and resigned themselves to doing what was expected of them. That's why you hear of women leaving their husbands now and setting up home with another woman. It's the first time in their lives they've ever felt able to do that.'

'And Rob was there at the right time and the right place with a ready-made family,' said Carl.

'Yep. I mean, it was no great love story, you've seen that. But I was too much of a coward to break cover and scandalise Halifax. It seems ridiculous now, I know that. Hebden Bridge is only a few miles down the road and it's always being touted as the lesbian capital of England. The irony is not lost on me.'

'It's like you were way ahead of your time,' I said. 'If you'd got together with Nina, you'd have been a lesbian icon. We'd probably have learnt about you in PSHE lessons.'

'Thanks for making me feeling ancient,' she said. But she managed a smile with it.

'But when things got easier,' said Carl, 'when it wasn't such a big deal any more, why didn't you get in touch with Nina?'

'I did try,' Jules said. 'Not very hard, I admit, but I searched for her on Facebook and googled her and that. I drew a blank, though. And I figured she's probably married and changed her name, maybe had kids and the last thing she'd want would be me raking up embarrassing stuff from our past.'

She went quiet again. As Jules didn't do quiet very often, I knew she must be hurting.

'It didn't mean she didn't love you back,' I said. 'Her running off like that. Maybe she was scared too.'

Jules frowned, as if she'd never contemplated that before.

'But you heard her. She said no.'

'Twice actually,' chipped in Carl.

'You can butt out of it,' I said. 'You're not female, for a start.'

I turned back to Jules.

'It was probably just a shock. She wasn't expecting it. And she may have been worried someone would come in at any moment.'

'But she pulled away and said no.'

'Twice,' repeated Carl.

'Shut up!' Jules and I said at the same time.

'People do all sorts of crazy stuff when they're scared and shocked. It doesn't mean she didn't have feelings for you. She might have regretted it afterwards. You don't know.'

Jules looked at me doubtfully.

'Have you still got the letter?' Carl asked her.

'Yeah. Never opened it. I couldn't bring myself to read what I'd written.'

'And did anyone else ever know what happened?' I asked.

'Nope. You guys are the first.'

Carl looked down and shook his head. I stared at Jules, realising now why she'd said all that stuff about some people never experiencing the love me and Harry had.

'Hey guys.' I looked up to see Faz had finally emerged from his sound booth. 'I don't want to pressure you but I'm, like, finished for the day now.'

I glanced at the digital clock on the wall. It was gone six.

'Jeez, sorry,' said Jules. 'That's my fault for having such a long life story.'

'But it's nowhere near finished yet,' I pointed out. 'You've only just left uni.'

'Yeah, Suzi said to let you know we're going to do this as a two-parter over a couple of days,' said Faz. 'We'll resume on Monday after we all have a day off. Sounds like you're the queen of significant moments,' he added, smiling his ridiculously bright teeth at Jules.

'I suppose that's one way of putting it,' replied Jules.

'So, what can we expect in the next instalment?' asked Faz.

'It goes dark,' said Jules. 'Like the seventh Harry Potter film. All the fun and joy have been sucked out, everybody's as depressed as fuck and there's a sense of hopelessness and impending doom.'

'Right,' he said, not seeming at all sure if she was joking or not. 'As long as you've got Neville Longbottom on your side in the final part.'

'I'm afraid Neville was conspicuous by his absence,' said Jules.

We filed out of the studio. It felt like a weird kind of intermission in Jules's life. Usually, I would stuff myself with popcorn and get an ice cream but that didn't appear to be an option here.

'Anyone hungry?' asked Carl.

'Yes,' I said.

'I don't want to go to Food to Die For,' said Jules. 'I can't cope with being surrounded by old dead people this evening.'

'Where else can we get food?' I asked.

'Well, Carl here is the food delivery expert,' said Jules.

'We can't get a Deliveroo, can we?' he replied. 'How are we going to order, pay, or collect?'

At that moment, the lift doors opened, and Suzi emerged, holding three flat boxes.

'Pizzas to go,' she said. 'Your regular delivery orders were on your files, so no arguing over whose is whose. I figured you probably just fancied chilling out tonight.'

She handed us a box each with our name written on it.

'Wow, I never had you down as the fairy godmother type,' Jules said to her.

'I'm more like the sharp-tongued one Jennifer Saunders voiced in *Shrek 2* than the everyone's favourite granny one from *Cinderella*.'

'Never mind that, how the hell did you get hold of these?' asked Carl, examining his plain brown pizza box as if looking for clues.

'I can't reveal my sources,' said Suzi. 'But let's say I have contacts on the outside. Emily, the drinks are in your room and your evening's viewing is teed up on your TV, ready to roll.'

'I thought we'd done with watching films for today?' I said.

'Yeah, well, this one's a bit on the short side but you can blame the director for that.'

She looked at me pointedly as she said it.

'Is it my director's cut of *Finding Nemo*?' I asked.

'It certainly is. But eat your pizzas quickly or it'll be over.'

We squeezed into the lift with Suzi and headed up to the sixth floor.

'Sure you don't want to join us?' Carl asked her when we stopped outside my room. 'We've got enough pizza for four.'

'You're OK, thanks,' said Suzi. 'You know what they say, four's a crowd. Anyway, I've got plans.'

She headed off along the corridor.

'How can she have plans?' I asked. 'I mean, she's just got a room like the rest of us, and I can't imagine her hanging out with the oldies.'

'Who knows?' said Jules. 'But I want my pizza before it goes cold, so will you please let us in?'

I did as I was asked, glad I'd made my bed that morning.

'Take your seats then,' I said. Jules and Carl sat sideways across the bed with their legs out and their backs against the wall. I handed them their pizzas and drinks before grabbing my own and the remote control and climbing into the space between them.

'I can't work out if I'm excited or dreading this,' I said, pressing play.

'We'll give you our verdict at the end,' replied Carl.

I'd forgotten how sad the opening to the film was. Probably because the first few times I watched it, my dad fast-forwarded past the bit where Coral and all her eggs, apart from one, were eaten by the barracuda. He just started it at the bit where Marlin promised Nemo he would never let anything happen to him. I still remembered the first time I watched it from the beginning on my own when Dad wasn't around and being absolutely traumatised by what had happened. So, maybe Dad did have a point, although I never told him that.

I glanced at Jules when we got to the barracuda bit. She had her head bowed while wrestling with some particularly stringy cheese.

'This is excellent pizza,' she said, as if she was too engrossed in eating it to watch.

'Wow, I'd forgotten how brutal this is,' Carl said. 'It's a long time since I watched it with Lewis.'

'The first day of school bit is coming and that's awesome,' I replied. And sure enough, a few minutes later, both of them were laughing at Marlin as he kept returning to the safety of the sea anemone.

'Marlin is literally my dad,' I said. 'Always looking for danger. Trying to protect me from stuff that no one else had even thought of. And then, taking his eye off me for one moment and the worst thing imaginable that even he hadn't thought of happens.'

We watched as Nemo swam out over the drop-off while Marlin was talking with his teacher about him not being ready for school. We all shouted 'no!' as the diver scooped Nemo up in a net and took him off on the boat.

'It's OK,' I said between mouthfuls of my pizza. 'Marlin's going to bump into Dory in a moment and she's going to sort everything.'

'Oh God, I'd forgotten,' said Jules, 'you've given her a working memory, haven't you?'

'Yep,' I replied. 'And here she comes now.'

Marlin bumped into Dory and asked if she'd seen a boat. She immediately replied she had, set off after it, avoiding Bruce the shark – because she remembered to look out for him – and leading Marlin straight to the boat.

'But they've still got to get Nemo out,' pointed out Carl.

'Hey, I've got faith in Dory,' I said. At which point Dory made a loud noise to attract Bruce, watched as he attacked the boat, spotted Nemo as soon as he swam free of the plastic container as the boat overturned and brought him safely back to Marlin.

'It doesn't look like it ended well for the diver,' said Carl as the sea turned a funny shade of red.

'It's only his foot he lost. But it means he can't dive any more. Which is fair enough as it would stop him kidnapping other sea creatures.'

'Fair point. We should have asked Alice to come and watch this. She'd have loved it,' said Jules.

We watched as Marlin and Dory shepherded Nemo safely back to school. There, he was greeted as a hero, Dory agreed to stay on as a school lunchtime supervisor and entertained all the creatures with her tales from the deep ocean and Marlin was looking on relieved, knowing he could safely get back to doing whatever it was adult clownfish did, as the credits rolled.

'So, what's the verdict?' I asked Carl.

'Started badly, tailed off a bit in the middle and less said about the end, the better,' he replied, giving me a playful dig in the ribs.

'I know I spoilt a perfectly brilliant film and the sequel, for that matter. But hey, Marlin got his kid back and was spared all that pain.'

'And that's what it was about for you,' said Carl.

'Yep,' I said. 'And I consider it worth the sacrifice.'

'Right,' he said, closing his pizza box and shuffling off the side of the bed. 'If the main presentation is over, I'll be heading back to my room.'

'That's fine, we'll do all the girly gossiping when you've gone,' said Jules.

'I thought as much,' Carl replied with a smile. 'Thanks, Emily. It was a grand director's cut. You're a good kid, you know.'

'Stop calling me a kid!' I shouted after him as he closed the door.

Jules turned to look at me, an unusually serious expression on her face.

'I think I know what you're going to do with your actual director's cut,' she said.

'Do you?'

'Yep. And I'm not going to try to talk you out of it because that's not my place. But I am going to ask you if you're absolutely sure about it.'

'I am,' I said. 'I've never been so sure of anything in my life.'

'Afterlife,' corrected Jules.

'Yeah. That too.'

21

CARL

I didn't go back to my room. I went straight down to the studio. There was something I wanted to take a closer look at. It was only a hunch, but I'd been the sort of police officer who'd always had pretty good hunches. And if there was even the tiniest chance I could do something to help Jules, I wanted to try.

Faz struck me as the sort of guy who would walk off thinking about entirely trivial crap without giving a second thought to locking the studio. Fortunately, I was right. I reached for the light. Everything was as we'd left it. I may not have been a cool tech kid like Faz, but I was confident that I'd be able to find my way around the editing programme to enable me to do what I wanted to without waiting for his help.

I logged in and found the footage of Jules's significant moments that we'd been watching earlier. I rewound to the point where she got into the cab. As it set off, the camera followed the cab, but by slowing down the video and zooming in along the route, I was able to see the people they passed. Actually see their faces, rather than a succession of blurry blobs on the pavement.

It took nearly an hour but that didn't bother me. I was used to painstaking work. And the whole point was that if you were thorough, you wouldn't have to do it again. It was all about the reward. You wouldn't remember how long it took, in years to come. You would only remember the result.

And there she was. Unmistakable, on account of her wearing a purple and black ballgown. Nina had been heading towards the bridge as Jules had been driven away.

I dashed back upstairs and knocked on Emily's door. I had a strong suspicion there'd been wine in Jules's cup, so I hoped I'd got to her before the alcohol had.

'Emily, Jules, you need to come with me,' I hissed.

Jules opened the door.

'Bloody hell, if this is some kind of police raid, I'll have you know that no illegal substances have been consumed on these premises,' she said.

'I want you to come with me. Now.'

'Am I being arrested?' she asked. 'Because I'd like to see you try to handcuff me, if so.'

Emily appeared at the door, as ever, the adult in the room.

'Come on,' she said. 'Let's go and see what it is.'

They followed me down in the lift to the studio.

'Isn't this classed as breaking and entering?' asked Jules.

'Faz left the door unlocked. Anyway, I've been investigating, and I think the end justifies the means. Sit down and watch closely.'

I rewound the tape and played from the cab stopping next to Jules.

'God, do we have to watch this again? It's like a *Groundhog Day* of my most embarrassing moments.'

I froze the frame at the point I'd marked and zoomed in.

'There,' I said. 'Look who I found.'

There was a pause before the shriek. It came from Emily, which I was not expecting.

'Oh my God, it's Nina! Jules, you know what this means? She was looking for you.'

I zoomed in further to ensure Jules could see without her glasses. It was a while before she was able to speak.

'It doesn't mean anything,' she said. 'She might have still been furious at me.'

'She didn't seem the sort of person who would be,' said Emily. 'She came across as fun and kind and like the best friend you'd most want to have on your side. What if she was trying to find you to say sorry and to explain her reaction?'

Jules looked from Emily to me in turn. It was almost like she didn't want the little nugget of hope I'd offered her.

'Look, I know what you're trying to do here,' she said. 'And I do appreciate it. But it's highly unlikely it would have changed anything. She probably just wanted to smooth things over. She wouldn't have wanted us to part on bad terms. She might have apologised that she didn't feel the same way but said "no hard feelings". Something like that.'

'But you don't know that for sure,' said Emily.

'I don't. But if there's one thing life has taught me, it's that Hollywood endings only happen in films. The rest of us get the bog-standard, unremarkable ones which they rejected.'

Emily looked pleadingly at her but there was nothing else forthcoming.

'Thanks again for trying, Carl,' she said, touching my arm as she headed for the door. 'And excellent detective skills.'

Emily looked at me.

'What do we do now?' she asked.

'There's nothing more we can do, is there? Not if she's adamant that it wouldn't have changed anything.'

'I'll work on her,' said Emily. 'Tell her it may help Nina if she'd give her the chance to part on better terms. She won't do it for herself, but she might do it for Nina.'

* * *

I wasn't expecting to get the opportunity to put my detective skills to use again so quickly, but when I woke early the next morning and decided to escape the hotel for a breath of fresh air, I found an unexpected item in the foyer area.

'What are you up to?' I asked Suzi, who was, for once, not dressed in her regulation leather jacket and tight trousers, but the more casual Sunday morning attire of jeans and a hoodie.

'I could ask the same of you,' she replied.

'Just needed some air. It gets a bit stuffy in there sometimes. A bit sterile.'

'You can say that again,' she replied. I waited for her to go on but she didn't, glancing down at her watch instead.

'Are you waiting for someone?' I asked.

She rolled her eyes and looked at me.

'You really don't give up, do you?'

'Nope. Trained to grab on and not let go, like a Rottweiler,' I said.

'Now there's an image. And there,' she said, nodding towards the main gates where a red car was pulling in, 'is your answer.'

I frowned as Majid pulled up in front of us. He looked as surprised to see me as I was him.

'I didn't think you filmed on Sundays,' I said.

'We don't,' Suzi replied. 'Our friend Majid does a little freelance work for me on the side. Turns out he's the afterlife's answer to Uber, only he still charges 1990s prices, which suits me just fine. And it all goes to a good cause anyway.'

'Jules told me about his family's good fortune on the People's Postcode Lottery.'

'Looks like they might get lucky again,' she said with a wink.

Majid stuck his head out of the driver's window.

'Morning, Carl. Are you coming too?' he asked. I looked at Suzi for an answer.

'Come on then,' she said, nodding her head towards the car. 'As long as you promise not to wear me down with one hundred questions.'

I got in the back. Suzi was in the front next to Majid. They chatted about music (seventies), cars (seventies) and football (seventies). It was like some weird retro podcast dedicated to that decade. And then Majid turned down a lane which led to a football pitch with a tiny stand on one side and turf which was definitely not Wembley standard.

'Right, thanks Majid,' Suzi said. 'Payment will be made through the usual channels. See you in a couple of hours.'

She got out of the car. I followed her, still not having any idea what was going on.

'Are you going to explain all this now?' I asked, waving my arm around.

'I'd have thought it was quite self-explanatory. I've come to watch a football match.'

I'd not had her down as a football fan previously, but she had just spent five minutes arguing with Majid about who was best, Kevin Keegan or Kenny Dalglish. However, this was definitely not Anfield.

'Who's playing?' I asked.

'Boothtown Girls Under-10s. I'll have you know that they're shit hot,' she replied.

'Right. And are you going to explain your connection?'

'What do you mean?' she said, taking up a prime position on the touchline.

I looked around at the other spectators who were starting to gather nearby.

'I don't think these people would have got up early on a Sunday morning unless they were coming to support family members.'

Before she had a chance to answer, a couple came to stand next to her. Obviously, they had no idea she was even there, but she turned and smiled at them. The woman had a friendly face and blonde bob and the man a fine head of unruly dark hair and eyes so vibrantly green they reminded me of—

'That's your son, isn't it?' I hissed at her, still unable to bypass the instinct to lower my voice in case other people heard.

'Whatever makes you think that?' she replied. But she couldn't disguise the smile and proud mum face. I was about to launch into my list of 101 questions for her when two teams of girls ran out onto the pitch, long hair pulled back into ponytails, apart from the one girl who didn't have long hair, but a mass of thick, short-cropped dark hair.

'Come on, Iris, kick their arses into touch!' Suzi bellowed.

'Suzi! You can't say that, they're only little girls.'

'I can say anything I want because they can't fucking hear me and I tell you, it's the highlight of my week. Who needs all that mindfulness crap when you can do this?'

I started laughing. I couldn't help it. The very idea that Suzi's stress release involved tearing a strip off little girls playing football.

'I have questions,' I said.

'Thought you might. I'll answer what I can, but I won't take my eyes off the action because the last time I did that, I missed our Iris score a cracking header and I've never forgiven myself.'

'OK,' I said as the girls took up their positions and the match kicked off. 'You've so far revealed nothing about your life, so I'm going to do this chronologically, as you'd expect. We'll start with the father of your son.'

Iris was already running around the pitch with such energy and zeal that I wondered if she'd be able to last the full ninety minutes.

'Complete waster. Cameraman by the name of Shaun. We met when we were both working on Calendar TV news. In defence of my twenty-six-year-old self, he was good looking and drove a fast car – we were going to cover a big peace march once and he took the corner so fast he nearly took out half of the marchers, which, admittedly, would have been a big story but a terrible waste too. Anyway, we eventually shacked up together, I was promoted to producer. Within a year we were married and a year later I was pregnant.'

She broke off as Iris surged through the midfield and slid into a tackle, which made everyone watching wince and look away, including her father who was standing next to us. The girl in question went down with a yelp and did not get up again.

'She's OK,' said Suzi. 'Just needs to toughen up a bit.'

'She's nine or ten, Suzi, and she has legs like a sparrow. And your Iris has got a tackle as hard as Roy Keane.'

'How dare you?' she said, turning to me. 'She's at least as hard as Ron "Chopper" Harris.'

Iris's victim gingerly got to her feet, limping badly, and there was a relieved ripple of applause from the spectators – all apart from Suzi.

'Made a bit of a meal of it, if you ask me,' she said.

I shook my head.

'So, when was your son born?' I asked.

'New Year's Day, 1985. Nathan was the first baby of the new

year at Calderdale Royal. Nearly split me in half arriving because he weighed in at nine pounds, but he was good as gold from then on. Happiest baby you've ever seen. I was left to do everything, of course. Shaun never even changed a bloody nappy.'

'And what about when you went back to work?'

'He wasn't any better. My mum looked after Nathan and when I got home from work, I took over while Shaun went to the pub.'

'That doesn't sound fair,' I said.

'It was what being a working woman and mum in the eighties was like. We were told we could have it all, they just forgot to tell us we'd be working sixteen hours a day doing it.'

'And you stuck with Shaun?'

Suzi fell silent for a moment. She kept her eyes on the game, following the play for a few minutes before she answered.

'I should have kicked him out. Especially when his drinking got worse. I know that now. But at the time it were just one more thing on my to-do list I never got around to. The years passed, Nathan became a pretty self-sufficient teenager and then an adult – which is one good thing I managed to do for his partner, Leanne.'

She nodded towards the woman with the blonde bob holding Nathan's hand.

'She seems nice.'

'She is. Best thing that ever happened to him. I was so excited when he told me they were expecting. Started buying clothes for my first grandchild...'

Suzi's voice trailed off.

'What happened?' I asked.

'I was working for an independent film production company by then. Shaun was still with Calendar. I think he felt a bit crap about that. He was drinking more heavily. He phoned and asked if I wanted a lift home after work one night, said he'd been working late. He hadn't been, he'd been in the boozer with his mates.

'I had no idea how much he'd drunk. Like most people with a drink problem, he was very good at hiding it.'

I looked down at my feet, knowing I was in no position to pass judgement.

'Anyway, he lost control on a bend on the way home. Smashed into a wall. We were both killed instantly.'

'Oh, Suzi, I'm so sorry.'

She waved away my sympathies, still unable to look at me.

'So, you never got to see Iris?'

'Nope. I would have been the best grandma ever, that's what Nathan said at my funeral.'

'You went, then?'

'Yeah, wasn't going to miss my biggest directing gig. At least they didn't do a joint one with Shaun. Nathan made sure of that. I wasn't even buried in the same cemetery.'

I turned and took another look at Suzi's son. He really was the spitting image of her. I couldn't get my head around how weird it must be for her standing next to him, knowing he couldn't see or hear her. And that she'd never be able to hug him or have a chat with him. Or ever touch her granddaughter.

'That's why you stayed, isn't it?' I asked.

She shrugged, which I took as an admission of guilt.

'How could I leave without seeing Iris? It was bad enough not being able to hold her, but I could never have walked away completely. When I got here and they saw my CV, they offered me the new position of executive producer with End Credits, which has worked out perfectly, as it's meant I've been able to see her grow up. I used to come here to watch Nathan play footie every Sunday. Fucking dreadful, he was. He's a theatre set designer now. Says it all, really. But her' – she nodded towards Iris – 'she's got what it takes to go all the way.'

As if to prove the point, Iris won the ball off an opponent, powered her way towards the eighteen-yard box, dodged two tackles and buried the ball into the bottom corner of the net.

'Yeesss!' roared Suzi, leaping up and down on the touchline. 'You go, girl!'

Iris celebrated with her teammates then turned and ran over to her parents, arms aloft, a huge grin on her face. They were whooping in delight too. I turned to look at Suzi, who was wiping away a tear.

'That's my granddaughter, that is,' she said. 'Future Lioness, you mark my words.'

'So, you're not going anywhere then?' I asked.

'Only to Wembley,' she replied.

* * *

When Majid dropped us off at the hotel later, I turned to Suzi.

'Thank you for sharing your family with me,' I said. 'Never had you down as a doting grandma.'

'Oi,' she replied, 'if I catch any of you calling me that, you'll be in trouble.'

'I don't suppose you have any vacancies for security officers or food delivery guys here?'

She looked at me seriously.

'We now prioritise those with children for new vacancies. Fairest way to do it. Anyway, you three will be moving on soon.'

'Have you finished all our paperwork then?'

'God, yes. I did that a couple of weeks ago.'

I frowned at her.

'So why didn't you tell us? Why are we still here?'

Suzi looks at me, her face as serious as I've even seen it.

'It was never really about processing your applications. More about you guys processing your emotions, finding some kind of peace, so I knew you were ready to move on.'

I stared at her.

'So, you've basically been playing God?'

'I thought you were an atheist?'

'You know what I mean.'

She sighed.

'If you mean, is it in my job description as exec producer, the answer is no. If you're asking if I think it would be right to let people move on when they haven't taken the steps needed to find peace, friendship and self-forgiveness – things that will stand them in good stead in the future – the answer is also no.'

I stood, thinking about what she'd said for a moment.

'And the moonlighting as a deranged hotel chaplain in the room of reflection?'

'Also not in the job description but bloody good fun.'

I smiled.

'Thank you,' I said. 'You did a damn sight better job than God, to be honest. When are we leaving?'

'Tuesday. After you've all made your director's cuts.'

'How do you know we'll make the right decisions?'

'I don't. But I do know that you've helped each other through an incredibly tough few weeks and come a hell of a long way during that time.'

I nodded and headed towards the lift.

'Tonight's film for your viewing pleasure is in your room,' Suzi called after me. 'You're another one who's ruined the original, but my expectations weren't high.'

* * *

We sat on my bed later that evening, Jules and Emily still struggling to take in what I'd told them about Suzi. 'I can't believe how tough that must have been, never holding her own granddaughter,' Jules said. 'All that hard as nails stuff and not giving a toss about anyone is just an act, isn't it? She can't risk all that hurt pouring out if she lets her feelings show.'

'I'm glad she got to stay with her family,' said Emily. 'I love the idea of her still looking out for them.'

'After standing next to her on the touchline, I certainly wouldn't mess with any member of her family,' I said. 'She's like a matriarch, ready to charge.'

I thought of Mum, sitting at Lewis's bedside, watching over him, having already lost me. I'd be able to relieve her of her duties soon. She could go back to just worrying about him because he could be a dick sometimes, which is what all mums did.

'And we're really leaving on Tuesday?' asked Jules.

'That's what she said. After we'd done our director's cuts. Talking of which, are we going to watch *The Lion King* or what?'

'Yeah,' said Emily. 'I think it's going to be a bit weird, though.'

'I think it's going to be a complete bore-fest,' said Jules.

I pressed play – it was the only way to shut them up. I'd kept Elton John's music, of course, and the whole opening scenes in the Pride Lands were as spectacular as ever. Scar remained evil enough to entice Simba to explore the elephants' graveyard and nearly get eaten by hyenas. But after being confronted by Mufasa, my version had Scar being racked with guilt and offering to give up his claim to the throne and leave the kingdom in disgrace.

'It's basically like Prince Andrew, bypassing the whole

Woking Pizza Express story, admitting he screwed up big time and voluntarily disappearing from public life and getting a one-way ticket to Siberia,' said Jules. 'Which is why it entirely lacks credibility.'

When Scar then plunged to his death accidentally, Mufasa died trying to save him. Jules pressed pause and leant over to me.

'I see what you did there,' she said.

'I hated not being able to save either of them.'

'I know, but you get to save Lewis in the real director's cut, which is all that matters.'

'But does that mean Simba doesn't run off and make friends with Timon and Pumbaa, because that's my favourite bit,' said Emily.

'No, you're OK. Simba gets put into childcare while his mum—'

'Sarabi,' interrupted Jules.

'Yes, don't worry, I gave his mum a namecheck. Sarabi rules the kingdom on his behalf. And Simba meets Timon and Pumbaa in childcare and they still became firm friends.'

'OK, you might just get away with it,' said Emily. 'Let's see the rest.'

* * *

As they got up to leave when the film ended, I won a lukewarm round of applause (I was well aware I'd scuppered any claim I had to Ridley Scott's throne).

'You might be nominated for the Oscar for directing scenes of mild peril,' Jules said.

'That's fine,' I replied. 'Mild peril is very underrated.'

22

JULES

I'd been dreading this day from the moment we'd been told what was going to happen. Seeing Nina's rejection of me had been bad enough; this was going to be unbearable. I was glad I'd told Carl about Grace's stillbirth but worried now that I should have told Emily too. Why hadn't I? To protect her? To protect myself? Whatever the reason, it was too late now, she would just have to watch it unfold on screen.

I was aware my life had been the wrong way around for a film too. The fun, exciting bit full of love at the beginning, followed by the biggest loss a woman can suffer, and then the slow extinguishing of my life. It was very much lacking in the 'uplifting ending' department. I'd never been going to get a Hollywood ending, or a Disney one, come to that. But a suicide was about the worst way you could end something, short of a nuclear explosion.

'Think of this as *Jules-heimer*,' I said when I joined the others in the studio. 'The first part you saw was basically the fun *Barbie* bit, even though that went desperately wrong at the end. And today you're going to see my life being nuked. Strap yourselves in, it's going to be a fun ride.'

Faz laughed uproariously. Carl and Emily looked down at their hands. I went to press play.

'Don't we get a "previously on *Jules-heimer*"?' asked Carl.

I looked at him, wondering if he was angling for Faz to rewind the cab footage to show Nina again. But I'd made up my mind. I didn't want to go there. What was done was done. And I simply wanted to get the rest of it over as quickly as possible.

'Sadly not,' I said. 'It'll be like an entirely different film anyway. Forget Bristol and beautiful suspension bridges. This part's set in Halifax. And I suspect it will have skipped forward at least ten years.'

'What, nothing significant happened in your life in all that time?' asked Emily.

'Nope. Moved back here. Got a job with the council's environmental health department. The need to start earning so I could get out of my parents' house and get a flat of my own was too great. Dreams were dumped and the hard realities of earning a living and keeping a roof over my head kicked in. And as I recall it being deathly boring and it was my bloody life, I've no doubt it hasn't made the cut.'

I pressed play. I was right. Faz had even put a '2009' on the screen to denote the massive passing of time.

'A thirteen-year void. That takes some doing,' said Carl.

'Yeah, I worked hard at that.'

'So, what's going to happen to break that?' he asked.

'A stupid bet,' I replied.

I'm with my friend Kim from work. We used to laugh about that. I'd go in somewhere first and say, 'I'm looking for my friend. Kimberley.' It only worked if they were a Victoria Wood fan, of course, but it had a pretty high hit rate. We're in a pub together. She's telling me that the guy at the bar is called Robert Smith. He used to be her brother's mate at school. She knows I love The Cure. She doesn't know that men aren't my type.

She dares me to ask him out on a date. We've had a few drinks. I wouldn't even entertain the idea otherwise. Still, I refuse. I then make the mistake of asking what's in it for me. A moment later she offers me equal shares in her black leather jacket if I go on a date with him. It's too good an offer to refuse, although I do insist she lets me put the jacket on to go and ask him.

I saunter up to the bar and gaze across at him, trying to appear as casual as possible. He clocks me looking, though, and flashes a smile. I guess he can't have women approaching him that often if he appears flattered by the approaches of a thirty-four-year-old woman who's had a few drinks.

'What are you drinking?' he asks.

'Depends who's buying,' I say. He smiles and nods, acknowledging my quick thinking.

'That'll be me then.'

'And I'll have a vodka and Coke. My friend Kim there will have the same, thanks.'

He doesn't protest. Simply orders the drinks.

'She says her brother used to go to school with you. Darren Jarvis, his name is.'

'Oh aye, I remember Daz. Haven't seen him around for a while.'

'He moved to Barnsley.'

'I'm sorry to hear that,' he says. We both laugh. The barman passes me our drinks and Robert Smith pays for them.

'Thank you,' I say. 'If you fancy going out sometime, I'll buy you a drink back.'

'You're on,' he says. I scribble down my phone number on the back of the receipt and hand it to him.

'Just so you know,' he says, 'I've got two little boys so I'll have to get babysitting sorted first.'

'Sure,' I reply, trying not to sound taken aback or flustered in any way. 'Thanks for the drinks.'

He smiles and I head back to our table.

'I'm going out with Robert Smith,' I say. And all I can think in my head is how much Nina would have laughed at that.

The film skips forward to me meeting Thomas and Noah for the first time. Thomas was five and had recently started Reception; Noah was three and at nursery. Rob introduced me to them as 'my friend Jules'. I got that, although it did make me feel a bit like a nanny at the time.

Noah took one look at me and went straight back to his Duplo. Thomas brought a picture book up to me and asked me to read it. It was called *Fix-It Duck* and had a lovely rhyme and rhythm to it. I'd never read a child a book before. It was such an intimate thing to do. And as I finished the story and Thomas ran to get another one, I had the strangest sense that I was locked in now. Had made a solemn pledge to be a part of this boy's life and therefore part of Rob's.

There was no going back, and, in some ways, the children made it easier for me. I could tell myself I was needed, that I had a purpose in life. Something that had been lacking for the past thirteen years. And the fact that I didn't love Rob, not in the way I'd loved Nina, was an irrelevance rather than something that should have prevented it.

We cut to my wedding day. I was getting ready in our bedroom; I'd moved in with him six months after we met, mainly because it made looking after the boys easier. It was, in all ways, a marriage of convenience.

'Didn't you ever love him?' asked Emily.

'Not really. Not in the way you're supposed to. Not like I'd loved Nina.'

'But didn't that break your heart?' she said.

'My heart had been broken a long time ago,' I replied.

I'm standing outside Calderdale Register Office. It is, at least, a beautiful gothic building with a tower and turret. Nina would have loved it, I think. Which is not what you're supposed to be thinking about on your wedding day. Dad is standing next to me. I don't know it yet, but he'll be dead within a year, from a heart attack. Not that it will leave a big hole in my life, as we'd never been close. I had no idea whether he thought I loved Rob or not but clearly, he didn't think it was his place to enquire or advise caution. I was finally getting married at thirty-five, he was walking me into the register office, and he could cross that duty off his to-do list.

I'm wearing an ivory lace dress that stops just below the knee. It was the only thing that didn't make me look like a milkmaid but appeared vaguely bridal. It's not me. None of this is me. I may as well not be here. I'm going through the motions. Doing what's expected of me. Not ruffling any feathers. And all I can think of is the gown I wore to the graduation ball and how that was *me and that somehow I lost myself after that night.*

I hear Nina telling me how beautiful I am. That I have lovely shoulders. They are covered up today and I do not feel in the slightest bit beautiful. I've put on weight since my Bristol days, changed my hair dye to a reddish brown because black looks too severe at my age. And yet I still see Nina looking at me, radiating love and care and kindness.

'Are you ready?' Dad asks, and I say yes, because what else can I say? But every step of the way into the registry office, I'm trying not to think of Nina and trying not to cry. Thomas and Noah are pageboys. They look unbelievably cute. It's a bit of luck I don't know that in ten

years' time they will think of me as nothing more than a huge embarrassment.

Rob is standing there. He's scrubbed up well. I could have done worse. So much worse. But I could also have done so much better.

We skip on past our wedding, not stopping for our honeymoon (Scarborough, unremarkable. I would have rather gone to Whitby). There are glimpses of me trying to adapt to life as a stepmum; having to do everything a mum does but not being their mum, the 'evil stepmother' title always dangling above me, waiting for the opportunity to descend. Rob simply getting on with his work, safe in the knowledge that he has taken on the services of a wife, cook, cleaner and substitute mother. There was a brief scene where I mentioned that I wanted to try for a baby before it was too late, carefully avoiding the words 'of my own' or any suggestion that Thomas and Noah were not enough.

Whoever selected these moments had cut the actual 'trying', for which I was grateful. Instead, there are glimpses of my growing bump. Already, my hands felt clammy at what was to come. I glanced at Emily and saw she was frowning, clearly not understanding what was about to happen. I reached out and took her hand.

'I'm sorry,' I said. 'I still find it really hard to talk about.'

The baby stops moving at 3.38 a.m. on a Friday morning in July. I look at the digital display on the alarm clock radio, not realising at the time that this will be imprinted in my head for the rest of my life. I'm forty weeks pregnant, which is why I was awake as my baby has taken to doing some kind of aerobics routine in the early hours of the morning and I'm far too big and uncomfortable to get restful sleep.

I'm not unduly concerned at first because the same thing happened two days ago. I went to the maternity unit, and they checked it out and found me a reassuring heartbeat. Nothing to worry about. Quite common at this stage in pregnancy. The baby hasn't got much space. I suspected they had written 'anxious mother' on my notes as I left.

I sit up in bed. I'll go and get it checked out again. Get the reassurance I need, even if they now write 'neurotic mother' on my notes.

Rob is sleeping soundly beside me. He's been doing this throughout the wakeful nights of my pregnancy, and it pisses me off. I rouse him enough to tell him.

'The baby's stopped moving again. I'm going to the hospital to get it checked out.'

His eyes open wider.

'Do you want me to come with you?'

'You can't leave the boys, can you? And I don't want to wake my mum at this time in the morning. I'll be back within an hour. I'm sure it'll all be OK.'

He looks for a moment as if he might protest but thinks better of it.

'If you're sure,' he says. 'Call me if there's a problem.'

I nod and haul myself up out of bed. I pull on my maternity knickers and bra and my maternity joggers and top. There is no dignity at this point; you are just fucking huge and need specially made clothes. I squeeze my swollen feet into my Crocs. I don't know why I pick up my 'go' bag on the way to the door. It has been packed and ready for weeks. I suppose I think it will be a shame to waste that readiness if I do end up needing it.

It's only a five-minute drive to the hospital, which is why I decide to squeeze my bump behind the steering wheel rather than bother calling a cab. There and back within the hour, I tell myself. The streets are quiet. There are sporadic flags and bunting; it's the London Olympic opening ceremony this evening. I'll probably watch it later in case it's not as crap as these things usually are. Danny Boyle is directing it, which gives me hope.

It turns out that getting a parking space in the hospital car park is also straightforward at four in the morning. I approach the desk in the maternity unit. I'd rung before I set off so they're expecting me. I'm taken into a room by a chatty midwife and asked to lie on the bed. She examines me, checks for a heartbeat. She stops chatting. I see her face change. She calls for a sonographer, and I'm taken for a proper scan. The gel is cold on my belly but I'm not caring any more, because I know. Even before the stillness of the baby is on the screen, before the silence of where the heartbeat should be. I know my baby is dead.

I'm taken into a private room. A doctor comes and tells me what I already know. I'm asked if there's anyone who can come in to be with me. A partner or family member, perhaps? And I make that call to Rob. He answers groggily. I can't bring myself to say the word 'dead'.

'It's me. The baby's heartbeat has stopped,' I say.

There's a delay in him leaving while he waits for my mum to come and stay with the boys before he drives to the hospital. When he enters the room, he's already crying, and I realise I've never seen him cry before.

He bends to envelop me in a hug and all I can say is, 'Don't squash the baby.'

* * *

They've given me some medicine and sent me home. I'm to go back tomorrow to have my baby. Apparently, a vaginal birth will be best for me. Less risky than a caesarean. And that is why I'm sitting on the sofa, still with one hand on my bump, watching the Olympic opening ceremony. Rob is sitting next to me, but our bodies aren't touching. Thomas and Noah are on either side of us. Rob has told them. I don't know exactly what he said but they are quiet and can't bring themselves to look at me, although Noah keeps glancing at the bump.

On TV, Kenneth Branagh gets out of the carriage. We're told he's playing Isambard Kingdom Brunel.

'Who's he?' asks Thomas.

'An engineer. He designed lots of bridges and railways and other big things.'

I think of running over the Clifton Suspension Bridge with Nina. I wonder if she'll be watching this now and remembering the same thing.

Kenneth Branagh is quoting from The Tempest. *Talking about not being 'afeared' and waking from a long sleep.*

'The baby that's sleeping,' says Noah, out of nowhere. 'Will it never wake up now?'

I can't answer. Tears are pouring down my cheeks. I want to run from the room, but I don't think I can get up off the sofa.

'No,' says Rob softly. 'No, it won't.'

* * *

Everyone is being very nice to me at the hospital the next day. They're trying to involve me, asking how I'd like things to be. And all I can say is that I want things to be over. The idea of having to push out a baby who is already dead is abhorrent to me. Like some ghoulish freakshow. No one should have to do that and yet somehow, they do. The midwife suggests I have a think about what I'd like to do afterwards, tells me what other couples have chosen to do, and I want to scream at her that I want the baby to be born alive, that is all I ever wanted. But that option is no longer available.

When the pain comes, I try to bear it. That's the one thing I feel I can do for this baby, bear the pain of its birth as stoically as possibly. So, I refuse all offers of pain relief. I will birth my own baby without any fuss. There'll be no need for intervention. I owe it a calm and dignified arrival in this world. The world it will never live in. It's the very least I can do.

I've been told already not to blame myself. That it was nothing I did or didn't do. That these things 'just happen'. That may be the case but I'm finding it hard to accept right now. Everything that's gone wrong in my life has been my fault and I'm struggling to see why this should be any different.

The contractions are coming harder and faster. The midwife examines me and tells me it won't be long now. Rob is in the room with me, but he doesn't touch or speak to me. This whole thing feels like I'm having an out-of-body experience. Looking down on myself giving birth to a dead baby.

I push again and the pain is excruciating. Not just at one point but across my entire pelvis.

I'm panting and screaming and feel like I'm going to explode.

'I can't do it!' I shout. 'The baby's stuck.'

The midwife examines me again. She calls a doctor. There is a whispered conversation. I hear the words 'too late' and 'in the circumstances'.

'Baby's nearly there,' she says to me. 'Just coming out slightly awkwardly.' And with a final primeval howl from me, the baby emerges, silently, into the world. No gasp of air. No piercing cry. Simply born sleeping.

'It's a girl,' the midwife says, and I hadn't thought about this, that I'd get told the sex.

'Do you know what you were going to call a little girl?' she asks, and I do.

'Grace,' I whisper.

'Would you like to hold Grace?' she asks. And that is how I find myself holding my dead baby. I didn't think I'd be able to. The mere thought of it had turned me cold. But now she is in my arms, she is still warm. Her tiny rosebud lips slightly parted. And I see that she is perfect. Absolutely perfect. Apart from the fact that she is not breathing.

The midwife asks if we'd like hand and footprints taken. Perhaps a lock of hair? And photos of her, so we can keep them in a memory box we'll be given. I say yes to everything because it seems the easiest thing to do.

Another midwife is called to examine me, and she takes charge.

'We're going to have to take you to the theatre for some stitches,' she says.

'Can't you do it here?' Rob asks.

'I'm afraid not. Your wife's suffered an obstetric anal sphincter injury. The baby came out with its arm over its head, causing fourth-degree tears along the birth canal and bowel wall. It will need surgery to repair the damage.'

'You're not going to take her away while I'm gone, are you?' I ask.

'No. Perhaps your partner can hold her until you return.'

Rob nods, although he looks terrified, and the midwife hands Grace to him, wrapped in a blanket. And my bed is wheeled away as he sits there, shoulders shaking, holding our beautiful daughter in his arms.

Emily sniffed loudly next to me. I realised she was still holding my hand, and I gave it a squeeze.

'I'm so sorry,' she said. 'I had no idea.'

'It's OK. You wouldn't do, would you? I only told Carl because I wanted him to understand why I did it. Well, some of why I did it.'

'Is there worse to come, then?' she asked.

'Nothing as bad as that. It's simply that I never recovered from it. Not mentally or physically.'

I started the film again. I was glad they had spared me the surgery and the thirty-nine stitches and the epidural I had to have for it, having gone through the whole birth without pain relief. Instead, I saw myself kissing Grace goodbye before we left the hospital and arriving home carrying a memory box instead of a baby. I'd been told to rest in bed for a fortnight after the surgery, easier said than done when you have two small boys in the house. When I did move, the pain was still excruciating. After two weeks, when Rob went back to work and the boys were both at school, I finally plucked up the courage to enter Grace's nursery.

It's the colour that hits me first, a gorgeous sun-like yellow. It had seemed perfect when I'd chosen it. Not so perfect now, for a nursery which had become a shrine. The memory box was on the changing table, where I presumed Rob had left it when we came home. I hadn't seen it since. The Winnie the Pooh mobile hung forlornly over it as if Piglet and Tigger had been left wondering who was supposed to be looking at them. Everything bathed in sunlight yellow. A room which had been so full of hope and now smelt of past-their-best 'In sympathy' flower arrangements, which Rob had also presumably put in there in case throwing them away had been the wrong thing to do.

I lay my hand on the memory box but can't bear to open it. One day at a time. That's what everyone keeps telling me. Apart from Rob's mum, who had said, 'It wasn't meant to be,' the casual cruelty of it presumably not apparent to her.

I glance up at the Winnie the Pooh curtains, which have been drawn as a sign of respect. Eeyore was right all along. It was better to expect the worst, to avoid being disappointed. I draw back the curtains. The sun is still poking through the clouds. But it will probably rain later.

The film stopped. Faz came out of his booth.

'What's happening?' I asked.

'Is there a technical hitch?' asked Carl.

'No. Suzi will explain,' said Faz.

The door opened and Suzi walked in.

'Welcome to the Intermission,' she said. 'For those of you too young to remember, this is what used to happen, usually at the most exciting part of the film, and would completely ruin the build-up of tension. However, I'm calling an intermission on humanitarian grounds.'

'I never had you down as a UN Ambassador,' said Carl.

'Fair point, but one of my many jobs as an executive producer is to ensure we take our responsibility to our employees' well-being seriously, so with that in mind, may I introduce Eric.'

A screen at the back of the studio that I'd never even noticed before drew back and an elderly man seated at an organ rose up through the floor.

'What the actual fuck,' said Emily.

'Eric was the resident organist at Elland Picture House for many years and delighted audiences with his repertoire during the intermission. On this occasion he'll be playing music from the first day of Jules's significant moments and I'll be coming around shortly with refreshments for your enjoyment.'

Eric started playing the first notes of 'Boys Don't Cry' by The Cure and I found myself inexplicably crying with laughter. The others took one look at me and started laughing too. Suzi returned to the studio with Slush Puppies and an array of Pick 'n' Mix sweets.

She leant over and whispered in my ear.

'I've cut Grace's funeral scene too. It's too much in one day and I've no doubt you know it's available to you should you want it.'

'Thank you,' I said. 'I just wish I'd have known about Eric before because I'd have had him playing a Cure medley on his organ at my funeral.'

Suzi smiled and left us to it. I let Eric play his full repertoire and we gave him a standing ovation when he'd finished before he disappeared back below the floor.

'Now I have seen everything,' said Carl.

'That guy had rizz,' said Faz, before returning to his booth.

'OK, are you ready for the rest?' I asked. 'I can't promise much of an uplift but we're over the worst.'

'OK,' said Emily. 'And for what it's worth, I think you're amazing.'

The film continued, ignoring the fact that my life had, to all intents and purposes, ended there. I'd been in too much pain, both physically and emotionally, to even think about trying again for several years. By the time we did, I had a sense that it was already too late. There were clips of visits to the GP and a hospital. And after a few more years of nothing happening, me hitting my forties, the doctors unable to find a medical reason and people saying, 'At least you've got the boys', I resigned myself to the fact that the nursery would forever remain a shrine.

It skipped forward again then, to ten years after Grace's still-birth. That was when my perimenopause symptoms started, as if in some kind of sick tribute act. Although I didn't realise they were perimenopause symptoms at the time, because no one tells women the important stuff. You had to find it out yourselves.

There were clips of me shouting. A lot of shouting. If someone had done a portrait of me at the time, they would have simply called it 'Rage'. That or 'Tired'. Because I was permanently tired after a fitful night's sleep grappling with night sweats, insomnia and multiple toilet visits.

'What's happening?' asked Emily.

'It's called the perimenopause. It basically means your life being shit for a considerable number of years while your hormones go bonkers, your periods get heavier and erratic, you can't sleep or remember basic words and you're riddled with depression and anxiety.'

'I guess that's the one silver lining for me then,' she replied. 'Missing all of that.'

I smiled.

'I guess it is.'

And then things got worse. The shooting pains across my whole pelvic area took hold. There were shots of me writhing in agony in the loos at work, sticking ice packs between my legs and in my knickers. Sitting in the GP surgery and being told I was imagining it, that it was 'just' period pains. That I was too young for the perimenopause and should eat healthily and try to exercise. Although they never explained what exercise you could do while clamping your legs together and screaming in agony.

I'm sitting in King Street car park in Halifax on a Saturday afternoon. I'm waiting for Thomas to finish his guitar class. Rob has gone to watch the football because of course he has. I've got to the point where I know I need to go for a wee but almost instantly I know I've left it too late. I open the car door, try to put one leg out but have to stop and squeeze. Only I can't squeeze because the pain is unbearable. I know if I wee myself in the car, Thomas will be able to smell it when he comes out so I do the only thing I can; I swing both legs out quickly, try to stand up and crouch behind my car door, the gush of warm urine flowing down my leg and pooling on the ground next to me.

I wait until it has finished, because there's nothing else I can do, and then I pick up my bag, lock the car door and walk across to M&S where I buy a pair of leggings, knickers and socks, trying to stand at an angle where people can't see or smell the urine, before going into the loos and changing, discovering I've also soiled my knickers, putting all my old clothes in a carrier bag and dumping them in a bin on the way back to the car, still getting back in time to greet Thomas with a smile and ask how his lesson had gone.

Carl was looking down at his feet, clearly embarrassed.

'I don't understand,' said Emily. 'Does that happen to everyone?'

I shook my head.

'No, although it took me a long time to find that out. I finally paid to see a women's health physio, and she explained that the scar tissue from the surgery after Grace's birth had hardened and contracted with the lack of hormones. It was pulling everything out of shape down there, pressing on my pudendal nerve, causing a prolapse and affecting the nerves in my bowel.

'I felt like a little old lady who smells of pee or worse. It was horrific and I couldn't talk to anyone because, well, you wouldn't, would you?'

'So, was there anything they could do?'

'A bit. I had some sessions with the physio. I won't go into details, and you won't see it on here because it would violate all their privacy rules. And I went on HRT and local oestrogen, which eased things a little. Until earlier this year when the GP said that as things had improved, he was going to stop prescribing HRT and see how I got on. As if the thought of going back to that level of pain and discomfort wouldn't be enough to push me to do something extreme.'

'Did Rob know any of this?' asked Carl.

I shook my head.

'We'd hardly talked since Grace died. To explain what I was going through, I'd have had to mention her birth, and he didn't want to go there. Never had. I put the photo of her in a frame and put it up in the living room on what would have been her first birthday. But the next day it was back in the nursery. He left me a note. It simply said, 'too soon'. And we never spoke about her again.'

The others were silent for a moment.

'Did you get any support?' asked Carl.

'Sands, the baby loss charity, were great. I joined an online support group. Just talking to others who had been through it helped. But nothing from family or friends. I don't think people knew what to say.'

'But Rob never got any support either?' asked Carl.

'No,' I said. 'I gave him the details. They even have football teams for bereaved dads, but he wouldn't or couldn't. You know what men are like.'

Carl nodded.

'Anyway,' I said. 'I think we're nearly finished now. I suspect it's just my fiftieth birthday to go.'

I pressed play. I was right.

I'm sitting in a restaurant. It's a nice restaurant in Leeds. I'd never been there before but a couple of people from work had been raving about it and if you couldn't push the boat out for your fiftieth, when could you?

I was all dressed up too. It was not often I got the chance. A new frock which Rob had given me. Or more that he'd given me the money and told me to get something nice for myself for my birthday.

And here I am. Early, of course. Because the next train would have been cutting it fine, but I have a drink in my hand and the menu in front of me, so I'm OK. It will just be the four of us. Mum's been in the dementia home for more than a year now and no longer knows who I am, so I couldn't invite her, even if I wanted to. And the other person, the only one I actually want to be with, well, I've no idea where she is. Living her best life, I hope.

The text from Thomas comes first. He's really sorry but he's got a gig. The money was too good to turn down for a student. Can he take me somewhere at the weekend instead? Although it will probably only be Wagamama because that's all he can afford.

I reply, 'Yes, that's fine.' Noah's text comes hard on its heels.

Because Thomas has told him to send it, I'm in no doubt about that. It's shorter and to the point.

'Sorry. Got a deadline for uni. Enjoy your meal. See you at weekend.'

'No problem,' I reply.

It is a problem, though. Everything is a problem. Because this fragmented, make-do-and-mend family is all I have now. And we may not talk or eat or laugh together but tonight we were going to do all those things. For one night only. Then we can go back to being sullen and dysfunctional and uncommunicative. But tonight, my fiftieth birthday, we were going to paper over the cracks and pretend everything was OK. For me. Because I need it. That is all.

My phone rings. I look at the screen and see it's Rob and know instantly what he's going to say. Or at least what the end result will be; the particular excuse will be up to him.

'Jules, I'm really sorry, but my work meeting went on miles later than it was supposed to and now I'm stuck in traffic on the fucking M62. There's been an accident, there's massive tailbacks. I'll probably be at least an hour and a half yet, maybe more and I'm shattered, to be honest. I'll get something from the service station. You guys go ahead without me.'

He rings off without giving me a chance to say there is no 'you guys'. That it's just me. I sit there for a moment, unsure what to do. The waiter comes up and asks if I'd like another drink.

'I'm sorry,' I hear myself saying. 'There's been a family emergency. I'm going to have to leave.'

He says it's no problem. He completely understands. It seems you get treated nicely at expensive restaurants. I pay for my drink and stand up, blinking back the tears. He probably thinks someone's died. And they have. It was a long time ago but a part of me died with her. And what remains of me has festered and been eaten away inside since. Leaving what? I'm not sure any more. I don't know who I am or what the fucking point is. I'm treading water, passing time, trying to hold things together until what? The end? Is that all I have to look forward to any more?

I leave the restaurant. The tinkling laughter and aromatic smells irritating to me now. I walk back towards the station. Get a Greggs on the way. Because this is what my life has come to. Me, eating a steak bake on a bench at Leeds Station, while a guy further along the platform – can in hand – vomits straight onto the tracks. 'Happy Birthday, Jules,' I say out loud. 'And may there be many more to come.'

And that's when I realise. That's when I make the decision. That I don't want to spend another year in my shitty, empty life simply in order to see in my fifty-first on my own like this. I don't even want to spend another day in agony. I'm tired. The pain has taken its toll. The loss has left me wrung out. I have nothing left to give this world and it has nothing left for me. It's best we part company sooner rather than later, so there are no hard feelings. I finish the steak bake as the train pulls in. As last suppers go, it really wasn't the best.

The film stopped. The studio was silent. They knew what happened the next morning.

'I'm sorry,' Emily said eventually.

'What have you got to be sorry about?'

'I judged you, didn't I? I was so full of pity for myself that I didn't have any left for you.'

'Why would you? I'm still not proud of what I did. I know it was wrong. That it hurt people. There's no excuse for that.'

'You probably had PTSD,' said Carl.

'You what?'

'You don't have to be in the emergency services to get it, you know. What you went through with Grace must have been so traumatic.'

I shrugged. I knew he was probably right, but I didn't want to let myself off the hook that easily.

'It was still wrong. I'd take it back in an instant if I could.'

'Except none of us can do that,' said Carl. 'Those are the rules.'

'Which reminds me,' I said, 'Suzi said my film's ready to play in my room. *Bambi 2: Revenge Just Got Real.*'

Carl groaned.

'I'd almost forgotten about that. So basically, I'm going to have to sit there while anything with balls gets humiliated or destroyed.'

'Pretty much so,' I replied. 'But before that, Suzi did say they'll be serving a special last supper for us at Food To Die For.'

'I'm up for that,' he said with a smile. 'As long as there are poppadoms. I could eat my bodyweight in poppadoms.'

* * *

They'd decorated our table in the restaurant with flowers and party favours. The other diners clapped as we made our way to it, as if we'd done something to celebrate rather than simply come to the end of the road.

'No sign of Jesus, yet,' I said as we sat down. 'I imagine he must be caught in traffic with the twelve disciples.'

'Did Suzi tell you what exactly they do for our last supper?' asked Carl.

'No, but Elsie is on her way over and if we can hang in there until she arrives, I suspect she might enlighten us.'

'Hi Elsie,' I said when she finally made it to the table. 'Seen any good films lately?'

'I have, as a matter of fact,' she replied. 'That one with all the nudey men at the end.'

Emily and Carl looked at me, clearly alarmed.

'*The Full Monty*, is that the one?'

'Oh yes,' said Elsie. 'A proper eyeful that were.'

'Well. I'm glad you enjoyed it. Now, can you tell us what's on the menu this evening, because there aren't any on our table.'

'No, that's because you'll each have your special menus. All your favourite foods brought to your table. And it will be in a proper order because we're not like one of those new-fangled places I've heard about that say, "we'll bring dishes out as soon as they're ready", because that's just them being lazy sods who can't be arsed cooking things so that they arrive at your table on time.'

'Couldn't agree more,' said Carl. Emily appeared to have been rendered speechless.

'I'll have other waiting staff helping me this evening, else you'll still be here tomorrow morning,' Elsie explained. 'Can't be doing with all this fast food lark.'

'You do it in your own time,' I told Elsie. 'It's been a pleasure having you as our waitress.'

My prawn cocktail came first, alongside what did indeed appear to be Carl's bodyweight in poppadoms and yogurt raita and chutneys, and chocolate sourdough for Emily.

'Chocolate for starters?' questioned Carl.

'You can never go wrong with chocolate,' she replied. And she really did have a point.

* * *

Afterwards, when we'd polished off everything they'd thrown at us, including the after-dinner mints, I turned to the others and raised my glass.

'Thank you,' I said, 'for being the best afterlife buddies imaginable.'

They grinned and raised their glasses.

'Although that doesn't stop me being pissed off with Jesus and his mates for not making it.'

Later, when Faline had told Bambi to get stuffed and Miss Bunny had given Thumper Myxomatosis, renamed herself Persephone and run off with Faline, Carl turned to me and said, 'I see what you've done there.'

I smiled.

'You've still got a chance tomorrow,' said Emily.

'What, to give someone Myxomatosis?'

'No,' she replied. 'To give someone a chance to explain.'

23

EMILY

It was such an odd feeling. Less than a month ago I'd arrived here unable to get my head around the place and the people or even understand what Suzi had been on about. Now it was time to leave, I couldn't help feeling kind of sad. These people who I'd never even met had become my surrogate family. A very weird and mixed-up family, admittedly, but still the closest I'd had to one here. And I presumed that once we'd seen our directors' cuts, we'd go our separate ways and never see each other again. And that bothered me.

Plus, I knew what I had to do today before I left. I still had no doubt that it was the right thing to do – the only thing I could do in the circumstances – but that didn't mean it was going to be easy. I was starting to feel sick already. Like I was waiting to have one of my limbs amputated and I knew I'd never feel whole again.

Do it for Harry, I told myself. Again and again and again.

* * *

We had breakfast together in the restaurant. Even that felt strangely normal now. And it was only the previous day's arrivals who gave me a pitying look. The others had grown used to me being there. Perhaps, in a way, I made them think they were lucky. Sure, they'd gone too soon but not as soon as me.

'So,' said Carl. 'Are we all ready for this?'

'I have no fucking idea,' replied Jules.

'I can't believe it's all over,' I said. 'Where are we even going to go?'

'You haven't got to worry,' Jules told me. 'I reckon they'll put you up in a luxury hotel with room service on demand, all the streaming channels and they'll give you your phone back.'

I laughed. Because a few weeks ago, that was my main concern.

'But I won't have you two to annoy the hell out of me,' I said.

'What, and screw up your favourite Disney films? I think you'll be just fine.'

'And we've got the screening to look forward to first,' said Carl. 'I do believe Suzi promised popcorn.'

'Right, well, finish your breakfast,' Jules said, 'and let's go and do our worst in the editing studio so we can get going.'

* * *

When we got to the studio, Faz had put presents on each of our desks.

'Just a little something to say thank you for sharing your lives with me,' he said.

'Bloody hell,' replied Jules, giving him a hug. 'I thought you were a cool tech bro who couldn't wait till he got shot of us.'

'Get in the bin,' said Faz, hugging Jules back. 'You three have broken me more than any Disney Pixar film I've ever watched and that's saying something.'

I wasn't sure if we should feel flattered or sad about that. I unwrapped my present. They were *Finding Nemo* chocolates, Jules had *Bambi* ones and Carl *The Lion King* selection.

'Thanks,' I said, 'these are amazing.'

'I set up a site when I got here, kind of like Etsy but for the afterlife. It's called Deathsy. People can make you anything.'

'Do you also run an online food delivery service including pizzas and Indian takeaways for the afterlife?' asked Carl.

'How did you know that?' asked Faz.

'Just a hunch,' said Carl.

'Is that how you get paid?' Jules asked. 'We know about Elsie and Majid. Do your wages go towards building your online business empire?'

Faz smiled.

'Rumbled. I always wanted to have a side hustle as an entrepreneur.'

'What stopped you?' asked Jules.

'My e-scooter collided with a bus while I was checking my phone.'

The three of us all winced.

'And I thought my method of departure was stupid,' said Jules.

'Fair comment,' said Faz. 'Anyway, your significant moments are loaded. You can make your director's cut whenever you want, just put a marker at the point you want to cut from and to. If you need to leave a note on the marker about what you'd like me to do, please do so. And if you want to come to the sound booth to do some ADR, you're very welcome.'

'What's that?' asked Jules.

'Additional Dialogue Recording. So, if there's a different line you want to record, you can do that.'

'And what about the new material after the change? How does that work?'

'CGI is very good these days,' said Faz. 'And I take it you've all heard of AI?'

'Hang on, no one mentioned anything about me being played by a robot,' said Jules.

'We could do a very hot AI representation of you?' said Faz.

'I'm in,' said Jules.

'Right,' said Faz. 'I'll leave you to it then.'

I stared at the controls and the screen in front of me, suddenly aware of the fact that power was in my hands. I couldn't remember ever having power or control before. All I knew was that I'd use it wisely. I set the marker at the exact point I wanted, wrote a note for Faz on it and stood up to go to the sound desk to record my additional dialogue.

'What are you doing?' asked Jules.

'Making a change,' I said. 'And setting someone free in the process.'

I didn't even script my lines, just spoke from the heart. When I'd finished, Faz looked at me.

'You always were the brave one,' he said. 'And you're also a one-take wonder.'

I went back down to the others. Carl had finished. I could tell that by the relief etched on his face.

'Sorted?' I asked. He nodded.

'And no extra words needed. Sometimes silence is all you need.'

We sat down either side of Jules. She was rewinding and fast-forwarding back and forth.

'What are you thinking?' I asked.

'Whether to change the steak bake for a sausage roll.'

Carl and I both laughed.

'I know you'd save Grace if you could,' I said. 'But you could still save Nina. No one should have to live their life thinking about what could have been.'

Carl stood up.

'She's right. We'll be outside when you're ready,' he said.

It was a while before Jules joined us. I couldn't decide whether that was a good or bad thing and her face gave nothing away.

'Well?' I asked.

'I've never had a vegan sausage roll,' she said. 'So, I thought I better had before I died, to see what all the fuss was about.'

Me and Carl looked at each other. Clearly, Jules wasn't going to reveal what she'd done. Suzi stuck her head out of her office door.

'Aaahhh, I see my three musketeers have accomplished their mission. Please join me in my office.'

We did as we were told. Everything had seemed so strange and wrong the first morning we'd been here. Now, it seemed almost ordinary. And Suzi, who I'd thought was a cold-hearted cow who spoke a different language, had been revealed to be a complete star in the meantime.

Jules went straight up and gave her a hug.

'I'm sorry about what happened to you,' she said.

'And I think your granddaughter sounds awesome,' I added.

Suzi looked at Carl and raised her eyebrow. There may have been tears glistening in her eyes, although I was sure she'd have denied it.

'So, it really is "all for one and one for all" now,' she said. 'You guys have clearly taken this bonding thing to heart.'

'We can only help and support each other if we're honest

about what we've been through,' said Jules. 'I was the last one to learn that but I'm finally on board.'

'Then I do believe you're ready,' said Suzi. 'In which case, it's time for the awards. Please take your seats.'

She gestured towards the black and chrome chairs, dropped her projector screen down and an image of an Oscar appeared.

'Shouldn't you wait until you've actually seen the finished directors' cuts?' asked Carl.

'I don't need to. These aren't for the films,' replied Suzi. 'Our first category is Best Person to Cheer Everyone Else Up, Having Initially Pissed Them Right Off.'

We all turned and looked at Jules. She smiled and stepped up to accept the imitation Oscar figure Suzi held out.

'I'd like to say thank you to everyone I know but that wouldn't be honest, because a lot of them were complete eejits. But you two,' she said, pointing at me and Carl, 'thank you for putting up with me.'

We clapped as she sat down.

'Next up,' said Suzi, 'is Best Guy to Have on Your Side When You Need a Problem Solved. Stand up please, quiet guy.'

Carl went up and accepted his award, accompanied by whoops from me and Jules.

'Lewis, this is for you,' he said, raising it in the air.

'And finally,' said Suzi, 'Best Person to Make You Rethink Your Views on Gen Z. Step this way, Emily.'

I walked up to accept my award to more whooping.

'Right,' said Suzi, 'that concludes our award ceremony. By the time you reach the cinema where your directors' cuts will receive their world premiere, Faz will have sent the digital version of your films to them and an old-school souvenir film reel of it will have been left on your seats, along with your complimentary popcorn. Are there any further questions?'

'Can we go back to our rooms and change first?' asked Jules. 'Only I want to make an effort in case there are paparazzi there.'

'No need,' said Suzi. 'I'll ensure you arrive in appropriate attire for the red carpet.'

'Are these your fairy godmother powers again?' asked Jules.

'Think of it as my final parting gift,' Suzi replied. 'Now, it's time to go.'

'Is Majid taking us?' asked Carl. 'Another bit of freelance work?'

'Oh, even Majid can't get to where you're going.'

'So how do we get there?' I asked.

'Follow me,' she said.

Suzi led us outside and back along the basement corridor to the very end.

'But this is just the glass lift,' Carl said. 'I've seen it from the front of the building.'

'And that's where you'd be wrong,' replied Suzi, pressing the call button. The doors slid back. Inside was a huge panel of shiny chrome numbered buttons stretching from floor to ceiling.

'Why so many buttons?' I asked.

'So many places to go,' Suzi replied.

'You mean it's not just Heaven or Hell?' asked Carl.

'Oh God, no,' said Suzi. 'Because life isn't black and white, is it? There are a lot of grey areas in between.'

She looked at me as she said it. I nodded slowly.

'So where do they all go?' I asked.

'It's more a question of what people they're for,' explained Suzi. 'You know that saying, "I hope there's a special place in Hell for you"?'

We nodded in unison.

'Well, this one,' she said, pointing at number 12, 'is for people who designed trousers for women in only one leg length. I mean, I may be a short-arse, but I refuse to believe we should put up with one-length-fits-all trousers when men don't have to.'

Jules high-fived her for that.

'And this?' asked Carl, pointing at button 29.

'For those men who think it's OK for women to have to spend a ridiculous percentage of their lives queuing to use the toilet in their building or the one they designed.'

'Let me guess,' I said. 'Their special place in hell hasn't got any toilet facilities?'

'Better than that. It has only one cubicle for men and it's made of glass.'

'It would almost be worth going to Hell to see them suffer that,' Jules said.

'And what about this?' Carl asked, pointing at number 1.

'Bosses of companies that have recorded messages saying they're experiencing an unusually high call volume at the moment but that your call is important to them.'

'Where does it go?' I asked.

'It doesn't. They simply go up and down in the lift forever while a message plays telling them we're experiencing an unusually high lift call volume at the moment, but their journey is important to us,' Suzi said.

'So, what button's ours?' Carl asked.

Suzi pointed to the one at the top which said 'Up and Out'.

'It's a little nod to Roald Dahl,' she explained. 'Because just like his glass elevator, this one is not restricted to this building.'

'Are you sure it's safe?' Carl asked.

'Quiet guy, you're already dead, remember?' she replied. 'Now, come on. Get in. I haven't got all day.'

'Aren't you coming with us?' I asked.

'I have new arrivals to welcome. Besides, I've got complete faith in you three. And if in any doubt, they should listen to you because you've got an amazingly wise head on your young shoulders.'

'Oh God,' said Carl. 'This is like the bit when the scarecrow, the tin man and the lion have to say goodbye to Dorothy.'

'Except you have courage, heart and brains by the bucket-load and I don't possess the girlish charm of Judy Garland, or a pair of sparkly red slippers and a dog called Toto, come to that.'

'You should get a Toto,' I told her. 'It would suit you.'

'I'll bear that in mind,' Suzi said with a smile before we gave her a group hug and got in the lift.

'I hope Iris plays for the Lionesses one day,' Carl said to her.

'And I hope you knock the musical theatre on the head and listen to some proper rock music,' Suzi replied.

'Oi, I had AC/DC at my funeral,' said Carl. Jules and I looked at each other. Suzi nodded at me. I knew what to do. I reached up and pressed 'Up and Out'.

The lift doors clanged shut and we started heading up, far faster than I'd ever thought a lift could go.

'Jesus, it's like being on the runway before take-off,' said Jules, hanging on to a rail.

The glass elevator whooshed out of the top of the building without the expected noise or devastation.

'What happened?' asked Jules.

Carl looked down below. 'The building's got a retractable roof,' he said.

A button marked 'Comms' flashed red. Carl shrugged and pressed it.

'Had you worried there,' came Suzi's voice.

'What's keeping us up in the air now?' Carl asked.

'Suzi power,' she replied. 'That or sky hooks. You can take your choice. Enjoy the show!'

I finally plucked up the courage to look down.

'Wow, the town still looks shitty from up here,' said Jules.

'But then your heart was never here, was it?' said Carl.

Within a few moments, we were through the clouds and heading towards space.

'Knowing my luck, we'll bump into one of Elon Musk's rockets,' said Jules.

I stared out into the blackness. Harry always liked looking at the stars. It made me think of him.

'It's beautiful,' I said. The others fell silent. A minute later, there was a clank, and we started to slow down.

'I think we're coming into land, or dock, or whatever they call it,' said Carl. 'You'd better brace yourselves.'

But there were no bumps; we simply glided to a halt and the lights went out.

'Do you think that was supposed to happen?' asked Jules.

'I don't know,' said Carl.

'And does anyone else feel like they're now taking up the whole of the lift?' asked Jules. At which point, the lights turned back on to reveal that she was dressed in a mad red and black gothic ballgown with her hair piled up.

'Oh my God,' I said, 'it's your dress from the ball!'

Jules looked down and felt her petticoats, as if to make sure they were real.

'It fucking is too!' she said, laughing and twirling as much as she could do in a confined space. I looked down to find myself wearing my emerald-green prom dress, which I'd never got the chance to wear. Even Carl, dressed all in black with a trendy biker jacket, looked the part.

'Wow, it appears we're all going to the ball,' said Jules. Carl pressed the button to open the lift doors. The one thing I wasn't expecting to see on the other side was a yellow brick road.

'Suzi's sense of humour at play, I think,' said Carl. We

stepped out, me in the centre, Jules and Carl with their arms threaded through mine.

'I'm not doing the dance, though,' said Carl.

'Spoilsport,' said Jules. We followed the yellow brick road around the swirls and off to the right. When we got around the corner, we saw it was leading up to a cinema in the distance. Not a big multiplex like the one in town but a beautiful independent picture house, like the one in Hebden Bridge.

'Get in,' said Jules. 'They do proper mugs of tea there.'

'But where even is this?' I asked. 'Like, is it supposed to be Heaven?'

'I think,' said Carl, 'that it's wherever we want it to be. Whatever we make it.'

'So, you don't reckon we're going on anywhere afterwards?' I asked.

'No, I think this is it. But there are worse ways of spending the afterlife than watching films all day, I suppose,' he replied.

When we got closer to the cinema, the yellow brick road stopped, and a red carpet continued. There were even a handful of photographers and a camera crew there, although disappointingly, it wasn't Gerry and Alice. We went up the steps to the entrance, and a woman welcomed us, took our drinks orders and showed us into our own private cinema, where three directors' chairs were set up with our names on the back.

'Looks like you've finally made it,' Jules said to Carl, pointing at his chair.

'I'll take that,' he replied.

We sat down in the order the chairs had been put out: me, Carl, then Jules. I guessed that was the order the films were going to be shown in.

'The last time I went to a triple bill it was an all-nighter at a cinema in Bristol with Nina,' Jules said. 'I think we saw *Grease*, *Fame* and *Hairspray*.'

'I reckon these will be better,' said Carl.

'There'll certainly be less singing and dancing,' replied Jules.

They came in with our drinks. I picked up my popcorn and as the lights went dark, prepared to watch me star in a rewritten version of my own life. And even though I knew the lines I had spoken and the impact they would have, I still found myself wondering how it would actually play out. And how I would feel about it at the end.

Faz had done as I asked. Turned all the video clips at the beginning into an *Up*-style sequence. Except it said 'Emily's Story' on it, because that's all it was now. The story of me.

Everything was the same as I remembered from the significant moments as we edged closer towards my edit. It was like watching a creepy film when you know something bad's coming but you somehow can't bear to look away. And then we were there. The day at school when Harry turned to look at me and Ava and she hurried away as he walked over to me.

Harry smiles. I have seen that smile many times before, but it is still somehow the most dazzling thing on the planet.

'Hey,' he says.

'Hey.' It's all I can do to get the word out. My brain and mouth appear to be struggling to communicate with each other. My brain is struggling to do pretty much anything other than stare at him.

'I've got a couple of tickets for a gig next week—'

'I'm sorry, I'm busy,' I say, before he has even finished asking me. He stares, as if not quite sure he has heard right, and then he starts laughing.

'You don't even know which day yet,' he says. I feel the colour rising in my cheeks. Worry it's come out wrong, and I've sounded dead rude.

'No, all week. I'm really sorry but I've got some family stuff on.'

I see him deflate before me. Feel like such a cow for saying that.

'Maybe another time then?' he asks.

I hate doing this to him but I'm going to have to stand firm.

'The thing is, Harry,' I say. 'It's like, super nice of you to ask but my dad's kind of strict. He's always said no boyfriends till after my GCSEs. He wants me to concentrate on, you know, school stuff first.'

Harry frowns at me, like he's not sure if I'm joking or not.

'I'm sorry, but can we just be friends?' I ask. 'I think it's better that way.'

'Oh. Right. Sure,' he says, not seeming sure about any of it. 'It's no biggie.'

It is though. I know that and I need to find some way of softening the blow.

'Look,' I say. 'It's also a bit awkward because Ava really likes you.'

'She does?'

'Yeah. So, if you are at all interested, you could maybe leave it a bit, and then, you know, ask her out. Only if you want to, mind.'

He smiles at me. The same beautiful smile.

'Are you trying to set us up here?' he asks.

'I might be,' I say. 'Isn't that what friends do?'

'OK. I will leave it a bit though. Because I'll need to get over you first.'

I blush and stare at my feet, unable to look him in the eye in case he sees how I really feel.

'Right. That's sweet, thanks. If you're not taking the piss.'

I look up to see him shake his head.

'And just so you know,' I go on. 'Her parents will be cool with it, so you'll get no hassle there.'

He nods. 'That's good to know.'

'Sorry again, about my dad, I mean. You know Finding Nemo*? He's a bit like Marlin. Can't quite bring himself to let go.'*

Harry smiles.

'But we can still be friends,' I say.

'Good,' he says, 'I'd like that,' before turning to walk away.

The snotty sob came from Jules. She reached out a hand across Carl, who was also sniffing loudly, to clutch mine.

'You brave, brave girl,' she said.

The film continued, though I watched the rest through watery eyes. Me telling Ava I didn't fancy Harry any more. That I didn't want the hassle of going out with anyone, not till my dad got off my back. Harry leaving it a respectful few months then asking Ava out one day when I wasn't around.

I'd already told her to say yes. Though she hadn't believed he was interested in her at the time. When I met her after school, she had a huge stupid grin on her face. She asked if I thought she'd done the right thing. I told her she'd never regret it.

And my life carried on. I got used to being the third wheel with Ava and Harry, or as used to it as I could ever be. And then we got to the point where I became ill and had all the tests. And I watched myself get the diagnosis all over again.

I FaceTime Ava later that evening to tell her. I should probably do it in person, but I can't help thinking that would be more brutal. I know Harry's with her, and this way I can tell her, say I'm tired and end the call and he can comfort her, which is far better than us two wailing and hugging each other for two hours in person. She starts crying when I tell her, as I knew she would. I try to do the brave 'it'll all be OK' thing. I don't know if she believes me though. Or whether I believe myself.

I see Harry's arms around her. Know she has his support, her scaffold, and I make my excuses and end the call.

It was just my parents there when I died. I missed the Harry-sized hole by my bed. Missed his head on my chest. His whispering in my ear. It was the right thing to do though, to spare him that pain. I wished I could have spared my parents it too, but that wasn't an option.

I watched my own funeral for the second time. Harry sat next to Ava, behind my parents. He didn't sing or play. He didn't make people cry. He held Ava's hand. I watched her grip it tightly. They did not let go of each other at any point, which was exactly as I'd wanted. And why I tried to ignore the hurt inside as I whispered, 'I love you, Harry Sanders.'

Harry and Ava are standing by my graveside. The other mourners are walking away. Even my parents, who are heading off to the wake.

'I still can't believe she's gone,' says Ava.

'I know,' says Harry. 'It's all so unfair. She was so brave, though. I could never have been that brave.'

'So, what do we do now?' asks Ava.

'We go to the wake. Mum's waiting in the car outside.'

'No. After that. Like, what happens next?'

'We do what she asked us to do. We go off and live our lives. Do everything she never got the chance to do.'

'We go to Liverpool next year, then?'

'That's what she said. She wanted us to follow our dreams. So, I'll do my music and you'll do your nursing and we'll see where that takes us.'

'We were so lucky to have her, weren't we?' says Ava.

Harry takes one last look at my grave.

'We absolutely were,' he says.

24

CARL

I couldn't have been prouder of Emily if she'd been my own daughter. She'd done it. Our amazing Emily had done the hardest thing imaginable and given up her Harry to save him from the pain of losing her. I wrapped an arm around her and squeezed her shoulder.

'You're incredible,' I said to her as the film finished. 'I'm utterly in awe of you.'

Jules left her seat and practically threw herself at Emily.

'You broke me. That was worse than the beginning of *Up*. You deserve a fucking award for that.'

Emily wiped her eyes. She was still shaking.

'You're not regretting it?' I asked. She shook her head.

'No. Because Harry's got his life back. His hopes and dreams are still alive. Him and Ava will support each other. They'll be fine.'

'That's one hell of a sacrifice, though,' I said.

She shrugged. 'That's what you do when you love someone, isn't it?'

We sat in silence for a moment. Our untouched popcorn tubs still sitting by our sides.

'It wasn't really a popcorn kind of film, was it?' said Emily.

'Nope,' I agreed.

'I hope yours is going to be a bit more uplifting,' Jules said to me.

'What, up until the point where I die, you mean?'

'Yeah, but we know that's coming. We've been through your pain. Now we want the payoff.'

'Right, popcorn at the ready, then. Let's see what happens.'

* * *

I'd given myself an edgy opening. I'd asked Faz to find the footage from the camera I used to wear on my bike helmet. It may not have been significant to them, but it was to me. I was still using what was already there, which was allowed. Everything on screen after that proceeded as expected. I steeled myself for the school minibus crash. I felt strangely detached from it this time, like I was watching someone else go through it. Thinking, poor bastard, that's going to really screw him up.

The funerals were still tough, though. You'd have thought I'd have been to enough over the past month to have developed some kind of immunity to grief. But that wasn't the case. I whispered 'sorry' as each of the girls was laid to rest. Not because I thought it was my fault but because I was sad the rules had prevented me rescuing them and saving their parents from their grief.

I struggled to recognise the man I became after that. The one who drowned his guilt in alcohol and rejected every offer of help that came his way. I understood that he was suffering – far more than he had realised at the time – and I wished someone had been able to get through to him, had taken control and not allowed him to wriggle out of it. Watching a grown man wreck his own life is never easy. But watching him wreck someone else's, that was unbearable. Which was why I'd made sure no one had to sit through that again.

I take the vodka bottle from the cupboard. I hide it behind cereal packets so that Lewis doesn't see it. I take my first shot neat. And the second. The third gets mixed with orange juice because it's all I have in the fridge. It's only as I shut the door that I remember I have an optician's appointment that afternoon. It's too late to cancel now and I don't do no-shows. Never have done. Besides, I know I need new glasses. I've been noticing my vision isn't as sharp when riding at night.

I start to get my things together. It's less than ten minutes into town. And I'll be fine. Absolutely fine. Besides, if I get pulled over by the police, I'll probably know the officer and they're hardly going to breathalyse a former colleague, are they?

I'm pulling on my boots and picking up my helmet when I hear Lewis shout from the landing.

'Are you going into town? Only I need to get to the job centre, and I'll end up sanctioned if I'm late again.'

'So, get the bloody bus,' I say.

'The buses are crap. Anyway, I've just checked, and the next one isn't due for half an hour now...'

His voice trails off as I let myself out of the back door, climb onto my bike and am gone before he even realises.

Jules and Emily cheered.

'Hey, that's a bit much. I'm about to die.'

'Yeah, but you saved Lewis,' Jules said. 'You looked after your kid brother, just like you promised your mum you would do.'

My death was as dramatic as before but this time there was

only one body on the bike, one figure tumbling down the steep side of the road.

I was relieved it stopped there. That I didn't have to watch Lewis identify my body, as I knew he would have done. But when I saw him on the day of the cremation, standing next to Mum and supporting her as my coffin was carried into the chapel, I knew it would weirdly be the making of him. Because he'd have to step up now. Be forced to grow up. And hopefully, my death would have given him the kick up the arse he needed.

The turnout from my biker friends at my cremation was just as impressive, 'Bring Him Home' from *Les Mis* as rousing and Sgt Lockwood's eulogy just as moving.

During a quiet moment of reflection, the camera focussed on Lewis sitting there, head bowed, next to Mum, when his phone pinged with two notifications. I imagined Alice dangling her boom over them.

'Turn that bloody thing off, will you,' hissed Mum sternly. Lewis slid his phone out of his pocket and checked his screen. The camera zoomed in. Good old Gerry.

The notifications were replies to a post he'd made on a private Facebook group for Halifax musicians. A post in which he said he was forming a band, planning some local gigs and needed a singer and guitarist to complete the line-up. The two replies were from a Thomas Smith, who offered his services as a guitarist, and a Harry Sanders, who said he could sing a bit.

It was hard to tell who whooped loudest between Jules and Emily.

'They're going to be in a band!' shrieked Jules. 'They're going to be the next fucking Beatles.'

'I feel I should point out that Lewis has got a track record of not having much sticking power,' I said.

'And Harry will be going off to Liverpool next year,' said Emily.

'It doesn't matter, does it?' said Jules. 'Thomas will be back at Warwick soon too. The point is they're going to jam together. They're going to make friends and it's like we've somehow made these connections to help bring them together.'

And with that, she picked up her popcorn and emptied the rest of it into her mouth. I watched as Lewis walked out of that chapel. His body and his drumming dreams still intact and a fire in his belly that meant he might just make something of them. And if not, he'd have a bloody good time trying.

25

JULES

'Right then,' I said. 'I guess it's up to me to decide if we end this triple bill on a high or are plunged into gloomy darkness forever.'

I'd already made a decision, what happened next was out of my hands and my fate was already decided. It was someone else's life I may or may not have made better.

The film started in Bristol, because that's when my life started. That's where Nina lit up my entire world.

We ran across the bridge, we talked, we danced, we laughed ourselves silly and we had a cheeky try on of our gowns, imagining a spectacular day in the future when we would get to wear them. And when we did, we both looked as magnificent as ever. I saw the glint of excitement in my eye about what the night could bring, saw the breathless anticipation as I leant in to kiss her in the toilets and felt the pang of rejection as she pushed me away and fled the scene.

At which point, I made my escape too, to my special place and the only one I could think of running to.

The bridge is calling me closer. Beckoning me to shelter in its safety. I watch it growing larger as I approach. Its size and reach comforting and familiar. It's only when I'm standing on it, clinging on to the railings as I'm feeling a little unsteady, that I think of Sarah Ann Henley standing here over one hundred years before me. Broken hearted after being rejected by her love. All her hopes and dreams for the future in tatters and feeling so utterly wretched that she was driven to do something desperate.

I climb up onto the railings and look down into the gorge below me in the gathering darkness. It would be so easy. All so very easy to put a stop to the pain.

'You OK, love?'

The man's voice comes from behind me. I turn to see a cab pulled up, the face of a bearded middle-aged man sticking out of the open window.

'Yes,' I reply, my voice shaky. 'I'm waiting for someone.'

'Whoever he is, he's not worth it.'

I think for a moment about telling him that it's a 'she' actually. And that she is worth everything. But I don't want to make things any more complicated for myself than they already are.

'I'm happy to take you somewhere safe for free, if that helps,' he says.

I'm suddenly aware that I'm a slightly drunk young woman in a ballgown with tears streaming down my face. He's probably got a daughter around my age and hopes that someone would do the same for her if they ever spotted her climbing a bridge railing.

And I'm aware that a lot of cabbies may refuse my fare if I try to hail one later. They'd probably see the state of me and worry I was going to throw up in the back of their cab.

'It's OK, thanks,' I say. 'She's on her way.'

He pulls a face. A mixture of surprise and concern.

'OK. If you're sure, then. But don't do anything you'll regret.'

He waits for a moment then puts up the window and drives off.

I'm already wondering if I'll regret letting him go later. I have no idea why I said what I did about waiting for Nina. No reason to think she would come here to find me. She probably wants to be as far away from me as possible right now. I want to run after the cab, but he's disappeared from view now.

Nina will be back at the hotel with some of the other students. They'll be laughing at me. Finding it hilarious that I ever thought she could have feelings for me and appalled that I went ahead and acted on my *feelings. Forcing her away like that. Making her flee. She'll never return now. I can't say I blame her. At least Sarah Ann Henley was betrothed before she was rejected. At least he had loved her before he broke things off. I don't even have that. My life is a mess, and I have no one but myself to blame.*

I turn back to the railings and climb up. Higher than I was before. High enough to feel the wind in my face. To see the darkness of the water below. I could jump now. No one would really miss me. Not Nina, not my family. I'd be a sad footnote in history. The woman in a ballgown who did a copycat jump from the Clifton Suspension Bridge but didn't survive.

'Jules!'

The woman's voice is distant but full of fear. I realise at once that I'm having some kind of auditory hallucination. It's come to this now, I'm hearing the voice of my lost love. I climb a step higher. Wobble a little as the wind catches me. The voice comes again, breathless and more desperate this time.

'Jules, don't you dare!'

I could look around but if I do, I'll be disappointed. Reality will come crashing in and stop me doing what I have to do. Sometimes, there's only one way out. And no second chances. I let go of the railings with one hand and lean forward into the wind. There are footsteps behind me now. And breathless, panic-stricken shouting.

'Jules! You're a damn sight heavier than Sarah Ann Henley would

have been and you don't have sufficient petticoats. You'll plummet and your dress will be ruined, and I'll have to pay for the whole fucking thing.'

As hard as I'm trying not to, I find myself laughing. The hysterical sort of laughter people do when they're not thinking straight. I feel arms reach up and clasp my legs tightly, easing me back down to the ground. They're Nina's arms holding me, Nina's voice in my ear, saying, 'It's OK, I've got you,' over and over again.

'You came,' I say, still not quite believing that she's real.

'Well, I was hardly going to leave you there to jump, was I?'

'But you pushed me away, you said no, you ran away. Why would you come back?'

'Because I went back to our flat and read this,' she says, brandishing my letter. 'And because I want to say sorry for freaking out like that and running off.'

I stare at her, sure I'm still hallucinating.

'You took me by surprise,' she says. 'I wasn't expecting that. I mean, no one expects a declaration of love to take place in the ladies' loos, do they?'

I'm frowning now, because none of it makes sense.

'You mean, you didn't mind?'

'Mind? I bloody loved it. But I was also terrified. I mean, what if someone had come in and seen us? And even if they hadn't, have you thought about how difficult this would make our lives? Our families would probably disown us, we'd be shunned by society and have to shack up secretly, pretending we run a home for abandoned cats or something.'

'That sounds pretty appealing to me,' I reply. And then we're laughing. Both of us. Still a kind of hysterical laughter but we're holding hands and clinging on to each other as if we're both still up there, swaying in the breeze.

'But the letter,' I groan eventually. 'It told you everything about how I feel.'

'I know, stupid. And that's why I'm here now, waving it in your face. Because I feel exactly the same, only I'm not as good as putting it into words as you are. So I'm simply going to say, "same".'

All the feelings that have been churning around inside me start to settle. Joy and surprise push their way to the surface. I find myself smiling at her, a huge bloody great grin. Nina came back. My Nina came back for me.

'I'm going to kiss you,' I say. 'I just wanted to warn you this time. Are you sure this isn't too public, because we can go somewhere else if you want to?'

She leans in and kisses me first. And that is my answer. The only answer I need. Her lips are much as I remember, except they are sure now, sure of what they're doing. When we finally break for air, she says, 'If anyone ever asks, if we ever get to a point where people can ask such a thing and we can break free from the cat sanctuary cover story, can we tell them that was our first kiss?'

I nod.

'Sure,' I say. 'I'll never speak of the other one again.'

'Good, although I reserve permission to write about it in a book one day, because it did have good dramatic value.'

I smile, lean my head into her.

'And will you promise me you'll never attempt to throw yourself off that bridge again? Or any bridge, for that matter. You'll be no good to me at all in a splatty heap on the floor.'

'Promise,' I say. 'Although I did find a kindly cab driver who stopped to check I was OK and ask if I wanted a lift anywhere.'

'Only because your dress wasn't covered in mud,' says Nina.

'Yeah,' I reply. 'That's probably true.'

26

EMILY

I'd been crying so much until that point that I hadn't been able to speak. But now the tears had morphed into laughter and I let out a whoop.

'I told you!' I shouted. 'I told you to wait for Nina. I always knew she loved you. I absolutely did.'

I leant forward and reached out over Carl for Jules's hand. That was when I screamed.

'She's not there!'

'What?'

Carl turned to look for himself.

'She must have gone to the loo, or to get another tea or something.'

'She wouldn't have done that,' I said. 'Not in the most important scene of her director's cut.'

'Maybe she just couldn't bear to watch. She didn't think it was going to end well.'

'But we'd have heard her get up and go. She never did anything quietly, did she?'

I checked the front of the cinema, half expecting Jules to

stick her head out from behind the curtain, playing some sort of practical joke on us. She wasn't there though. Not present-day Jules. Only the twenty-one-year-old version on screen, walking slowly hand in hand with Nina back to their flat, as the camera gradually zoomed out.

'She's gone,' I said. 'Actually gone. She's not in the afterlife because she didn't die. That's why her film is ending here. Her life story hasn't finished yet because she's living the life that she always should have.'

'But where's your evidence for that?' asked Carl.

'Come on, you're supposed to be the former police officer,' I said, gesturing towards her empty seat. 'She's disappeared because her director's cut saved her.'

'But we weren't allowed to save ourselves.'

'She didn't. Nina saved her. Her cut was simply to refuse the offer of a lift from the cab driver and stay on the bridge to hear what Nina had to say. But when Nina stopped her jumping, it prevented her death. Not just then, but a few weeks ago too.'

Carl thought a moment.

'So, you're saying she's lived a completely different life as a result?'

'Yes. Because Nina's love saved her. And that's why she's not here. The Jules we knew doesn't exist any more. Her life from that moment on the bridge was wiped. I'm hoping she's living her best life in Bristol, with Nina and a whole heap of cats.'

'Jesus,' said Carl, as if he'd finally caught up. 'I think you could be right. But what about Rob and the boys?'

'They'd still have existed, they just wouldn't have had Jules in their lives. They probably had a cleaner right from the beginning.'

Carl laughed.

'So, what do you reckon her life in Bristol will have been like?'

'Exactly how she wanted. They'd have moved into a flat together after uni and got a rescue cat which she'd have named Robert Smith.'

'He'd probably have been more fun than her husband,' said Carl.

'And she'd have got her zoology master's and ended up working as a big cat keeper at Bristol Zoo.'

'I like it,' said Carl. 'She always had mad cat lady potential.'

'What about you?' I asked. 'Any predictions?'

He thought for a moment.

'They'd have moved to a bigger place, with a view of the Clifton Suspension Bridge from upstairs. And they'd have adopted a child when the laws changed to allow them to do so. And probably got married when the same-sex marriage laws came in too.'

'I like that,' I said. 'Her having the happy ending she never thought she deserved.'

'If she was still here,' said Carl, 'she'd probably be annoyed. Say that it should have been you and Harry getting the happy ending.'

'But I had my love story,' I said. 'She never got to live hers, so it's only right that she's the one who got a second chance.'

'I think she'll be living that life to the full,' Carl said. 'And she won't be taking any crap. Remember what she did to *Bambi*?'

I laughed and stood up, picking up my empty cup and popcorn tub.

'What are you doing?' asked Carl. 'The credits haven't even started yet and I never leave a cinema until they've finished.'

'Why not?' I asked.

'I kind of think it's rude. All those people worked so hard on the film. The least we can do is stay and acknowledge their input. And in this case, we actually know them.'

'Fair point,' I said, sitting back down again.

'And sometimes, you get rewarded with a post-credits scene. You never know, I wouldn't put it past Suzi.'

We cheered as 'End Credits Productions' came up on the screen, and I clapped all the names. Faz, Gerry and Alice, Majid. The catering staff at Food to Die For, including Elsie. Even the company they'd hired our trailer from and other names we didn't know, no doubt including the crew that had shot our deaths.

'I'm still not sure about the David Attenborough rule of not intervening,' said Carl.

'I stand by my point about the camera crew being allowed to build a ramp for the penguins.'

'Anyway, I guess what's done is done,' he said. 'At least for us.'

The credits finished. I was about to get up for the second time when Carl pointed at the screen.

'Look,' he said. 'What did I tell you?'

POST-CREDITS SCENE

'I don't think I've ever married a couple in matching dresses before,' the registrar says with a smile, clearly trying to break the ice, as we wait before the ceremony.

They're not matching though. One is red and black, the other purple and black. Not the original gowns we'd worn to the graduates' ball, obviously, but they are close enough.

'And who's this?' asks the registrar, smiling at the best bridesmaid we could possibly have wished for.

'Lizzie, our daughter,' I say proudly.

'I wasn't made with a turkey baster, if that's what you're thinking,' Lizzie says to the registrar. 'They adopted me.'

'Right. I see,' he says, seemingly struggling to know where to look. 'That's quite an outfit you've got. I don't think I've ever seen a black bridesmaid's dress before either.'

Although part of me wants to slap him for that, I know that I don't have to because Lizzie is perfectly capable of dealing with it herself. She scowls at him.

'I'm a drama student,' she says. 'I'm allowed to push boundaries.'

I smile because our Lizzie certainly does that. She's not carrying a traditional bridesmaid's posy, either. Instead, she's holding the knitted toilet-roll holder doll. The one Nina had given me that Christmas. Only Lizzie has given her full goth make-up for the occasion.

Nina and I are each holding a single rose, in a corresponding colour to our gowns. It will undoubtedly be seen as romantic, although the truth is it was a good way of saving us a fortune on wedding bouquets.

'Are you ready then?' asks the registrar.

'Oh, we've been ready for a long time,' says Nina. 'We've just been waiting for the country to catch up.'

I smile at her and we walk out onto the terrace of the Clifton Observatory; the suspension bridge towers across the skyline behind us. A director couldn't have asked for a more fitting backdrop.

'Lovesong' by The Cure plays as we make our way up the aisle. The small congregation claps when we reach the front. I turn around to face them.

'You see that?' I call out, pointing to the bridge. 'That's where we had our first kiss eighteen years ago today.'

Nina smiles knowingly, as does Lizzie, because she knows the truth too.

'Right, let's begin,' says the registrar, appearing more nervous by the second and no doubt wishing he was officiating at any wedding but ours.

'Oh, this isn't the beginning,' I say. 'It's more like a sequel.'

* * *

MORE FROM LINDA GREEN

BOOK CLUB QUESTIONS

1. Did the concept of setting a novel in the afterlife appeal to you and how did their afterlife compare to any you may have imagined?
2. How did the relationship between Jules, Emily and Carl develop during their time at End Credits?
3. How did your initial impressions of the three main characters change during the novel?
4. Did the novel make you think differently about death and our attitude to it?
5. Who was your favourite of the other characters we meet in the afterlife?
6. Which character surprised you the most?
7. How do you feel the author managed to balance the humour in the novel with the sadness and grief?
8. Who would you reserve 'a special place in Hell' lift button for?
9. Did Jules and Nina get the ending you had hoped for?
10. Has the novel made you think about any regrets of your own and what your director's cut would be?

ACKNOWLEDGEMENTS

Huge thanks to the following people: my brilliant editor Francesca Best for believing in this book, letting me write a novel that doesn't fit easily into any category/trend and helping me get the best out of the story and characters. And to all at my publishers Boldwood, especially Nia Beynon, Marcela Torres and Ben Wilson, for getting it out into the world and into the hands of readers.

My wonderful agent Maddalena Cavaciuti for stepping so ably into the big shoes left by my previous agent Anthony Goff, and for her passion, skill and determination in supporting me every step of the way. And to all at David Higham Associates for their ongoing support and getting my novels to readers overseas.

Sarah Durham for so brilliantly voicing the audiobook and bringing my characters to life, Debra Newhouse for her keen-eyed copy editing, Jennifer Kay Davies for her excellent proof-reading and Alice Moore for the great cover.

The Royal Literary Fund for the grant which has enabled me to keep going as a writer; their support is vital to writers like me from a working-class background.

My family and friends for their support, especially my husband Ian for all the promotional videos, photographs and putting up with me on my plot walks! My son Rohan for my great website (www.lindagreenauthor.com), his girlfriend Alice for lending her name to a character and her steak knife injury story for me to embellish!

The wonderful book community, the author friends who continue to support me and keep me smiling, the book bloggers and book clubs for spreading the word and readers for recommending and reviewing. The librarians and booksellers who get my books into readers' hands and a special thank you to Leeds Waterstones and the wonderful independent bookshops The Book Case in Hebden Bridge, The Book Corner in Halifax and The Grove Bookshop in Ilkley for stocking my books – get your signed copies from them!

And most importantly, you, the readers, for keeping me going with your messages and appreciation and taking my novels to your heart. If you're a first-time reader, the good news is I have twelve previous novels for you to enjoy! Please do get in touch with me through my website www.lindagreenauthor.com, Facebook: Author Linda Green, Instagram: lindagreenbooks, Bluesky lindagreenauthor.bsky.social and the site formerly known as Twitter, where I remain (until he tries to get me to pay for his rockets!) @lindagreenisms. I look forward to hearing what you think of this novel. I appreciate some of the content in this one is difficult but I hope you'll understand that the more we talk about grief and loss, the more we can support those going through it.

Note for people not lucky enough to live in Yorkshire: my novels are set here and most of my characters were born and bred here, which means they may speak differently to you (e.g. dropping the odd 'the', using 'were' instead of 'was', 'owt' instead of 'anything', etc). These are not typos or grammatical errors, simply how some folk speak and I like to celebrate the rich and varied dialects of these islands, rather than pretend everyone speaks the same way. Thank you for embracing this and come and visit, it's glorious up here!

ABOUT THE AUTHOR

Linda Green is the million copy Sunday Times bestselling author of more than ten novels including *The Last Thing She Told Me*.

Download your exclusive bonus content from Linda Green here:

Visit Linda's website: www.lindagreenauthor.com

Follow Linda on social media:

x.com/LindaGreenisms
facebook.com/LindaGreenAuthor
instagram.com/lindagreenbooks

ALSO BY LINDA GREEN

The Woman with All the Answers

If I Had My Time Again

www.ingramcontent.com/pod-product-compliance
Ingram Content Group UK Ltd.
Pitfield, Milton Keynes, MK11 3LW, UK
UKHW011327110526
12398UKWH00032B/718

9 781836 339830